DEAD OF NIGHT

An absolutely addictive crime thriller with a huge twist

(DI Temple Book 2)

DEBORAH LUCY

JOFFE BOOKS

First published 2019
Joffe Books, London
www.joffebooks.com

We hate typos too but sometimes they slip through.
Please send any errors you find to
corrections@joffebooks.com
We'll get them fixed ASAP. We're very grateful to eagle-eyed readers who take the time to contact us.

Please join our mailing list for free Kindle crime thriller, detective, mystery books and new releases.

ISBN: 978-1-78931-148-8

PROLOGUE

The body in the boot of the car shifted slightly as the speeding Audi swerved into the bend in the road. In the dark night, the road was awash with sheeting October rain. The driver was unfamiliar with the twists and turns of the desolate, endless criss-cross of roads that spread over Salisbury Plain. His disorientation was made worse as the rain beat like rods on the windscreen, obscuring his view.

He was already at a disadvantage as he squinted at the windscreen, the manic motion of the wipers useless at clearing the deluge. It was pitch black out there. When his passenger looked through the window, out into the night, he saw nothing but his own reflection. There was nothing to guide the way: no lights, no road markings. Even the bright white xenon beam of the headlights failed to alert the driver to a large mass of water pooling in the road ahead.

The water dumped onto the screen with unexpected force and the car aquaplaned, hitting the verge. The driver had no control as the Audi skidded off the road and plunged into the darkness of a plantation of sturdy birch trees. He grappled with the wheel as the lights shone through the thicket. His foot was on the brake but it was useless. Noise filled the car as the metalwork glanced off snapping branches. The car spun as if part of a wild split-second fairground ride, before thudding sidelong into a tree.

The force threw the passenger sprawling across to the driver's side. Dazed, the two men took a few seconds to get themselves sitting upright, and to regain their orientation. It had all happened so quickly. They looked at each other and silently assessed their surroundings. The car was a hissing mess.

'*Fuck it!*' The Albanian driver beat both his fists on the steering wheel.

The passenger side of the car was pressed hard against the trunk of a tree. After shouldering the driver's door open, they emerged into the rain. In the darkness they stumbled on the soft, sodden earth and tree roots as they went to the front of the Audi.

'You got any flame?' the driver asked his passenger in his broken English, as the rain beat into their faces. His passenger looked back at him.

In the dark, the rivulets of rain ran down the driver's face and obscured the long scar normally visible across his cheek. But nothing could obscure his opaque right eye. In this light, it was as if he were wearing a mask.

'No.'

He cursed. Suddenly, they knew they had to get away, and fast. Neither knew exactly where they were, except that they were in the black of the countryside. They could have gone by a more direct route from Swindon to the south coast but decided to go across country, to avoid any police patrols. But they'd soon got lost, taking one wrong turn after another; the dark, twisting roads made for tricky driving in torrential rain, especially for those not familiar with them.

'Let's get the fuck out of here,' said the passenger in his London accent.

'And the cargo?' asked the Albanian. The rain was saturating them.

'Leave it. There's nothing here to trace back to us once we wipe the car down.'

The driver wasn't so sure but there was nothing he could do about it now. They used their wet sleeves to vigorously wipe the steering wheel, door handles and the outside of the boot.

A quick look of acknowledgement between them and both started to run in the rain, through the thicket of trees and out the other side to a sodden field, away from the road. They were gone.

* * *

The police patrol car pulled up slowly. The marks in the verge of a vehicle leaving the road were clear. In the dark, amongst the trees, the faint outline of the Audi was visible. A police officer got out of the passenger side. He put his hat on and, torch in hand, slowly walked into the dark void, talking into the radio strapped to his shoulder. His colleague remained in the car and activated the strobe lights on the roof as a warning to any approaching vehicles.

The hard rain had stopped but heavy drips came off the leaves and high branches, and he felt the cold splashes on his exposed hands as he held his torch out. The officer looked in through the open driver's door, the light of the torch illuminating the front interior. Seeing the area did not contain any passengers, he moved the light to the rear seats. Nobody there. He relayed the number plate into his radio and back to the control room. They would soon know who the vehicle belonged to and could knock on their door.

Standing at the rear of the vehicle, he tried to lift the boot open but it wouldn't move. Thinking it was jammed from the impact, he walked back to the patrol car to fetch a wrench. Continuing his search, he put the end of it under the edge of the boot and levered it.

As it opened, a barn owl let out its cry, flying low across his eyeline. Almost feeling the flap of its wings on his face, he jumped back, his heart leaping wildly from the unexpected movement. Distracted, he quickly shone his torch inside.

Happy that the boot was empty, he slammed it shut, his heart still racing from the surprise of the owl. He walked back to the patrol car, fallen leaves squelching beneath his feet.

'Anything?' asked his colleague, as the officer sat back into the passenger seat.

'Nothing in the car,' he replied. 'Whoever was in there is long gone. The engine's cold. The plates are moody, nothing on PNC. Fucking owl coming out of nowhere nearly frightened me to death though.'

'Don't get comfortable – there's some tape in the boot. I'll ask the control room to call out vehicle reclamation.' The officer looked back at his colleague. 'That's if you're not too scared of the dark.' The driver had no intention of getting out of the warmth of the police car. Besides, he was the one wearing the stripes. 'Remember, it's nearly Halloween. . .' he added sarcastically as his colleague left his seat.

'Oh fuck off.' It had been a long night and the last of a five-night shift. The officer walked to the boot of the patrol car and retrieved a roll of blue-and-white tape, stamped with POLICE. He took it back to the Audi and used the trunks of the trees to create a taped cordon around the car. It would stop another report of it being sent into the control room. Job done, the patrol car resumed its journey.

* * *

Not long after noon the next day, the recovery lorry unloaded the Audi at a breaker's yard. From the call, Fin Chadwick knew enough to go over the vehicle with a gimlet eye for anything that the police hadn't retrieved. On many occasions he had discovered money, jewellery, drugs and weapons that he'd been able to sell on. In his opinion, the police were blind or lazy bastards because if he could find it, so could they.

He enjoyed this bit because he never knew what he was going to find. He ran his hands under the seats, pedals, roof lining. He'd have the front dash and side panels off and flooring up before it was crushed. Top locations for stashing any amount of gear. He lifted the boot. He pulled at the boot floor to reach the spare wheel where many a hoard had been found, but his access was restricted by a clump of dark-coloured blankets.

As he pulled them towards him, the blankets slipped off what they were covering. He stiffened, taking a step back. His eyes remained locked onto the object and he stood for a few seconds trying to process what was in front of him. He'd exposed a body, tucked in a foetal position. He was now staring at perfectly formed vertebrae running along a small, purple-grey back.

He stretched his arm out to the blanket the body was lying on and tugged at the edge of it, already worried by the colour of the skin. An arm slipped towards him. The way it fell told him there was no life in it.

He looked closely. It was a small arm, the grey colour of dead flesh. Slim. Small. Not a man's. *Fuck*. What was this? He took half a step back and then stood, eyes fixed on the arm, trying to weigh up what to do next. The last thing he needed was the police crawling all over the yard.

Chadwick hesitated. Slowly he stretched out his arm again and tugged at the blanket, hoping against hope that this was a trick. It was nearly Halloween after all. It might be a dummy, someone's idea of a joke. This time the body moved onto its back and the head flopped to the side at an awkward angle.

Suddenly, the wide eyes of a young girl stared into his, looking straight at him. Her dead face had captured the pain and horror of her last moments of life. Her mouth was set in a grimace and her teeth were bared. Under her chin he saw a wide, deep slash across her throat, almost through to the back of the neck.

He slammed the boot shut and retreated to a nearby Portakabin.

CHAPTER 1

He killed animals for a living and that's where the kernel of the idea had begun. The small abattoir that he now struggled to run on his own served a new purpose, what had now become his purpose in life. As he saw it, the end for so many animals provided him with the means to dispose of the problem.

He looked at the man sitting next to him in his car. He was a drunken, stinking heap of sleeping piss and shit. The smell emanating from him was vile, and in the confines of the car it became concentrated. It came from the man's mouth when he exhaled and from his body, his clothes, his skin. Every pore, every inch of him, gave off a foul-smelling odour. He couldn't wait to get him out. He smelt worse than any animal.

He had slaughtered thousands of cows, sheep and pigs over the years, each time returning expertly butchered meat, sausages and burger products to eager street food vendors, smallholders and hobby farmers. He'd learnt his trade, knew all about the anatomy of the animals he butchered, and knew exactly how to use his knife.

He preferred game to eat and he caught this himself. He was good at patiently stalking his prey and laying traps. And he was a good shot. His favourite was deer; instinctively shy animals that wouldn't have been touched by a human hand until dead. He liked to eat animals that lived in the wild and had had the least human contact possible. Because, as he saw it, that was the problem. Human contact.

He wasn't good at it. He didn't really get on with people; didn't like them. He much preferred animals. People left too much behind; everywhere he went he could see traces of them from discarded cans, bottles, food, packets, clothes, dirt, shit. Everywhere he looked, every time he drove or walked through the town. It was true, litter had become an obsession, he acknowledged that, but that was because it was out of control. The more humans there were, the bigger the issue was becoming. But now there was something else.

There was a new and growing problem – a different kind of litter that couldn't be picked up and put in the bin. This wasn't just wrappings, discarded paper or plastic. This was flesh and blood. Human litter he called it. And it was everywhere.

They called them 'homeless' but it was a misnomer because they were making their homes on the streets, turning doorways into bedrooms and precincts and streets into their living quarters. Men and women sat or lay on pavements, in doorways, on corners and alleyways, like discarded fag ends of society waiting to be swept up. He saw their draggled bodies covered by their fetid clothes, their shoulders slumped with the weight of their existence.

He watched them like he watched his animal prey, watched the things they did, how they reacted as people passed by. He saw how they looked up through cold, empty eyes as they asked again and again of each passer-by through their cracked lips to be given money. Or they just sat and said nothing, shivering against the cold, hoping the mere sight of them was enough to provoke pity and elicit the drop of coins onto the pavement in front of them.

He tried to calm his thoughts but the complete apathy they displayed towards their own lives made him rage. He looked across at the man in the seat next to him. The smell of him was making him gag. As he drove he took an off-white cotton handkerchief from his trouser pocket and pressed it to his lips. The feel of the material calmed him. He had to calm down.

The abattoir was situated in a remote corner in the far north of the county, and it was his mother who had said that it suited his personality. What she meant was the lack of it. She knew he needed to be kept out of society. Society didn't suit him. He needed his own world.

'Brian, you stay inside your head and think too much,' she said. He could still hear her saying it. 'That's why you've got all those little tics.' That's what she called them. Tics. The endless washing of his hands. The constant need to wipe his mouth with a cotton handkerchief. Always picking things up off the ground.

She had been right though, it did suit him. He loved his job, loved the animals; he relished seeing how they came in alive and once he'd killed them, how he turned them into meat. The process of it gave him a good deal of satisfaction. It was no different with humans.

Eventually he arrived, able to pull the car right up to a side door. He was only too pleased to get out. He'd turned the heater on in the car to help keep his passenger in a comatose state, but the stench it generated was evil. *The dirty bastard.*

He got out and went round to the passenger side door and opened it. Holding his breath, he took hold of the man's arm and yanked him out of his seat, half waking him in the process. In a drowsy but compliant haze, he came out easily enough. Getting him through the side door into the small lairage area was also easy. The alcohol had rendered the man's mind incapable of registering where he was, never mind any danger he might be in.

Offered a simple metal chair to sit on in the half-light, just while he told the man he had to find the key for the room he could stay in, the beggaring fool didn't even feel the cold steel of a captive bolt pistol against the side of his head. On firing, he slumped forward instantly. Pushing the man back on the chair he fired another bolt into his chest. Dead.

Halloween and Bonfire Night were approaching and there were any number of community firework displays and football matches in the area over the next few evenings. The distraction of a goal or people gazing up at firework displays would ensure no one paid too close attention to the hotdog or burger in their hand.

CHAPTER 2

It had been the television programme Prayer Taylor saw a year ago that had first sparked her curiosity about her identity. Her adoptive parents Patrick and Fiona Taylor had been very good about it. Of course she should know the truth; of course she should go. They knew that at sixteen, Prayer was of an age now when these things started to matter.

The Taylors had always been open with her and had explained to her when she was very young that she had been adopted. They felt it was important for her to know; they didn't want her to find out in the school playground. It was important for them to explain that she was special and had been chosen by them. And besides, they knew this day would come eventually. They had spoken of it often, although never in her presence. They spoke of it so they could prepare themselves for when it came, as they knew it would.

With the help of the charity and adoption service, they'd traced her birth mother to Swindon. Patrick and Fiona Taylor had dismissed the need to know about the background of their daughter's mother at the time of the adoption; frankly, they didn't want to know right then. They didn't want to spoil their moment and have to consider her, about how she might be feeling having given up her beautiful five-day-old baby daughter, the most perfect thing they had ever seen. The three of them were starting a new future together, and they didn't want it marred by such thoughts as how the mother might be coping.

Since they'd brought her home when she was just days old, she had been the answer to their prayers – and so that's what they'd called her. Five desperate rounds of non-productive IVF had left the two high achievers shattered. They had everything except their own child. When they finally accepted defeat and considered adoption, they knew they had to have a newborn. It would feel as if the baby were almost their own flesh and blood that way.

And she had been an absolute joy to them ever since. Seemingly wiser than her years, the Taylors told anyone who would listen of her academic achievements at her expensive private school. With top grades in her year, she was fluent in French and Mandarin. Not only that, but she was very socially rounded and could talk to anyone with confidence and empathy, thanks to drama and debating classes.

She was very smart and savvy, already taking an interest in politics and the wider world. She was developing a social conscience and was keen to help those less fortunate than herself. She wanted to become a lawyer and she had set her sights on a law degree at university.

She was a credit to her successful architect parents, who were extremely proud of her. From their home in affluent Little Aston, Sutton Coldfield, they had nurtured Prayer and watched with wonder as they saw their pretty teenage girl take confident strides towards adulthood. She was full of the promise of a successful life and future.

Prayer conceded that it must have been very difficult for them when she asked to find her birth mother, but they couldn't have been nicer about it, or more supportive. They were the best parents to have been adopted by.

When she had explained that she'd prefer to meet her biological mother without them, they were understandably apprehensive. This was something she wanted to do on her own, she said. She wanted to keep them both separate – her parents and her biological mother. When she explained that she would be staying under the guidance of the Salvation Army and that there would be a member of the Salvation Army with her at all times, they were much happier about her request and understood completely. They would be supporting her, she told them, acting as an intermediary. She'd never lied to them before, but she'd lied then.

She also told them her biological mother was a nurse who lived on her own. Another lie. Prayer had no idea what she did for a living, but she knew that saying she was a nurse would have a positive influence on her parents. All Prayer knew was that she wanted to meet her biological mother and question her.

The burning question she wanted to ask, of course, was *why*? Why had she been given away? She needed to know. Typical in the circumstances, she also wanted to know who her father was. What had happened to cause her own mother to give her baby away to two strangers? What sort of person was she to do that?

She talked it through with her parents and she reassured them that once she knew about her biological parents, she could put it behind her. It was merely a case of putting a missing piece of a puzzle into place and then closing that part of her life forever.

The Taylors understood; they would give her space and time and wait for her to call them, such was their trust in their amazing daughter and the bond they had with her. She had never given them any concern, or a moment's worry. She was so very sensible.

Prayer knew this. She knew how they viewed her and like most teenagers her age, she was beginning not to share quite so much, to keep things to herself; starting the process of breaking away, of independence from her parents. She was a product of their successful nurture, but Prayer was already making plans for a life at a university as far away from the family home as she could get. Unknown to them, she was starting to make her own decisions, hungry for life on her own terms. She loved them dearly but needed to be her own person.

Such was their trust in her and her ability to handle the situation, they were prepared to step back and in a week's time, welcome her home and listen to her news. As much as it hurt them to do so, as much as they wanted to continue to protect her from the wider world, they knew they had to start treating her like an adult – the last thing they wanted was to lose her now.

This, they decided, would best be done in the half-term break. Prayer's private school broke up earlier and for longer than state schools. This would allow her to spend the time away from them in Swindon that she wanted, and also leave them able to make the best of the second week.

She'd chosen to go by train, as she could travel on her own and it would give her time to gather her thoughts and imagine what was to come. She kept her parents informed of her two changes at Birmingham and Gloucester. They promised that after they knew she had arrived safely, they wouldn't bother her with their calls or texts.

The Great Western train was approaching Swindon and she was full of excitement and trepidation. She texted them: 'I'm here! Love you. Big hugs xxx ☺'. She was wearing an expensive leather biker jacket over a roll-neck jumper and jeans. As Prayer looked at herself in a small mirror she kept in her smart handbag, she took a lipstick and applied it, pouting as she did so. She'd wanted to look good, make the best impression. *What would her birth mother look like*, she wondered? Would they have similarities? In a few minutes she would know; she would be meeting her for the first time.

The train came to a halt at Swindon station, where they had arranged to meet. The other passengers stirred and stood up to retrieve their bags from the overhead luggage space. There was a sense of anticipation as they all reached their destination. Suddenly, Prayer was nervous. Her usual unwavering confidence uncharacteristically deserted her.

She deliberately didn't look out of the window as she retrieved her pink case from overhead. It was becoming all too real. There would be no going back from this point. She would always know where she came from. Who she came from. She had a thousand questions, but right there and then, wondered if she was doing the right thing after all. She counselled herself. She was here now. How bad could it be, the truth? She had to know it.

She waited patiently for an old couple barring her way as they gathered their things from their seats. They stood in the aisle hurriedly putting on their coats. Still she didn't look out of the windows. She wanted to get off the train first. The old couple muttered their apologies and chided one another for their slowness. At last they were ready and started to move down the aisle.

This was it, thought Prayer, *the point of no return*. Nervously, she stepped out onto the platform, paying attention to her case, and at last looked up. There was no one there. She walked forward and looked around at the people that had just come off the train. They were all busy helloing and waving to people. Then suddenly she saw her. Standing alone with her hand up, a slight figure in the distance. Prayer walked towards her.

CHAPTER 3

'MEGON – PLEASE COME HOME' the bold print pleaded. A photograph of Megon Wallace in a school uniform accompanied the piece, along with a picture of family members, concern etched in their faces. The text included the words, 'We all love you. You're not in trouble, just get in touch with us, please.'

The *Evening Standard* had run the report on the seventh page; the thirteen-year-old girl had left home in Hackney one late September morning to go to school and hadn't come home since. It was a depressingly familiar 'runaway' story that readers would have read time and again. The only reason it had managed to get into the *Standard* three weeks ago was due to the fact that one of the paper's reporters lived in the same block as Megon's parents.

The piece went on to explain that Dad, Paul Wallace, had just been made redundant, and Mum, Leonie, was recovering from chemotherapy. Megon's two younger sisters and Nigella, the pregnant family Rottweiler, all missed her. The reporter had tried hard for the sympathy angle.

Wallace held a cutting of the report in his hands; he'd carried it with him for three weeks, folded in his wallet. He read it again and again. It was a nightmare he couldn't quite believe they were all in. The flimsy paper was already becoming worn, but there it was. In black and white. His daughter had left home and not returned. He was gutted, literally. When he could get it, sleep was the only respite he had from a raw fear that had lodged firmly in his stomach ever since she'd gone. He was literally sick with worry. She was the only thing he could think of.

The police had taken the missing report and had said all the right things. But Megon had been one of twenty-six reports of missing people across the capital they had received that day. The day before there had been twenty-nine and the day after, another thirty-two, many young truants amongst them. While most returned home within twenty-four hours, some remained missing.

They signposted the family to Missing People, the charity set up in memory of Suzy Lamplugh, the estate agent who'd walked out of her office one day in July 1986 and had not been seen since. It had been Missing People who had immediately printed posters of Megon and provided ongoing support to their family. They assigned them a caseworker, who told them they could ring her whenever they needed to – and they did. True to her word, the caseworker was there for them. Especially when Paul Wallace was sleepless at stupid o'clock in the morning.

Megon then joined the hundreds of other people who featured on the charity's website. And as Wallace scoured through the endless stream of faces of other missing people – missing since last week, last month, last year; five, ten years ago, longer; twenty years, thirty years – he began to wonder if their quest was already futile.

Where did all these people go? Where were they all? There were hundreds of them, thousands. Some were old, some middle-aged, some in their teens, twenties, thirties – all ages. Some were infants, and there were even babies. How could they all be missing? *How can a baby be missing?* How could so many people be displaced? How come he hadn't known about all this until now? He was shocked by the sheer scale of it all.

A huge wave of despair washed over him as he looked at the faces on his laptop screen. There were teenagers like Megon who'd left home one day and never returned. How come this wasn't in the news? Why hadn't he known about this? Where were the police investigations? How could teenagers simply go missing?

They couldn't all still be missing, he thought; not after ten, twenty or thirty years. They had to be dead – taken, killed, murdered – but what was being done about it? Because if they weren't dead, where were they? How could kids vanish and there not be a public outcry?

Paul Wallace was determined Megon would not be one of the faces that would look out at people in a year's time. He began to think that it was just as well he had lost his job. He could put all his efforts into finding Megon. She had been missing for four weeks and already it felt like four months.

The police didn't seem overly concerned – they could see that her life wasn't ideal. Friends had reported they'd seen her; she was alive and apparently well. But not at home. She'd regularly stayed out late and they suggested that going missing was another step further, probably another symptom of her unhappiness and general teenage hormones. A cry for attention.

Paul was the first to admit that their domestic set-up wasn't conducive to happy families. The five of them and the dog were all cooped up in a small flat, and the last six months had seen enough frustration and tension to test even the most contented. Having to support his wife through her cancer diagnosis and then the treatment had seen him take his eye off the ball at work. There had been little in the way of sympathy there – there was no room in small companies to carry people like him.

He'd had to look after the girls, take on the household chores as well. He'd put his family first and it had resulted in his redundancy. He'd worked at the company for fifteen years, always on time, the last to leave and at the first sign that he needed some support, he was gone.

With a couple of thousand pounds in redundancy money, Paul was at least able to concentrate on looking after Leonie. He'd thought he was going to lose her and that terrified him. With her cancer now in remission, it felt like they'd turned a corner. As they were about to count their blessings, without being able to draw breath, they'd gone from one nightmare to another. He'd lost Megon. They'd fought the cancer so now he was determined they'd fight for Megon. He had to find her and bring her back.

Leonie wasn't strong enough to join him in the search and the girls had to go to school, so he continued to go out alone every day. He went back in the evening, made sure they were all right, fed them, fed the dog, and then at about 10 p.m., went out again until 2 a.m. He was back out again at 6 a.m.; his body wouldn't let him rest any longer than three hours. Very quickly this became his routine. His job.

He'd put up the posters of her all around the locality and in the Tube stations. Her young, pretty face looked out, her dark hair falling on her shoulders. She looked older than thirteen – he saw that now and it frightened him. It annoyed him if a poster was taken down, so he'd put another in its place. He made sure all the neighbours knew about Megon's disappearance.

This had paid off when he discovered one of them was a freelance journalist for the *Evening Standard*. She said she'd help Paul with publicity, get Megon's picture out to thousands throughout London and beyond. He was pleased with the piece, which had given the number of the charity and asked people to ring if they'd seen Megon.

From day one he had taken to the streets himself, walking around, convinced that he'd see her and be able to take her back. He'd walked so many miles. His feet ached at first and then they just seemed to become part of his shoes, as he barely took them off.

He had to go to every place he thought she might be or anywhere her friends had told him she might go. She'd had a mobile that the police had rung the day after they reported her missing. She answered once, but the line immediately went dead. He tried but with the same result.

His regular visits to the Missing People website made him wonder how on earth people continued to function when their loved ones remained missing. As the weeks went by, he knew the answer to this. As much as he tried to remain cheerful indoors with his family, he knew he was only just hanging on.

At the same time as his heart was heavy and felt like it was breaking, his head was awash with dark thoughts. Paul's mind was his biggest enemy; he knew if he listened to the voices in his head, played out the worst nightmares of what might be happening to Megon, he would quickly go mad. These were the things that deprived him of sleep. He felt that he was on a knife edge. He daren't speak to Leonie about it; he didn't want to hear her nightmares too. Besides, they hadn't spoken much since Megon had gone. The pain was etched raw on Leonie's face; there was no need for words. The girls cried. He knew what he had to do. Find her. For all their sakes.

He had to carry on searching because if he gave in, if he gave up, not only Megon would be lost; they'd all be lost. Every time he went out to look for her, Paul had every hope that *that* day, *that* night, he would find her and take her home. He knew he hadn't seen his little girl for the last time. He knew that it was up to him to find her.

Every day, her friends, neighbours, even strangers who were shown her picture said they saw her here and there. This sent Paul all across London. As a result of the newspaper appeal, the police told him she had been seen as far afield as the Midlands, Cornwall and Brighton. He soon realised she couldn't be in all these places at the same time and so he chose to stay local for the sake of Leonie and the girls, refusing to believe that Megon would leave them to go miles away.

As the weeks went by, he spoke to people, people he wouldn't otherwise have passed the time of day with. In his bid to reach anyone who might have seen Megon, his quest saw him speaking to the homeless, those who sat out all night, wrapped up in rags and cardboard, using anything they could find to fight against the cold. He came to respect them, if nothing else but for their sheer tenacity for continuing to live a life of hardship with little or no apparent comfort.

He became good at people watching, spent hours at it until those he watched became familiar. He watched and observed so many kids pouring onto the streets and at railway stations such as King's Cross and Euston, and saw how they were approached by those who hung around those places, watching, like him. Once, he spoke to a young lad, Mitch, at King's Cross, who'd come down from the north a year ago.

Paul told him he worked for a charity, and for a Big Mac and Coke, Mitch told him the names of a few of the people that Paul had seen, and what they were doing. Mitch said there was a trade in the young and vulnerable who were literally bought and sold. The boy spoke matter-of-factly about it.

'I see these kids about a few times and then I don't see them no more. They disappear. Because they've been taken. Taken and sold on to someone for money, so another person can use them to make money.'

'But how can they disappear? What about their families? Why doesn't anyone want to find them?' Paul struggled to understand.

'They've run away, like me. We're trouble at home, we don't want to be at school, so we come here. When trouble goes away, no one goes out and looks for it to bring it back, do they? But when they come here, the kids, they don't know about these people. They make promises and kids get sucked in. They're good at it; they make it sound good and the kids go with them. I wanted to make my own way, live my own life, that's why I came here. But I watch this other shit going on all the time.'

Paul was incredulous. 'But how do you live? How do you survive?'

'They approached me to do the toilets, going up to men. I told them to fuck off. So I steal. I take mobiles, laptops and iPads, wallets and handbags. People are careless. I do good trade at train stations.'

Mitch explained he didn't lose any sleep over what he did, just hoped that in time he would somehow no longer need to do it. It was still better than what 'they' would have him do.

'Couldn't you go home?'

'There was five of us kids at home. Being here, I'm one less mouth to feed, one less to tidy up after. I wanted my own space. Freedom. I don't want to be surrounded by kids. I've grown up now. I can live life on my own terms. I'm not going back. I won't do this forever.'

'You might get caught and end up in prison,' Paul cautioned.

'I won't. Have you seen this lot?' He gestured towards a police officer walking through the concourse. 'They'd have to catch me first.' He gave Paul a cheeky grin, thanked him for the burger and left.

Paul wondered if Megon had been preyed on by the people he'd seen. The thought of that made his heart ache. He knew Megon always thought she was so streetwise, but witnessing this underworld for himself, he knew she wouldn't stand a chance. His beautiful Megon, the baby he'd cuddled, taught to talk, walk, ride her bike, taken to school and helped with her homework. She was still his baby, his and Leonie's. Why had she gone?

He went over and over the last time he saw her. What had he missed that day, what clues were there that she was not going to come back that evening as she always had done? He didn't want to believe anything bad had happened to her. But equally, he couldn't believe she would want to hurt her mother in this way. She wouldn't. So what the hell was going on?

In only four weeks, the sightings of Megon became less and less frequent. Paul knew he would have to cast his net wider. He had saturated the locality with posters and he had to admit that if he were Megon, he would have left to escape the pictures of her that were everywhere, but what could he do?

* * *

One day a breakthrough finally came. A friend of Megon got in touch to say another friend had had contact with his daughter. They said that Megon was no longer in London – she was in Swindon. Paul didn't even know for sure where Swindon was.

CHAPTER 4

Detective Inspector Temple pulled up outside a row of terraced houses in the shadow of a block of 1960s flats in Park North, Swindon. He peered out of the windscreen, searching for the number on the front door. Looking at the numbers on the houses either side confirmed the house he had to go to. The plain, unpainted wooden door gave a hint of what lay behind. Underneath the key latch there were deep, dirty scars from the paws of a strong dog. The base of the door was blackened by boot marks and a tall spike of thick-stemmed thistles stood guard to one side.

Temple had seized the routine enquiry following the morning briefing. A fourteen-year-old girl had been reported missing by her school friend, who had rung in saying she hadn't seen her for three days. Unusually, there had been no report of the girl missing from home by her parents. He had no doubt a few quick enquiries would establish that this was the latest teen prank to plague the emergency number.

A couple of phone calls and a PNC check quickly established the missing girl came from a chaotic family. Dad was long gone, leaving the unemployed mother – who was known to social services – nursing a chronic alcohol habit as she struggled to look after the missing girl and her ten-year-old brother. An unemployed twenty-two-year-old son who no longer lived at home had an old conviction for possession of Class A drugs.

It should be simple enough, and Temple had to take any opportunity to get out of the poky office. But he resented that it should have to come to this, picking up an enquiry that could easily be done by a PCSO or constable just so that he could get out in the fresh air.

He was miserable. He was sick of feeling like a pariah, having spent the last six months marking time away from front-line policing on 'project work' that had stopped just short of counting paperclips. The suicide of a teenage boy after police contact during a previous murder enquiry he'd led had seen him placed under investigation by the Independent Office for Police Conduct. Temple gave himself a hard time over it; he wished it had turned out differently. But it hadn't.

The deputy chief constable would let him know the outcome of the investigation that afternoon. Temple hoped for 'management advice' and a return to detective duties that, for anyone else, might be a fair assessment. But he knew there was too much bad blood between him and his boss to think he'd be treated fairly in this process.

As well as moving him to back-office functions, the hierarchy had also put him back into uniform. Back in the white shirt and black clip-on tie, Temple knew it was all part of the punishment but it pissed him off; being turned out of the CID office was a clear sign to all of his fall from grace. He was in the shit, back in uniform, with a rubbish job and a long investigation ahead of him, and the loss of control that came with it. The drip effect.

It poured fuel on the inevitable canteen gossip, and the Chinese whispers ensured that when it was all put together, a stink of suspicion and lack of trust hovered about him. He quickly noticed that no one with promotion prospects would openly be seen talking to him, no matter how many times they might have passed the time of day or worked together in the past.

Professionally, he was a leper; death following police contact was to be avoided at all costs and was guaranteed to put a large dent in any career. He found that when colleagues saw him approaching, or he rang them on a work-related matter, they behaved as if he had something they didn't want to catch. Held at arm's length by the organisation and many of those in it, after six long months, Temple was feeling hypersensitive to his situation.

Then almost a month ago, the same hierarchy took the decision to lump him together in an office with a few more of the force's black sheep who were under disciplinary investigation. In comparison with his three other colleagues, Temple considered himself lucky. His new 'project' was auditing historic missing person reports. The others were working on auditing stop-and-search figures and charging decisions. It would keep them all out of operational duties and distanced from other colleagues.

Although Temple was grateful for more meaningful work at last, the natural by-product of disciplinary action was a heightened sense of paranoia. He analysed every sideways look, every word spoken for anything that could cut through the secrecy and give a clue as to what the hierarchy had in mind to sanction him. It always leaked out somewhere to someone who would tell others.

As such, Temple viewed his three fellow officers with quiet mistrust, and they returned the compliment. Quarantined into one windowless room that had previously been a storage area, they all felt the size of their cramped conditions. Each of them was suspicious enough of the others and the Professional Standards Department to think that there was a reason they'd put them all together in such a confined space. The room was either bugged or there was a mole amongst them.

The three others were variously accused of assaulting a neighbour, racist comments and sexual harassment of a colleague. Now and then, each would make a throwaway comment, with no other motive than to put the theory of a mole or covert surveillance to the test. It made for a tense atmosphere, broken only by taut bursts of humour.

A bout of food poisoning running through the station as a result of a shift sergeant's attempt at a prawn curry the previous night meant that by the morning, the shift was decimated and a number of low-level enquiries had to be divvied out. Temple had grabbed the chance to get out into the fresh air.

The prospect of conducting a safe-and-well check on a young schoolgirl who'd been reported missing by her friend would get him out for an hour. He had every expectation of finding the two friends together, giggling at him for taking the report seriously.

He thumped his fist loudly against the door.

'Mrs Lewis? Answer the door please.' He banged again. He figured 10.30 was a decent enough time to wake anyone.

His knock was sufficiently loud to rouse her and to open the door as far as a heavy padlocked chain allowed. She peered through the gap.

'Mrs Barbara Lewis? I'm DI Temple. I need to talk to you about your daughter. Can I come in please?' Through the narrow opening, he could see a portion of her drawn and lined face. He had seen many faces such as hers, haggard and weighted by the unrelenting misery of her liquid life. From his basic enquiries, he knew she was forty-three, but on sight of her she looked easily twenty years older. She wasn't registering the uniform so he took his warrant card out and put it close to the opening in the door.

For a moment she stood looking back at him blankly, before closing the door to release a chain that banged heavily on release. Dressed in a once-white flimsy cotton vest that ended at the top of her bare thighs, she let him in and walked back into the living room without a backward glance. Closing the door, Temple examined the thick chain and heavy-duty padlock that had barred his entry.

'Who are you expecting?' he called after her, but she ignored him.

Temple followed her into a living room where he was greeted with the stale smell of body odour. A multi-stained carpet lined the floor and empty cider cans stood sentry against the legs of wooden armchairs. Yellowing net curtains were hanging at the windows and spray from what was presumably cider stained the walls.

Even if he'd wanted to sit, Temple could see all the chairs were occupied either by clothes, dog hairs or newspapers. He could see that any notion of domesticity had bypassed Barbara Lewis. She continued on through to a small square kitchen and Temple followed. Standing with her back to him, she flicked the switch on the kettle.

'Don't bother on my account,' he said as he looked about him, taking in the filthy surroundings. He didn't want to risk drinking anything offered to him in a cup by Barbara Lewis. She killed the noise of the kettle.

'I'd like to ask you about your daughter – she's been reported missing by her friend. Is she here?'

Fully expecting her to say she was in her bedroom, he continued to look around. The kitchen was in disarray, with all the work surfaces covered by various cooking items, tins and the remains of old food. There was a strong smell of something rotting in an overflowing waste bin that she seemed oblivious to. The place was a health hazard.

She snorted, 'She's not been here for weeks.'

'What do you mean? She does live here, doesn't she?'

'Yes,' she said, irritated at being questioned. She kept her back to him.

'So how can she have not been here for weeks? If she's not here, where is she?'

'I dunno,' she shrugged.

'So, how long has it been since you last saw her? Two weeks, three?'

'Yep. That's about right,' Barbara Lewis slurred, uninterested. She remained turned away from him, busy with something he couldn't see. He wasn't sure who was more confused now, him or her. Was she really saying she hadn't seen her own fourteen-year-old daughter for weeks? Being an alcoholic, perhaps she'd got it wrong; perhaps she hadn't understood what he'd said. He persisted.

'She was reported missing today by a school friend who hasn't seen her for three days, but you say you haven't seen her for weeks?' He watched as Barbara Lewis shrugged again.

'You don't appear to be that concerned. Do you know where she is?' asked Temple, slightly raising his voice as if she was hard of hearing.

'No, I don't know where she is.' Barbara turned around to face him with a cup clutched in one hand, cigarette in the other. He looked at her standing in front of him, her dirty feet bare on a faded, sticky lino floor. If her feet were anything to go by he couldn't guess when she'd last had a bath.

'Don't you *want* to know where she is?' Temple asked. He found it strange for a mother not to be concerned about the absence of her fourteen-year-old daughter. He wondered if she was on drugs as well as booze.

She was silent before letting out a sigh. 'No, I don't think I do.'

'You *are* Barbara Lewis, the mother of China Lewis?'

'Yes,' she sighed again.

'When did you last see her?'

'I don't know, I can't remember exactly.' She looked up to the ceiling as if she was trying hard to remember. Her grey, lank, greasy hair fell back like curtains either side of her haggard face. Watching her, Temple had no doubt that her lack of recall was genuine.

'What's she like, China?'

'Gobby,' she slurred, looking at him.

'Is she in any trouble?'

'She's always in trouble. And I don't want it here.'

'Have you had any contact with China since you last saw her?'

'Nope.' Her heavily bagged eyes betrayed no concern. 'And I don't want to hear from her.'

'And why would that be exactly?'

Barbara Lewis shrugged and with her wrinkled mouth clamped round her cigarette, she concentrated on taking a deep draw of nicotine. Temple couldn't make her out. She showed a genuine lack of interest in where her daughter was. In fact, looking around, she showed a lack of interest in everything except for what was in the cup she was holding.

'Do you know where she is, Barbara?'

'I've said I don't know.'

Temple moved towards her. 'Barbara, you *need* to know. You should want to know where she is.'

'As I said, I don't know and don't want to know.'

'You are her mother, her legal custodian. You should be looking after her—'

Before he finished, she slammed the cup down on the edge of the work surface, sending some of the cider inside spilling out. Suddenly she rounded on him, the fingers holding her cigarette jabbing out at him as she shouted.

'I've had enough of this. You lot should be looking after her. I don't want her back here. *You* find her. *You* look after her. You lot. You're supposed to be so fucking good at it.'

'I'm trying to find out where she is, to see if she's in any danger, to stop her being in danger. To do that, I need your help,' Temple said in an attempt to placate her. The last thing he wanted was for her to become violent and for him to have to lay hands on her to restrain her.

'I don't care.' Her voice was hard. Her face twisted as she spat the words.

She wrapped one arm across herself and glanced towards the small window in the kitchen that looked out onto the approach to the front door. Temple was starting to lose patience. It was clear he was an unwelcome intrusion into her day and he was getting nowhere with her. He decided to change tack.

'Show me her bedroom.'

Barbara Lewis led the way up the stairs, leaving Temple to step back and avert his eyes as it was clear she was wearing no underwear under her long vest. She showed him to a room at the top of the stairs. Again, the scars of clawing dog paws were evident on the door.

The room she showed him to was small, dominated by a double divan bed pushed up against the wall, giving access from one side. A creased, plain grey duvet cover was neatly arranged on the bed. He lifted the mattress and ran his hand underneath. He felt nothing. Opposite the end of the bed, Temple searched through a chest of drawers.

It contained the usual teenage clothing of Primark tops and leggings. As Temple searched the bottom drawer, he put his hands through the clothing to the back board. There he discovered a stash of condoms and morning-after pills.

'Does she have a boyfriend?'

Barbara Lewis stood in the door frame, looking down on him as he squatted in front of the drawers. To the side of her, Temple's eye was drawn to the end of a small barrel from a bolt lock on the door frame. As he looked up at her waiting for an answer, she sucked deeply on her disappearing cigarette and Temple watched as a column of ash fell onto the carpet. She lifted her bare foot and rubbed it in with her toes. Looking at the condoms in his hands, she shrugged her shoulders.

'She's *fourteen*.' He hoped his words might penetrate through the cider. Temple knew this wasn't just a sign China was having sex.

'I don't know, she must have a boyfriend, mustn't she?' she slurred. He stood up and faced her.

'You see, my problem is that you've got a completely different reaction to most parents whose kids go missing. They're usually distraught. They're usually straight on the phone. They help the police to find their kids and bring them back. You've not even bothered to report her missing. From what you're telling me, you don't even want her back, is that right?'

A sarcastic cackle showed her stained brown teeth. 'Oh, at last, he's got it.'

'Whether you're bothered or not, I still need to find China. If you don't want her back here then we'll deal with that when we've found her. So if you know if any harm's come to her, you better say now because I will find out.'

Barbara looked at him. 'You don't get it, do you?'

'Then help me, Barbara. Tell me.'

'She's safer away from here,' she murmured. Temple let a silence settle between them.

'Are you in danger? Is that what you're trying to tell me?'

She gestured that her own safety wasn't an issue.

'Then what is it? Who or what is the threat, Barbara? Tell me, why isn't China safe here in her own home?'

'I don't want her back,' she hissed. She turned and went downstairs.

Temple finished his search of the bedroom and went out onto the landing. Above him was a loft hatch. Using a rickety stool he snatched from the bathroom, he slowly pushed the board up to open the loft. As he lifted the hatch, he heard the soft break of thick threads of cobwebs. He stuck his head into darkness. In the little light there was, he could see nothing significant. Familiar with the smell of decaying flesh, he was satisfied that China Lewis wasn't dead and hidden in the house.

As he returned the stool to the bathroom, his eyes flicked around. The room was filthy. The rim of the bath had a dark, dirty tide mark around it and it certainly hadn't been recently used. The room smelt, but not of bleach or any other cleaning products that might be a telltale sign of something befalling China in her own home which might necessitate a scrub down.

He looked in on two other bedrooms before he went back downstairs into the kitchen, where he found Barbara Lewis at the sink with her back turned.

'Where's your phone? Your mobile, where is it?'

She looked around her, found it by the sink and gave it to him. Looking through the grubby screen he found China's number and rang it. There was no answer. He sent the number to his own phone.

Just then, Temple heard the front door slam shut. A Staffordshire bull terrier padded its way down the hall and came trotting into the kitchen, followed by its tall, shaven-headed owner. The rolled-up sleeves of his shirt revealed a brightly inked eagle and dragon tattoo that extended all the way to his neck. His slim but strong physique was no doubt a result of twice-weekly visits to the gym. In his hand he carried a Tesco bag containing two large bottles of cider and a cheap bottle of vodka, which he set down on the floor.

'Who the *fuck* are you?' he asked, eyeing Temple, not welcoming the sight of a stranger. He slammed a chain-link dog lead onto the only available space on a kitchen worktop to mark his displeasure. 'I thought I fucking told you,' he said to Barbara. 'You don't let anyone in here.'

'It's the police, Gary, and he's just going – he's here about your sister.' Barbara Lewis was suddenly animated, going towards the bag.

'I'm looking for China.' Temple faced Gary Lewis, who continued to eye him.

'Oh yeah?' His features were sharp, his nose and chin protruding from his face as if they were trying to get away from it. He tipped his head back slightly so that he could look at Temple through half closed eyes.

'When was the last time you saw her?'

'I don't have to talk to you.' Gary Lewis drew his shoulders back as he spoke.

'When, Gary? As soon as you tell me, I can get the fuck out of here.'

'A few days ago.'

'You see, your mother says she hasn't been here for weeks. So which is it, Gary? Days or weeks?'

'This silly cow's confused. We haven't seen her for a few days, that's all.'

'How come you haven't reported her missing?'

'Because she's not.' Lewis couldn't believe his mother had let a fucking copper in the house. Stupid drunken bitch couldn't be trusted. He wanted Temple out. More than that, he wanted this copper to stop poking around, which he would if his mother would keep her mouth shut.

'So which of you two is telling the truth? Your sister China was last seen by a friend three days ago. Your mother says she hasn't seen her for weeks and doesn't want her here. Who's she been staying with if she's not been here?'

'I don't know where she's been staying. With a friend, I suppose. I don't know where she is. Look, she's not fucking missing all right and that silly cow there doesn't know what she's talking about. She's around; she's probably been back here without us knowing.'

'Where did you last see her?' asked Temple, watching as Gary Lewis looked at him through his small, slit-like eyes. As Temple kept eye contact with Lewis, he was suddenly conscious that he could feel the dog's snout sniffing closely at his shins.

'Here. The little cow fucked off with some money of mine. I'll find her, don't worry. I'll get her back. She's only local, people have seen her. They've told me. You can stop looking for her – she's not missing. Now get out, copper, there must be some traffic you can go and play with.'

Ignoring his offer to leave, Temple was trying to work out what to do if the dog attacked him.

'What people? Who?'

'Just people, people like her friends. I don't know how many times I have to tell you, she's not missing. Now fuck off out of it.' Lewis started to twitch his shoulders. He didn't want any police looking for China. He could handle it himself.

'Has she ever run away before?' Temple persisted.

'She's always running. We just haven't bothered reporting it because she always turns up. Now, I said fuck off.' Lewis leaned in towards Temple and an eager growl sprouted from the dog, whose gaze seemed to be fixed on his calf. Temple looked down. The dog was a solid mass of muscle. He didn't fancy its jaws clamping onto one of his legs if it was incited by Gary Lewis.

'You need to let me know if she comes back.' Temple left his card on top of the dog lead and left the house. Perhaps this was still two friends giving the police the runaround, but from what he'd seen, he wouldn't be happy until he'd seen China Lewis for himself.

CHAPTER 5

'Kostya, we *have* to inform the police. She's been missing for four days now. No one has seen her.' Darya Petrenko's anguished face betrayed any attempts not to panic as she pleaded with her husband. She'd give everything she had just to have her daughter back. And that was it – it seemed *he* would not.

She couldn't eat or sleep with the worry. Her daughter had never run away before, but the driver said that when he dropped her off on the last day before the half-term break, instead of going through the wrought-iron gates into the grounds of the £15,000-a-term school, she had turned and run in the opposite direction, leaving him to watch her in his rear-view mirror.

He had explained to her that the traffic of Bentleys and Porsches dropping off had prevented him from reversing and driving after Katya. Despite his anti-kidnap and hostile-environment training, by the time he had got out of the car to run after her, he couldn't see where she had gone. It was the last thing he had thought would happen that morning.

Avoiding looking at his wife's pale, agonised face, Kostya Petrenko paced around the plush drawing room. For the first time in his life he was unsure what to do, but he was equally aware that he shouldn't show signs of weakness, not now, not even to Darya. He reminded himself he was a very successful businessman, a multi-millionaire. He had provided his family with every luxury and he couldn't understand why his thirteen-year-old daughter Katya would go missing.

Kostya made sure that she had everything. He even made sure she wasn't contaminated by the toxic London air, as he saw to it that she was ferried everywhere in an armoured black limousine. He'd tried to see to it that she was virtually hermetically sealed so that no contaminants touched her life. And now this. But the timing of it couldn't be worse for him.

'I cannot inform the police. You know why. I have people out looking for her. They will find her. She will quickly miss her life here with us and return, I'm certain of it.'

'How can you put your business interests before your own flesh and blood? Your daughter went out of that door four days ago and we haven't seen or heard from her since. What kind of man are you, Kostya?' Darya spat back in Russian, her face wet with angry tears.

'And just how do you think it will look to the people I have to make the deal with? They will think that I can't even control my own family, my own daughter, so why would they do business with me? I sign the contract on Friday. If she hasn't returned by then, I will inform the police on Saturday. More time, that's all I ask.'

'You are *inhuman*!' she screamed at him.

He was as concerned as she was, but the last thing he wanted was to involve the police. His wealth had bought him an exclusive address and privacy, and he risked all of that by reporting Katya's disappearance to the police. He had no intention of letting police officers through the front door of his Belgravia house to poke their noses into his world. He could imagine their questions, them searching his home, taking his laptop away, asking about his business dealings, his money. Invading their private space. The thought of it appalled him as much as thinking of Katya on the streets of London.

He decided that he would go to the Russian Embassy if Katya hadn't returned by Friday – after he'd signed the contract on his latest business for financial consultancy services. In the meantime, his security staff would comb the streets looking for Katya. He was sure they would find her. They had to. Until then, he had to control Darya.

He walked to her and put his arm around her. She pushed him off and ran up the stairs shrieking at the top of her voice. He had secreted her mobile phone so he knew she couldn't make any covert calls to the police. They just had to sit tight and wait.

When Katya came back, no doubt he would find out that she'd run away due to some imaginary slight she felt and had wanted to frighten them. But Darya was becoming hysterical and it unnerved him. He wondered if this whole thing was some kind of test to see how he'd react. But he didn't know how much longer he could hold out in Darya's company; she was making him nervous.

He even wondered at first if his new business partners had kidnapped Katya, but he had the evidence from the dashcam that clearly showed her running off on her own. And there'd been no ransom demand. Although not all his, he had hundreds of millions of pounds sitting in the bank. Why did that not guarantee things like this wouldn't happen to him?

His eyes fell onto a gold photo frame of Katya. She was very slight and looked younger than her thirteen years. She had access to money; she had her own bank account where a monthly allowance was paid. It had never occurred to him that she might be exploited, but right then it did. He'd already checked it and saw that two days ago she had withdrawn £250 from an ATM at Paddington station.

* * *

Temple sat in the head teacher's office at the Park Academy. It was the first day back from the autumn half-term break and the school was buzzing with the noise of 300 pupils.

Approaching him through the door in kitten heels was Amy Davidson, the best friend of China Lewis who had reported her missing. She was medium height and slim, wearing a too-short blue school skirt, a tight white shirt, blue blazer and school tie that hung in a lazy knot more like a necklace. In contravention of the school no make-up policy, she was wearing lots of near-orange foundation and under strongly defined eyebrows were heavily lashed eyes. She had a tiny diamond nose piercing and pale lipstick. The handles of a large pink handbag nestled in the crook of her arm.

'Have you found her yet?' She barked the question, aiming it straight at Temple without waiting for introductions.

Her voice was loaded with attitude and had little of the strong West Country twang of the other pupils. Amy had made slavish efforts to eradicate it to sound more like the people she followed on social media, more Estuary. She hoped it would make her sound as if she meant business, particularly in this scenario surrounded by adults.

She shot a look of barely disguised loathing at an accompanying teacher who had followed behind her. Sitting in a chair opposite Temple, she crossed her legs, which had her skirt rising further up her thighs. She couldn't care less. All she wanted was to find China.

Temple introduced himself. The teacher stood in the open doorway, as if to bar Amy's escape.

'No. I've been to speak to her mother and to see if she'd returned home,' Temple explained. He knew he had to get her onside somehow as she could be a valuable source of information.

'That's a waste of fucking time,' Amy spat. Her association with China had given her confidence and she'd taken on board some of her best friend's attitude. The teacher nevertheless admonished her for swearing. Amy took advantage of Temple's presence and flashed her a look of contempt.

'Tell me what you know, Amy. When did you last see China? I want to find your friend. I'm very interested in what you have to say.'

She pulled a face at the teacher. 'I'm glad someone is.' Amy warmed to being taken seriously and Temple made sure she had his full attention. He knew he could be dealing with a heap of teenage hormones, jealousies and petty arguments, but given what he had witnessed at Barbara Lewis's house, he was ready to hear what Amy had to say.

She focused on Temple. 'I last saw her three days ago and I've heard nothing from her since.' As he questioned her, he wrote in his small notebook.

'Where did you see her?'

'Round at my house. She stays with me, sleeps over.'

'How frequently would you say she stays over, Amy?'

'Oh loads. All the time. And we're always on the phone, texting, FaceTiming, Snapchat and now nothing. It's like she's not there.'

'So you're very close, you and China?'

'Yes, we're more like sisters than friends.' It was true; they shared most things in the confines of their private world in Amy's bedroom. Clothes, shoes, make-up, secrets. But Amy felt that lately China seemed to be holding back.

'What time did you see her? When exactly did she leave yours?'

'She went about seven-thirty last Friday, in the evening. Said she was going into town – only that, "going into town". Said she'd be back.'

'So what did you take that to mean?'

'That she was going into Swindon.'

'So you were expecting her to stay at yours last Friday, three nights ago?'

'Yeah. She didn't come back that night and I haven't seen or heard from her since. When she didn't turn up for school this morning, I called you lot. 'Cos someone's gotta care about her, for fuck's sake.' Amy shot another look at the teacher standing in the doorway listening, daring her to admonish her again for swearing.

'Could she be staying somewhere else? With another friend? Her mother says she hasn't seen her but her brother Gary says that people have seen her and he is looking for her,' said Temple. Amy was put out by the suggestion that China would have another friend that she could stay with.

'We're best mates, she only stays at mine. And she wouldn't go back home. She's run away from there. That's the last place she'd go.'

'Why's that, Amy? Why doesn't China want to go home?'

'Her brother. Gary fucking Lewis. She hates him. *I* hate him.'

'And why would that be?' he asked gently.

She looked from Temple to the teacher still in the doorway. 'He controls her. He's a nasty bastard. She's missing because of him.'

'Does he hurt her? Is that what you're saying?'

'Oh, he hurts her all right. I'm not saying any more in front of *her*.' She gestured at the teacher. Then she looked back at Temple. Suddenly, pricks of angry tears sprang in her eyes, betraying her hard facade. Quickly blinking them away, she leaned forward, pointing her finger at him.

'Now – you find my mate.'

Temple told Amy he would arrange for a video statement to be recorded from her that afternoon at Gable Cross police station with female officers. Satisfied, Amy stood up and walked away, pushing past the teacher standing in the doorway. Temple heard her kitten heels clack on the wooden floor as she left. He was a little frustrated Amy had clammed up – he needed to know what she knew about Gary Lewis.

Having spoken to the head teacher, he established that China was a frequent truant, with letters to her mother going unanswered. The school had no direct means of contacting

Barbara Lewis other than by letter and so another was already in the post to her, asking her to explain where her daughter was after not showing up after the half-term break.

Academically, China was described as bright but lazy, not showing the slightest interest in lessons. School was a means of meeting up with her friends and socialising through the day. She had little time for teachers and the school in general, and it seemed they had little time for her.

Temple still couldn't be sure he wasn't being given the runaround. But Amy hadn't flinched when he invited her back to the station for a video interview. Between her mother, brother and teachers, Amy seemed to be the only one who cared about China's whereabouts right now. And what was Gary Lewis's part in this, insisting that China wasn't missing? Missing or not, he had to find out.

CHAPTER 6

Back in the office he shared, Temple set about emailing and texting a photo of China that Amy had sent to him to the PCSOs and police mobile units, telling them to circulate her image, ask around for information and look out for her during patrol. The photo showed China with short bleached-blonde hair, her long fringe swept to one side, wearing a bright pink jumper. She was pouting a moody pose for the camera. As he looked at her, he was reminded that she didn't look too much older than his own daughter, Daisy. He'd seen many such attempts by Daisy on her phone to emulate the same pose that China had seemingly perfected.

He was suddenly conscious of the time and looking up at the clock, he knew he had to keep his appointment with Deputy Chief Constable Buller regarding the outcome of his disciplinary investigation, before he could watch Amy's video interview. He wasn't looking forward to it; he hated exchanges with senior officers at the best of times. He wasn't good at fawning, as was generally expected by the higher ranks. 'Just play the game' colleagues often told him, but he couldn't.

The general consensus was that chief officers were a different breed. Their well-honed sense of self- and pension-preservation seemed to take priority above all else. The so-called

College of Policing Strategic Command Course had a lot to answer for in churning out these clones, but whatever else took place to train chief officers, one thing he knew for sure: it included a form of yoga that was so far advanced that no matter what their size or shape, it showed them how to shove their heads right up their own arses.

Temple was sick of being under investigation and being kept away from detective duties. It would have been a senior officer decision by someone somewhere to put him back into uniform duties. That, he felt, had been punitive, particularly as there was a shortage of detective officers in the force.

And as much as it rankled with him, he knew he now relied on a positive outcome from his meeting with the DCC if he was ever going to get back to CID duties. He was hoping Buller would tell him the investigation was over and that he would receive 'management advice'. That was what his Police Federation Rep had advised might happen. But Temple's paranoia was rampant and the reality was chief officers were a capricious bunch. As he went along to Buller's office, he didn't know what outcome to expect. Perhaps now was the time for him to 'play the game' if he wanted his job back in CID.

From behind the computer screen on his desk, Buller indicated with his head for Temple to take a seat at the round meeting table in the corner of his office. Recently promoted, Buller assumed the superior demeanour of a man who was comfortable and confident in his new position.

Now in charge of discipline, Buller was sure this was where his speciality lay. He liked the detail of misdemeanours and made sure nothing was left out. Most of all he liked the feeling of power that came with the nature of the role: the confidential meetings with Human Resources, the Police Federation and UNISON; the closed-door and off-the-record conversations, the need-to-know basis, reading sensitive files, the fact that he could order investigations into any member of staff – including the chief constable. He liked his new role.

Temple took his place at the meeting table, momentarily looking round the room as Buller seemed engrossed with what was on his computer screen and in no hurry to join him. On the wall were the usual framed photographs with colleagues from various courses Buller attended in the early years, mainly taken outside the Police Staff College at Bramshill, all geared towards showing everyone that this was evidence of a career that had always been on an upward trajectory.

Temple's eyes skimmed over the various photographs of Buller's family members on the wall that had been grouped together for all to see. Photos with his second wife, two sons and daughter on expensive holidays. At a barbeque held in an expanse of expensive garden. On a speedboat. At a party and a wedding. They were posed like scenes from *Hello!* magazine. All chosen and designed to impress and show his success.

Temple saw that, separate to these, on top of a cupboard were two small wooden frames with photos of two other children, old photos of two boys. They were from his first marriage. They didn't feature as part of the happy family up on the wall. They were separated by divorce. They were from another time and place, the children of the first wife. The wife who'd paid the price for the relentless climb in rank.

Although concentrating on replying to an email from the chief constable, Buller was able to keep Temple in his peripheral vision; he could see him looking around. He could have dealt with the email later, but this was all about management psychology. Asserting authority. Keep them waiting; let them know who was in charge, particularly where disciplinary decisions were involved. Make their arse sweat.

Email sent, Buller deliberately cleared his throat as a way to gain Temple's attention. He didn't want to engage in small talk. Eventually he broke the silence in the room, ensuring his voice had the appropriate edge it should for this encounter.

'You know why you're here, Inspector Temple?'

Buller referring to him as 'Inspector' without acknowledging his detective training wasn't lost on Temple. He *thought* he knew why he was there; however, knowing how the current management culture worked in the force, he was always on the alert for the unexpected ambush. There were a few things he'd done that he knew would interest the Professional Standards Department if they found out about them. Things he'd done that he would deserve being investigated for. He instantly recalled the bloodied and battered face of Roger Hunt, his wife Leigh's former boyfriend. So far, Temple had got away with that one. Despite what Temple had done to him, and as he'd discovered afterwards, done unjustifiably, Hunt hadn't complained to the police. Temple had wondered why ever since.

Temple eyed Buller, trying to read his demeanour. Everything about Buller was thin: thin physique, thin-lipped and equally thin character. Like many who parachuted their way in from other forces, their reputations always preceded or would catch up with them; Buller was no exception. Temple knew they could say what they liked on their CVs and in their promotion interviews, but a few well-placed phone calls by the detective ranks always got the dirt on the so-called 'carpetbaggers'.

Stunted promotion prospects at the home force suddenly calling a halt to somebody who had already been promoted way beyond their abilities was usually the precursor for a force move. If it could be disguised by promotion, it was guaranteed to make someone look better than they were. A move to a new force always allowed for a large degree of reinvention, especially with inflated endorsements by a force keen to get rid.

Temple knew the anecdotes of Buller's career skeletons included all the usual suspects his CV would fail to acknowledge – investigative fuck-ups, fingering other colleagues to keep himself out of the shit, claiming successful jobs that he was nowhere near and Olympian arse-licking. It always amazed him to think that senior officers wouldn't give the lower ranks the credit of doing their own 'due diligence' before they arrived. They always did. The thin face that contained his small, pig-like eyes betrayed no emotion to help Temple read what was likely to follow.

'James Ashton-Jones?' Temple ventured tentatively.

Buller wrenched himself away from his computer, getting to his feet. He didn't join Temple at the table. Moving towards the only window in the room, turning his back on Temple to look out, he rested his hands on the window sill. It was designed to give a message and the gesture wasn't lost on Temple. Whatever was coming, it wasn't good news; he was already being blanked.

'I've been speaking to Clive Harker,' said Buller without turning around.

Temple now knew where this was going. He stayed silent and looked at his watch; he could be back at his desk doing something more meaningful. This conversation was only going to go one way. *Just play the game*, he told himself.

'He says that DS Simon Sloper had no idea of the reason you sent him to visit James Ashton-Jones before his death. If he had known your intention, he would have ensured that safeguards were put in place for him. He is certain that course of action would have prevented James's suicide. What do you say about that?' Still Buller kept his back to Temple, who knew what he'd said was a lie.

'I asked Sloper to capture fingerprints and DNA from James Ashton-Jones, his father and his father's friend. We had DNA evidence and I had to go through a process of elimination. I couldn't know or predict what James Ashton-Jones was going to do. DS Sloper couldn't either. Having been the one who saw him, DS Sloper gave me no indication that that was a prospect.' Buller turned around, his back resting against the window frame.

'You see, I take a different view. DS Sloper says you were prone to going missing during the enquiry, that there were times when he just couldn't find you and he had to defer to Clive Harker on many occasions. He says that you knew more than you let on and that it hampered him in terms of progressing the enquiry. What do you say to that?'

Temple knew that Sloper was informing Detective Chief Superintendent Clive Harker from the moment he took on the investigation. He'd deliberately been provided with a skeleton staff and felt he'd been set up to fail, which he would have if he hadn't bucked Harker's instruction on finalising the enquiry.

That was what this was about – that and the long vendetta Harker held against him. Yes, Temple had had to address some pressing personal issues during the enquiry but it was his effort, not Sloper's or Harker's, that had got the eventual result, the capture of a serial rapist and murderer. That being the case, Harker was now trying to cover his tracks for giving him the wrong direction.

Without Temple's intervention, without him going against Harker's instruction, an innocent, albeit dead lad would have been labelled a murderer. Harker had wanted him to wrap up a so-called domestic murder around someone who couldn't answer back because he was dead. Temple had used his own judgement to reject this and as a result had convicted Ian Turner, who, but for his intervention, would have been able to carry on his crimes.

He could see why this placed Harker in a difficult position. Temple also knew this now placed *him* in a particularly vulnerable position. Harker wanted no witnesses to his failure, least of all Temple. He knew Harker was a proud man, and along with his friend DS Simon Sloper, they usually managed most things between them, regardless of them being at opposite ends in terms of rank. Knowing the truth of what had happened put Temple in a spot.

'We were short staffed. With everything that was going on at the same time—'

Buller cut him off. Temple could see that any explanation he offered wasn't going to make a difference.

'You took your eye off the ball during a murder investigation,' Buller's voice had a hard edge to it, 'and a lad died, a lad that had had police contact. You sent Sloper in to retrieve DNA and fingerprints without the full facts as you knew them. Simon Sloper maintains he could have affected a different outcome – that's the problem here, Temple.'

'If I could have prevented what happened, of course I would have. I never saw it as a possibility – there was no reason to at that time.' Temple knew he was being judged by the magical perspective of hindsight, always used by hierarchy when something went wrong to make them sound like wise men.

'You see, the IOPC have finalised their report and have recommended management advice.' Buller paused, and for a second, Temple's mood brightened. It was what he'd been hoping for. Buller spoke again.

'But on thinking about it, I'm not so sure. I'm inclined to take matters further. As I say, I've spoken to Clive about you and he tells me that you're one of those officers who are in the "difficult to manage" category. Have you heard that term before, Temple?' Buller made for the chair behind his desk.

'Yes I have, and with respect, sir, if anything, I'd say the term should be "different" to manage instead of "difficult".' He knew he shouldn't have answered. He was being reeled in but he couldn't keep his mouth shut.

'Well, that's just it, isn't it, Temple? Where's the respect?'

'I have a difficult relationship with DCS Harker—'

'As I said, Temple, difficult, so we agree. Clive said that he gave you instruction during the course of the enquiry, and you ignored it. Is that right?'

Temple had walked right into a trap and he was angry. Sloper and Harker had worked a pincer movement on him. Yes, he'd ignored Harker's instruction because he had to. Harker was obviously claiming credit for the case to cover his own tracks and Temple was left wondering how he had ended up being made out to be the bad guy. Temple could see he was on a hiding to nothing.

'We had a difference of opinion as to who the main suspect was. If I'd followed Mr Harker's direction, we would not have made the arrest and it's likely that Turner would have got away with murder. So yes, I did ignore the instruction because I thought differently and, as it turns out, rightly, which was proved with the subsequent conviction.'

Buller leaned across his desk.

'Let me tell you now, Temple, that I have actually seen the policy book and what Clive Harker has written tells me a different story, so I'd be very careful if I were you. It was you, not Clive Harker, who identified the lad Ashton-Jones as the murder suspect. Clive Harker told you to think again, look at the evidence and that brought us to Turner. You wanted to close the enquiry down when the lad committed suicide because you thought he was the murderer.

'Clive told you not to close it, to keep looking, and you disobeyed that order. You kept disappearing – God knows where – thinking the case was closed. You disobeyed Clive Harker's instruction to keep the investigation live until he expressly had to tell you again to continue. It was Clive's experience that got us Turner. You were all over the place thinking it was Ashton-Jones. I think that there's a case for you to answer here for failing to follow a lawful order.'

Temple couldn't believe what he was hearing. He'd given Harker the policy book and Harker had written his own narrative to cover himself. Temple couldn't help but smile at Harker's audacious lie. He was good, very good. Now Buller was adding to the invented story, telling him his own thought processes.

'With respect, sir, that's not how it was at all.' But Temple's plea was cut short.

'I believe Clive Harker, a senior officer with exemplary service. Do you need disciplinary action to be taken against you in order to know what a lawful order is and when to carry it out?'

Temple had had enough. 'No, *sir*,' he said, leaving a pause between the two words. It wasn't lost on Buller.

'Well, I think perhaps you do. Proceedings will be instigated against you on that basis. There'll be a misconduct hearing next Tuesday. We've informed your fed rep. There'll be two charges for you to answer.'

Temple struggled to keep his cool. He had seriously underestimated the depth of Harker's feeling towards him. He was a man with a grudge that hadn't blunted with the passage of time. But Temple hadn't expected him to lie. Harker had waited a long time and now he had him.

'Clive also tells me that you've been asking about Op Acre and whether the investigation will reopen?'

Temple looked back at Buller and said nothing. He continued.

'As you know, a DNA profile was gained from the blue T-shirt. This was run through the database with no result. The case is over thirty years old and we need to be realistic as to what can be achieved. I'm satisfied with the level of effort that's been put into Op Acre to this point but we will not be progressing things further at this stage.'

Temple shook his head in disbelief. 'You can't expect me to be happy with that.'

Buller was stony-faced. 'Happy or not, you may have to reconcile yourself to the fact that you will never know who the killer is. You *will* have to reconcile yourself to the fact that, in the current climate, resources are finite. The old days are gone. We can't spend money on a thirty-two-year-old cold case when we have more pressing current issues to deal with.'

Temple watched him; he was in full flow now.

'We have to prioritise and cold cases have to succumb to that process of prioritisation. Let me be clear, Temple, Op Acre is closed pending new information. If you have anything in your head with regards to mass screenings, you can forget it. It's not happening. The DNA profile will sit on file. You can't have any further involvement, not least of which for reasons of cross-contamination of evidence, as you well know. I won't have any more force resources spent on this, and that includes *you*.'

Temple looked back at him. 'But I'm already involved.'

'Not any more,' said Buller.

'But I was there, I had physical contact with the murderer, so how can I not be involved? Of course I've been careful not to contaminate the case – that's why Paul Wright's been between me and the enquiry and he ran everything past DCI Rees—'

'Chris Rees – ha!' Buller didn't welcome the reminder of the former DCI and the increasingly bitter exchanges he had had with the man before he died. Rees had tried to advocate that Op Acre receive more resources. 'Chris Rees is dead and I have to prioritise—'

Temple cut across him, standing up both to reinforce his point and to make for the door. He'd had enough. He had to get out before he said something he shouldn't. He was also thinking of Amy Davidson's interview, which would start shortly.

'A young woman – *my mother* – was found murdered, strangled, her throat stuffed with contaminated pills. There's now a DNA profile and you expect me to not want to pursue that?'

'We've taken things as far as we can. Without new information, there's little more that can be done. There is no known suspect and we don't have the resources to continue on that basis.'

Temple wanted to grab Buller and choke the words in his throat. Buller had all the control and knew it. Control over Op Acre and control over him. Harker was bound to have had a hand in this, he was sure. Temple hadn't been expecting this.

'If this is to get at me, it's not just about me; as well as my mother, she was also a sister. Her brother, Richard Temple, will also need to be informed of that decision. Sorry, I thought we were the police.' He couldn't stop himself; he was furious. 'I thought we were interested in catching killers. My mistake, obviously.'

Buller looked at him archly. It had gone better than he expected; he was pleased with himself. He'd managed to deliver a shit sandwich and wrap it up as a bollocking.

'I'm going to ignore that. No further involvement, Temple, and to be clear, that's a lawful order. I'll write to Richard Temple and let him know the force position.' He looked at his watch. 'My next appointment's due,' he said by way of dismissal.

Temple's heart raced, the rapid beat of it knocking against his chest. He was fuming. He hadn't seen it coming; he hadn't considered for a moment that they would call time on Op Acre or that Clive Harker would lie and actually write that lie in a policy book. Of course, as the head of department, Harker would want to claim the prize of catching a killer and serial rapist. DCS Clive Harker had screwed him. He was facing a hearing and it came down to Sloper and Harker's word against his.

He was angry with himself; he'd been stupid. And caught unawares he had no response prepared. He'd just let Buller walk all over him. He'd been pathetic. That's what rankled with him most. He guessed that was why they were in the positions they were. They were ruthless and they were good at it. No doubt enjoyed it too.

He considered what sanction he would get for being found guilty of an offence related to his performance of duty and disobeying a lawful order – a fine perhaps, a written warning, although it might be deemed serious enough for demotion. Harker would surely relish that sanction most of all.

But how could Buller seriously expect him not to be angry at being told not to have anything further to do with Op Acre, to reconcile himself to the murderer never being identified? This was something Temple couldn't stomach. If Buller thought he was going to take that, he was mad. But Buller was right: things *were* different. Temple had to acknowledge that even he had different priorities now.

Growing up and seeing no progress being made into the case, as a teenager, Temple saw it as his mission to track down the killer. The need to know never left him. It hung over him like a constant black cloud. It was a puzzle, a mystery that needed to be solved, not shelved.

And yes, Temple had been expecting to do some kind of mass screening now they had isolated a DNA profile. But Buller was closing it down. They weren't even going to bother running DNA tests on a number of drug dealers that Temple's own enquiries had thrown up.

Ignoring his warning, Temple left Buller's office, went straight to the custody unit and picked up some DNA kits.

CHAPTER 7

Temple shook off the anger of his meeting and watched the video interview of Amy Davidson. He'd quickly briefed the two female detectives and they interviewed her in the company of her mother, Linda. At the start of the interview, they told Amy where the camera was and every now and then, Amy looked directly at it. He watched as Amy sat at a desk opposite the detectives, still in her uniform, with her mother beside her, telling them of her last sighting of China Lewis three days earlier.

China had regular extended sleepovers at the Davidsons' as the two girls were at school together. They had been friends since infant school and China was always welcome at the Davidsons'. Amy didn't stay at China's house as it was a chaotic household and Linda Davidson didn't like Barbara Lewis on account of her drinking problem and lifestyle.

Linda said that China didn't say too much about things at home to her, but it was obvious to Temple that Amy knew much more than she let on to her mother. The reason China spent so much time at the Davidsons' was because she hated going home. Amy said this was because of her brother, Gary Lewis.

He had a nasty reputation in the community, she said. He was known to carry a knife and not be afraid to use it to protect himself and mete out summary punishments to anyone he thought crossed or slighted him. It was well known, she said, that he was a dealer who had graduated from selling drugs at school gates and street corners. She said that, from a young age, China had been used by Gary Lewis as a drugs mule, getting her to take 'packages' to people in and around Swindon, even sending her on trains when his dealing went further afield. As China got older and realised what it was that she was carrying, she refused to do it. Gary had to resort to threats and violence to make her do his bidding.

Amy cited an occasion when China was eleven years old and had refused to take a package across town. She'd woken the next morning to find that Gary had entered her room during the night and had spitefully cut off her beautiful long hair, leaving it on the pillow. She had been distraught at this and had kept her hair cut short ever since. Amy told of how he would burn China's arms with cigarettes and punch her so she did what he asked.

She said China had felt protective towards her younger brother Tommy and had tried to look after him, as Barbara Lewis spent most days out of her head on vodka and cider cocktails. But China had lost the battle for influence with Tommy and he was rapidly heading the same way as Gary. This was when she started to have extended sleepovers at the Davidsons'. She liked it there. It was a proper home. Linda Davidson smiled at the compliment.

Amy said that China would still 'run errands' for Gary but that she had become more secretive about what these were. Sometimes she would go and Amy would have no contact with her for twenty-four hours. She wouldn't answer her phone or text messages. When she saw her again, it would take her a couple of days to get back to her 'old self', as if she'd been somewhere and it had taken its toll on her.

She also said she smelt of chlorine when she returned. She told Amy that she couldn't or wouldn't take a bath at home, and would go to the local swimming baths as it was somewhere she could stay for hours and use their showering facilities.

Rumour had it around Swindon that Gary Lewis had quietly managed to climb higher up the pecking order and was now making a lot of money. Asked if she knew anything about China being seen around Swindon, as Gary Lewis had told Temple, Amy was adamant that if anyone was going to see China, it would be her, and she hadn't seen her. When asked if she knew about China taking money from Gary, she said she often took £10 or £20 from him for going on errands, but nothing larger.

As Amy spoke of her friend's hardships and abuse for the first time, she became increasingly angry and tearful. She was scared for China. She wasn't answering her calls and this just wasn't like her. The interview ended with her shouting at the police officers and looking directly into the camera, demanding to know what they were going to do to find her.

Temple had already confirmed Gary Lewis had a conviction for drug dealing five years ago, but Amy alluded to much more than a one-time possession of drugs. And there'd been no fresh intel recorded on Lewis. How could all this be known about him on the streets and not be recorded on intel records? This was what happened, Temple concluded, when detectives became office-bound – there was no one out there walking amongst this lot, talking to them and bringing back the information.

Temple recalled the lock he had seen on China's bedroom door. He had no doubt that Amy knew exactly what China did when she went missing, and suspected Gary Lewis of more than using his sister as a runner. The condoms he'd found served the dual purpose of secreting the drugs, and going to the baths was probably her way of washing the filth off her. But if Amy had said as much in front of her mother, China probably wouldn't be let through the door of the Davidsons' again. Temple had to speak to Amy without her mother being present.

The officers retrieved China's mobile number from Amy's phone. It matched the one Temple had got from Barbara Lewis. The poor kid was in deep and now no one seemed to know where she was.

He looked through the command and control system on his computer. He scrolled through, making a list of teenagers who had been reported missing in the last few days in Swindon. China had been one of twenty-three reports of missing people in the last three days, ten of whom were of similar age. Four of the ten had returned home within one to two hours of being reported, a further three had returned home between two and three hours after the report. The other three reports were one male and two females, thirteen to fifteen years old, who had returned home between 10 p.m. and 1 a.m. in the morning.

Temple made a note of their addresses, all local to Swindon, one of which was a children's home. Checking their names, the girl from the children's home, Molly Wicks, aged twelve, had been reported missing on nine previous occasions in the last few months. She was close to China in age and he had an idea she would be worth seeing, as she may know of China and her whereabouts, having been reported missing so frequently in Swindon.

But speaking to Gary Lewis again was now his priority. He grabbed a set of handcuffs from his drawer. It was clear China was being exploited and he had to find her fast to get her the help she needed.

CHAPTER 8

Paul Wallace had had to look on a map to see exactly where Swindon was. He had arrived at Swindon railway station earlier that cloudy morning and had been walking around Old Town, trying to familiarise himself with the surroundings. He'd walked along Station Street and onto Corporation Street, looking at the various small businesses in jerry-built disparate-looking low-level buildings. The place seemed run-down, in a stuck-in-time sort of way. He then turned onto Fleming Way and eventually found himself in the Parade Shopping Centre.

As he walked along, he tried to imagine Megon here and looked for her in the faces of the young girls that passed him. He heard the thick West Country lilt of their chatter as he walked close behind them, talking about their boyfriends, shopping, things he knew Megon would talk about and find interesting. He kept his ears open for any snippets that might help him track her down. They mentioned another shopping centre, the designer outlet – he would need to find that too.

Like most teenage girls, Megon loved to shop, and if he were to see her anywhere, he knew it would be where shops were. He stopped himself thinking about where she might find the money to go shopping – she would probably be stealing, like Mitch had been back at King's Cross station. Anything more than that he couldn't contemplate. She was only thirteen and the thought of her having to fend for herself on the streets like some kind of feral cat or dog, hurt him. What had they done as parents that was so bad that she would prefer running away and living on the streets to being at home with them? Suddenly, emotion caught in his throat and tears stung his eyes. That was how it crept up on him; one minute he was fine, the next he would have to wipe tears away.

He was used to pounding the streets and covered a lot of ground in just a few hours. He walked through the Brunel Shopping Centre and across to the modern designer outlet, all the time looking around him, scanning faces, familiarising himself with the surroundings. He had run out of posters and would need to ask Missing People for more so that he could put them up around Swindon. But he was able to brandish a photo of Megon on his phone and he approached a number of shop assistants and security members asking if they had seen her. They hadn't.

He couldn't stay in Swindon overnight. His return train ticket was timed for 8.20 p.m., and it would take just over an hour to get back to Paddington; this would give him time to get home and see the girls before they went to bed. The evenings had started to draw in early and it was dark by 5.30 p.m. He allowed himself to stop briefly for coffee in a small café; he couldn't afford the likes of Caffè Nero or Starbucks. He'd be sitting down all the way home so he didn't need to rest, he just needed a coffee to keep him going.

Looking out the window of the café, Paul Wallace noticed how different the atmosphere was on the streets as soon as it went dark. It was the same in London. It was as if there was a shift in gear; the environment put on its evening face and changed pace. It was this time in the evening that he liked. The change in tempo from day to night recharged him; he felt the energy of the movement of the night-time economy, people going to and from the pubs, the clubs, the restaurants.

Again, he felt that early evening was another time when he was likely to see Megon. It was funny and he couldn't explain it, but he had a good feeling about Swindon. It was almost as if he could feel her, sense her near. He hadn't felt that lately back home in London. It was almost as if she was calling to him, 'I'm here, Dad, come and find me. Come and take me home.' She had to be here.

* * *

Just across the town, Temple pulled up outside Gary Lewis's two-bedroom luxury flat in Eastleaze. It was dark by now and the cold meant the street was quiet. Outside the communal entrance, Temple found the intercom and the flat number and kept his finger on the buzzer.

'Who is it?' came the gruff response.

'Police, Gary. DI Temple – we met earlier. I need to speak to you.'

'Fuck off, filth.'

The intercom went dead. Temple applied the buzzer again.

'I said fuck off.'

'I'm not going away. If you don't speak to me now, I'll get on the radio and bring the response group down.' Temple knew the shift was stretched to breaking tonight and that only two response cars were available for the whole of Swindon and outlying areas.

There was no chance of them responding any time soon to any request he might make. He'd be lucky if they turned up within the hour for a shout for immediate assistance.

'I'm trying to find China and I'm concerned for her safety. Now, you can do this nicely or I can get a van down here and we'll take you in. They'll be here in two minutes. Your choice.'

'Wait.'

Lewis left his flat and came out of the door of a communal hallway to meet Temple on the street outside. It was dark and the only light was from a street lamp across the road.

'Make it quick,' Lewis demanded. Temple was struck again by his rat-like features. He also adopted the same arrogant stance of looking at Temple with his head tilted back.

'That's not how this works, Gary. I need to find China and you told me that she had been seen by people. By who? I've only got your word. You haven't seen her and can't find her. So where is she?'

'I told you she's not missing. Are you fucking deaf or something? She stole money from me and she's keeping her distance.' Gary Lewis had to get rid of this cop. He didn't want him turning up here and he wanted him off his back.

'Who told you they've seen her? Give me their names, who are they?'

'I can't remember.' Lewis was shifting on his feet.

'I know you're lying, so either you remember who told you she's been seen, or what you said was a load of bullshit.'

'I asked about, asked people if they'd seen her and they told me they had.'

'So, who are the people? Names?'

'No names, just lowlifes.'

'When was the last time you saw China?'

'Can't remember. I'm going.' This cop was now becoming a fucking nuisance.

Temple ignored him and continued. 'She was last seen three days ago. Did you send her on one of your errands?'

Lewis momentarily looked down at the floor. He was sick of answering questions.

'What's happened to China, Gary?'

'I don't know. But you need to leave it alone. She's not missing.'

'I'm not going to stop looking for China until I find her. Have you got her in your flat?' Temple could see Gary Lewis knew more than he was saying.

'*What?* No. When I say I don't know where she is, I'm telling you the fucking truth. Now, you need to leave it, filth. Go and investigate something else.'

'Why do I need to leave it, Gary, eh? I found condoms in her bedroom, loads of them. Why would a fourteen-year-old need so many condoms? What errand did you send her on? She hasn't come back, has she? You've sent her off with a load of drugs and you've lost her. You're pimping her too, aren't you? She's your mule, isn't she? Got her on crack too, have you, Gary? You're coming to the station with me.'

'I'm going nowhere, you fucker.' Lewis moved swiftly, putting his hands behind him and swinging them back round.

Suddenly, Temple saw the flash of a long blade with a curved end and instinctively jumped away. Lewis was waving the long-bladed knife in his direction and as Temple held his hands out in a bid to keep him at a distance, the curved edge sliced into one of Temple's fingers. The pain of it made him take a leap back.

With Temple distracted, Lewis fled, running down the road. Temple wondered what had happened and with a stinging injury to his finger, he was suddenly dripping blood all over the pavement. He instinctively clamped his fingers around the source of the pain. Looking on the pavement and satisfied that he wasn't missing part of his finger, he berated himself for letting it happen.

He couldn't understand where the blade had come from. Where the fuck had he been hiding that? His hand quickly filled with blood as his fingers failed to stem the bleeding. Holding his hand out away from him, Temple went back to the unmarked police car under the street light. Standing by the side of the car, Temple held out his right hand to look at it. There was a deep slice down the middle finger. With his left hand, he pulled at his clip-on tie and wrapped it tightly around his injury. He then contacted the control room and asked for obs to be put out for Gary Lewis for his immediate arrest for assaulting a police officer.

CHAPTER 9

It was imperative that Brian Porten kept the slaughterhouse meticulously clean. Not least for public health reasons and to increase the length between visits from the Food Standards Agency. He liked cleanliness. Cleanliness and order. Porten & Sons was a small but long-established concern, where he'd started as an apprentice to his cousin Tom, a small, older man who, in hindsight, was a lot like himself. He'd taught Brian all he knew, and as Tom was the last of the 'Sons', he had been pleased to have Brian alongside him.

A loner, old Tom had taken him under his wing when Brian's mother had asked Tom to find him a job at the abattoir. They'd worked together for years before Tom's death three years ago at the age of sixty-nine. At the time, Tom had recognised a lot of himself in the lad; Brian wasn't stupid, he just wasn't a socialiser.

Like Brian, Tom hadn't been much of a talker, but they both shared an interest in what was in the news and what was around them. When Brian's mother died, it was Tom who quietly organised him, moved Brian in to share his two-bedroom bungalow not far from the abattoir. They'd lived there together for years. Yes, Tom had looked after him, and but for the twenty-year gap in their ages, they could have been brothers. So they had lived together and worked together and had never really had a cross word between them either.

When Tom died, Brian took it hard. The business hadn't been the same since; it wasn't the same without Tom. It couldn't be. He missed Tom dreadfully, missed his steadying influence, and since then he had withdrawn more into himself. Into his *project.*

Brian had had to reduce the workload; there was only so much one person could do, and without Tom, he had to acknowledge his heart wasn't in it to the same degree. Killing days were now just once a week, on a Tuesday. That meant he only had to have a vet and inspector on site for one day and so everyone knew Tuesday was when they brought their animals. It kept things simple and allowed him to focus more on the task at hand.

The last FSA inspection had been a month ago – that's why now was a good time to take some more people off the streets because they wouldn't do an unannounced visit in such close proximity to the last inspection. No, he knew he would have a good run now. And he had to be careful. The reason he had removed so many already so successfully was because he was careful.

That and the fact that nobody actually missed these people. Who would? Who would miss a beggar? No one. They were a public nuisance. The more he could get off the streets, the better society was for it. But for every one he removed, it seemed another took their place. That's why he had to keep going until that stopped. It had to stop. His heart started to pound in his chest.

He decided he would try again tonight. One more homeless person should do it, then he could release the meat to his customers.

* * *

Megon Wallace had been left in a locked room in an empty flat in the dark. She was naked and cold, lying on a dirty mattress. There was no bulb in the light fitting that hung from the ceiling above her and the windows were boarded up. She knew that she was in something way too deep and she had no choice but to deal with it. She didn't know how, but she had to get herself out.

More than anything, she wanted to be back at home, in her shared bedroom with her sisters and their dog, with her mum and dad. This was so far away from that comfort and she didn't know if she'd ever see them again. The thought of that made her feel so sad she wanted to cry.

Despite everything that had happened to her in the last few days, it was that thought that really got to her. They told her she had a debt to pay and that they intended to collect every single penny of it, and some. This was what happened to girls like her who were careless, they said. It would teach her a lesson she would never forget.

She had nothing left, nothing, not even her dignity. They had taken her clothes to stop her running away. She had no phone, no possessions of any kind; they had stripped her of everything – even the thin silver ring she wore on her thumb.

She had nothing to put round her to keep her warm against a draught that came in under the door. The only other thing in the room was a galvanised bucket for her to go to the toilet and be sick in. She was sick quite a few times a day but she didn't bring much up. She'd been left to wait, wait for the footsteps. She both welcomed and dreaded the footsteps. The footsteps would bring food for which she was so grateful, even though it was always so very little and never warm. Drink was equally restricted because they didn't want her having to go to the toilet too often. But mostly the footsteps meant that men were being brought to her.

Megon couldn't bear to think about how she'd got here. She had run with her friend – they'd had to because they'd lost the drugs and the money. The last she'd seen of her friend was when they caught up with them both. Megon was going to go home but they found them and split them up. It got really serious then.

Up to that point she'd been doing as she was told, ferrying drugs and money from London into the country areas, staying in trap houses, selling users the drugs and taking the money. Once she sold her stash she took the money back to London and repeated the exercise. She'd earned £200 for it. It made her feel useful, independent; she could do a lot with £200.

This was her third journey and she'd met a friend doing the same thing. They'd met in the trap house and quickly became mates. Then it had gone wrong; the money and drugs had been stolen from them. She'd been warned what would happen if she lost either the drugs or the money. She'd have to pay it back. There was a logic to it. It stopped anyone helping themselves, she could see that. They brought her here and it was then that she realised what they meant by paying her debt. She had no idea they would make her do this.

It was a flat above a small betting shop. She could hear the muffled sounds of a television and electronic slot machines with their endless mad circus-like music ringing out. No one could hear her against that din. She was left cold and hungry, really hungry. Then she would hear footsteps, big heavy footsteps against the bare wooden floorboards, coming up the stairs and along a short landing. One set of footsteps meant she could anticipate food, two sets meant fear. She knew there were thirteen steps up the stairs as she'd counted them. Then they would unlock the door. There was light outside as it shone through when they opened it.

They would let a man in. As soon as the man was inside, they left a small lamp in the corner that illuminated the whole room in a soft sort of light. Then they locked the door. More often than not, the men spoke in a foreign language; she had no idea what was being said between them or what they said to her. At first she had visions of running at them, pushing past them and escaping down the stairs. But they were big and threatening and they told her she was doing it to pay off her debt, to keep herself alive. If she didn't do it, she was dead. Her choice.

When it became clear to her what this meant, she'd fought back, but that got her slapped and punched into the bargain. A big fat man had held her face in his hand and squeezed so tightly she thought her jaw would break. So she decided to just lie there, let them do what they wanted. Let them thump their bodies into hers. She did what they told her to do, got it done, got them out.

When they finished, another would come in. The same. Then another, the same. Another. One after the other they came: old, young, dirty, fat, thin, stinking, leering, vile, foreign, black, white, African, Asian, English. They came in, used her and left. She knew when the last one had gone because they took the lamp away. It was later that they brought food. Always cold food.

This was day four but it felt like a month. She'd already lost count of how many men had come into the room – twenty, thirty, more. It was like a conveyer belt. She was so scared of these people she dare not even scream. Each time they left her in the room with a man, she was so fearful, wondering if she'd be left alive. She just wanted to be herself again. Reclaim her body, her soul. But she couldn't see a way of getting out.

Because most of the men who came in couldn't speak English, she couldn't even appeal to them, appeal to any shred of decency they might have. What was wrong with them? Couldn't they see her, didn't they care that she was so young, trapped, filthy, dirty, unwilling, being made to do the things they wanted? But it was precisely her youth and her naked prettiness that they wanted.

So she lay there, shivering with cold, the only warmth coming from her own imprint in the dirty mattress. She shifted and laid her cold back on the warm patch. That little bit of warmth was her only comfort. But she took it and took comfort from the fact that she had made it. She wanted her mum and dad. She wanted home. She waited to hear the steps on the stairs.

* * *

Temple went back to the office. He had his finger still wrapped in his tie and as he entered, two of his colleagues looked up from their laptops.

'Fuck, someone's tried to cut his throat.' DS Sam Mendoza immediately saw blood around the neck of Temple's white shirt. 'What *have* you done?'

'Christ, either that or he's trying out his Dracula look.' Inspector Bruce Jackson started to laugh. 'You're too early for Halloween. It's not for a few more days yet.'

Temple held up his hand. 'I was questioning Gary Lewis when he drew some sort of bloody machete out of nowhere. Nearly took my fucking finger off.'

'You've lost your touch; been a while since you've been outside. You'd better stay indoors in future.' They both laughed out loud at his discomfort.

Temple explained why he'd been out all day and that he was on the hunt for Gary Lewis. It was the end of his day shift, so Mendoza, who was on 2–10, said he would keep an eye on command and control logs and custody to see if anyone brought Lewis in during the evening. Temple said nothing to his colleagues about his meeting with DCC Buller. He couldn't trust himself not to rant and them not to report it back. Looking at his watch, he made for home.

'Give our love to Ana,' Jackson shouted after Temple as he left. Without turning round, Temple held up his uninjured middle finger and carried on walking.

CHAPTER 10

Temple parked up on High Street, Avebury, in the only available space near St James's churchyard. Fine rain had started to come down, making the cold air cling to him. He walked through the lychgate of the churchyard. He could have gone the long way round using the road but this was the quickest route in the rain. Looking to his left, he saw lights shining from the small windows of a thatched cottage behind a low brick wall. It was a cosy and inviting sight, which belied the cramped and crooked layout of a house built over 200 years ago, not designed for modern living.

He walked through the wooden door into the welcome smell of food cooking in the oven. He stepped onto a narrow, tiled hallway with a stairway opposite. To the left was the kitchen and to the right a living room. He could hear the television and the familiar sound of a *Thomas the Tank Engine* DVD. He quietly put his head around the living room door.

The small room was made smaller by the largeness of the television balanced on a table in the corner. He saw his three-year-old son dressed in pyjamas, sitting on the floor in front of the television with his back to him, transfixed by the moving figures. Temple ducked back out of the doorway, careful not to disturb him, conscious of the blood on the neck of his shirt.

He went into the kitchen, over to the sink. Coming in behind him from the utility area, a young woman carried dried washing in a basket. She had smiling eyes and her black hair was held back with a faded red ribbon at the nape of her neck.

'I thought I heard you,' she said quietly, smiling at Temple.

'Had a good day, Ana? How's he been?' Temple looked over his shoulder, and as he spoke he started to unwind the tie from around his finger.

'He's been fine. He went to nursery this morning. He ate his lunch and then went for a nap for an hour. When he woke, we went out for a walk to the pond at the manor and fed the birds.' She smiled as she spoke and stood folding clothing. Temple listened, now used to the lyrical tone of the au pair's soft Portuguese accent. There was a lovely softness about her face that followed in her personality.

'Any progress?'

'Not today. I was hoping that feeding the ducks might have helped. I wanted him to see you before he went to bed.' She put her basket down and went into the living room to check on Ben. He was still engrossed in his programme and she didn't disturb him.

On the face of it, the little boy had seemed to accept and adapt well to his new environment. The tragic loss of his mother and upheaval of losing all that was familiar to him had seen him understandably withdrawn to begin with. But in the four months since he'd moved here, Temple had not once heard the boy laugh. Despite any antics he or Ana tried, they couldn't get the little lad to chuckle. They had hoped that putting him in the company of other little people at nursery might help.

Ana returned to the kitchen to see Temple looking at his bloodied hand. The tightness of the binding had just about stopped the flow of blood, but it was a deep gash. He ran it under cold water.

'What have you done?' she asked, concerned, looking at the blood-soaked tie in the sink and examining him for the first time since he'd come in.

'I didn't want Ben to see this. I couldn't go in to him with my shirt and hand covered in blood. Could you look in the box for me and see if there's a bandage or something?'

Ana went straight to a green first-aid box and gathered the necessary cotton pad and bandage.

'You should get it looked at, it does not look good . . . What happened?' She dried and tended to the wound.

'A man pushed a knife in my direction and I didn't move fast enough.' He held a thick cotton pad in place while Ana wound the bandage round, tying it neatly and tightly at the bottom when she'd finished.

'Thanks, that's better. I'll change quickly and put Ben up to bed. I'll read him his story.'

Having quickly pulled on a jumper, Temple went into the living room and gently tousled the boy's hair. Ben looked up immediately at his touch but was solemn. Temple scooped him up and sat on a sofa where they chatted, the boy noticing Temple's bandaged finger. Ben was clearly tired after a long day and it wasn't long before Temple carried him up to bed and sat and read him a story. He didn't get to the bottom of the page before the boy was sound asleep. Temple sat awhile in the silence and stared at him. He looked utterly angelic.

He had dark hair like Temple, with dark, feathery eyelashes. His chubby little hands lay on top of the duvet cover. He sat and listened to him breathing perfectly soundly. Temple gently got up from the bed, kissed the sleeping boy's head and turned off the light. Leaving the bedroom door open, he went downstairs to the kitchen.

Ana had laid the table and put out a salad. She produced a lasagne from the oven. Temple sat down as she put their plates in front of them.

'There! I hope you like it.'

'You don't have to do this,' he said, feeling as though he should say it but not really wanting to discourage her. The smell was delicious.

'Yes I do. You go out to work, so I cook and clean and look after Ben. It's a good life, I like it,' she said, smiling.

'This is great,' he said through a mouthful of hot lasagne. He was pleased he'd found Ana; she was a godsend. And Ben seemed to respond well to her.

'Jane visited today. She wanted to make sure we were settling in OK. It's all fine here, yes?'

'I suppose we've just about squeezed in.' He already hated it here. It had been a mistake to move to Avebury. The cottage was tiny, but it had been available at short notice. As an added incentive, his landlady Jane had knocked £50 off the monthly rent, making it a financial no-brainer. Jane had a soft spot for him and had helped Temple when his wife Leigh had thrown him out by renting another of her houses to him. When that was fire-damaged, she had Temple stay at her house temporarily.

If it hadn't been for Ben, she would have had Temple move in with her permanently, but she wasn't mother material and having a three-year-old around the house wasn't her idea of fun. Still, she hadn't wanted to lose contact with him, and taking a slight hit on the rent was one way of ensuring that.

However, as cheap as it was, Temple was beginning to wish he'd taken more time before accepting the tenancy. God knows he'd needed to save money, and what Jane had offered was a help. His wife Leigh had made it quite clear she was expecting a very healthy divorce settlement and his finances were already strained to breaking point with the bills of two households. He tried not to think of his money problems. His three credit cards were nearly maxed, which would mean he would need another soon.

But in hindsight, no matter how cheap, he should have looked for somewhere else to live. The house was almost part of the churchyard so had very little privacy and an open fire wasn't ideal with a three-year-old. He also had to watch that he didn't bang his head on a beam in the tiny bathroom.

But it wasn't for these reasons he wished he'd not taken the house. It was Avebury itself. He knew now that he didn't want to be here. If it wasn't for the fact he'd disturb Ben, he'd move in a flash. They both carried on eating and talking and Temple said nothing more about the cottage.

'I'll probably have to work late tomorrow evening, will that be OK?' Temple asked.

'Sure, it's fine. I'm going to the pub tonight, so it's good.'

'You can bring your boyfriend here you know, this is your home too.'

'No, the pub is fine, I like to meet him there,' she smiled. She was grateful for her job. She felt lucky working for Temple and she already loved little Ben. They had all been together for four months now and had established a routine. But she needed to get out of the house and make a life outside too.

As they ate, Ana gave Temple a rundown of the day's events, telling him of all the necessary details to enable him to imagine his small son's day. It was his third week at nursery school and he had cried every day when Ana left him. On his return today, after the half-term break had disturbed their routine, there had been the same tears but thankfully with less intensity than before. They discussed Ben and the gradual introduction to nursery. They decided to continue until the end of next week to see if the situation improved. With their meal done, Ana took herself to the pub to meet her boyfriend.

'Take your key; I'll be in bed before the pub shuts.' Temple was tired. It felt good to get out of the office today, away from the computer screen and back to some proper work, even if it had cost him an injury. Sitting in front of the fire alone, he went back over the incident. Gary Lewis was dangerous and was lying about China's whereabouts. Temple felt sure Lewis knew where she was.

CHAPTER 11

He had to try a different town. He never took two from the same town; that would be too risky. So he tried somewhere else. He drove to Chippenham. Under the cover of the night sky, he parked up in an unlit spot down near the river. Once he was out of the car, he could hear the fast flow of the Avon and feel its icy temperature as the wind blew along with the flow. The rain had stopped but the dampness in the air made it seem much colder than it was.

Pulling up his coat collar against the cold and pushing his hands deep into his pockets, Brian walked up High Street looking at the shop fronts and the recessed doorways. There were a few people walking about, the pub-goers, those walking home from working late. As he walked slowly up the gradual incline, he couldn't isolate a lone sleeper; they seemed to be huddled together in twos and threes.

It was particularly cold; the rain had left everything wet and he thought, given these conditions, someone would be grateful for the offer of booze and a warm bed for the night. If he could find someone on their own, his journey wouldn't have been wasted.

He continued on to the top and walked around the back streets. He went to where he knew there were some smaller recesses. It was still no good; there was no one on their own in an isolated spot. He decided to cut his losses, go to a different location, so he walked back to his car.

He drove across to Trowbridge but unknowingly chose the wrong night there. A soup kitchen was in operation at St Mary's Church. The local homeless charity had gone out and rounded up all the homeless they could find to get them out of the cold and take a hot meal. His evening had been wasted after all. He had run out of time tonight. He'd have to come out again. Tomorrow.

* * *

Temple woke and lay alone in the dark, staring up at the ceiling. His fingers went to the base of his neck, trying to manipulate it and stop it from tightening as he listened to the strange sounds the old building made in the dead of night. Just for a moment, he lay concentrating on the little creaking noises and how the building reacted to the wind and rain so that he could learn how he might distinguish the various natural sounds from those of an intruder.

Not for the first time since he came here, he wondered how many other people had lain awake at night in this room over the years. There was a date carved into the mantle above the small fireplace in the living room. It said 1801. He'd tried to calculate how many people might have stared at this exact spot in the dead of night since then, disturbed by their troubles or thoughts of intruders. But lack of sleep was the least of his worries.

Staring up, the low, uneven white ceiling acted as the screen on which his mind ran and reran the last few months like a mad, fast-forward projector that he could do nothing to stop. He couldn't help himself but watch, going over it all again, night after night, like a slow motion car crash. Since it had all blown up, he'd made himself a hostage to this method of processing what had happened.

He'd hoped that by going over it again and again, a solution would find its way out of the dark. What was it that Leigh had said? That he had rolled a hand grenade into their lives and was hoping that it wouldn't go off. If he could just go back, he'd do things differently. That was the only impossible solution that offered itself up.

But he couldn't go back. *It was a total fuck-up*. He thought immediately of Ben and felt guilty for even thinking of his endearing little boy in that same moment. But Temple knew he *had* fucked up. Big time. And he couldn't change it. He'd had to wreck his family in order to save Ben, save him from living in care, being fostered or adopted, having someone else bringing him up. He couldn't have left him to the fate of the state, and in rescuing him, he'd had to hurt and lose those he loved.

It had been both an obvious and difficult choice to make. As soon as the social worker told him of Ben's existence, the product of an extra-marital two-night stand between Temple and Ben's now dead mother, he knew he wouldn't be able to abandon him. It reminded him too much of his own situation as a young boy. His uncle Richard and his grandfather, both of whom had been almost strangers to him, had offered him the same lifeline, or else he would have suffered the fate of living in state care when his mother was murdered.

They hadn't had to take him in. His grandfather was old and Richard was a single man, but they'd come together to give him a home. And there was only one thing he could do given similar circumstances. Even before he'd broken the news to her, he knew Leigh would not be able to forgive him. Newly reconciled and back living together, they were happy and he didn't want to spoil that. So he'd waited six weeks before he told her, after the DNA test he'd requested had confirmed he was Ben's father.

Recalling the moment he'd told her, he saw her face again, the hurt and anger, the tears. He hoped that she might accept the situation for what it was and manage to bring Ben into their family. There was no threat to her from the boy's mother; she was dead. But Leigh was massively wounded by the revelation. And she said that wound wouldn't grow any less if she had to keep seeing Ben. He was asking way too much.

How would Ben's sudden presence be explained, she said, to their family, their friends – any new friends? They would all have to be told. She refused to lie and said she would spend the rest of her life explaining and seeing the reaction on people's faces, seeing them feel sorry for her, having them talk behind her back. Pitying her. No, she wasn't prepared to do it.

He had to make a choice – he couldn't have it all. It was her and Daisy or it was Ben, and even before she said it, because of his past, she knew what Temple would do. She had been so angry with him. Not for the first time, she screamed at him that these were the consequences of his selfish actions and now they'd all have to live with them. As he lay there, remembering their conversations, he recalled how they escalated with them both shouting at each other and Daisy crying. Once again, Leigh threw him out.

Then came the news. A further twist of fate. News that Leigh was furious about, but that he'd hoped would give them a lifeline; that might change her mind. She was pregnant. He again asked her to reconsider their position – things were different in light of this, they should all be together, they could make it work. He loved her, for God's sake. She was adamant. No, they couldn't make it work. What's more, she would go it alone with the baby. *Fuck you*, she'd said.

So he had a decree nisi, with an absolute shortly to follow. Such was her anger with him she told him she would move away, putting miles between them, knowing this would mean he wouldn't have ready access to his ten-year-old daughter Daisy or the progress of Leigh's pregnancy.

While Daisy was bewildered by her parents' behaviour, she had been excited and readily accepting of Ben, her new-found half-brother. But Leigh wouldn't countenance any notion of playing happy families under such circumstances. She didn't care if it was what Daisy wanted. She was reeling from the situation he had left her in and wanted to teach Temple a life lesson: when you fuck up, there are consequences. She wanted to hurt him in every way she could. *Really* hurt him. Leigh knew taking Daisy away from him and cutting ties with her and the new baby would do that.

She was house hunting in Norfolk, hoping that going to the other side of the country would signal just how much she wanted to break contact. And she wanted to screw him financially. *More hurt.* To pay for how he'd hurt her.

Daisy was tearful and sad at the thought of being wrenched away from her school, her friends and her daddy. She was starting to fail at school, misbehave. She was giving Leigh a hard time, saying she would refuse to move. She would live with her dad; she didn't want to go and she couldn't make her. If she did she would run away; she wouldn't stay. And so Leigh was also left having to cope with Daisy's growing resentment towards her and her misbehaviour.

And Ben, Temple's little boy, was in the middle of all this mess. Under investigation anyway, Temple had taken a month off work to see him settle into his new surroundings. The boy had been upset and confused and obviously missed his mother. 'Reinforce your relationship to him at every opportunity,' said the social worker. 'Remind him that you are his daddy and he will come to accept it.'

Almost overnight, Temple's life had been turned upside down. He had to make a home for Ben, a son he had no prior knowledge of and to whom he was a stranger. With the help of the social worker, he set to work. The boy was a good little soul and after the inevitable initial ups and downs, he had quietly settled into a routine.

Then Temple thought of Ana, the au pair who had moved in with them. Now he was living in a place he hated, in a tiny, rickety old cottage, with two people who only a few months earlier he'd had no knowledge of, while his angry ex-wife, their unborn child and his daughter whom he loved were in their old family home, his little girl crying herself to sleep at night. He was at a loss as to what he could do to put things right, but he had to do something. He'd lost Leigh but he couldn't and wouldn't lose Daisy, despite Leigh's attempts to keep them apart.

As he lay there, his bandaged finger started to pulse. His thoughts turned to China Lewis and all he'd heard about her. He had to try and find her. The sudden thought of tracking down Gary Lewis appealed to him far more than going over things he couldn't change. He decided to go into work.

CHAPTER 12

Darya Petrenko lay prostrate on her bed. She couldn't bear to look at her husband Kostya so she had taken refuge in her bedroom. He would know better than to disturb her there. She was out of her mind with worry for Katya. She had never run away before; it had never entered Darya's head that she would even think of doing such a thing. She was almost paralysed with fear of what might be happening to Katya. She could only think of bad things; the thoughts flooded into her brain like devils designed to drive her mad.

Her perfect world had been turned upside down and she was existing in a new reality. She didn't know what to believe anymore. She just wanted Katya back. She physically hurt knowing her daughter was out there, somewhere, without her, without any protection. Kostya said that he had the security team out looking for her and that they would find her. Well, the hours and days had ticked by and she hadn't returned.

He refused to contact the police and she felt helpless. Did he think that his business associates had something to do with it? But they had both viewed the recording of the driver taking Katya to school that day. They had seen for themselves that she had got out of the limousine and had literally run in the opposite direction of the school. They hadn't seen her since.

Her mind went over and over the morning she had last seen her. She had seemed perfectly normal. She thought back further – was there something she'd missed? Was there an undertone with Katya that she'd failed to spot? Was she unhappy with something in her life? Something must have been wrong or else why would she have run away?

Darya just wanted her daughter back. She wouldn't be able to move until she knew Katya was home. She was going to stay there, laid on her bed, wanting to black out and be rendered unconscious until that time. The not knowing was too much for her to bear. The tears started to roll down the side of her face and into her hair. She needed her back. She was going out of her mind.

She wanted the police to be looking for her daughter and she hated Kostya for preventing that. The last seventy-two hours had shown her a different side to her husband that she had never seen before. And right now, she hated him with every fibre of her being. She never thought she would feel this way towards him but she did now.

He'd prioritised his business partnership over his own daughter, his own flesh and blood. She would never forgive him for that. She marvelled at how her feelings could change in such a short space of time but they had, perhaps irrevocably. She didn't know if they would survive this and she no longer cared. There was only one thing she wanted more than anything in the world, and that was Katya back with her.

* * *

In the quiet darkness of the early morning, Temple pulled up outside Gary Lewis's flat. The lights were still on, as they had been when he'd looked up at them only hours before when Lewis ran off. He rang the buzzer but there was no answer. Perhaps he'd been picked up and was in custody.

Back at Gable Cross police station, Temple went to the custody unit. He then checked his emails and the force log. No Gary Lewis and no return or sign of China Lewis reported from any of the PCSOs who'd gone out with China's photo. He would escalate the case today, particularly in light of the disclosures from Amy Davidson. Temple started to plan for teams to go in and do a thorough search of Barbara's and Gary Lewis's premises and make a wider media appeal for information on the whereabouts of both Gary and China.

The police station was quiet at this time of the morning. Temple was one of only a handful of people there. He'd have to wait for the 8 a.m. shift to come on duty before being able to put any of his plans into action. He had nearly two hours to wait. He looked at the address of the children's home that he had put in his pocket, and the name of the girl who'd gone missing about the same time as China. He looked at his watch and left the station.

The Brook was a large Victorian double-fronted terraced house in a nice residential street in Swindon. Nothing from the outside marked it out as a children's home. The manager of The Brook, Kay Riley, who welcomed Temple inside, had been on a sleepover and was in the process of ensuring the four children in the home were being organised for school.

As he stepped into the hallway, Temple was greeted by strings of coloured bunting. It was warm and inviting and went against his perception of a children's home as a cold, utilitarian environment. As he followed the manager, he saw heart-shaped pictures pinned to the downstairs doors.

Amongst the noise upstairs of staff chivvying children from bathrooms to bedrooms, Kay showed him into a large kitchen-diner extension where he sat at a pine table while she made him a cup of coffee. The room was unexpectedly modern in design, bright, clean and well decorated. The same colourful bunting was here too, pinned around the dining area walls, along with kids' drawings. It felt like any other happy home.

'As I said, I'm interested in one of the kids that ran away two days ago,' Temple explained. 'According to my records, Molly Wicks was returned just after midnight after being reported missing for six hours.'

'Yes, Molly's going through some difficult times at the moment. They seem to hit double figures and start pushing at the boundaries to see how far they stretch. We only have girls between the ages of eight and fourteen and we've increased our intake from three to four in the last few months. The kids find this a challenging time in the home. I'm sure things will settle down but in the meantime there will be the inevitable disturbance that another child coming in brings. Just as they get used to another child being in their home, after a short while, along comes another.'

'So the dynamics change?'

'Yes, so you can start to see our challenges. We try and match them as best we can before taking them, but for all that you never really know how it's going to work out until they actually move in and start interacting with the other girls. As you can imagine, it takes a while for things to settle down.'

'What makes them want to run? This feels like a nice home.' The more Temple saw of the place the more impressed he was. His preconceived ideas about a children's home being a dark and threatening place were clearly wrong.

'We do our best here to make it homely but the reasons for running away could be any number of things. For a start they could just be "runners"; it could be their default position. It's our job to try and break that as a pattern of behaviour. Or it could simply be the upheaval another arrival brings. There are also trust issues to overcome – Molly had a very difficult time at home before coming into care.'

'So what happened here?'

'Molly's upset by the new girl, Shona – perhaps she sees her as a threat at the moment. The new girl's quite a handful. She's somewhat violent; lashes out, throws things, screams. She hasn't settled in yet. It's a new place, new people, new kids. She's unsettled, scared even. She takes a lot of our time. It's all behaviour we expect to deal with, but it can be quite upsetting and unsettling for the other kids.'

At that moment, Kay Riley looked past Temple to acknowledge a staff member who had just come on shift.

'Hi, Callie, thanks for coming in.'

Temple turned round. A tall, slim woman with red hair looked back at him with a broad smile.

'I'll just go on up and get started,' she said, and turned out of the room.

'Callie's had to come in to cover a shift for us,' Kay Riley explained. 'Our new girl lashed out last night and one of our carers was injured. You want to speak to Molly, did you say?'

'Yes, if that's possible. I'm looking for another young girl who's gone missing in Swindon and I just wondered if I could show Molly a photo of her, see whether she could tell me if she'd seen her or knows where she might be. Do you know where Molly went while she was missing?'

Kay handed Temple a cup of hot coffee and they moved into a small office away from the kitchen.

'Of course we spoke to her when she returned but she was non-committal. Her social worker's supposed to conduct a "return home" interview with her, but that might not take place for another few days yet. She may disclose to her where she went, but kids can be very secretive. She's told us in the past that she hangs around the train station. Apparently kids feel safe at railway stations – can you believe that? She's also said before that she's hung around the Parade Shopping Centre. I'll go and ask Callie if Molly's ready and see if she'll talk to you.'

Kay left Temple sitting in her office. He looked round the room as he finished his drink. On the wall there were some paintings by the kids, menu plans, rotas, a poster with company values, framed qualifications of staff members. It all looked well run. Kay returned to her office and sat behind her desk while in the hallway he could hear Callie trying to coax an unwilling Molly along the hall.

Callie was at the door with a shy Molly who stood just outside, reluctant to come across the threshold. She didn't want to go any further inside. She was a pretty, still sleepy-eyed, dark-skinned girl in a school uniform.

'Would you speak to this police officer please, Moll? And then you can get yourself some breakfast.' Callie was trying her best. 'It won't take a minute. He's wondering if you can help him.' She spoke gently. 'He's very nice, he won't bite.' Temple and Callie exchanged glances at that point, with Molly looking at the floor.

Temple introduced himself. Molly rubbed at her eyes with the back of her hand, all the time avoiding any eye contact with him, then looked down to focus on the floor. She didn't speak.

'I won't keep you long, Molly, I just wondered if you might have seen this girl. Have you seen her around Swindon at all?' Temple offered up his phone with the picture of China for her to see. She still didn't speak, but she was unable to resist looking at the screen, dragging her eyes from the floor and studying the photo for a couple of seconds.

Temple watched her closely as her eyes flicked over China's image. Molly hoped she showed no obvious sign that she recognised the girl. She shrugged and looked away over her shoulder, appearing disinterested but not able to mask the merest hint of a smile.

'She's not in trouble. I want to help her. I'm worried about her. I take it you don't know her, otherwise you'd tell me?' There was no answer from the girl except a slight shrug.

'Well, thanks for looking. I won't keep you from your breakfast.'

Temple shut down the image and put his phone in his pocket. He didn't want to press her. Callie made an apologetic facial gesture back to Temple and followed Molly as she sloped off to the kitchen.

'I'll leave you my card. Could you let me know please if Molly discloses anything you think might help me?'

Kay took it from him.

From her slight smile, he felt sure Molly had seen China and knew who she was. He was frustrated. It had been a long shot but he thought speaking to Molly might have reaped some reward, some shortcut to finding China Lewis. It might have worked had she not been so vulnerable herself. There was definitely a hint of recognition when Molly saw China's photo.

Back at the station, Temple rang Molly's social worker to see when the last return home interview had been conducted. Molly hadn't been interviewed for three weeks, which covered five of her missing episodes. This, explained the social worker, was due to her heavy workload; she just hadn't had the time. But from previous notes, Molly had disclosed that she hung around Swindon railway station and the shopping centre area until late at night, just as Kay Riley had said.

Temple's phone rang. It was the control room.

'There's a lady on the line for you, a Mrs Linda Davidson.'

'Put her through.' He heard the call connect.

'I need to speak to you about China Lewis. My daughter Amy gave me your name, says you spoke to her at the school yesterday.'

'Yes, that's right, she reported China missing.'

'That's just it. China's not missing. She was here last night, at our house with Amy.'

CHAPTER 13

Temple straightened. 'Where is she now?' He was looking forward to meeting China at last.

'She's gone again,' Linda Davidson explained. 'She left early this morning.'

'Gone where? Is she coming back?'

'I don't know. She left before I got up.'

'Did you see her last night?'

'Yes.'

'How did she look, what did she seem like?'

'She seemed OK. In fact, more than OK. She looked well.'

'Did she say where she'd been?'

'Only that she'd been keeping out of her brother's way.'

'And you definitely saw her?'

'Yes,' she confirmed.

'So why didn't you ring last night?' Temple felt frustrated with her.

There was a slight hesitation in Linda answering. 'I was going to ring last night. But I thought I'd leave it until the morning. I didn't know she would go again. So I'm ringing now.'

‘I’ll come and take a statement if you don’t mind.’ Temple didn’t give her a chance to answer before telling her he would be straight there.

He started to wonder again if he’d been so desperate to get out of the office that he had stupidly got caught up in some silly teenage game. But there was something about this that he didn’t like. Why did Gary Lewis lash out at him and tell him to lay off trying to find China? Even if she was no longer missing, Gary Lewis would still need investigating over the things that Amy Davidson had said about China and her brother, never mind Lewis drawing a knife and assaulting a police officer. Still, if China had been at the Davidsons’ house last night and, as per Linda Davidson’s account, was very much alive and well, there’d be no need for the searches that morning or a press appeal. If she was there last night, there was every chance she might turn up there again that evening.

A short while later, Temple sat at a small pine table in Linda Davidson’s spotless kitchen. She had to be at work she said, so couldn’t take too long. As if to emphasise the point, she was wearing her coat and her handbag sat on the table in front of him. She didn’t sit with him. He watched her busying her hands with small tasks: bleaching the sink, wiping the kitchen counter tops, things she needed to do while facing away from him.

‘So when did China turn up?’ Temple asked, his pen ready for her response.

‘Last night, about eleven-thirty,’ Linda told him over her shoulder.

‘What, and you were up at that time?’

‘Yes, I don’t go to bed until about midnight. Amy was in her room playing music when we got a tap on the door, and there’s China, asking if she can see Amy and if she can stay the night.’

‘And you let her in and she stayed over?’

‘Yeah, of course. She slept in with Amy.’

‘Amy pleased to see her?’

‘Yeah, really pleased.’

'So what time did she go this morning then?'

'When Amy woke up, China was already gone.'

'Just gone?' Temple was forced to aim his questions with Linda turned away from him. He could sense he wasn't exactly welcome and she wanted this conversation over as quickly as possible.

'Yeah, no goodbye or nothing.' Linda was pushing away at a seemingly stubborn mark on the kitchen work surface with a paper wipe.

'Do you think she's gone to school today?'

'I've no idea. Really. Why don't you call the school and check?'

'And you said she seemed OK to you, looked well?'

'Oh yes, just the same normal China, happy enough.' She half turned to him at that point.

'Did she say where she'd been, who she'd been with the last few days?'

'No.'

Temple was finding this hard work. 'Do you know if she said anything to Amy?'

'I don't, no – they went to bed. I don't know what they said to each other in there.'

'So what was China wearing?'

'Um, jeans and a top, a red top.'

'What sort of top?'

'A jumper.'

'You sure?'

'Of course.'

'And what about a coat?'

'A short black leather-looking jacket, scruffy-looking thing.' She had now run out of things to keep her hands busy with.

'I'll have to speak to Amy to see what was said when they were together.'

'But Amy's at school,' she said.

He continued to press. 'I'll call round tonight.' Temple sensed Linda Davidson's eagerness to leave the house.

'Now, back to China, tell me again, what did she look like when you saw her?'

'Look, I've said all this. I really have to go now,' she insisted. 'I've got to be at work, they'll be short without me.' She picked up her handbag, a signal that she clearly wanted Temple to go.

'I'll call again this evening and speak to Amy. Perhaps we can finish off then?'

'If you really must, but we're going out tonight. To the pictures, to see a film.'

'Oh yeah, what are you going to see?'

'Don't know yet, but it's our picture night. We always go on a Tuesday.'

'About five then, I'll call back then.'

She nodded and left the house with him, after reluctantly giving him her mobile number. Temple watched as she got into her car and drove away. Perhaps she *was* eager to get to work, but she certainly hadn't wanted to go into too much detail about China.

He remembered watching her on Amy's video interview and his impression that Amy hadn't disclosed all she knew in front of her mother. And why hadn't Linda Davidson called the police last night? Officers would have attended to do a safe-and-well check and the missing person report would have been closed.

Linda Davidson obviously thought that, on the basis of a telephone call to Temple this morning, it would be case closed. She clearly hadn't anticipated or welcomed his visit, but there she was telling him that China had turned up. So why did he have the distinct impression that throughout the exchange they'd just had, Linda Davidson was lying?

* * *

Temple went to the Park Academy where he made his way to the head teacher's office. A quick enquiry established that neither Amy Davidson nor China Lewis were at school that day. Linda Davidson had rung in saying that Amy was sick. He rang the mobile number that Linda had given him – there was no such number. He went back to the Davidsons' house and knocked on the door. No one answered.

Shortly after, Temple was looking at the dirty front door at Barbara Lewis's house, wondering if Gary was inside. His finger continued to throb as a result of their last meeting; he knew he had handcuffs with him but no other means of protection. He banged his fist on the door.

'Come on, Barbara, open up.'

There was no response so Temple hammered again. Eventually he heard the sound of the heavy lock being undone from inside. She opened the door an inch or two.

'I need to speak to you again, Barbara, can I come in?'

She didn't say anything but opened the door a fraction wider as she turned and walked unsteadily down the hall. *She'd started early this morning*, he thought. Temple followed her back into the kitchen.

'I need to speak to Gary. Do you have his phone number?'

She looked around the room for her phone. Temple found it before she did and interrogated it, finding the number and ringing it. There was no answer.

'Did Gary come here last night?'

'No.' She was already slurring and reeked of alcohol from her cider and vodka breakfast.

'Do you know where he goes when he's not here or at his flat?'

'You think I'd tell *you* if I knew?' She spat her words at him. Temple knew he was wasting his time so he left. When he arrived back at his desk there was a message for him to contact a Swindon PCSO. China had been seen in Swindon town centre.

'We saw her this morning, me and my colleague. It was from a distance but it was definitely her,' they told him down the phone.

'Where was she?' he asked.

'She went into Primark. By the time we got in there, we lost sight of her again. The place was heaving.'

'Was she alone?'

'She seemed to be.'

'And you're sure it was her?'

'Yes.'

'Keep looking for her – if you see her, at least take her photo with your phone or get her on your body cam if you can. Speak to her, tell her we've been looking for her. Invite her back to the station and contact me. I need to talk to her.'

Temple knew that sometimes people could be mistaken when reporting sightings but with Linda Davidson saying she'd seen China last night and now two PCSOs saying they'd seen her that morning, perhaps she was flitting around the town, just trying to keep out of the way of her brother Gary, as Temple had been told. In light of what the PCSOs had told him, he cancelled his plans for the house search of Gary Lewis's flat and the media appeal. Despite the sightings, he still wouldn't feel happy until he'd seen China for himself.

CHAPTER 14

Paul Wallace arrived back in Swindon. He felt optimistic today. The early morning mist had subsided and the sun was climbing in a cloudless blue sky. As he stepped off the train he felt the weak warmth of the sun's rays, despite it being late October and it getting colder. He had to find Megon before long, before the winter. He couldn't bear the thought of her still being missing in the winter. The sun made him feel optimistic. It felt right being here. He felt as though he was close to Megon. He felt as if he could feel her there, like he would see her.

He'd covered much of the town centre and its parameters yesterday and felt he'd got the size of the place. He'd even located a church close by to the station, St Mark's, a proper Victorian church. Somewhere he could go to for a quiet moment if needed, to ask for Megon to come back, just as he'd done at their local church when Leonie was ill. He wasn't a religious man but he'd gone into the church when he was at his lowest ebb and it had worked. It might work again.

He could walk the town centre systematically now, follow a plan. He'd pick up a local newspaper and see if he could get a feel for what sort of place it was, see where the trouble spots were, see if it would provide him with any clues to where Megon might be drawn to. He planned to catch a late train back tonight. He set off towards the town centre, down the now familiar streets, all the time looking about, looking at the young faces that approached him. He'd read about positivity in an article in the *Metro* on the train that morning: thinking about what you wanted might make it actually happen. He repeated a plea in his mind: *Where are you, Megon? Draw me to you, let me find you.* As he walked along, repeating his mantra, he fell into his stride.

He looked around as he walked. It was such a bright, almost warm day that he felt in good spirits. Today was the day; today he felt he was going to find her. He had rarely felt this close to finding Megon since she'd disappeared. His step was light as he continued walking. He would think positive.

Walking down the street, he approached a group of men standing around on the pavement outside a bookies. One of them, a young, light-haired man in his early twenties, was stripped to the waist. As Wallace got nearer, he could see the man had a livid red welt from a scratch down his back. He stood proud, as if he wanted all to see his newly made scar. He was standing next to a fat man, by an open narrow doorway with stairs leading straight up. As Paul Wallace passed through them, he heard their foreign talk and coarse laughter, and wondered where they were from. Along the road he went into a small newsagent's where he bought the local Swindon newspaper. When he reached the town centre, he sat on a bench in the sun and flicked through. The front-page headline was 'COUNCIL TO RECONSIDER BIN COLLECTION' with a smaller one in the corner – 'WHERE'S MUTTLEY?' – a plea to find a missing dog not seen for a few days.

Apart from that it was the usual fodder he normally read about in the *Evening Standard*: a community wail about burglaries, drugs, thefts and stabbings spread amongst the advertising for garden centres and pine furniture. There were pictures of community and charity events, which he scanned in case Megon appeared in the background. He noted the places and streets mentioned where the thefts had occurred and wondered if Megon was amongst the culprits, fending for herself as Mitch had told him he'd had to do.

Another news story featured which mentioned the growing problem of pop-up brothels and the influx of foreign prostitutes. It said that young girls were trafficked into prostitution across Swindon. He knew how this worked; there was enough of it in the *Metro* and in the *Evening Standard* back home. Brothels were advertised online and communicated through texts and WhatsApp messaging until there were queues of men lining up.

His mind flitted back to the group of men he had seen earlier. He couldn't bear the thought of Megon caught in that world. What sort of place was this that attracted so many men to use these women? He had to find her. He started to walk again, keeping to a grid system he'd mapped out. In his head he began to repeat his mantra: *Come on, Megon, come out, let me see you, let me find you and take you home. Come on, love.*

* * *

'Get up.' The fat man spoke in his broken English. He'd stood there for a while watching her on the mattress. She didn't move. He knew he could have her if he wanted, but she wasn't arousing him. She was young enough, but she wasn't his type, curled up naked in the foetal position; she was too small. Megon knew he was there. She stayed stock-still and closed her eyes. The last thing she wanted was any attention from him.

He kicked again at the mattress Megon was lying on. Megon had already had to deal with five men that morning. The last one had been young, foreign, and he'd been vile to her. The insides of her thighs had red marks from where his fingers had roughly grabbed her, which she knew would turn to bruises. As he'd continued to treat her roughly, she had scratched him down his back. That hadn't helped; he hurt her then. Curled up, she nursed herself.

Now the fat man was standing over her. She was shivering and wanting to hide herself from his gaze. He threw a cheap tracksuit top and trousers at her and watched as she uncurled herself and put them on, seeing the red marks on her body as she did so.

Megon was grateful for it; it almost felt luxurious to have something to cover her skin at last. She zipped up the front of the top to her neck and pulled the hood up over her head. She wanted to hide as much of her as she could from the pig's gaze. They were all pigs. They weren't human.

'You are going, dirty bitch. You need to wash – *mirosi* – you smell. We are moving you.'

He grabbed her. His thick fingers encased her upper arm, squeezing hard as if trying to hold the bone itself. He pushed her forward and manoeuvred her out through the door and down the stairs; all the time his hand was bolted around her arm. At the bottom of the stairs, the door was open and they went outside onto the sunlit street.

Standing barefoot on the pavement just for a brief moment, she experienced normality. Fresh air, the sun in her eyes, people coming and going about their business. She could hear the sound of the slot machines clearly now. The clarity of seeing and hearing things almost took her by surprise. She'd lost track of the outside world, shut up in the room. She couldn't even tell how long she'd been in there. The dark did that. The sunlight, the noise, as disorientating as it was, it did something to her; it invigorated her.

Before she could acclimatise to the outside or even get used to the fresh air, she was pushed forwards into the back seat of a waiting car. There was another girl in there. The fat man got into the front passenger seat and the car drove off.

Megon took a sideways look at the girl next to her. She didn't recognise her but she was wearing a similar tracksuit. Her head was bowed and she was looking into her lap. Megon gently pressed her elbow into hers but she gave no reaction.

Megon looked out of the window. No longer in the dark room, the change of scene caught her interest. She was alert now, aware of her surroundings. She heard the noise of the traffic, watched the cars going by and people walking. Normality had never looked so wonderful and she wanted to join it.

It energised her and made her realise that she was supposed to be out there, walking on the pavements, talking to her friends, smiling, laughing. That was the real world, not this underworld, hidden from sight, away from decent people who would not use her in the way she had been used.

Suddenly the car slowed, forced to stop in a line of traffic at a pedestrian crossing. She heard the bleeping of the crossing and watched as people filed across the road, oblivious to the cars waiting, oblivious to the drivers and their passengers, and oblivious to her.

If she could just get out she could run across the road with them. Now she was out of the room for the first time in days, she could think about getting away. She was barefoot but that didn't matter, she could still run. She stole a glance at the fat man in the passenger seat – he wouldn't be able to run after her. He didn't look as if he was capable of running even if his life depended on it. But hers did. If she could just get out she could run; before they even realised what was happening, she'd be out of sight. Megon felt suddenly emboldened.

She would have to be fast. She could open the door and quickly push it wide and leap out. Then she just needed to run, run anywhere, just run. As fast and as far as she could.

With her plan in place, she readied herself. All the time looking forward, she slowly extended her arm, her hand finding the door lever. Watching for any sign that her movements could be seen, she put her fingers round it and pulled at it gently. It had no leverage and moved freely in her hand. She hadn't heard the central locking engage when they drove off. Her heart sank.

Again, she looked at the people crossing the road, their animated faces, the bags they carried, the sun on their faces, the optimism they generated. She could hear their muffled voices. And then she thought she saw him. No, it couldn't be. She was mistaken. She looked again. It was. It was him. It was her dad.

CHAPTER 15

Following his grid system, Paul Wallace needed to reach the outlet village for around 1 p.m. This meant he could linger in that area and watch the afternoon shoppers and still do another loop of the Brunel Centre before closing time. He made his way to the pedestrian crossing where he stood with the many other shoppers waiting for the lights to turn red. The traffic was slow, but it was moving.

He'd continued to repeat his mantra and had fitted it into the rhythm of his stride. Now he had come to an enforced stop, he waited impatiently, needing to meet his goal. He looked at the people on the other side of the road, waiting to come towards him, making sure he didn't miss any one of them. Then he scanned the people who had merged with him at that point from their various directions. Old people, mothers with prams and young children, some teenagers. All now waiting at the crossing.

He looked to his left, up the line of traffic waiting to go north. An HGV carrying hardcore with one male driver, an SUV with a female driver with kids in the back, a Mini Cooper. Idling the time, he looked to his near side, to the line of traffic heading south.

As he stood behind a woman with a pram trying to herd her children towards her as she waited, he saw a boy racer at the front of the queue of traffic, foot on the accelerator, revving his engine noisily, ready to put some space between him and the car behind. His eyes flicked further down the queue of traffic. A dark-coloured saloon with two male drivers and two people he could just make out as back seat passengers. Behind that, a park-and-ride bus. He scanned the nearside passengers. A pair of PCSOs walked up behind him just as the lights turned red and the bleeping sounded. Everyone surged and the PCSOs crossed the road by the side of him.

Megon watched as her dad walked from the pavement across the road a few cars in front of her. He was looking straight ahead. Her initial reaction on seeing him was to duck down in case he turned and saw her. She didn't want him to see her like this. But then she wanted to call out, bash her hands on the windows, draw his attention to her. After trying the door, she now felt for the button to lower the window. It didn't move; it was locked. Her heart beat faster. It was now or never. She had to do *something*.

Suddenly, she lunged forward, pushing herself in between the two front seats, her outstretched hand landing on the centre of the steering wheel. As a little girl her dad had sat her on his lap and let her steer their Renault Clio. Part of the fun had been pushing the horn and delighting at the sound.

Now she found the spot exactly and the horn sounded. She managed to pump it again and again before the driver or the fat man could stop her. As the fat man struck out with his arm, his eyes were on the two PCSOs and he thought it was their attention she was trying to attract.

People's heads turned at the sound of the horn. The PCSOs looked hard right as they crossed the road, as did Paul Wallace. Everyone looked and presumed it was the boy racer in front of them, still revving his engine. Paul didn't see the man in the passenger seat in the car behind, pushing the girl and turning round to her in the back seat.

The lights turned back to green and as the pedestrians cleared, the cars moved on. Megon punched her hands on the window near her, calling out, but this was drowned as the boy racer screeched off the line into fifty yards of traffic space. She watched through the window, looking at the back of her dad as he walked away towards the outlet village. She urged him to glance back, turn around and look at her. He didn't. He was striding out away from her. The car was moving.

But he was in Swindon. He was looking for her, trying to find her. She knew she had to escape, but she had no idea where they were taking her and what they were taking her to. Right then, she had to deal with the fury of the fat man.

CHAPTER 16

Temple looked at a pile of buff-coloured files on his desk. There were an equal number of electronic files in his inbox. Looking at historic missing persons for the force had been a long-neglected task. While they were in the system and still 'live', the investigations into them were non-existent due to no new information being forthcoming. On that basis, he reasoned they were likely to sit there forever.

One of the cases was older than he was; others were five, ten years old, a few more recent. Men and women who had been reported missing and had seemingly just disappeared. A daughter reported missing by her mother, a man not seen for many years reported missing by his sister, and so it went on. He had taken a cursory glance into all fifty-six files in order to prioritise them.

He'd also wanted to get the size of the issue nationally and to put those he was now looking at in some sort of context. He'd spoken with the Missing Persons Bureau within the National Crime Agency. They recorded all reported incidents of missing people, which amounted to more than 250,000 reports a year, equating to an average of ninety reports per day into each police force across the country by worried friends and relatives. The numbers were staggering.

The Bureau kept a detailed record of people reported missing. They also went further and showed pictures on their website of the unidentified bodies of people who had been found dead or had been washed up on beaches. Any identifying information such as tattoos, scars or birthmarks were uploaded so that anyone searching might be able to recognise the bodies. It had been a bold, if somewhat gruesome step to take at the time, but had allowed officers or people with loved ones who were missing to regularly check to see if they had been found, albeit dead. The grim remains of people who had taken themselves off to commit suicide were regularly found at rivers and beauty spots by walkers in the country. The website was a way of helping to reconcile those with missing person reports.

Looking at the Missing People charity and UK Missing Persons Bureau websites, Temple saw the gap in figures of those still missing against unidentified bodies found.

He did further research into the figures and saw that the majority of those reported missing every day returned within twenty-four hours and most of those were children, many in care. But there were approximately 1,000 or so reports of missing people that remained outstanding year on year. That meant that of all those reported missing, approximately three people a day vanished from home and never returned.

He wondered how many of those people did indeed walk out of their lives to start a new one elsewhere, as suggested by some press reports and the Missing Persons Helpline. Some did; dissatisfied with their lives, troubled or burdened by finances, they just walked out, away from their families, never to return, only to exist in another location, to make another life without a backward glance. Those they left behind just had to deal with their shock, the aftermath of forever wondering what had become of them and not knowing if their loved one was alive or dead. Living in the limbo of not knowing.

He wondered how many of those reported missing ended up on the streets, sleeping rough, barely existing.

Where were they among the numbers? And how many people were missing as a result of a criminal act? Murdered, with their bodies hidden, buried or destroyed, but forever regarded as missing.

He felt as if he'd wandered into some kind of no man's land where people seemed to disappear from view. It looked as if there was no logical answer, yet sadly there was acceptance of the situation. For whatever reason, as his files told him, people vanished.

He figured that if one person a day – a third of the 1,000 people who remained missing each year – created new lives for themselves away from their homes, family and friends and another third committed suicide but their remains were yet to be discovered, that still left over 300 people a year. What happened to them – were they dead as a result of criminal activity? Some had to be, or else where were they? There seemed to be no 'official' answer to how or why so many people remained outstanding year on year.

Just as he was going to sit down and start wading into the files, a pain shot through his bandaged finger. As it began to throb against its tight covering, Temple picked at the knot that Ana had tied to try and release it. The throbbing worsened and he had to cut the knot to loosen it. He unwound the bandage until he could see his finger. The deep gash had started to turn an odd shade with yellowing pus around the edges and the finger had swollen. Ana had been right. This wasn't going to heal of its own accord.

'Fucking thing,' Temple muttered, thinking that the knife was probably the source of any number of bacteria.

* * *

He sat in A&E amongst all the other sick, wounded and broken. Having decided to wear his own navy-blue mac instead of anything with a police badge on it, he'd flashed his warrant card and told them he'd been injured on duty, hoping that he might jump the queue, but they were having none of it.

The place was heaving and as he sat there he wondered if he should just go before being seen, but the throbbing had given way to pain and more pus. Even so, he kept telling himself he should just get up and go back to the nick. As a queue formed at the desk, he stood up to go. He could be here all day. Just then his name was called.

He was shown to a cubicle where a male nurse cleaned and stitched the wound. It was showing sure signs of infection, he said, and gave Temple some antibiotics with a prescription for more. It was a good job he came when he did, he was told. As Temple was leaving the cubicle he noticed a female pass by, her flash of red hair familiar to him from earlier that same day.

'Hi, it's Callie, isn't it?' Temple called out.

As she turned, he saw that she had a cut and swelling on the bridge of her nose and two bruises were starting to form around her eyes.

'Woah, what happened to you?' As he spoke, he extended his undamaged hand.

'Hello again.' Shaking his hand, she looked slightly self-conscious. Despite her obvious injuries, she flashed him a smile.

'This? Oh, it was one of the kids. I was in the way when she threw a chair across the room. Nothing broken, thankfully. Bloody hurts though.' She had a very proper accent that he hadn't noticed before and there was a soft huskiness to it. 'Sorry, I'm not exactly looking my best at the moment.' Callie's hand went into her hair.

'You look fine to me. Your eyes are going to be a great shade of purple. Someone must have been quite worked up to want to land a chair on you.'

'It was little Molly actually. I was going to ring you. Kay gave me your card. Molly told me she had seen the girl you were looking for.'

'Did she say where?' Temple wasn't surprised as he'd suspected as much.

'She said she'd seen her around the train station. Then she threw the chair.'

'That's what provoked her? I am sorry – now I feel responsible.'

'It wasn't just that. She's having a few problems at the moment and obviously didn't take kindly to me asking questions. So what brings you here?'

'I got in the way of a blade.' He held up his bandaged finger.

'Work or home?'

'Work. Like you, I should have moved faster.' They started to walk together towards the exit. As they walked she explained that she'd started to question Molly about her whereabouts and if she'd seen the girl Temple had shown on his phone. She said she had and then got herself into a rage. Once outside they stood looking across the expanse of car park. She suddenly put her hand up to the side of her head as if she was in pain.

'Are you OK to drive? Is there anywhere I can take you?' he asked. He felt protective towards her.

'No, it's OK, I'm sure I can manage.' She turned to face him. 'Tell me, how bad does it look?'

Temple looked at her pretty face, now marred by bruising. 'Your nose is starting to swell a little, but the cut will heal quickly.'

'Oh God, he'll be so angry.'

'Who's that, your husband?'

'No,' she smiled, briefly looking down. 'No husband. No, I meant my father. He doesn't like it when this happens. Makes him angry and then he goes on at me to give it up.'

'Do you have far to go?'

'Not really, just back along the A346 and then down to Huish. You?'

'Back to work, Swindon. Look, I could take you home. You could pick your car up from here later tomorrow. You've taken a bit of a knock there.'

Callie took a few seconds and then conceded. 'If it's not too much trouble. I mean, it's in the opposite direction to where you're going.' She recovered her earlier self-consciousness about how she looked. She'd wanted to help him since seeing him at the home. She was attracted to him and he seemed to care about the girl he was looking for.

'It's a pretty straight run and I'd feel happier knowing you actually got home safely. It's the least I can do since you were trying to help me when this happened.'

He saw her to his car and they set off towards the small village of Huish. During the journey he asked her about working at The Brook.

'So, tell me about Molly, about the kids there,' he asked.

'Molly's like most of the kids we look after who are generally dealing with a range of issues. A lot of them have suffered physical, psychological and sexual abuse and are deeply traumatised by it. Others might have experience of abusive and neglectful parenting. It affects how they behave.' She stopped and looked across at him.

'Go on,' he replied, 'I'm interested.'

'Many of them have been mistreated; often in the most awful way, but sometimes in more subtle but nevertheless damaging ways. The back stories of these kids can be absolutely harrowing. Just when you think you've read the worst case you'll ever come across, there'll be another that's worse still.

'When we get them they might have been in many other placements. They're hurt, confused, frightened and angry. All from the way they've been mistreated and what they've been exposed to by their own reckless and dangerous parents. They need to relearn to trust adults, but that may never come. Hence me ending up like this.' She gestured to her face.

'We can only try and show them what a normal life should be like and provide the nurturing and psychological help they'll need to deal with the past. We've got to try and fix them, undo the damage. Reset them.'

'Back to factory settings,' said Temple, not meaning to be flippant. She acknowledged the metaphor. He listened to her as she continued.

'If only it was as easy as touching a few buttons. It costs time and money, but if you don't put that in now at their age, you end up with a lot of screwed-up adults later down the line, repeating the same behaviour on another set of kids. They're also growing up too, with all the usual hormones kicking in. Then, if they have a bad day, if someone new comes to live in their home for instance, that's another thing they have to deal with.'

He caught himself then thinking back to when he was young, with his mother and the latitude she'd given him to explore the world around him. He knew he'd had more freedom than most kids growing up.

Thing was, he'd had no idea then about the company his mother kept or ultimately the danger she had placed them both in. Looking back, the memory of his mother was brought into sharp relief by the parents that Callie was describing to him. 'Reckless and dangerous,' she'd said; his mother had definitely been both of those.

'So tell me about the girl you're looking for. How long has she been missing?'

'Well, that depends on who you speak to. People tell me they've seen her and that she's not missing; her friend tells me another story. It may turn out to be something and nothing.'

'Does she come from a good home?'

'No, having been there I'd say it was one of the worst.'

'Kids respond well to love and nurture. That's what we find. You can mend a lot with that.'

They continued to talk and when they reached the turning for Huish, Callie directed him through the village until they had gone on to the outskirts. She then directed a sharp turn left which took them along the long drive of a large old-style country house. Temple looked across at her.

'You live *here*?'

'Yes,' she said, almost embarrassed.

Temple drove across a cattle grid onto a wide driveway and pulled up by the front entrance. The house was a large, elegant Regency pile that had been built and owned by the principal landowner of the village in the early 1820s. It was constructed from Bath stone and had a portico across the door, flanked by two grand Doric columns.

Callie invited him inside and as they walked through into a grand, square hall, they were met almost immediately by a tall, slightly overweight, well-dressed man with a thick head of white hair.

'I was just on my way out,' the man said as he looked at her, 'but now I'll change my plans. What on earth has happened to you?' Temple assumed that it was her father. He couldn't quite work out why, but the man seemed familiar to him.

'Have you been involved in an accident?' he asked.

'No, I haven't—' She didn't get a chance to explain before he went on.

'Calypso, has this happened at the home?' He had taken her by the shoulders and was looking at her face. Temple could smell his strong cologne from where he stood, looking at his surroundings. There were a number of military prints hanging from the walls around him.

'Don't worry, Father, there's no harm done. It looks far worse than it is. Yes, it did happen at the home but it's only bruising. No bones broken.' She tried to make light of her injuries, but Temple could see he was having none of it.

He looked over his daughter's shoulder to Temple. 'And are you from the home? Is this how you want your staff treated? It's a disgrace.'

'No, I'm not from the home; I met Callie at the hospital. I'm a police officer, sir.'

'Oh, so the police are involved this time, are they? At last, you've seen sense. So, officer, what charges will be brought?'

Callie quickly cut in. 'This is my father, Theo St George. Father, this is Detective Inspector Temple.'

Temple held out his hand, which Theo St George shook with an efficiency that suggested he was a man with a military background.

'I'm just bringing Callie – Calypso – home, sir. I was also at the hospital and just wanted to make sure she got home safely. I'm not here to bring charges; there have been no complaints made.'

St George turned his attention back to his daughter. 'Well I'd like to bloody make one. For Christ's sake, Calypso, I wish you'd give it up.' Her father looked into her face, his eyes examining the cut on the bridge of her nose.

'It looks far worse than it is, really it does. There's no need to worry.' She gently tapped her father's cheek with her hand and changed the subject by offering them both tea.

With Theo St George striding behind them, she showed Temple into a drawing room off the hall and made sure he was ensconced on a large, low sofa before going off to the kitchen. Theo St George plunged into a sofa opposite him.

Temple suddenly realised who he was. 'You're an MP, Theodore St George – I thought you were familiar. Sorry, I should have realised.' There had been an article recently in the local paper regarding St George and a local MP in a spat over immigration that had spilled into the national press.

'Was, Inspector – I've been relegated to the House of Lords now. That's how I see it anyway. What do you make of Calypso's injuries? It makes me bloody angry. Can I press charges?'

Temple could see he had clearly walked into an ongoing situation and was now being asked to take sides.

'From what she's told me, sir, the home where Callie – I mean Calypso – works does a lot of good work with children who badly need their input. She clearly loves her job.'

'That's as may be, but I don't like it. I fear for her.' Calypso was his only daughter, along with two sons. St George still felt protective of her and had never been impressed with her career choice. He knew the pay was awful and he knew that she did it in spite of that. She'd told him it was because she had so much herself that she wanted to help others less fortunate. It was doing something meaningful, she said. He could understand that all right but he drew the line at her getting hurt. This wasn't the first time and he was sure it wouldn't be the last. That's what bothered him.

'Look.' He leaned forward in his seat and shot a look at the door. 'While she's out of the room, whatever you can do to influence her to give up this job, I'd be very grateful. She frequently comes home with cuts and bruises.'

'We've only just met, Mr St George, and from what I've heard Calypso say about her job, I don't think I'd stand much of a chance.' Temple found himself enjoying saying her name; he liked the unusualness of it and how it sounded. It suited her.

'I just don't want her hurt. She's precious to me. She was once very ill you know, as a child, very ill. I don't like seeing her like that.' Theo St George was trying to keep his voice low but couldn't help himself. 'Do you have children, Inspector?'

'Yes, I do.' He hesitated before going on. 'A girl . . . and a boy.' The question caught Temple momentarily off guard. He was used to talking about Daisy. Now there was Ben. He realised it was the first time he had acknowledged that he had a *son* and daughter to a stranger. He suddenly thought of Leigh, pregnant with another of his children, and again the realisation hit that they would never all be under the same roof. Breaking this thought, Theo St George continued.

'And what would you do if someone used your daughter as a punch bag?'

'I'd intervene, sir.' As he said it, Temple remembered Roger Hunt again and how he'd reacted when he thought Hunt had hit Daisy. He'd certainly intervened then, using Roger Hunt as a punch bag only for Daisy to admit that she'd made it all up in an effort to reunite her parents.

'Yes, thought so. This happens at her place of work for God's sake. Who goes to work to get beaten, I ask you? It's the twenty-first century, not the bloody eighteen hundreds.'

Calypso came through the door with a tea tray and had obviously heard Theo speaking.

'That's enough!' she chided him.

Theo crumbled instantly. 'I'm sorry, darling, really sorry. It's just. . .'

'I know, I know. Just let's talk about it later. I'll listen, but I'm not promising anything.' She wasn't angry at all, just apologetic to Temple who had obviously come in on a long-standing issue between the two of them.

The rest of the time over tea was taken up with keeping off the subject of her work, and Callie and her father both managed to lighten the mood with more general conversation. They were good hosts and Temple could see it put Theo's uncharacteristic outburst into perspective. They were interested in Temple, his work, his home life. The work bit was fine, he was used to interest in that, but on the home front, the most he confided was that he lived with an au pair who helped him look after his son.

Their company was easy and Temple found himself becoming increasingly attracted to his hostess as she sat across from him. Despite the evident bruising, she was very attractive, with her red hair in a long bob to her shoulders. She had a ready smile and seemed really pleased for him to be there. She had certainly brightened since she'd been at home and showed no signs of a headache, as she had earlier.

The room they were sitting in felt very grand and although his hosts had made him feel extremely welcome and relaxed, Temple felt that he'd stepped into a different world. Apart from Callie working at the home, he wondered what worries Theo St George could possibly have as he looked around and admired the comfortable surroundings. After nearly an hour, Temple made a move to return to the station. Callie walked him back to his car.

'Sorry about my father earlier. That's not how he typically greets people he meets for the first time. I hope he redeemed himself.'

'There's no need to apologise. He cares, that's all.' Temple looked into Callie's bruised eyes. 'I can quite understand why he'd want to protect you. It's easy to see why.' They smiled at each other.

'Thank you for the lift back, it was really very kind of you.' She was so glad he'd made the offer.

'That was no problem. I've enjoyed myself, meeting you . . . your father. He's a bit of a character.'

'Yes, he is,' she said softly. 'He's a pussycat really.'

'I've also enjoyed finding out that your name is Calypso. I haven't met anyone called Calypso before.' He liked saying it again.

'Callie's a bit more conventional.' There was a brief silence between them. As they both looked down and back at each other at the same time, they seemed to acknowledge the mutual attraction they felt. They smiled at one another, saying nothing momentarily. Temple noticed the fullness of her mouth and how her teeth were now slightly biting her lower lip. It was Callie who broke the silence with a slight laugh.

'You could always come back later,' she said slowly. 'When you're off duty.' She'd reinforced the invitation by reaching out and squeezing his hand and holding his gaze for a few seconds. 'We can continue to get to know each other.' Temple had been wondering how he could finesse another meeting between them and suddenly it had been done for him. 'I've texted you my number,' she said.

He smiled and got into his car.

CHAPTER 17

The sunny day was quickly turning to evening by the time Temple arrived back at the station. The shift was changing and he knew if he was quick enough, he could get inside and speak to some of the local patrol teams to see if they'd seen either China or Gary Lewis.

Negative. No one had seen either of them.

He went back to his desk where his files lay just as he'd left them. His heart wasn't in it to start picking up the threads at this time of day. He logged in to the laptop to check his emails. He scrolled through them, looking for any that might give a clue as to the whereabouts of China Lewis. There was nothing.

Although he hated working behind a desk, up to now his days had had a quiet monotony of file reading, online form-filling and making phone calls to the Department of Work and Pensions and social services, tracking down the people in his case files. He'd found three of his missing persons were now dead, having drawn their old age pensions in the time they had been reported missing, the consequence of no one taking the time, trouble or interest to make the most basic of enquiries which would have closed the files long ago.

As he flicked through his inbox, his mind wandered back to Callie and their meeting. He wondered if he could have misunderstood the invitation she had extended – 'Come back later, when you're off duty.' He checked his phone – there was the text with her number. He thought of their meeting. She was obviously from a very privileged background and yet chose to work with children at the opposite end of the scale; in fact, the circumstances of the kids that she'd described couldn't be more different from her upbringing. And yet she felt she had to help them. He liked her for that.

He put her name into Google, which revealed some scant details. *The Honourable Calypso Andrea St George, 33 years old, daughter of Right Honourable Theodore St George, Baron St George, former MP for South West Wilts. Following his retirement as an MP he was appointed a Life Peer.*

Temple clicked on a few of the online references for Theo, which mainly focused on his past military and political activities. He found a useful biography that told him Theo had been in the 1st Regiment Royal Horse Artillery, ending his career as a captain before following family tradition and becoming an MP. He had been married to Calypso's mother, Fiona, for twenty-five years before she died in a boating accident off the coast of Corfu during a family holiday. His father, Gerald St George, also an MP in the 1950s, had managed to marry the only child of a rich landowner in 1946, which was obviously where the money had come from.

Looking at the screen, he could see Callie was in a different league. She'd definitely shown an interest in him, but from what he'd read about her background, he couldn't think why. They were worlds apart. But then perhaps that was part of the attraction for her. Perhaps that was what she was after; maybe it was a cop thing, a uniform thing?

He suddenly thought of Leigh. He tried to remember the last time he'd seen her – it must be more than three weeks ago. She dropped Daisy off in the road by the lychgate, which meant he didn't even get to see her. God, she was angry with him. Just the sight of him was like lighting the touch paper.

He didn't blame her. She'd made it quite clear to him their marriage was over, dead. And he'd killed it; she made that crystal clear. There was no going back. He'd never meant to cause her such pain, but in the circumstances, they were hollow words.

But Callie, the lovely, pretty Callie with her milky white skin and red hair, was like catnip. It was difficult to fight the attraction and her invitation. Wasn't he almost a free agent? He knew she was out of his league, that nothing would come of it. Even so. He was intrigued.

* * *

With the onset of early evening and still bothered by China Lewis, he left the station and drove round to Linda Davidson's house. Despite it being 5 p.m., like he'd promised, as he drove by he saw that the house was in darkness. They must have gone to the cinema early, or gone out for something to eat first. He'd have to come back later; he was determined to speak to Linda, but more importantly he needed to speak to Amy to ensure China really did go to the Davidsons' last night. Temple was not convinced and he wanted to catch Linda in her lie about China.

Back in the town centre, remembering what Callie had said about where Molly had seen China, Temple parked outside Swindon railway station. The evening was drawing in and it was dark now. There were commuters standing on the platform waiting for trains but it was past rush hour, so passengers had thinned out to the overtime workers.

He sat on a metal bench on the platform and watched those coming and going around him. Looking around for any signs of China, his mind returned again to Callie. 'Come back later,' she'd said. Should he? His thoughts were broken by a loud announcement over a tannoy system of the arrival of the 19.14 train from Paddington.

As it pulled in, Temple watched as the commuters with their business suits and briefcases stepped from the train.

Their breath hit the cold night air as they walked quickly to their cars, some greeted by waiting relatives. Among those that stepped off the train was a hard-faced man in his twenties, a woollen beanie hat pulled over his head. He was with a girl much smaller, younger and more delicate-looking than him.

She had to be thirteen or younger, in a maroon school blazer with gold trim. He had his hand around her shoulder. Temple watched them walk out of the station, trying to get a look at the badge on her jacket. The colour of the uniform was unfamiliar. In the short time he'd seen them, he knew they weren't right and he was up on his feet, following them.

As they walked down the street, the man walked slightly behind the young girl. As they walked on, he dropped his arm from around her shoulder and moved his hand around to the base of her neck. It was clear to Temple that he was controlling her, and in this way he steered her down the streets and across the junctions, walking around the feet of the dossers sitting on the pavements. She was carrying a Marks & Spencer 'bag for life' and looked straight ahead. As they walked down the street, they said nothing to each other. There was nothing to give Temple the impression that they were in any way emotionally connected. They behaved like a couple of strangers. He didn't like it.

Temple continued to follow them from a distance. They were heading towards Manchester Road. Keeping back, he watched as they turned right out of his sight. He knew Manchester Road so didn't quicken his pace. He decided to follow them and watch until they went into a premises, and then he could go in. If he could just follow them to wherever they were going, he could check out the address.

As he went round the same corner, he saw the girl standing alone now in the distance. She'd somehow lost her minder and was standing on the edge of the pavement as if waiting for someone. As Temple went to approach her, he was aware of someone in the darkness appearing out of nowhere from his right. Suddenly, he saw a fist swinging out and the pavement heading towards him.

CHAPTER 18

In deflecting the blow, Temple took a sharp punch to the side of his body, underneath his arm. The suddenness of the movement and awkwardness of the angle made him lose his footing. Before he could understand what had happened, he fell heavily onto the pavement, just managing to avoid his head hitting the side of a wall. When he looked up, a man was standing astride him, with fists clenched.

'What the fuck do you think you're doing, you perverted bastard.'

'Who are you?' Temple shouted back angrily as he lay on the pavement, winded. His assailant continued to look down on him as if ready to hit him again, his face contorted as he continued to shout at him.

'You scummy shit. Fuck off home, leave these girls alone. Go on, go home, you bastard.' The man gave him a half-hearted kick while he was still down. Temple looked up at the snarling face. He had to get up.

'I'm not after girls, you fucking idiot.' Temple scrambled to his feet. He looked down the street to where he had last seen the girl on the pavement. She was gone. There was no sign of the man who was with her. 'Who *are* you?' he asked his attacker.

'Never mind who I am, it's none of your business. I've seen the likes of you. I know what you do and what your game is—'

Before he could finish, Temple cut in. He'd caught his breath and was back on his feet. With his side still smarting from the blow, he slowly straightened up.

'My "game" is to arrest you for assaulting a police officer.' Temple took hold of the man's arm while fishing for the handcuffs in his pocket. The man jerked his arm free.

'Take your hands off me, scum, don't think I'm falling for that one. Where's your warrant card, eh? Where is it?'

Temple pulled out his wallet showing his warrant card and pushed it into the man's face.

'You are under arrest for assault.' Temple read the man his rights. Looking at him, Temple could see he was still not clear whether to believe his identification. 'I am a police officer and you'll have to come to the station with me. Now, what's your name?' Then the man saw the handcuffs in Temple's right hand. His aggression instantly disappeared and he almost crumbled in front of him.

'Look, mate, officer, I didn't know, did I? It was a mistake. You was creeping and just about to approach that young girl. I've only been here two days and I can see what's going on here.'

Temple ignored him. 'What's your name?'

'Paul Wallace. Look, please don't take me back to the station. I'm sorry I punched you. I wouldn't have done it if I'd known you were a copper. Of course I wouldn't. Please just don't take me to a bloody station. I'm sorry. *Please*.' Paul Wallace knew he had to plead his case if he wasn't going to waste his entire evening stuck in a cell, possibly not getting back to the girls that night. He might even end up on a charge of assault. Worse still, he might miss Megon. If she was here, tonight could be the night that he could find her. He'd get on his knees if he had to.

'Why are you here?' asked Temple. He had no more of a wish to get Wallace back to the station and start form-filling than Wallace had. He wanted to go back and see Linda and Amy Davidson, and taking Wallace into custody would scupper that.

'I'm here to find my daughter. Look, please, sir – take a look.' Paul Wallace had taken a flyer out of his backpack and put it into Temple's hands. It was a picture of Megon with her name beneath it.

'There's more in here,' he said, gesturing to his back. 'She's only thirteen and she's been missing from home for four, nearly five weeks now. I got a text from one of her mates to say that she'd come to Swindon. I've been looking for her for weeks around London. I'm from Hackney and now I'm here, walking the streets trying to find her. I must find her. Please don't stop me looking. She's my baby and she needs me to look for her.' The words just tumbled out, so desperate was he to win Temple's favour.

Temple looked at the flyer and back to Paul Wallace.

'Please don't arrest me. I'm sorry. I thought you were after a girl and I wanted to stop you. I wanted to keep her safe. *Please* don't arrest me.'

Temple could see the desperation in his face. As Temple stayed silent, Wallace carried on.

'I *swear* I'm here looking for my girl.'

The bloke looked knackered, with dark rings around his eyes and almost frightened since Temple had thrust his warrant card in his face and flashed his handcuffs.

'Yeah, all right, calm down. It's your lucky night. Look, you're de-arrested, but only because I've got better things to do. I suppose there's no harm done.' Temple rubbed the side of his body where Wallace had landed his punch. It was tender.

'Can I get you a cup of coffee by way of saying sorry?' Paul Wallace nodded towards a street vendor at the end of the road. 'Try and make up for it?'

'Yes you can.' They walked further down the road to a white van with a counter flap on the side. The warm, spicy smell and sound of onions and burgers frying hung enticingly in the air and drew in customers. Wallace bought two watery-looking coffees in polystyrene cups. Temple took a sip and winced at the bitter taste.

'I'm also looking for a missing girl,' Temple confided. 'Well, at least I think she's missing. Have you seen her about anywhere?' Temple showed Paul Wallace a photo of China Lewis on his phone.

'No, sorry I haven't. There are so many young girls out here on the streets at night. I've just got this real feeling that Megon's out here, you know, as if she's willing me to find her.'

'How long did you say she's been gone?'

'Getting on for five weeks now. Her mother's going mad with worry. She'd be with me, only she's recuperating from breast cancer treatment, the bloody chemo, and she's got to look after our other two little 'uns, Megon's sisters. We've got a dog just about to have pups too.'

Temple felt sympathy for him. It sounded as if he was really up against it.

'You need to watch yourself out here, especially around this area. There are men dealing in drugs and women who won't think twice about mugging you. Lots of Romanians and Albanians and they're violent bastards.' Looking through the steam the coffee generated, Temple took another sip.

'It's the same where we are.' Wallace shook his head. 'We've got the estate gangs, boys and girls taking drugs, knifing each other. It's everywhere. My Megon didn't stand a chance really, growing up where she did. I know why she ran away – she ran away from her life.

'A shitty London estate, rife with drugs, violence and gangs and then her mum gets ill. Her mum doesn't even look like her mum anymore, she loses her hair and gets all thin and she thinks maybe she'll die. Her dad works all day and has barely got time for any of his daughters and she's got to take all this, look after her sisters, watching her mum lying sick on the settee, walking the bloody dog amongst the scum and their knives and needles.

'And then I get made redundant, so then there's no money coming in. I can't even feed them properly, let alone buy her and her sisters the clothes they need just to keep their heads up at school. She's thirteen and her life's already shit.'

Temple felt glad he hadn't pursued the arrest of Paul Wallace. Listening to what he said, he knew that it was likely that Megon had succumbed to some kind of peer pressure back at home, especially if money was tight and she was trying to survive on a tough London estate.

Kids were being lured and trapped into drug-running on a large scale by London dealers, on the promise of earning large sums of money. It was a sinister and evil world where kids were cynically exploited. One of the signs of this was that kids were going missing for periods of time. He knew that if Megon was caught up in this, no matter how shit Paul thought her life was before she ran away, it would be ten times worse if she wasn't found – and fast.

CHAPTER 19

Temple walked around the streets with Paul Wallace, looking for Megon. They stopped by some homeless men and asked if they'd seen her. Paul left them a flyer. They spoke to some members of the Salvation Army and left Megon's flyer with them. Temple showed him where she might be likely to hang out and told him he would make sure Megon's photo was circulated with PCSOs and response teams. Temple felt genuinely sorry for him and before he left, said that he would keep a look out for her. They swapped mobile numbers.

Linda Davidson's house was dark when he got there. Temple parked further up the road so that he could observe from a distance. She'd said that she and Amy were at the cinema tonight. He was on a rest day after this so really needed to speak to Amy to find out what she knew about China Lewis from the visit the night before, and what China had disclosed to her.

Temple wasn't cut out for surveillance; he couldn't just sit still in a car watching for very long before getting bored. He needed to keep things moving. After an hour of them not showing, he drove off back to the Manchester Road area to see if he could spot the girl he'd seen coming off the train.

He parked up and went back to the street where he'd literally bumped into Paul Wallace. Where had the girl disappeared to? He hadn't seen a car pull up for her to get into, but then he'd been upside down on the pavement. And her minder had disappeared before she had. Terraced houses lined one side of the street; on the other side were some shops and small commercial buildings. He walked up and down the pavement looking at the fronts of the houses, trying to form an opinion of what might lie behind. He crossed the road and kept out of sight in a doorway, watching for any activity.

It wasn't long before three young men emerged out of a house not far from where Temple had last seen the girl standing on the kerb. Dressed in jeans and T-shirts despite the cold, one was shouting down a mobile. They were arguing but their language was foreign and as he walked across the road, he couldn't make out what they were saying. They were tall and lean and as they shouted, pushed and shoved each other, their language sounded more frantic and raised in volume.

He drew closer, under the illumination of a street light. Temple could hear that they were Eastern European. They started to jostle one another; it looked as if a fight was about to ensue. Two of the men traded blows as the third looked around and ran down the road. As the lookout saw Temple approach, he tapped one of his friends on the arm and shouted something. They broke from their fight and looked around; seeing Temple, they turned, running off down the street. Temple knew better than to run after them and instead stopped outside the house they had come from. It was a nondescript run-down terrace with a forecourt, not far from where Paul Wallace had grounded him.

Just then, the door of the house opened. A large man stepped out and walked towards him. Even with his head down, Temple knew him. DS Simon Sloper. They'd last worked together six months ago, on the same murder investigation that had resulted in Temple now facing a disciplinary hearing. Sloper, the chief witness against him. Sloper, the lying bastard.

Sloper was also a good friend of Harker. Seeing him now reminded Temple what a pincer movement Sloper and Harker had him in. In just a few days' time, he'd be standing in a hearing facing Sloper and Harker, and have to listen to their lies. It would be time for Harker to settle the score sheet, as he'd never forgiven Temple for the long-past relationship with his daughter Gemma. As Sloper looked up and saw Temple in front of him, his face changed.

'What are you doing here?' he asked. Sloper showed no respect for the man holding a higher rank than him.

'Working,' Temple replied. 'You?'

'Making enquiries.' Sloper seemed in no mood for talking. In fact, for once he looked a little rattled.

'What's going on in there?' Temple nodded towards the door of the house.

'Just some little druggy scumbag who was helping me with my enquiries. Nothing for you to worry about.' Sloper moved his twenty-stone bulk towards Temple as if he was just going to charge into him. Temple stood his ground.

'Is there a girl in there?'

'No, it's empty now. I'm off.' Sloper pushed his bulk past Temple but then suddenly stopped. He stepped back, putting his face close to Temple. 'So, why *are* you here?'

'Nothing that concerns you,' Temple replied. Sloper snorted in response, and drawing himself up, walked off to his car without a backward glance.

Temple hung around Swindon for a while before going back to the station. With a rest day looming, he'd have to pick up on China Lewis in two days' time, when he was back on duty. In the meantime, he hoped she would be spotted.

* * *

'Hey, girl. Come over here. Come and sit by me. Come on.' The man spoke to her in broken English.

China Lewis looked over to him. He was vile. They were sitting in the back room of a tiny terraced house. The room was a rectangle shape with two cheap and dirty sofas against the walls at right angles to each other. She was sitting on one sofa, as far away as she could get from the male sitting on the other sofa, but given the size of the room, that wasn't far. They were both alone in the house.

She had been there for four days now. She was being held there because she'd lost some drugs and money. She knew this sort of thing happened, of course she did, she'd been around long enough, but she had actually no idea of the danger she was in. Danger no longer registered with her.

'Come and make friends with me,' he said with a half-smile.

The man was Eastern European – she didn't know exactly what country he came from. They all sounded the same to her whether they came from Romania, Estonia, Croatia, Albania. It amounted to the same. To her, they were evil, nasty bastards.

She looked at him with his close-shaven head. She could see white scars visible on his scalp, tiny ones and larger ones. But that was nothing compared to the one on his face. It started by his ear and snaked across his cheek, ending by the corner of his mouth. It was wide, as if it had healed without being stitched together properly.

But it was the other side of his face that held the horror for her. His right eye was dead and unseeing, like an opaque, grey, wet marble had been fixed in its place. She was both transfixed and terrified by it as it stared out of his face.

When he spoke, his attempts at smiling revealed a tooth missing from the upper left side, the dark hole giving his grin menace. Put altogether, he repulsed her. He wasn't old – she guessed he was about twenty-five – but she found him so ugly that any attempts at being friendly made him seem even more menacing than he already was.

He'd told her they were his battle scars: battles for territory, turf battles and fights for survival. He wore his scars with pride; they were the marks of the man he was. They showed his resilience and his fearlessness to fight. They were a warning to others. But there was something more than the scars.

He'd told her that he had killed men, and she believed him. She could feel he had. There was something so cold, so empty about him. He was just a shell. There was nothing human, nothing remotely feeling about him. He was dead. Alive, but at the same time dead. And she couldn't bear the thought of this man lying on her. But that's what he was after now.

It wasn't that she was scared of him. It wasn't that. She'd seen so much in her short life, so much that had threatened her very existence, that she had ceased being scared.

In these situations, she looked to her future; that bright future where she lived a perfect life, with all this behind her as if none of it had ever happened. There she was in her perfect home, with her perfect husband and their two adorable children, where she had everything she ever wanted. She saw it as clearly as she saw this ugly man before her now. She was sure that was the life she was destined to live, she just didn't know how she would get there. But it didn't seem like such a giant leap. All it would take was one of the many men she encountered to love her and want to protect her.

He fingered the scar running across his cheek. He wanted sex now and this girl was here. He was waiting for some friends and he wanted to have her before they arrived. He had been alone there for nearly three hours; left to watch her, make sure she didn't leave. He had watched her, talked to her and now he wanted her. Still seated, he unzipped his trousers.

'China. China.' He coaxed her with her name. 'Come to me, China. Come and see what I have here for you.'

She gave him a sideways glance. He looked across at her, his half-smile like a grimace.

'You've got no fucking chance.' Her mouth never let her down; it just came out, her spirit leapt up and came out of her mouth. She heard the words like they had been said by someone else. She was sick of being used and she wasn't going to let this ugly man use her. He chimed her name again.

'China, I'm being nice to you. Come over here. Sit on my lap, China. Do as you're told for the nice man.' He was mocking her. He knew she knew all about men, had done from an early age, no thanks to her brother. He was giving her a chance for this to be mutual between the two of them. But his patience would run out if she didn't shut her mouth and do as she was told.

'You can just fuck yourself, go on. Fuck. Your. Self,' she retorted, her words spat across to him like a slap in the face.

His mood changed instantly. Like all the rest, this stupid bitch didn't realise that he would just take what he wanted. He flew across to her, enraged by her. He would show her how she should treat him. He wanted to choke the words in her throat. He wanted to hurt her, badly. This was not how he should be spoken to. More than once he'd killed for less than this.

She was taken by surprise, by the speed of his move towards her. There was no time for her to get to her feet. He grabbed her by the throat with one hand while she was still seated and squeezed tightly. She was looking up at him now; he had her full attention. His face was contorted. She could see the gap in his teeth as he grimaced, and the milky white eye in its socket. He continued to squeeze as her hands pulled at the hand at her throat.

Her eyes were wide and her mouth was open as she fought for breath. She was pulling hard with both hands to try and get him to release the grip round her throat. He was strong. As he continued to throttle her, he was also kicking at her legs, trying to force them to open until he was standing in between them. She felt his free hand tugging at the top of her tracksuit bottoms and her hand instinctively moved there to stop him. He squeezed her throat tighter still, but she would not give up fighting his hand trying to get between her legs. She could see that his jeans were unzipped.

He was leaning down on her now and she was trapped against the sofa. But she still continued to fight him. He knew she was a hair's breadth away from losing her life. But he didn't want to fuck a corpse. His hand then went behind him and from his back pocket he drew a flick knife, pressing the button on it close to her face. As the blade flicked up, her eyes widened in terror.

At that moment the front door opened and Megon was pushed inside the narrow passageway. With direct line of sight to the pair on the sofa, Megon saw the attack and screamed out her friend's name. The fat man gripping her arm and the man behind him also saw what was happening.

'Hey, hey, hey! Tarek, no!' Both he and the fat man behind pushed Megon along the narrow passageway and rushed over to pull him off, leaving China gasping for breath.

'She's no good to us dead, man, she's no good to us dead.' They were trying to calm their friend Tarek, who was visibly angry. He shook off their hands. Megon went over to China to comfort her.

China was rasping, but she was not prepared to let his assault on her go. With all her energy she let out another rant at him, squeezing the words out through her tight, burning throat.

'You filthy bastard . . . you dirty, filthy bastard. . .' He went to lunge at her again, the knife still in his hand. The men restrained him, pulling him back, one of them speaking to him in his own language. Before Megon and China had a chance to speak, the fat man clamped hold of China's arm and took her out of the room and upstairs to a back bedroom.

'Stay in there where he can't see you. Don't come back down.'

She sank down onto a stained and dirty mattress on the floor, her hand at her throat. Megon was downstairs; they had been reunited. But he was down there too. Megon wouldn't be safe. She could hear raised voices.

Suddenly she leapt up again and kicked the closed door in anger before slumping back down on the mattress. Her heart was racing; it had all happened so quickly she hadn't had time for tears. Now they came, hot and angry. She tried to stop them as she didn't want anyone to know she'd been crying, but she could still feel his squeezing fingers around her throat. She choked back the tears before fear took hold. She had to escape.

CHAPTER 20

Brian Porten was at the abattoir, hosing down. He was putting things in place ready for later. He had every intention of coming back with someone later tonight. He had seen the local newspaper that morning. Shopkeepers were up in arms at the council, asking them to do something about the numbers of homeless people who they had to step over in order to open their shops in the morning.

The police weren't interested in moving them on and the problem was reaching crisis point. Not only did the shopkeepers have to step over these vagrants every morning, but even if they could get access to their premises, when they opened their doors, the people were still asleep, putting customers off entering. Where a shop was vacant, they piled up their bedding in the doorways before going off for breakfast and returning to beg in another spot. The place was becoming a mess, an eyesore, and very shortly people wouldn't want to shop there. What were they paying their business rates for? He had to stop reading.

Brian was incensed by the inaction. He knew it to be true; there were steadily more and more homeless people pouring onto the streets. He was trying to help the situation; without him they would be in a worse state. But he would have to do more. Someone had to. It enraged him and he knew he had to keep himself in check. He suddenly felt the beats of his heart flare and bubble up into his throat, as if they would spring out of his mouth at any moment. He recognised the makings of a panic attack and before it took hold, he coughed. The flutters in his throat disappeared. He had to watch that.

He thought it out. If he went out tonight, he could find one from Salisbury and find another from Swindon the following night. It would mean him working harder, but two together, so close, might help the situation. There were certainly enough events coming up to help with the distribution of meat and he could even spread the products further afield. He'd make it work like he had done before. No one had been any the wiser that they had eaten human meat.

He reminded himself that no one suffered from what he did. There was no long, lingering death. It was quick and clean. He gave them a good death, better than the death they were otherwise sure to have. Better than dying freezing in a shop doorway, or from alcohol poisoning. No, just before he killed them, they were full of hope; hope that he was going to give them a bed, food and warmth. That's what they thought he was offering them. Their spirits were lifted. And when he killed them, he freed them of the misery of their rotten existence.

* * *

Temple drove in the darkness of the countryside until the road narrowed. It all looked different in the black of night. He took a right turn into an obscured driveway. Further down, he heard the rattle of a cattle grid under the wheels of the car. It was nearly midnight and every sound seemed to be magnified in the quietness of the still night. He reduced his speed to crawling and very slowly he continued to drive, looking out into the darkness, nothing familiar to him.

He carried on driving slowly until he came to a stop in front of a tree. He turned the engine off. As he looked out, he could see the faint light of a door opening. He got out of the car into a cold, still night and walked across a lawned area towards the back of the house.

'Won't your father be curious about who's arriving at this time of night?' he asked in a low voice as he approached.

'No,' she smiled. 'I have these rooms at the back of the house for a reason. He'll be in a deep whisky sleep and he snores like a bear.' Temple stepped inside and Callie closed the door behind him.

Once inside, he could see he'd entered a living area, the focal point being a large, stone fireplace aglow with a real fire in the hearth. The low flames threw a gentle light across the room. Callie had placed her hand on his arm and he turned back to her. He noticed that she was wearing not much more than an oversized cardigan that he guessed by the soft feel against his hand, was cashmere. Under that seemed to be something more flimsy and silken, but he couldn't quite make out what in the low light. She was dressed for bed. He distracted himself.

'This is all very nice,' he said, looking around the room. She took his coat from him and laid it across a chair. They turned to each other. The bruises under her eyes were softened by the light of the room.

'How are you feeling now?' he asked, wanting to touch her but reminding himself he hadn't been invited to.

'I'm good. I'm glad you could come by. I was hoping you would.' They were standing facing each other. He could smell her light perfume. Whatever it was, it was working its magic. He focused.

'I wondered if you'd still be up,' he said with a smile, looking into her face. 'I'm sorry it's so late, I hoped to be here earlier.'

She smiled back at him. 'I'm glad you sent your text. It was a little clichéd but yes, I'd love to help you with your enquiries.' She quickly moved in to him and taking him by surprise, she planted a lingering kiss on his lips. As she did so, he could feel her hands on his body, exploring over his shirt. As her hand moved over the tender spot where he had been punched by Paul Wallace, he flinched involuntarily, breaking the kiss.

'Sorry about that,' he said quietly. Her hands had now moved to the top of his trouser waistband. Her lips again brushed against his. He responded and felt her body press into him. She was moving fast, faster than he'd anticipated. He wasn't sure what he'd hoped for when he decided to see her that night, but her enthusiastic welcome was taking him by surprise.

He hadn't had this effect on a woman in a while. He was caught in a seductive mix of her perfume, her red hair and her lips on his. But as grateful as he was, he felt he had to at least make an effort to check the situation. He put his hands gently over hers and stopped them in their busy endeavour.

'Are you sure you know what you're doing? You don't know me.'

She looked back at him with her head to one side. Her hands were now still and nestled in his. She spoke softly.

'I know what I want to know. You're not a murderer because you're a police officer. I'm guessing you're not a sicko or weirdo because you wouldn't be doing what you're doing. You catch the bad guys and that makes you one of the good guys. That's all I need to know.'

'One doesn't necessarily follow the other. There are a few weirdos, as you say, amongst us. Besides, that's not exactly what I meant. I'm not even sure I should be here.'

'But you *are* here.' She moved to kiss him again. 'And I'm very pleased that you are. As for anything else, I don't really care right now.' She was looking into his eyes. He could see that he wasn't going to interrupt her mission. Shrugging the cardigan she was wearing off her shoulders, she pressed her mouth against his. This time he didn't hold back.

She deftly unbuttoned his shirt. He moved the thin spaghetti straps of her satin slip off her shoulders. She let it fall and he felt her naked skin on his. She was just as he imagined. Pale, smooth, soft skin. He kissed her neck, breathing in her scent, feeling her lovely copper hair across his face.

Taking his hand, she led him further into the room by the fire. As he watched her lay herself invitingly on a rug at his feet, the firelight flickered across her naked body. She beckoned him. He couldn't resist her.

CHAPTER 21

It was a crisp morning and it was early. Temple could see a light frost had settled on the grass as he looked out of the kitchen window across the churchyard. Looking out onto the lychgate, his mind wandered back a few hours before, when he'd held Callie in his arms. She was a delight, the stuff of dreams.

When they'd eventually moved from the rug in front of the fire to her bed, he told her that his domestic commitments meant that he couldn't stay with her overnight. She completely understood, she said. He'd promised he'd return to see her the following night and slipped away two hours later as she slept.

As he went over their time together, he'd unloaded the dishwasher and was setting cups on the worktop. Ana and Ben hadn't yet stirred and he used the quiet to think. As he waited for the kettle to boil, he looked again out of the small, square panes of window. This time his gaze went across the churchyard to a more distant spot in the landscape. The sight put an abrupt end to his more pleasant thoughts of Callie.

It hadn't been a good idea to move to Avebury, even though it was near to Leigh and Daisy at Beckhampton. Moving here had been a mistake. He wasn't sure right now whether it was good to be this close to where he'd found his mother murdered. Since they'd moved in, he'd been resisting the urge to revisit the spot. Of course he'd been back to the site since; he'd visited with his uncle Richard and he'd been there alone. But now he only had to look out of the window. Now the place was in sight, every day.

He should have asked if Jane had another property or, better still, he should have cut his ties with her and gone to another landlord. Maybe he still would. Maybe they wouldn't stay here for much longer. Since Ben had arrived in his life, he was slowly starting to feel differently about a lot of things. He'd started to view his life from a different perspective and this included his mother's murder.

With no suspect, not even his determination had made a difference to Op Acre. He could see now how ridiculous his notion had been of taking hold of the case, looking through the evidence, finding the clues that no other detective could find and finally resolving the enquiry. Loss of evidence and the gap of over thirty years had made this more difficult than he'd imagined.

Even joining forces with Richard at various stages hadn't moved things on. As an archaeologist, Richard was used to unravelling mysteries. He was used to waiting years for discoveries and answers. But even he wanted closure; to know what happened the day his vivacious younger sister, Gabriella, was brutally murdered.

Richard referred to her as his 'untameable sister'. They'd discovered she had been fearless – daring and reckless. But that had been part of the attraction for her 'alternative' lifestyle as a free spirit. As they'd tracked down and spoken to the people who knew her back then, a picture emerged of a woman who was playing with fire. Her friends told of how she would seek her thrills from the adventure of travelling around and meeting new people. They also said that she occasionally carried drugs around and made deliveries.

This sat at odds with Temple's memories of a happy childhood. When he looked back he could only recall endless summer days and camp fires. Yes, he could remember seeing her smoke cannabis on a regular basis, but he'd never seen her take pills or inject drugs. He never saw large amounts of money, although they always seemed to have food and fuel. He realised from what people told him that she must have been a drugs mule and that he had been with her when she was carrying her cargo around the country. In doing so, she'd put them both at risk. But to him as a seven-year-old, she'd been fun and he'd felt safe and loved.

Until he'd found her dead. Strangled, surrounded by small white pills. And as he'd stood by the side of her, the same hand that had choked the life out of his mother reached out and grabbed him. Over the years, he'd examined his memory of that moment in minute detail, looking for anything that would lead him to her attacker.

Try as he might, he couldn't wring out any more information about that moment. In a split second a hand came towards him, took full hold of the T-shirt he was wearing and shoved him backwards. No matter how many times he reran that moment, there was nothing more to gain. With the passage of time and his own maturity, he could still bring nothing more to mind. The hand of her killer had touched him and walked away.

It had haunted him ever since. He could still feel the man's hand on his chest as he shoved him, even after all this time. Why had he been left alive that day? He couldn't fathom it. But he wanted to reciprocate; he wanted to find who it was that had grabbed him that day and put *his* hand on him – on her killer – and bring him to justice. That's what had driven him on all these years.

And all this had occurred in a spot he could see from where he was standing now. He'd already recounted it more times than he could remember since being here, and it made no difference. But coming here with Ben made him realise the futility of his quest. It put the last thirty years into perspective. The last few months even. But it was the conversation he'd had with Callie that made this suddenly resonate. When she'd talked of the consequences that bad parenting had on children, it had made him think – about everything. He was starting to think he should let go of the past in favour of the future with his boy. Maybe now was the time to let it go.

Perhaps there was nothing more to be done. Perhaps with Leigh divorcing him and talking of moving away to start a new life without him, it was now time to sort himself out, leave the past where it was and concentrate on the future. Perhaps it had taken him coming back here to realise it. To accept there would be no resolution. What Callie had said had really struck a chord with him. Why had it taken someone he had only just met to make him see? He couldn't afford to screw up with Ben. And somehow he had to sort Daisy out.

Suddenly he felt the touch of his little boy's hair against his hand. Ben's upturned face looked up at him and as Temple gazed down, he saw the faintest signs of a smile. He knew then that he'd gladly give up the past to give his little boy a life untouched by his own tragedy. Yes, that tiny smile was all he needed to tell him it was time to let it go. He had to see Richard and explain, today.

As he made the short walk to nursery with Ben's hand in his, Temple was buoyed by an odd sense of optimism. With the early frost and mist burnt off by the slow-rising sun, it had the promise of a bright but cold day. With the little boy unusually chatty and happy to be walking with his daddy, Temple felt as if they might have turned a corner. He went inside the nursery with Ben, who did not cry as he had done previously, even when Temple waved him goodbye. Walking back home, it made him feel more relaxed about the boy.

Temple looked at his watch and was conscious of the time. He wanted to make sure he was back to be able to spend more time with Ben and he wanted to visit Richard. It was a long drive down south, but he had to see him. He'd made a decision and it already felt right.

* * *

Temple pulled up outside the home of his uncle Richard. His old yellow Volvo sat outside in a carport, so Temple knew he was at home. Hindon was a pretty village with a good pub, and the cottage with its thatched roof sat near the church. The door was answered nearly as quickly as Temple knocked on it. Richard was both surprised and glad to see his nephew.

'Come in, come in.' He stood aside at the open door. 'I was expecting a heating engineer, bloody boiler's packed up. Go through. It's good to see you. Long time, no see.'

'Good to see you too, Rich. Sorry it's been such a long time; we've got a bit of catching up to do. I want to tell you something so I thought I'd come in person rather than ring.'

Richard led the way through to a small kitchen where he put the kettle on. He was excited at seeing his nephew and tried to remember how long it had been since they'd last spoken. It must be two years. Yes, it was. The last time they'd met was on the thirtieth anniversary of Gabriella's death.

'So, what's keeping you busy in archaeology these days?' asked Temple, taking the initiative and the opportunity to give Richard a welfare check in the process. They had a good relationship that survived long periods without contact. Temple conceded that despite looking a little older, Richard was still in good shape for a near seventy-year-old. He seemed to be looking after himself; his grey beard was neatly trimmed and he looked healthy enough.

Richard's constant quest for knowledge of the unknown kept his mind sharp and he still looked slim and athletic, the slight stoop in his tall frame no more pronounced than usual. Years of trudging around fields and digging on archaeological sites around the world had kept him fit, with just a little of the usual inevitable knee and joint problems.

'I'm up and down to London at the moment, at the British Museum. I'm helping in a large study of Roman coinage that's going on. Do you know, just over a hundred thousand Roman coins have been found in England, not including hoards, of which there are well over a hundred.

To put this into context, millions of the Tetricus coin alone were struck. You see what I'm saying? There must be loads of Roman coins out there waiting to be discovered. It's fascinating stuff. Keeps me nice and busy.'

Temple smiled at him. He showed the same enthusiasm for his subject as ever.

'How's Leigh and Daisy? She must be growing into a pretty little lady by now.'

'They're both fine. Well, as fine as you can be when you're practically divorced.'

Richard stopped what he was doing and looked back at him. Temple looked sheepish and held his hands up.

'It's all my fault, all my doing. Leigh ran out of patience with me a long time ago.' Temple explained the circumstances that had Ben appearing in his life. 'I had to choose, Rich, and I couldn't leave Ben to a life in care or being adopted by another family. Not when I can bring him up. It's not Leigh's fault – I've caused all this. It's a mess. In choosing Ben I lost Leigh, our unborn and perhaps Daisy too.'

'I'm so sorry.' Richard patted Temple's shoulder. 'Are you sure there's nothing you can do? Is there no way you can all stay together?'

'Leigh can't even bear the sight of me, let alone talk to me. She won't countenance having Ben as part of our family, so I'm stuck with an impossible situation. I couldn't live with myself knowing Ben was in state care or being fostered.'

'You're a good man.' Richard gave Temple a mug of tea.

'If I was a good man, there'd be no Ben. I'd have been happy with what I had with Leigh if I was a good man. I screwed up. But I can't go on like this. It's really over with Leigh this time, but I still need contact with Daisy and the baby. To do that, I somehow have to have some sort of relationship with her.'

'I wish I could help you with that. Women and love and all that stuff are things that passed me by, as you know. Don't get me wrong, I appreciate a pretty woman and there's been one or two along the way, but who in their right mind would put up with me and all this?' Richard held up his arms and gestured around him.

Temple smiled back. The whole cottage was a homage to his archaeological career. It was cluttered with a lifetime's work on the subject with columns of papers and files and row upon row of books on a large span of floor-to-ceiling shelves.

'Besides, everything takes place on bloody mobile phones these days, all that texting and Facebooking – I haven't even got a mobile, so that counts me out, and that thing over there,' he gestured towards his laptop, 'is nearly steam-driven. At my age, I'd rather drool over a rare coin or a flint arrowhead. But if there's anything I can do for you or Leigh, let me know. You were good together.'

'I know. I didn't come here to bellyache to you though. I came here to give you some news about Op Acre. About six months ago, they found an exhibit, the blue T-shirt I was wearing at the time. It came to light in a loft clear-out at the home of the original SIO, Roy Filer. Op Acre was the last case before he retired. He's now dead.'

'I remember Filer, very gaunt-looking man. I remember him coming to see us, your grandfather and I. But surely that's what we've been looking for? Something tangible, some evidence at last, and now it's turned up.' He gave the cup he was stirring some celebratory taps with a spoon.

'Yesterday I spoke with the deputy chief constable who told me that they wouldn't be pursuing Acre any further. They have a DNA profile from the T-shirt but they're saying there are no suspects or new lines of enquiry and they have to prioritise other things. Case closed, pending new evidence. He's going to write to you.'

'Not pursuing it any further? Well he can shove his bloody priorities!' It was uncharacteristic of him but the unresolved murder of his sister made Richard Temple rear up. 'You can't just leave a case like that. You see it all the time in the news – a cold case is resurrected and with modern technology suspects are revealed. I'll write to him. We'll keep up the pressure. We'll carry on.'

'He's adamant that no more money will be spent. I've also been given an order to stay away from the case. I've got a disciplinary hearing coming up next week and I at least need to be seen to be following orders.'

'If you've been given an order to stay away, you have no choice. But that doesn't apply to me. What is it with your lot? Isn't it their priority to find a bloody murderer? Why stop now when there's hard evidence – are they trying to cover up? What's going on?'

'I can see where they're coming from; it would be resource intensive and other jobs keep coming in in the meantime.' Temple never thought he would find himself defending Buller. 'But as you say, there is still a murderer out there and now they have a tangible link to him. I agree, to call time on it now is bizarre.'

'Well, he'll get it in the neck from me, this DCC of yours. What are your chances at the disciplinary hearing?'

'Not good – they'll find me guilty, I'm sure of that. I just don't know what the sanction will be. A written warning if I'm lucky. Worse perhaps. I'm not exactly popular with the force hierarchy, so I'll have to be on my best behaviour from then on.'

'Of course you need to keep your job, but there's nothing to stop me from carrying on with it. They can't push me around. We've both been conducting our own enquiries for so long anyway, with no help from your colleagues in the police. Look, you came across a man in the caravan when you found Gabby and he grabbed you. We now have a DNA profile from the T-shirt you were wearing at the time. If that man didn't kill Gabby, then what was he doing there? Why didn't he raise the alarm? Why didn't he help you?

'Of course it was him and what we have now will lead us to him. Remember, it's not like the old days – we're not beholden to the police for everything now. We'll pay for our own DNA analysis. Archaeologists use private firms regularly now. Sod the bloody police.' He was animated.

'It's going to be like looking for a needle in a haystack—'

'We have his DNA. We can discount people; it's black and white now. All we have to do is find him.' Richard had started to pace around the kitchen as he tried to think of ideas to move forward on the DNA sample.

'We've been trying to find him for years. We can't DNA every man in England. And I'm tired of it, Rich. It's cost me. Dearly. I've got Ben and right now I have to concentrate on him. And Daisy for that matter. She's acting up with all this going on and I've got to spend time with her. I've spent so much time and effort on this for so little progress. Leigh put up with it and I missed out on time with Daisy because of it, time with *her*, chasing leads, dead ends. But I dare not risk Ben – he's too fragile.

'I can't afford to be absent and start going round the country again. I couldn't even risk bringing him here to meet you in case he thought he was going to be left again in another stranger's house. And it's more than that; this is a huge distraction and I need to be there for him. I need to concentrate on my kids instead of this. You of all people will appreciate what I'm trying to do. And correction, the police have his DNA, not "us".'

Richard stopped pacing and looked at Temple. He remembered the little boy he had first encountered. He'd been half feral and had hardly said a word for months when he and his father had brought him home. He'd also suffered with mood swings, which they eventually realised were a result of withdrawal symptoms from inhaling the strong weed that Gabriella and her friends smoked. He remembered how difficult those first months were and acknowledged that Temple was right to prioritise Ben. And Daisy. But he was damned if *he* was going to give up trying to find his sister's killer. He started to pace again.

'Yes, you're right, the police do have the DNA. That does give us a problem, as you say. We would need it for comparison. Without it, we're just collecting samples. So they've got us, I guess. They shut the case and we can't move forward on the DNA because we've got nothing to compare with. The bastards.' Richard's head dropped and he looked into his mug of coffee.

'There might be a way I could get it,' Temple offered tentatively. 'Not the exhibit obviously, or the lab sample itself. But leave it with me, let me think about it; phone a friend, as they say.'

Richard's enthusiasm was instantly reignited by his nephew's suggestion. 'As I said, if you've been ordered to stay away then I'll deal with it. We've conducted our own enquiries before – I'll carry on and keep you updated. Just one thing though. Can you get your hands on a number of DNA kits?'

'They're in the car.'

Richard stopped his pacing and stood in front of Temple, placing his hand on his shoulder. 'You see, you haven't given up, have you? You can no more give up than I can.'

'No, you're wrong.' Temple shook his head. 'I can't believe I'm saying it, but I have to step back. The DNA from the T-shirt is on the database now, so perhaps we'll get lucky. If he's still out there, perhaps he'll make a mistake and give us a match. Then again, maybe the murderer is already dead – who knows what might have happened in the last thirty-odd years. Or maybe we'll just never know, perhaps that's how it's meant to be. Maybe we just have to accept we'll never know. Get our heads around that instead. Try and come to some sort of peace with that.'

As the words came out of his mouth, Temple could hardly believe what he was saying. And in the presence of Richard too. The prospect of peace of mind and coming to terms with never knowing gave Temple a strange sense of relief. All he'd had to do was say it. It had to be the right thing to do.

Richard patted Temple's shoulder. He was right to think about stepping back from it all. It had cast enough of a shadow over his life. Both of their lives. But the injustice of it burrowed deep. It would ensure no true peace would be found for either of them.

‘Can you let me have a couple of those kits?’ Richard spoke quietly and softly.

‘Sure, if you insist on going on. Look, I’ll see if I can help out with the DNA profile, but I have to get the disciplinary out of the way first, get them off my back. And I have to make Ben and Daisy my priority instead of this.’

‘I’ll go over the names we’ve got already, do some poking around. Look, we know there were pills scattered around her and pushed into her throat. We know the pills had a tiny symbol of a feather stamped on them. I’m not sure what, if anything, we can read into that; take these pills and you’ll take flight, who knows. It was probably just some arsehole’s use of a random symbol. But that’s what we’ve got.’

‘We know all this, Rich, we’ve been over it all. The symbolism of using a feather with drugs, we got nowhere with it. You could read all kinds of stuff into it, but it’s not going to get us anywhere.’

Richard ignored the scepticism. ‘And the fact that the drugs were contaminated tells us a number of things: she was either peddling contaminated drugs and knew it, or she was peddling contaminated drugs unknowingly, or she was refusing to peddle them because they were contaminated.

‘The man that grabbed you was there for a reason. Perhaps he’d taken some of the drugs and had a bad reaction, perhaps one of his friends had. Perhaps he was angry and he killed her. Maybe he was the supplier and was angry with her. Whatever it was, he might still be out there somewhere, living his life, not paying for his crime.’

Temple was getting impatient. This was all old ground. Over the years they had talked about it and analysed it to death.

‘But we’re paying for his crime, Rich. You, me, Leigh, Daisy – it’s thrown a dark shadow, a black bloody cloud over all our lives and I don’t want it to cast a cloud or shadow over Ben’s life. I’ve got to be the parent he needs, the parent Daisy needs. I’ll see what I can do with the DNA sample, then I’m going to step back. I suggest you give it a couple more months, then enough is enough. We move on. This has to stop.’

CHAPTER 22

Back at home, Temple went over his conversation with Richard. The decision to call time on Op Acre made him feel as though a load had been taken off his shoulders. It had to be the right thing to do. He'd tried, Richard had tried and they couldn't make headway. His life was littered with the collateral damage and he couldn't afford for that to affect Ben. He'd have to somehow make it up with Daisy; it was too late for Leigh but not Daisy and his unborn child. He had to make sure they would no longer suffer the consequences of a murder that happened so long ago.

Feeling lighter than he had in years, he went out for a walk with Ana and Ben. It was a mild afternoon and the sky was blue. Temple was still in the process of familiarising Ben with his new surroundings at Avebury. The churchyard provided a couple of old stately yew trees with low-hanging branches that Ben could just about touch with his fingertips.

They ran around the large trunks of the trees and sat on the roots protruding through the earth. They walked to the lychgate, where they sat on the benches underneath its tiled awning. It was like a little house to Ben and he took delight in closing them inside, making sure the gate was closed. The boy was clearly cheered at the nearness of the three of them being together.

Then they took the boy across the road and over to the large standing stone circle, where they played hide and seek. Temple's own fascination with them was ignited as a child and now he was introducing Ben to them. As Ana hid and Temple and Ben looked for and found her, for the first time Ben started to squeal in delight. It was the breakthrough Temple had wished for: that his little boy had at last found laughter. *The stones had worked their magic once again*, thought Temple. He and Ana gave themselves a quiet high five, an acknowledgement of their love and care paying off.

It had been a good afternoon and as the sun began to sink, the air quickly chilled down so they went back into the confines of the small cottage. On the way in, Temple picked up some logs from an outside log store to make a fire inside. He was making their meal tonight to give Ana a break, and once he'd finished depositing the logs in the hearth, he went into the kitchen.

As they settled in for the evening, Ana was sitting at the kitchen table, Temple was at the stove putting the finishing touches to a cottage pie and Ben was driving his favourite tractor on the floor in between the legs of the chairs. Radio 2 was on and there was a Friday feel to the midweek day.

Temple was buoyed by his earlier decision around Op Acre and the rewarding sound of Ben's laughter. It was a moment to savour. Perhaps this was change happening, and happening for the good. Perhaps it would help him have a different perspective going forward. He didn't know. He looked at Ana and Ben, both relatively new in his life. He thought of Callie and last night. New beginnings, maybe. Perhaps all it had taken was to let go of the past.

Ana was watching Temple. There was something different about him today; he'd been the most relaxed she'd ever seen him. Not that she had any complaints about working for him; he was kind and considerate and she liked staying here.

He'd explained the circumstances with Ben when she'd first arrived and had added in somewhat blunt terms, 'I'm no good, Ana. I was a rotten husband and I'm as weak as shit around a redhead. The boy's mum, well, there's not much I can tell you. There's not much I can tell him either when he asks one day. We never got to know each other. All I can say is she was a pretty redhead and on that basis, we're now looking at Ben.'

Going back over the conversation, she thought he'd said that to her as much for her own benefit as anything else. Being an au pair, it was essential to quickly form good relationships with members of the family. And in one conversation he had let her know that although they lived together, she was safe as far as he was concerned. She was there to do a job and the priority was Ben. The result had so far meant they could both live in close quarters in the tiny cottage and be very relaxed around each other. And it created an easy trust between them. They worked as a team and it felt good.

They ate and sat by the fire for a while and then Temple bathed Ben and put him to bed. Joining Ana back at the fire, she had a glass of red wine ready for them both. They agreed it had been a good day and that it felt like a turning point, a breakthrough. To hear Ben laughing in such a carefree way showed that their care of him had been rewarded in the best possible way.

Temple was so glad he'd found Ana. She understood exactly what he needed and was so good with Ben. She'd also agreed to stay for at least another six months, which gave them all a bit of stability. They continued to talk and Ana took their glasses back to the kitchen. He hadn't forgotten his promise to visit Callie later that evening and was thinking he'd set off in half an hour.

As Temple stoked the fire, he heard a small scream. It was Ana. He leapt up and went into the kitchen. Ana was standing by the fridge while by the back door stood a figure he hadn't seen for years.

'Hello,' she said as she saw him. She spoke quietly, tentatively.

'*Gemma?* What the fuck's going on?' He was startled and immediately angry that someone could come in uninvited. 'How did you get in here?'

'Through the back door. It wasn't locked.'

Temple and Ana looked at each other. They had had such a good day and he'd forgotten something as basic as locking the back door. The least he could do was keep them all safe but here was Gemma Harker standing in the kitchen uninvited.

'I'm sorry to have to come here like this but you're the only one who can help me.' Her voice was tense, her face desperate.

'How the hell can I help *you*?' His anger at her appearing in the kitchen made him sound blunt and harsh. Ana hadn't seen him like this before. This woman obviously knew him but he didn't seem pleased to see her.

They all stood as if on points of a triangle. Gemma Harker looked back at them, her gaze now fixed on Temple. She looked distressed but she wasn't crying. Temple didn't offer her a chair; he couldn't believe she was there and wondered what on earth she could want from him. This was a blast from the past he could do without.

Looking at her, he saw that her once red hair was now a strange colour from over-dying and premature ageing. There was still just a tiny trace of her former attractiveness, but her long-lost pretty face was signed with all the markers of her rotten lifestyle. The drugs, the vodka, the pay-for-whatever-you-want sex – it had all taken its toll. The pretty young girl he had once fallen for was almost unrecognisable as the same woman who was standing in his kitchen now. It was strange seeing her there in front of him.

'I need your help so much,' she pleaded. Her knees were bent to emphasise her desperation. 'I don't know what to do. I saw you last night in Swindon and then I knew I had to come to you. I was running around all day yesterday and today. There's no one else I can go to. You must help me, please.' As well as her face pleading with him, her body moved too, as if she was physically aching. He watched her intently.

'I just don't know how you think I can help you. If you're in some kind of trouble, I haven't left the job, so I don't see what you think I can do for you.'

'I am in trouble. The worst. And I'm not asking for myself. It's not me that I'm here for.'

'Look, whoever you're here for, I am not the one who can help you. I'm sorry, Gem.'

'You're the only one who can help. And I'm not going from here until you do.' Gemma Harker looked as if she meant it. Temple wanted her out. He was thinking of Ben upstairs and he was increasingly riled that she had come in quietly through the back door without either of them hearing her. He didn't even know if she was alone. She was a well-known sex worker and drug user, and she could have any lowlife sitting outside, knowing where he lived. He wasn't moved by her pleadings.

'You need to go.' He went towards her.

She moved defensively. 'I said I'm not going until you help me. You need to listen to what I'm going to say.' She was ready to resist any attempts to move her. Temple was losing patience but he didn't want to have to physically remove her, at least not in front of Ana.

'Say what you have to say and go. How the hell did you know where to find me anyway?'

She hesitated. 'I followed you last night, after I saw you. Thank God I did. Look, can I sit down?'

Temple reluctantly pulled out a kitchen chair for her to sit on. Ana went to another chair and sat down. Temple stood as Gemma sat on the edge of the chair and rested her elbows on the table. For a few seconds she said nothing, as if deciding what it was she wanted to say. Temple stood against the stove with his arms crossed, waiting. He exchanged glances with Ana.

'Some money's gone missing. A lot of money. Drugs money. The people who it's owed to came round to my flat yesterday morning and took something from me. They said that they would only give it back when I paid them. They're dangerous and I need your help.'

Temple let out a sarcastic laugh. 'Why do you think I will help you? Have you come here for money? You're crazy. Get out, Gemma.' He moved to open the back door to show her out.

'No. I haven't come for money, that's not why I'm here. Listen to me. *Please*. I've been trying to help some girls. Drug runners. Young girls. I've been trying to help them get away. Now money's gone missing. They're going to punish me for it. They've got something that's mine and that's how they're going to punish me.'

'So . . . what? You want me to get involved in some kind of drugs spat you're having? Are you mad? If you've lost money, go down the local station and report it. See how much sympathy you get when you tell them it was drugs money.'

'You're not listening to me. I want you to help me get back what's mine from these evil bastards. I want your help in this because I can't do it alone and I don't want the police involved.' It was as if she was pleading for her life. She looked at him in a way that no one had ever looked at him before. There was sheer desperation in her eyes. And something else: fear.

'But I am the police – you know that. And to be honest, I don't care what they've taken from you. Why come to *me*? I couldn't give a shit. Why not go and speak to your dad? He'll get the cavalry in for you.' Temple looked at Ana. 'Her father is Clive Harker. He's a detective chief superintendent who used to be my boss, so he can help her, but she comes here, to me.' He turned back to her. 'It doesn't make sense, Gemma.'

'I haven't seen my dad for more than sixteen years. You're not hearing me. I don't want the police involved. You know what happens in drug vendetta kidnaps. They hardly ever get reported to the police. They get sorted out. Besides, I don't want my dad to know anything about this. That's really important. I *don't* want him to know.'

'You're talking in fucking riddles, woman. *What* drugs vendetta kidnap? You said they'd taken something of yours – like what?'

She looked him in the eyes as she spoke.

'They've taken my daughter. They've taken my little girl. That's the reason I'm here.'

CHAPTER 23

Ana let out a small gasp. Temple didn't believe her. Gemma Harker having a daughter would have been something he would have been aware of if it were true. It was inconceivable for it not to have been picked up on intel reports, and in turn, not be general knowledge amongst him and his colleagues.

'You're in trouble with your filthy mates and you've come here with some old moody story to get me involved in helping you. Nice try, Gemma, but the answer's no. So you can go now.'

'It's *true*,' she pleaded.

'So where's she been then, this mystery daughter of yours?'

Her head dropped and she looked at the table. 'She was adopted five days after she was born, sixteen years ago. I was in no fit state to keep a kid by the time I knew I was pregnant, let alone when I had her – the social worker saw that. I was on drugs and everything else.' Gemma looked across at Ana, not sure how much to disclose before she lost her sympathy. She went on, looking across at both of them, tears welling up in her eyes as she spoke.

'It was the best thing I could have done for her. She was adopted by a lovely couple in the Midlands who wanted a baby and there I was, able to give them what they'd always wanted. And they've done a really good job; she's lovely.

'Then a few months ago, I got tapped on the shoulder by one of the Samaritans. They handed me a letter that said she had traced me as her birth mother and asked if she could meet me. They handed a letter back to her from me and we had an exchange of letters. Even in this day and age, it had to be done by letter, no emailing or texting. Anyway, with the permission of her mum and dad, we arranged to meet; she wanted to spend some time with me, get to know me, in her half-term holiday. So I cleaned myself up over the last few weeks and she turned up. Oh, she's beautiful.' She sniffed into a tissue that Ana had supplied her with. 'The night before last, in they come, their faces covered with Halloween masks. It was terrifying. And they took her.'

'I don't want to appear unsympathetic but why didn't you just report it as an abduction to the police?'

'Because you know as well as I do that if I do that I'll never see her again. I need this sorted – fast. Without the fucking police circus. Under the radar – it's the only way I'll get her back. *You* know it and *I* know it. And I don't want my dad involved in any way. I don't want him to know about Prayer.' She was tearful now. She didn't know what she'd do if he wouldn't help her.

'Is that her name?'

'Yes, Prayer Taylor. I've got to get her back.' She looked at him, pleading with her eyes.

Temple didn't want to believe her. However, he knew that what Gemma said about drug vendetta kidnaps was true. They happened so frequently with gangs in disputes over money and drugs that they went largely unreported. Usually these situations were resolved without police intervention.

'Please help me. Please. If nothing else, for old times' sake.'

Temple looked at her. *For old times' sake.* Those four words suddenly took him back years and penetrated the anger he felt towards her for coming into his home. It was as if they were the only two people in the room. He hadn't seen her in years and now here she was. A ghost of the girl he'd once known. He now remembered their last meeting and seeing the way things had turned out for her, he had to acknowledge his part in that.

He recalled how he had loved her once, more than loved her; he'd been besotted with her and she with him. He remembered how they'd seen each other for six months without Clive Harker's knowledge. Gemma was a bright star academically but they'd fallen hard for each other and they both knew that Harker would take some persuading about her having a relationship with a probationer constable. They both knew Harker had his sights set much higher for her. She was his pride and joy, and she was going places until she met Temple.

Temple knew he should have taken the punch that night, that powerful, awful, knockout punch that Clive Harker threw in his direction. But out of instinct, he'd dodged out of the way, leaving Gemma to catch the full force of her father's blind fury. Harker's fist unintentionally smashed into Gemma's jaw, painfully breaking it and sending her flying when he'd found them together on his settee, embarrassingly caught in the act.

The violence, the ambulance, her being taken to hospital, the police being called, the then Detective Inspector Clive Harker being taken into custody for assault, the humiliation of being kept in a cell with the prospect of being charged by his own daughter. What had started as a romantic evening when they'd agreed to 'go public' had spiralled nastily out of control. Temple also knew he should have stood up to Clive Harker's subsequent threats to drive him out of the job if he saw Gemma again. But he didn't. He decided then that he needed his job as a new probationer constable more than he needed Gemma Harker.

He wanted to find his mother's killer and for that he needed to be on the inside. He wanted to progress to detective, learn the craft, be a good one. A detective who could ultimately catch killers, who would find his own mother's killer. And so, for the sake of that, he'd backed off as Clive Harker had demanded him to. He sacrificed Gemma, the woman he loved, for that unending quest.

Her response to her father's interference and influence on the love of her life had been to leave home, drop out of university, go on the vodka, heroin and cocaine, and disappear onto the streets as a sex worker. Temple had been 'the one' and she wanted to punish Harker and the love of *his* life – his job – and knew just how to do it to maximum effect. She became part of his world but from the wrong side, criminalising herself and becoming an embarrassment to him. And now here she was after all this time, coming to him for help to find her daughter.

She was a different person to the lovely girl he'd fallen in love with back then, but he had also changed. And maybe if he hadn't left her as he had, she wouldn't be like she was now. Now she was hard; there was a bitterness to her voice that hadn't been there when they were together. Maybe this was reserved for him because perhaps both their lives could have been so different. They were in love once and that should have taken its natural course. Maybe they would have married – it had certainly felt like they would at the time. Instead, she took her life off a cliff into drugs and prostitution, and he'd married Leigh and fucked her life up too. *For old times' sake.*

'I'm sorry about before, Gem. . .'

She knew what he was apologising for and was dismissive. It was odd being in his home, speaking to him after all this time, seeing him in a domestic set-up. She'd wondered now and then over the years how it might have been between them, imagining their life together.

She'd concluded that he couldn't have loved her as much as she'd loved him or he wouldn't have let her go like that. If only she could have moved on from him at the time, it might have been different. But she hadn't been able to. So she'd punished her father and punished herself for not being good enough for Temple to go after her, fight for her. She knew she was no longer the same person; she saw that in his eyes, in the way he looked at her. That Gemma was long gone. But it was right that she was here. He *had* to help her.

'I haven't got time to care about all that shit now. You made it quite clear you were following my dad's orders not to keep in touch with me. Detective Inspector Clive Harker pulled your strings then, probably still does. If he gets to hear about Prayer, I'll never see her again.'

'I hate to be the one to break it to you, but do you really think this is going to make her want to see you again? Go and see your birth mother and get mixed up in her world, and be kidnapped into the bargain – really? I think that ship's sailed, don't you?' She knew this was true but she didn't want to hear it. At least his voice was softer now.

Her head dropped. 'Let's just get her back.'

'You'd better tell me everything. What's that you said about helping some girls?'

'That's what this is all about. I've been trying to help these young girls. The Albanians have been moving in wholesale. Lots of drugs, lots of brothels, lots of girls. They ship them in from Stansted, Luton, Cardiff, other airports, and they're put straight on the game. But I also see a lot of young English girls – and boys – on the streets, used to drug-run for London-based Albanian dealers. There were these two girls, one of them's a local. They'd been ferrying bags of drugs and money around. I was trying to help them, stop them doing it, show them it wasn't worth it.'

'And how did you do that?' he pressed her, still sceptical. He knew about the surge in sex trafficking and kids being used by drug dealers, but Gemma had spent a long time on the streets. She knew every trick and scam going and this could be another one.

'I let them know they could use my place to stay. That it would be somewhere safe for them. When they stayed, I spoke to them, told them about me, what I was, how I ended up. There was still a chance for them not to make my mistakes. A week ago, these two girls came back to mine.

They had drugs and money. I don't know how much exactly. We hid it and popped down the shops, all three of us. I was going to make sure they had some food inside them. When we got back, the drugs and money were gone. Vanished. They were so scared they just ran out of the flat.'

'So how do I know that you didn't take the drugs and money and just set them up?'

'It wasn't me, stupid. I'm trying to get them away from all this. It's different now, not like it was years ago. The Albanians, they just don't give a shit. This is like wholesale, supermarket-sized organised crime, not what I used to get up to – this isn't prostitution. This is above the law, outside the law; the law can't get to them. Oh, I know who took the money all right. But they want it back and they've taken Prayer to make sure I get it for them.'

'So? Who took the drugs and money?' Temple was finding it difficult to get one step ahead of her.

'Simon Sloper of course.' She lived in this world so easily, she couldn't understand how others couldn't see what to her was blindingly obvious.

'What?'

'Simon Sloper took it. Detective. Sergeant. Simon. Sloper.' She spoke to him as if he was being too slow to take it in. Temple knew he had seen him last night in Swindon, coming out of a druggy's house. He remembered the men he'd seen outside, Eastern Europeans. The girl he had followed from the railway station had disappeared around there. Something occurred to him.

'Give me the names of the two girls you say you were helping.'

'China Lewis, she's local. You might know her – Gary Lewis's sister. He's shitting himself because they're leaning on him for the money too. The other girl I only know as Megon. She told me she was from London.'

CHAPTER 24

Linda Davidson had told Temple that China Lewis had turned up at her house a day ago, following Amy reporting her missing for three days. If what Gemma was saying was true, no wonder she was trying to keep a low profile. She'd been using the Davidsons' house to hide herself.

'How long was it before they realised the money was gone – the Albanians?'

'I don't know; they were in contact with the girls by phone. Hours, a day, I don't know.'

'So why don't you just ask Sloper to give the money back?'

'He wouldn't give it back even if I begged him to. He's done it before. It's what he does. His way of showing the Albanians that he's still in the game, to get respect from them, payment from them.' She was tired now. She'd given him more than she'd intended. But she was past caring. All she wanted was Prayer back safe.

'If you're spinning me a line, Gemma, I'm going to take you in. Stay here. I'm going out and I want you here when I come back, or I'm not going to help you; I'll go straight to the station and tell them everything you've told me. Ana, give her a cup of tea, no booze and keep your eye on her. Don't leave her alone.'

* * *

Temple headed off towards Swindon to see Linda Davidson. When he reached the street where she lived, he drove slowly and parked up. He walked to the house and saw lights showing above the curtains. He knocked on the door. A man answered.

'Mr Davidson?' Temple asked.

'Yes.'

'I'm DI Temple. I called yesterday and spoke to your wife. Is she or Amy in?'

'You better come in. I told her this would happen. I knew it.'

Temple went inside. Both Linda and Amy Davidson were in the lounge, reclining over a corner group settee, and surprised to see him. They sat up as he came in.

'Enjoy the pictures last night, ladies?'

Linda Davidson looked awkward.

'I told her to ring you and put you straight. Since you're here, she can do it now,' Mr Davidson said. He was standing behind Temple. 'Go on, tell him the truth.'

'So, what have you both got to tell me?'

Linda looked at her husband and spoke up. 'Gary Lewis came round here looking for China after Amy had been to the police station. He told her to contact you and tell you that she'd made a mistake – that China wasn't missing. He said she would get China into big trouble if she didn't. Amy wouldn't do it, would you, Ames?'

Amy shook her head. 'I hate that bastard. I'm not doing anything *he* tells me. And I'm not frightened of him either.' She shot a disapproving look at her mother.

'I told him that I would ring the police and tell them that China had turned up here, that she was no longer missing. It amounted to the same thing. He just wanted to make sure the police weren't involved in looking for China. We've had a hell of a row about it here, but I don't want no trouble. I don't want the likes of Gary Lewis coming round here, threatening us.'

'So let's get this straight. China wasn't here on Monday evening?'

Linda looked at Temple. 'No she wasn't.'

'Is Linda in trouble, Officer?' asked Mr Davidson, anxious for his wife.

'No. But you lied to me, Linda. Do you think you can tell me exactly what Gary Lewis said?' She looked sheepish, having been caught in her own lie.

'Of course I can. He turned up here on the doorstep, with his dog. He wasn't here long. Told me he knew Amy had reported China missing and to get her to ring the police and tell them she'd turned up here. Call the police off, he said. If we didn't do it, he said that China would be put in real danger. You know the rest.'

* * *

Temple returned home. He sat in the dark in his car, needing to think before he went back inside. Gemma Harker with a daughter. Prayer was an apt name considering the predicament she was now in, if Gemma could be believed. And if what she was saying was true, it didn't bear thinking about what was happening to her. There was one fast way to pay back drug debts and that was lying on her back. She could already be hundreds of miles away, trafficked, being drugged, raped and sold. Albanians were ruthless bastards and life was cheap. Money was king and if you were female, you were a commodity. Nothing more than a human slot machine.

Gemma said she was bright, had had a good upbringing. Why hadn't Gemma just left it at that? What did she hope to gain from letting her daughter into her chaotic and shit life?

Within twenty-four hours of meeting her, Prayer had fallen into more danger than she would ever have dreamt possible.

He thought about what Gemma was asking him to do. Not reporting an abduction in favour of getting a quick resolution. Taking on violent Albanians. What on earth did she think he could do by himself? And this was no longer just about Prayer, it was about China and it seemed Megon too. He had been really saddened by Paul Wallace's predicament. And suddenly, he could be in a position to let him know that Megon was indeed in Swindon, or at least had been, and who she was with.

His thoughts turned to Sloper. Simon *fucking* Sloper, whose actions in taking drugs and money had started this mess. Now he had a chance to expose Sloper. There had always been rumours about him being bent but Clive Harker had always stood by him, getting Sloper out of any shit he seemed to get into. And here he was now, with Sloper being handed to him on a plate by Gemma Harker.

Even so, Temple wasn't sure he could do what Gemma was asking. If it went wrong, it would be disastrous and he'd deserve everything he would surely have coming to him. All the girls could be either injured or worse; they'd be trafficked and their families would never see them again. Overt police involvement could swiftly guarantee their disappearance. But if he didn't do something and fast, he knew that could very well be the case anyway. If he decided to help, he knew he couldn't do it on his own.

CHAPTER 25

Temple went back into the house. Ana and Gemma were sitting around the kitchen table where he'd left them an hour and a half ago. They were deep in conversation, which stopped abruptly as he came in. He put his car keys on the table and sat down.

Ana was relieved Temple was back. Babysitting Gemma had been a revelation but she was glad to see him return. She looked at him as she leapt up and put the kettle on. Her gaze wasn't lost on Temple; no doubt Gemma had been giving her account of their past relationship. He sat at the table and looked at Gemma.

'You're going to tell me everything you know again. And I want to know all about Sloper.'

He watched Gemma's face. There was a slight cloud at the mention of telling all about Sloper. He knew he'd have to make sure he had it all. He couldn't trust her not to hold back, even now.

'When I think you've told me everything, I'll think about helping you. Now, start again.' Without telling her, he'd switched his phone on to record their conversation. He knew that she might change her story if eventually the police were involved so it was important that he capture what she told him.

During the course of two hours, Temple downloaded what he needed from Gemma. She told him how she was trying to turn her life around. She'd seen it on TV, people who had done bad things and who had redeemed themselves by doing good. It wasn't the same on the streets anymore. The older ones like her, they were beyond help. It was the young girls – far younger than she'd been. She'd seen girls just in their early teens being ferried into houses, hidden behind the doors of cheap hotels or rented rooms. The fear etched on their faces turned her stomach. They were so young.

They were treated terribly. She'd heard them referred to as just meat, meat for customers to buy. It was inhumane the way they were sold; they didn't even have the choice to sell themselves. Everything was taken from them. At least what she did, street sex, she'd had a say in who she went with and could keep the money – well, some of it anyway. In this new business these women weren't prostitutes, it was far worse – they were sex slaves.

Sometimes, she told him, the Albanians would use empty houses put on the market for sale to ply their trade in pop-up brothels. It ensured no one discovered what was going on as it was hard to pin them down. After looking online at websites, when they saw a house was vacant they drove by the location to check the place out. The longer it had been on the market, the more likely they were to use it. They would then discreetly break in and arrange for girls to be taken there. Then the customers would be told where to go. When they left, there was no trace of them so no one was any the wiser.

The girls in the brothels were so young and so scared; she could see that in some instances they had virtually been lifted off the streets. They weren't like her. She'd gone down a path. She was nineteen when she chose to turn her back on her home and her family. She knew exactly what she was doing. She chose to take drugs, chose to opt out of her former life, be a prostitute to punish her father. Punish him for being a police officer, for always putting his job first, for overreacting with her and Temple, for ruining what they had. What they could have had.

What was clear to her was that these girls were now being enslaved. In many cases they'd been brought into the country having been promised proper jobs, not a life of sex slavery. She saw that Swindon was being flooded with foreign girls, but she couldn't save them all. So she chose to save those who at least spoke her language and she could engage with.

She'd had some success and had already managed to turn some girls away from drugs and safely back to their families. But the stakes were higher than ever and it was dangerous. She'd seen that ever younger kids were now being used as drugs mules as they were 'clean skins' with no previous police involvement, and less likely to be stopped or come to notice due to how young they were. Over the years, she'd seen China being used in this way.

She knew Gary Lewis from around Swindon, although more *of* him than actually knowing him herself. She'd seen China with him a few times but no more than that. She wanted to help China, and as she was local she thought she could see it through, get her the help that she needed to make her safe and take her off the streets.

Because she knew her by sight, it was easier to talk to her. She'd asked China about her friend Megon and how they knew each other; China said that they had met the week before as they both worked for the same dealer in London. He'd sent Megon down to Swindon with drugs for sale. She was going to take money from drugs that China had sold back to London. When the drugs and money went missing from the flat, they both fled in fear. They'd have to pay the money back. They both knew what would happen to them.

Gemma knew it was no use them running – they would be picked up by people sent out by their dealer. Since they had run from the flat, Gemma had asked around for any sightings of them. No one had seen them. She guessed that maybe £3,000–£5,000 had been taken from the flat, including the drugs. She was convinced the girls would have been picked up by now.

'The girl, Megon – was this her?' Temple showed Gemma a photo of Megon that Paul Wallace had sent him. Gemma took the phone from him and studied it.

'Yes, that's her, that's Megon, the girl who was with China. How do you have her photo?'

'I'm trying to find China. She was reported missing by her friend a few days ago. Megon has also been reported missing by her family in London. So tell me about Sloper – how come he's got a key to your flat?'

'It's his flat.'

'You live in a flat owned by Sloper?'

'Yes, I moved in a while back.'

'So tell me how he fits into all this then?'

In her desperation to find Prayer, Gemma had turned to Temple but now as he questioned her about Sloper, for the first time she started to see how the world around her was going to unravel. She sat silent. She needed to think.

'So you say he took the money – how do you know?' Temple prompted her.

'Maybe I was wrong, maybe it wasn't him.' Her survival instincts kicked in. She'd been on the streets too long and this was dangerous. Her sudden reluctance to speak made Temple start to wonder about her whole story. Perhaps this was all about saving her own skin. Perhaps there was an element of truth somewhere in all this but that was all. Perhaps she'd been sent here by Sloper. She was living in his flat after all, so she could still be doing his bidding. He knew he couldn't trust her. He pressed her again.

'No, you said it was him, with some conviction. You said you *knew* he'd taken the money. You said this had happened before, didn't you? He's taken drug money from your flat before, hasn't he? Is this what you and him do, set girls up? Lure them in and take their drugs and money? Does he pimp girls out of the flat?'

'*No!* Look, this is wasting time; you could be out there looking for Prayer. The flat is clean, it's my home; no one comes back there unless I want them to. He pimped out of my old flat but not where I live now.'

'Oh really? Well nothing's going to happen until you tell me all about Sloper. Your choice.'

As she saw it, she had no choice at all. 'All right, all right.' Telling him about her life wasn't something she wanted to do. But then this wasn't about her, it was about finding Prayer as quickly as possible. She looked back at him and began.

'When I first started on the streets, Sloper said he was there to protect me. He said he was there to look out for me. But then, well, he used me too. Said he needed to know what the punters were paying for. That fat bastard gave me the drugs and took his fill. He said he'd keep the pimps at bay, that we'd be seen together and that I wouldn't get any trouble. But then he ran a couple of other girls and started to get into the drug side of things in a big way. When I lived in my old flat, he'd use that to deal and to pimp. He got close to what was happening, knew who was coming in, what they were doing.

'Sometimes, when the other dealers overstepped the mark and got in his way, he'd take what was theirs as a way of keeping them in check. These Eastern Europeans though, they don't give a shit about him. I took a beating one night on my way back to the flat and ended up in hospital the last time he did it. He's still trying to flex his muscles with them but they're too big; they're evil. They can't be stopped. He's taken the money, but it's the girls who'll have to pay it back, not him, and he knows it.' She started to weep. 'That's why they came that night. They came round for me but they found Prayer and took her instead. I begged them not to but they could see my fear.'

'And who are they, Gemma? Who came round?'

'Their faces were hidden by masks, I told you.'

'What kind of masks?'

'Halloween masks, just the kind you find in all the supermarkets at the moment. Horrible green ones, with hair on them.'

'Did they speak? Were they English?'

'They had foreign accents. He'll know who they are, or who sent them.'

'Who will?'

'Sloper. So, will you help me?' she pleaded.

He didn't know whether to believe her. She lived in Sloper's flat and she said he was taking money and drugs from drug dealers. How could he be sure this wasn't a set-up? And the girl, Prayer – perhaps she didn't exist at all, perhaps this was just all a story to drag him into her world?

'Won't her parents report Prayer missing if they don't hear from her?'

'She spoke to them on Sunday and said she'd call them again on Friday. She's supposed to be staying with me for the week, so we've got two days to find her.'

'That won't be the end of it – you do realise that, don't you? If we find her she'll be in a state; she probably won't want to see you again. And when her parents find out. . .'

He'd made up his mind; he didn't want any part of this. It was madness. It was her sleazy, dirty world and she wanted to drag him into it. Was she laying a trap for him with Sloper? Had there been any truth in anything she'd said in the past few hours?

'I know. Don't you think I *know* that?' She was now slumped in front of him, her shoulders bent in defeat. Then she looked up. 'But she must know that I did all I could to find her. Look, here she is.' Gemma opened up her phone to reveal a photo. Temple looked at the image. He looked back at Gemma. There was no mistaking it.

'That's why I'm here. That's why I've come to *you*. She's our daughter. Yours and mine.'

CHAPTER 26

Brian Porten drove into Salisbury, heading for St Saviour's Church. They ran a permanent soup kitchen every Wednesday night and would be open tonight. He'd rung them and promised them some sausages.

'Come in, Brian, bless you.' A grey-haired lady opened the back door to the small kitchen and he went inside with a large cooling box. 'It's so kind of you to come out in the dark. It's getting bitterly cold now at night.'

He went over to a work surface and put the box on top of it. Taking off the lid, the lady appeared by his side and peered in. 'That will be just fine. We will have enough there to feed them well for a week. You're a very kind man. They so enjoyed the last lot you brought. I hope they're the same.'

Porten said it was no problem and that he was glad to help and yes, they were the same recipe. He watched her unload the sausages into a small chest freezer, keeping some aside for that evening's meal. She asked him if he wanted to stay, have some food himself before he journeyed back. It was good fare, he should know. He declined. He wanted to get out of there. He didn't want to hang around anywhere that fed these bastards. He made his excuses and left.

Sitting in his car, he thought of what she'd said. *'They so enjoyed the last lot you brought.'* As when he'd first heard her say it, a picture of beggarly-looking men scoffing sausages sprang into his mind. And again, he felt a thin vein of sickness in the pit of his stomach. People feeding on people. But why should it be any different to people feeding on animals, he reasoned. Anyway, these were the guinea pigs; he tried out most of his human produce on them first. And there they were asking for more.

With the feeling of sickness subsiding, he turned the key in the ignition. He'd drive off into the city centre and park up for a bit. Have a walk, see who was about, who wasn't bothered with going to the soup kitchen. Knowing it was a long drive back to the abattoir, he'd brought his pistol with him tonight. It was under his seat. As soon as he had someone in the passenger seat, he could make sure they were no trouble to him on the journey back.

* * *

Deputy Chief Constable Buller sat in his office, putting the finishing touches to a statement. As his fingers tapped away on the keyboard, the sun's sharp early morning rays penetrated a grey, cloudy sky, causing the computer screen to go opaque. At the same time, there was a knock and Detective Chief Superintendent Clive Harker put his head around the door.

'I'm just about to send it over to you. Pull the blind across for me would you, Clive?' Buller didn't look up. Invited in, Harker strode purposefully to the window.

'Thanks, sir. I think we'll have everything ready today.' He spoke as he walked and pulled the vertical blind across the window. 'If we aim for ten this morning, we'll have made all the necessary arrangements.' His normally harsh Glaswegian growl was tempered for this exchange with his boss. And given the subject matter they spoke of, it took on an almost pleasant timbre.

'Make sure we reclaim any laptop and tablet devices.'

'I've already checked with IT – there aren't any. Just a phone, which we'll take immediately of course.'

'All the forms drawn up?'

'Yes, sir. There's a letter detailing exactly the reason and terms of suspension. It reads, "Disobeying a lawful order from Deputy Chief Constable Buller", and leaves it open for you to verbally explain the situation.'

'Yes. That's fine. I take it he's due on duty today?'

'I've checked. Temple's due in on a nine-to-five shift today. I'll have a message sent to him to report at your office at ten o'clock. Let's say it's about Op Acre, which of course it is.'

'I won't have disobedience, Clive, not at this level.' Buller continued to stab away at the keyboard.

'I think there's enough here.' Harker was looking over his shoulder. 'There's no way back now. We need to make sure we take this opportunity. It'll send the right message.'

'When's the hearing scheduled?'

'Tuesday, sir. Only five days to go and Temple will be dismissed from the force.'

* * *

Temple went into work early to check out some of the things Gemma had told him. He was reeling from her revelation about Prayer. Gemma told him that it had been the reason she had left Swindon all those years ago. She'd discovered she was pregnant with Prayer three months after she'd left home. Her wired jaw hadn't stopped her intake of cocaine, by which time she was also on the game.

Temple remembered their last meeting, how he'd told her that it was best if they didn't see one another again, that it probably wouldn't work out anyway. But why hadn't she got word to him that she was pregnant? That rankled with him and made him doubt what she had told him now. A few simple words then might have changed everything. Changed the course of her life. His.

No, instead of telling him, she'd left home and gone off to the streets on a drugs binge, then disappeared from town altogether. Now back at his desk thinking it through, the whole evening took on a surreal aspect; he hadn't slept at all and with a threatening pain currently shooting into his neck, he suddenly thought of Callie. He'd said he would meet her last night. He looked down at his phone. There were no messages. He texted her to say that he had been called away.

Temple thought of Leigh. Gemma's disclosure would give her all the justification she needed, if she didn't have enough already, that her course of action to divorce him was the right one. He'd be lucky if he ever saw Daisy on a regular basis again when she found out, let alone the newborn when it came. He could just imagine what she'd call him. He could imagine her face.

The revelation of another child was the last thing he needed right now. He put his head in his hands. But if what Gemma was saying was true, he also knew he needed to find Prayer and fast.

He'd been trying to formulate a plan of action, going back and forth over whether or not to just go into Harker's office and tell him what Gemma had said. But she'd pleaded with him not to and besides, any mention of discrediting Sloper, who was so crucial to Harker in Temple's disciplinary hearing and who was no doubt nicely lined up to say anything Harker wanted him to, just wouldn't be believed.

As for Prayer, his mind tried to reject the idea. It was insane. A girl he'd had no knowledge of, a girl he'd never met – who was apparently his daughter – was now caught up in Gemma's miserable life. If he could believe Gemma, Prayer had been missing for twenty-four hours and was in so much danger it made his blood run cold.

But *could* he believe her? Did Prayer even *exist*? Or was this just some old moody story to get him involved in getting some drugs and money back? His mind worked overtime. Was she playing him?

Gemma had spent so long on the streets that this could be a load of bullshit, but he couldn't think of what she'd have to gain by it, except setting him up. If that was the case, what was her motivation? Was it Sloper? Was he telling her to do this? Were they both trying to trap him? Perhaps it had suddenly occurred to her that she could embark on one hell of a revenge trip and get even with him for how he'd left her all those years ago?

Even if she did exist, was Prayer really his child? Gemma had shown him a picture and sure, the picture showed a pretty girl who resembled him, but was that what he wanted to see? It was certainly what Gemma had wanted him to see. She could have found any photo on the Internet to show him. What was it she'd said? She had been brought up well. If Prayer *was* his daughter, that was the only comfort he could find in all this.

He logged into his computer and checked the command and control log. There had been no sign of Gary Lewis or China reported. He started an Internet search of Land Registry on the address of Gemma Harker's flat. It was indeed owned by Simon Sloper. She had been telling the truth on that at least.

He knew what he should do was go to Harker, tell him everything. He would mount an operation and they could start getting Prayer and the other girls back. But he wasn't sure he would even get Harker to listen to him in the circumstances. Even if he could get Harker to believe him, Temple knew these sorts of operations took time to get going and were fraught with danger. He knew that time was running out and he had to act fast. The key to this was Sloper. Sloper would know exactly who had taken Prayer.

CHAPTER 27

Temple knew he had to find Sloper fast – that was the quickest way to resolve this. Looking at the computer, Temple found the shift record; Sloper was on duty.

His desk phone rang. It was the control room.

'We've had a message to pass on to you from the night crew. They think they saw lights on in Gary Lewis's flat last night and think he might have returned there. They had another call to go to, an RTC which kept them out until this morning. Sorry to have only just passed this on, we've been a bit busy.'

Temple knew it might be worth a visit just in case he had returned since he'd last seen him. What was it that Gemma had said? Gary Lewis was being leant on for the return of the money.

As Temple got up, his phone rang again. It was Buller's PA telling him to report to his office at ten.

With no indication given as to why he was being summoned, Temple wondered if Buller had changed his mind about closing Op Acre. It would be a bit of a climb down if he had, but perhaps Richard had been onto him. He looked at his watch. If he set off now he might have time to call by Lewis's flat first before his ten o'clock appointment.

Seeing Gary Lewis and finding out as much as he could from him was paramount.

* * *

As he pulled up outside Lewis's flat, he saw a couple of young women standing in the doorway to the building. He ran over and gained entry while they had the door open. He spoke to them both and asked one of them if, for £10, she would help him play a joke on a friend. They made their way up to Lewis's flat on the second floor and found the number. Prompting the woman, he tapped on the door.

'Hello? Gary?' she said. Temple listened. He thought he heard sounds of movement inside.

'I've got the money I owe you,' she said hesitantly. Temple whispered a 'thank you' and looking over her shoulder, the bemused woman went back downstairs pocketing a £10 note. It was a cheap shot but it was all Temple could think of. He heard the familiar rushed sound of a padlock being unlocked and the heavy clunk of a chain. In his hurry and greed, and the sound of a female giving him money, Gary Lewis had forgotten to look through his security door spyhole.

Temple put all his energy into rushing the door as soon as he saw a gap open. As wiry as Lewis was, he caught him off guard and with the momentum of adrenalin, Temple shoved his fist into Lewis's stomach and both of them crashed back into a narrow hallway and onto the floor. Pushing all his weight into Lewis, Temple made good use of his officer safety training. Pinning down a winded Lewis onto his front, Temple sat across his shoulders and managed to pull his arms up behind his back.

Although he bucked him, Temple freed the handcuffs from his pocket and snapped them around Gary Lewis's wrists. Being careful to avoid his kicking feet, Temple jumped out of the way with Lewis still on the floor. Leaning against a wall, Temple caught his breath.

'Right, you bastard. I've come to ask you some questions about China and the fucking mess you've got her in.'

Still winded and lying on his front, he glanced at Temple.

'Where's your dog?' Temple breathed. The last thing he wanted was to be attacked by the bloody thing.

Lewis didn't answer.

'Tell me where your fucking dog is or I'll taser it.'

'Having a shit on the balcony.'

'Right. Get on your knees and go in there.'

Temple grabbed hold of Lewis's T-shirt and pulled him up onto his knees. With his hands cuffed behind his back and Temple's hand pressed down on his shoulder, Gary Lewis walked on his knees along the floor into his lounge area. Temple told him to sit on the floor in the middle of the room.

From the tussle they'd had, Temple at least knew he didn't have the long knife he'd had on him at their earlier meeting. He needed to keep him where he could see him while he searched the flat. He looked out onto the balcony and seeing the dog, he locked it outside and drew a curtain.

'Now, you're going to tell me all about your mates and China and the money that's owing.'

'Fuck off, lunatic. I don't know what you're talking about.' Gary was angry with himself for getting caught opening the door and for someone like Temple getting the better of him. He should have had the dog with him at the door.

'I'm talking about money that's gone missing, drugs money that China had. I'm talking about your sister having to pay off a drug debt, a debt that they're probably also looking to you to pay too, since you're her brother. Where is she and who are the people who've got her?'

'I don't know where she is.' He watched Temple looking round as he spoke. Temple was looking at his things, pulling out all his CDs onto the floor, looking behind cushions, pulling up his sofa, kicking over a rug. He moved into the bedroom, shouting questions behind him. Temple pulled the bedclothes onto the floor and turned the mattress off the bed before going back to him.

'Who's got her, Gary? You know who's got her, don't you?'

'I don't know nothing.'

'Oh yes you do. You know exactly what's going on. And we're both going to stay here until you tell me. Because I've got all day – all night if that's what it takes. Now, tell me where she is. I know you know.'

'What if I do?'

'So why don't you give them the money so that they can let her go?'

'She's a thieving little bitch and she needs to learn a lesson. She needs to learn some respect.'

'That's some lesson you're making her learn, Gary. She's fourteen. You know what happens. She's your sister, your own sister. What kind of man doesn't want to protect his own sister? How do you expect her to behave when you took her into that world? So, she's stolen money from you in the past, and now you think she's stolen money from her dealers, the dealers who are asking you for money because they think you're controlling her and she's done this for you. Is that about right?'

Lewis didn't answer; his mind was working on how he could get himself out of the handcuffs and out of the flat. If Temple thought he could get to him by mentioning China, he couldn't be more wrong.

'I actually don't care what happens to my sister, I don't care how they treat her. It'll teach her a lesson not to fuck with me.' Lewis had no sentimental feelings for his sister. She was just something that had monetary value to him. He was such a dumb fuck, this cop. Lewis had no emotional connection to her at all. She was just a commodity. Something he could sell. And he'd been doing that for years.

He'd learnt long ago that he could exploit her for his own ends. He'd even auctioned her once, auctioned her virginity – got a fair price too. Since then he sold her regularly, so she meant nothing because, as he'd learnt, there were plenty more like her who would be far less trouble. No, he hated his thieving sister and he was right to hate her. She brought nothing but trouble. She was his Achilles heel. She was a pain in the fucking arse to him, so if she got sliced, or worse, he really didn't give a shit.

Yes, they were looking to him to pay the money she owed but he was fucked if he was going to give over three and a half G for her. In fact, it would enhance his reputation if he showed just how little he cared what they'd do. They could kill her for all he cared. And he really didn't. That's why he didn't want this cop looking for her. He didn't want the police to find her. He wanted her to stay exactly where she was because when he didn't pay, she would get sliced or worse and his kudos would skyrocket. He would have shown no weakness to these people. That's all that mattered.

'So I'm right. You do know who's got her. Do you think she took the money, the money that was in Gemma Harker's flat?'

Lewis looked back at him and said nothing.

'Because you're wrong. She didn't take the money – I know who did and it wasn't China. Who are they, Gary? Just give me a name.'

'She had the money and it went missing, therefore it's down to her. She knows that. She knows the score. She knows what happens then.'

'It was stolen from her, Gary. Stolen from her by a man I've got in custody. So I've got the money. Me. He didn't know what it was that he was stealing, he just saw it and took it. He didn't realise the trouble it was going to cause. And it's brought you and China to police attention, attention you can do without because of what you do.

'So here's what I'm going to suggest. At this point there's still only me and you that know I've got the money. If you tell me who's got China and I can find her, I'll give you the money, then you can pay the dealers. Everybody's happy. You won't know who took it and the person that did won't know what trouble they caused. What do you think about that?'

'And why would you do that?'

'Because China's been reported missing and I need to find her. And if I don't find her we will keep looking for her. In twenty-four hours' time, we'll be all over you and your mates, we will tear this fucking town apart to find her and it'll go on until we do. You won't be able to as much as take a shit without the police knowing about it. But that all takes time and police resources.

'Now, you know who's got her and I want her back. I've got the money you want to get her back, the money that was stolen from her, so we can either do this quietly between ourselves or the whole circus will be unleashed. All the little deals you've got going will be gone, all your networks gone; the place will be flooded with police. China's name will be all over the news and you'll be in custody.'

'What do you get out of it?'

'I've just told you – I get an easy life. China back, case closed. She's got a mate with her who was snatched from Gemma Harker's flat in retaliation. I need to get her back too.'

'How do I know you'll give me the money?'

'I've just told you I will. I have the money – let's just rectify the situation between ourselves.'

Lewis considered the proposition. Here was a cop saying he wanted to resolve a situation between dealers. To get China back. The thing was, he didn't want China back; he didn't care if she never came back. He did, though, relish the prospect of getting the money.

Temple could see Lewis was thinking.

'How are we going to do this then?' Gary Lewis was shifting on the floor. The handcuffs were biting and he was uncomfortable. But if he could work this situation to his advantage, he could get a few thousand pounds gratis. He could get this dopey cop to give him the money and still leave China where she was.

'All I need is for you to tell me who's got her and we can move this thing on.' Temple hoped he'd done enough for Gary Lewis to finally confide who was holding China and Prayer. Hopefully Megon too. They both looked at one another. The silence hung in the air.

'So let me get this straight. I tell you who's got her and then what?'

'As soon as I've had sight of China, you get the money. I have to see her first though.'

'Your plan's all very well but I don't know who's got her and I don't know where she is.'

'They're not going to go away, Gary. They will want their money whether they harm China or not and if I was them, I'd be coming after you. If I was them, I'd be after getting rid of you. Because if you don't tell me where she is, I'm going to start putting it around that you told her to take the money and you've got it. I'm going to confirm what they already think. You won't be able to walk down the street. You'll be a dead man.'

Lewis was thinking. The cop was right; he was already being leant on but there was no way he was going to pay up. But if this cop gave him the money he could pocket that and tell him the deal didn't come off. That way he'd have the money and tell the dealers they could do what they liked with China. Harming or killing her would settle the debt. Everybody's happy.

'I'll make a call. Arrange a meet.'

Temple undid the handcuffs and handed Lewis his phone. He stood and watched as he dialled.

'It has to be soon. Tonight. And if there's no China and her friend, no money.' Now Temple had to find Sloper.

CHAPTER 28

Back in his car, Temple wondered if his plan would work. It was pretty desperate; even if Lewis did contact him and set up a meeting, he had no money yet to complete the exchange. But he was thinking of a plan for that. He now had to wait for Gary Lewis to contact him.

Temple arrived at DCC Buller's office. He didn't have time for this right now; if Buller was going to change his mind about Op Acre, he could have emailed him. He was late. He knocked on the door. From inside he heard Buller tell him to enter. When he opened the door, Buller was sitting with Harker at his desk. Thinking he'd interrupted them, Temple went to wheel round and go back out.

'You're not interrupting us, we are both waiting for you. You're late, Inspector Temple. Shut the door and come and stand here.' Temple noted his tone and did as instructed. 'I've called you in today to serve these papers on you: a notice of disciplinary action for disobeying a lawful order and a notice of your imminent suspension from duty.'

Temple turned the words over in his mind. Disobeying a lawful order? Suspension? He hadn't been expecting this. His first thoughts were that he had to find Prayer and China. And then there was Megon too. He couldn't be suspended.

Perhaps PSD had caught up with him after all. His mind went immediately to Roger Hunt, Leigh's ex, whom Temple had beaten up months ago. Perhaps Roger had suddenly found his backbone and reported him? Or else perhaps it was the gun, his gun, the Chamelot-Delvigne revolver he'd disposed of; perhaps he hadn't cleaned it enough, perhaps they'd found his fingerprints on it? Both had the potential to get him a custodial sentence. His mouth went dry.

'Can I ask what this relates to?'

Buller drew himself up to his full height. Harker was standing beside him with a smug look of satisfaction that he did nothing to disguise.

'This relates to me giving you a lawful order to leave Op Acre alone and then you being seen on CCTV taking a quantity of DNA kits from custody.' The tone of his voice was officious and he was animated.

Although he shouldn't have been, Temple was relieved. It could have been much worse, but it was bad enough if it resulted in suspension. Suspension would render him unable to find the girls and unable to work, as he knew the next thing he would be asked was to surrender his warrant card. Without it he couldn't function as a police officer. Then they would ask for his phone. Thinking fast, Temple knew he had to keep his phone in order for Gary Lewis to get back in touch with him. He'd also given his number to Gemma and Amy Davidson for them to tell him any more information. Somehow he had to get out of there.

'Now, if you could hand over your mobile phone to Mr Harker please.'

'This has come as a bit of shock, sir. I need the toilet, now.' As neither Buller nor Harker were expecting this response, without giving them time to react, Temple made towards the door.

'If you could just sign—'

'I'll be straight back.' Temple moved fast and once out of the office, made straight for the gents' toilets. Expecting Harker to be hard on his heels, he didn't go to the nearest toilets but ones further away. He hoped the distance might buy him some extra time and make it take longer for Harker to find him.

He bolted himself into a cubicle and started to send telephone numbers to Ana's phone. After a few minutes, he heard the washroom door open and someone come in, but he stayed where he was until he finished the task. When he'd sent all the phone numbers he needed, Temple flushed the toilet. As he expected, when he opened the cubicle door, Harker was there waiting for him.

'I'll take that.' Harker's customary guttural growl was at its menacing best as he held out his hand for the mobile. 'If I were you, I'd start looking for a new job, Temple,' Harker continued in a low voice. 'There's no way back for you now. You can kiss goodbye to the next ten years as a police officer.' Temple handed over the phone.

It had been a long time coming but at last Clive Harker felt he had Temple over a barrel. He'd managed to choreograph a set of circumstances that had led to a disciplinary hearing and now there was a further charge to add to the sheet. Harker would have known that any mention of discontinuing Op Acre would see Temple disobeying an order to leave the enquiry alone and he'd been right. *Suggesting this course of action to Buller had been clever on his part*, he thought. He'd known it would only be a matter of time and that had come far sooner than he'd expected.

An alleged assault in custody by a detective officer had had Harker looking at the CCTV in the custody unit. When he saw Temple in the background making off with DNA kits immediately following his meeting with Buller, it was a gift. He knew he had him. Now there was direct chief officer involvement, Harker would see to it that Temple wouldn't survive. The hearing was scheduled for next Tuesday; by the end of that day, he'd be out. It couldn't come soon enough. The two men eyed each other. It was a showdown of sorts between them and Harker already thought it was game over.

All Temple could think of was that they were about to take his warrant card away from him and strip him of his ability to function as an officer. How could he find Prayer and China without it? He'd be neither in the job nor out of it, but stuck in a sort of no man's land of policing, useless without the powers and protection it gave.

They were standing close enough for Temple to see a small pulse beating in Harker's left cheek. Temple wondered what Harker would say if he knew Gemma had been to visit him. That she had a daughter, Temple's daughter, the only grandchild Harker was likely to have. He wondered what Harker would say if he knew that his only grandchild was now placed in danger because of the actions of his good friend Sloper and that by suspending him, Harker had just scuppered the best chance of her being found alive and well.

Even in that moment as he thought about it, Temple still wondered if it was true. The temptation to tell Harker, shock him and tell him that instead of suspending him, he needed to listen to him and work with him to get his granddaughter back, was strong. But he could hardly believe it himself, let alone convince Harker. And Temple remembered Gemma's strict instructions not to tell him. His mind raced. Was Gemma setting him up? Was this all part of it, a drive to get him out of the job? The sooner he could get out of the building the better.

Accompanied by Harker back to Buller's office, Temple was served disciplinary papers and was asked for his warrant card. He took it from his wallet and placed it on Buller's desk. Buller picked it up and Temple watched as he put it in a brown envelope. Harker then accompanied Temple to his car to retrieve the DNA kits he still had in there. He hoped they hadn't checked the inventory to see how many were missing or they'd know he'd got some elsewhere, the stash he gave to Richard.

Back in Buller's office, Temple was told that he needed to report any journeys he wanted to make out of the county to gain permission to do so. He was told he had no access to police stations. He wasn't permitted to wear his uniform except at the impending disciplinary hearing and contact regarding that would be made with him through his designated force 'welfare officer', a chief superintendent designated by Buller.

In a final act designed to humiliate Temple, Buller ensured he was escorted off the premises by a sergeant. As Temple reached the door to leave, Harker spoke.

'Temple.' He waited for him to turn. 'See you next Tuesday.'

CHAPTER 29

In the small, rank-smelling flat in Penhill, Katya Petrenko was waiting for her mobile phone to ring. She was sitting on a stained settee in leggings and a T-shirt while her uniform from her expensive school hung on a hanger over the door in front of her, the intricate gold-embroidered school badge on the breast pocket offset against the burgundy cashmere wool blend.

In the kitchen, the drugs were being cooked to make them malleable, easy to hide. In this state, they could be put into condoms and transported inside the body, hiding them from any police search. And dressed in her uniform, her very proper uniform, Katya was the perfect foil for drug dealing.

A local drug gang had recruited an older girl at her school, whom they had supplied with ecstasy and cocaine. She in turn had been threatened and forced to recruit more runners. She'd made it sound easy and exciting, which was what had lured Katya. Katya had all the money she wanted but it was excitement her life lacked. She lived her life through watching others on social media, and she wanted to have a piece of the action. This didn't seem particularly difficult, but it was the fact that it was illegal that attracted her. And there was such demand.

Suppliers were flooding the more rural communities with drugs; there was a healthy appetite for cocaine and it needed to be transported and delivered quickly and easily. There was a need to recruit younger, more respectable-looking kids; kids from good backgrounds, rich even. Posh kids who wouldn't readily come to notice. They could be used to deliver to the more well-heeled clientele as they would blend in easily.

And it worked. They were getting more and more drugs across the country with fewer losses. And kids were easy to frighten. It was quick and easy to make them feel responsible, scare them shitless with threats of reprisals against their families so that, in the end, they were doing it to keep anything bad from happening.

The trap house was known to be where local addicts could buy their gear and where Katya and the other runners could be replenished. The door opened with a key and another young boy came in. He was small for his age, with the added benefit that he therefore looked much younger than his fourteen years.

'Lordon? Lordon?' he shouted.

'In here,' came a voice from the kitchen. Lordon was 'cooking'.

The boy was holding his arm and Katya could see his coat was torn. He walked straight past her to the kitchen. He was in pain and he was scared.

'I've been cut. They've sliced me. Some other dealers attacked me.' The boy went into the kitchen clutching his arm across his chest.

Lordon stopped what he was doing and went to the boy. The boy's face was ashen and he'd obviously been frightened by the attack. But at least he was here; he'd made it back. He was alive. He gestured to the boy, his hands still in blue latex gloves from handling drugs.

'Take your coat off and let me see.'

The boy did as instructed and revealed a long livid cut and blood dripping from along the inside of his left arm and onto the floor. He winced as he revealed it, peeling his coat away, looking at Lordon's face.

'He had a fucking knife and suddenly sliced me as they asked me for my drugs and money.'

'They stopped you and asked you?'

'Yes, I didn't have any on me. I told them.'

'If you had and they'd taken it, you would pay for it.' It was important to get that message across, for the future. 'Oi,' Lordon shouted out to Katya. 'Come in here and help me.'

Katya got up from the settee and went into the kitchen. She was enthralled by her situation, which still felt like a game. A game where she was surrounded by young people going about their clandestine business, which was now her business. In the short time she had been involved in this, a whole new world had opened up to her. For the most part she was silent and wide-eyed, taking it in, doing as she was asked.

Lordon had the boy's arm across the kitchen table and it was bleeding heavily. The boy looked at his injury and felt sick.

'Am I going to die? I'll have to go to hospital.'

'You're going nowhere. I'll deal with this.' Lordon knew he had to do all he could to keep the boy away from hospital. Hospitals were to be avoided at all costs. Too many eyes looking, too many questions asked.

He looked across at Katya. 'Right, that's better. You hold the cut together and I'll close it. Now, stay still. It could have been a lot worse. You were lucky it was only your arm. They could have just done you in the street, man. Finished you.'

Lordon went to a drawer and brought out a sealed bag. From inside he took out a plastic bottle with a nozzle. Unscrewing the lid from the nozzle, he then squeezed the liquid. He had to stop the wound from bleeding and the sooner he got this done, the better.

'Right, hold the cut together,' he instructed Katya, and as the boy winced and groaned, Lordon dripped the contents lengthways into the cut and then in a criss-cross, anointing the wound. He made sure the glue was applied thickly, so that it formed a hard crust.

'There,' he said. 'Keep still for a minute, hold it. Hope that this works or I'll have to stitch you myself.'

'What is it?'

'Superglue. Just stay still, let it work.'

He packed the glue away and got back to business.

Seeing that the boy's wound was fastened by the glue, Katya retreated back to the settee.

Lordon addressed the boy, who was still sitting at the kitchen table, examining his handiwork. He was lucky he hadn't had to take a needle and thread to it. He had the means and he had been taught what to do by learning from another dealer stitching up his own injuries. It was a good way of swerving hospitals, especially for some of the younger kids.

'Don't go picking at it.' The boy winced. 'You'll get used to it. See it as a battle scar. It won't be the last you'll have – if you want to be like me in a couple of years' time, dishing the stuff out, you'll get a few more scars before then.' Lordon pulled up his top to reveal a raised scar across his left side.

'I survived that, see? And a few others.' He pulled up his trouser leg to reveal a scar on his shin. 'This one I stitched myself, learnt how to do it. Good thing you didn't have any gear or money on you, man. Now tomorrow, get some of this stashed on you and get back on the train. I'll give you a knife to carry, to defend yourself. And you,' he shouted out to Katya, 'get your uniform ready. He's going to wear the jacket.'

CHAPTER 30

Temple drove home, having first stopped to buy a pay-as-you-go mobile. He should have seen this coming and there was no way Harker wasn't going to capitalise on the situation. What were the chances of Harker seeing a clip of CCTV where Temple could be seen in the background picking up DNA kits? He sat in his car, his mind racing, going over it all. He was in a mess and it was of his own making.

Of course they must have been expecting him to do something; Harker knew he would react in some way when they told him Op Acre would be closed down. He'd handed himself to them, to Harker and then Buller. It would have been Harker's decision not to pursue Op Acre and he would have advised Buller. He had to hand it to Harker, he was good. And there was no way he was going to survive next week's disciplinary hearing now. Harker had already told him that. He didn't quite know what he was going to do but somehow he had to fight back.

He met Ana at the front door, who'd been wondering why she had received so many telephone number notifications. He explained the position to her, that he was now no longer a warranted police officer.

'What does it mean?' she asked.

'It means, Ana, that I need to do something to sort the situation out or I'll lose my job next week. They've taken my work mobile. I'll need to borrow your mobile phone, that's why I sent you the numbers. I've bought you a pay-as-you-go which will need charging; I'd use it but I haven't got time to wait for that.'

Ana tentatively handed over her mobile and Temple sat in the kitchen and put the numbers he'd sent by text into Ana's contacts, texting his new number to Amy and Paul Wallace. He then went into the small back garden and called Gary Lewis. He was impatient now.

'I haven't heard back from you yet, Gary. What's happening?'

Lewis wasn't taking orders from Temple. He was in no rush. 'I'm trying to fix a meet for tomorrow night.'

'Why not tonight? Tomorrow night's too late.'

'You got the money?'

'I can get the money, don't worry about that. All I need is the meet set up. Ring me back on this mobile. This is the number you reach me on now.'

He then used Ana's phone to make contact with his office. He wanted the others to hear of his suspension from him. DS Sam Mendoza answered and listened as Temple explained his exchange in Buller's office. As Temple spoke, Mendoza abruptly cut short their conversation. So that was the effect suspension had. He texted his friend DC Paul Wright, who rang him back immediately.

'The bastards have got you then, mate? I'll call round at the weekend, see if there's anything I can do.'

'No, I don't want you dragged into this, you've helped enough already. If I could ask you to help on another matter though, while I've got you.'

'Anything. What can I do?'

'I need the DNA profile from the blue T-shirt.' Paul Wright understood immediately without any further explanation.

'Leave it with me. I'll be in touch. Are you sure there's nothing I can help you with regarding the suspension?'

'No. One way or another it'll be over soon; the disciplinary hearing's scheduled for next Tuesday. Besides, I'm not giving up yet, there still might be a way I can turn it round.' He didn't want to say anything more on the phone as his paranoia was telling him that they could already be monitoring Wright's conversations with him.

Temple made one last call to his police fed rep to tell him of his suspension. Inspector Bob May listened intently as Temple informed him of his news.

'They're looking at three charges now then.' May was thinking through a worst-case scenario. That was his default position; he wasn't there to provide a shoulder to cry on, he was there to lay it on the line. If someone was facing the sack, best they get used to the idea sooner rather than later. He didn't offer agony aunt services.

'Three charges means they can go for warning, final warning and terminating the contract of employment. With the line-up you've got, I don't fancy your chances of coming out of it with your job. But that's the worst case – other than that, a bit of ritual humiliation with a demotion maybe.'

'Thanks, Bob, I knew I could rely on you to cheer me up.'

'My pleasure. I'll see you there then, on the day. In the meantime, I'll get some testimonials in for you. You never know, I could be proved wrong but I doubt it. I'll argue for you to be able to resign rather than be sacked. That's the best scenario I can offer.'

Temple hung up. Now the phone calls were out of the way, he could concentrate on the only thing that mattered. Finding Prayer, China and Megon.

Temple thought about his interaction with Gary Lewis earlier that day. He needed Lewis to set the meeting up for later that night. If he could only find the girls, Gemma might be willing to make a statement about Sloper and he might be able to gain himself an advantage. But without the return of Prayer, Gemma was unlikely to help. He knew he couldn't get the girls back on his own and now he was an exiled cop with no warrant card, no uniform, no radio and no backup. *Nada*, as Ana would say.

As he sat thinking through his options, there was a knock on the door. Ana answered it. The smallness of the cottage meant that he could hear the familiar voice of DS Sam Mendoza. He went from the kitchen to the front door.

'I wanted to come round, mate, and offer my support. I thought it best not to speak on the phone, in the office with the others listening in. I've told them you've been suspended. And I mean it, if there's anything I can do. . .'

Mendoza reached across the threshold and put his hand on Temple's shoulder.

'Come in.' Temple reluctantly stepped aside.

'I won't stay long, I just wanted to come out following your call to let you know that I sympathise.'

They went into the kitchen and stood facing each other. What was Mendoza really doing here? He could have said this on the phone. Perhaps he'd been sent to report back on how he had taken the suspension, see how angry he was. Temple knew he had to be careful not to give anything away. He tried to put on a philosophical front.

'It is what it is. The hearing's next week so I won't have long to wait.'

'Look, my own case is pretty hopeless. My putting my hand on a colleague's knee isn't going to bode well for me in the long term. Her word against mine, with me saying it was unintentional. Which it was. With all this #MeToo, I'm fucked. They've already asked me to consider resignation. The only reason I haven't is that it's taking them so long to bring the case, I may as well get a few more mortgage payments out of it. Here's my mobile number. If I can do anything for you, just call.'

'That's good of you, Sam, thanks. Will you resign?'

'Next month maybe. Perhaps it's time to get out anyway. Disciplinary aside, I've got ten years to do if I stay, and the job doesn't get any better. So what I'm saying is, I've got one foot out of the door anyway; if I can do you a good turn, just let me know. I'm out tonight, having a drink in Swindon if you want to join me?'

'Like you, Sam, I think I've pretty much had it. I should have been better at seeing it coming. If I think of something though, I'll call. I'll pass on the drink but thanks all the same. I appreciate it. I'm going to keep my head down and prepare for the hearing.'

Temple made all the right noises even though he wasn't sincere. He didn't feel like socialising or drowning his sorrows. He was angry. Mostly with himself.

Mendoza left. Even before he was out of sight, Temple wondered if Mendoza had meant anything he'd said. Perhaps Mendoza was one of Harker's spies, perhaps he'd been reporting back on their conversations in the office all along. He didn't know if that was fair or not; he didn't know what to think anymore.

He felt as if he was in overdrive, spurred on by adrenalin from the anger of his suspension. He was restless and with it, his mind burrowed away, trying to formulate a plan to deal with the impossibility of Gemma's request for help.

CHAPTER 31

Temple quickly changed into jeans and a jumper. He went into the attic space where he had stored some boxes following the move. As he looked in amongst them, he dug out a heavy dark overcoat that had seen better days, some old army combat trousers and old blankets. Back in the kitchen, he spoke to Ana as he laced up an old pair of Doc Martens.

'I'm going to be out the next twenty-four hours or so, do you think you can look after Ben without me coming back?'

'Of course.' She looked at Temple. She could see that he was trying to hide his anger and was at the same time strangely energised.

'A letter came for you today.' She passed him a white envelope. He finished lacing his boots and tore it open. It was the decree absolute. It was official and final; he and Leigh were divorced. He tossed the letter across to Ana, indicating for her to read. She read it and looked back at him without saying anything.

'That's that then,' he said by way of a response. It was turning out to be some day.

'If anyone calls by for you, what shall I tell them?' she asked softly.

'If anyone from the police calls by, tell them I'm out and you don't know when I'll be back. Only call me in an emergency.'

'Where will you stay?'

'In the car. I've got some blankets from the loft.'

He left and went to his car, putting the combats and blankets in the boot. He had to think through what he was going to do. Firstly, he had to go back to Gemma.

* * *

Temple found her at her flat. Her face looked harder today; she was edgier. She let him in and going into the living room, he could see a bottle of vodka and a glass on a coffee table.

'What do you think you're doing, Gem? You'll be no help pissed out of your head on that.' He was annoyed with her; he needed her to be able to function without drugs or alcohol. She picked up the glass and drained it.

'It'll take more than this. This is medicine. This is how I cope.'

'I need you to help me, tell me where Sloper goes, where he lives. I need to find him and quick. Is he due back here?'

'No, he won't come here until the weekend. You'll find him on the streets around Manchester Road, looking after his assets, as he puts it.' She walked away from him, showing no apparent signs of being the worse for drinking. Ignoring his instruction, she went to refill her glass.

'Assets? What – other girls?'

'Yes. His girls, two of them. If you can't find him, just go and bother them and they'll ring him. Go and find Claire and Justine.'

'Why didn't you tell me this the other night? I asked you to tell me everything.'

She rounded on him. 'I had other things on my mind more important than his tarts.'

'OK, OK.' He knew that getting her back up was not going to help. 'Where does he live?'

She calmed again. 'I haven't been inside. But I know where it is. He lives at Old Town, Marlborough Road. Don't know the number.'

'Right, you'll have to come out and help me. I need to find him. If you say he took the money, we've got to hope that he still has it. Get your shoes on, you're going to show me his girls and his house.'

She put her glass down and went into the bedroom as he looked around the flat. It was small, but bright and clean. The half empty vodka bottle and empty glass stood on a coffee table and there was an iPad on one of the two white sofas where Gemma had been sitting. There was a fringed Afghan rug on the floor, which gave the only colour to the room.

He went over to a bookcase and, leaning his head to one side, he read the spines of the books. Amongst some paperbacks, there were some second-hand medicine books. They should have been out of place but seeing them, he was reminded that she had been at university studying medicine when they first met. It felt like so long ago that it was almost like recalling someone else's life.

He'd never forgotten the first time he saw her. They had met at a pub during a retirement party for a police colleague. Temple hadn't known him well – he was eleven months into his probation – but the whole station had been invited. Harker attended with his wife, and Gemma, back on a Friday night for a weekend from uni, had tagged along for a late-night drink.

He remembered how he had been immediately attracted to her; her pretty, pale face framed by her soft, flame-coloured hair and her slim legs in her frayed jeans. He remembered that she wore a low-cut tunic that clearly showed she was braless. He remembered his eyes following the point of the V neckline down to a toned abdomen and being instantly mesmerised. She'd made such an impression on him, he'd never forgotten his first sight of her.

He'd also discovered that night that she intended to be a doctor; she was a smart girl, loaded with her own hopes and expectations, as well as those of her parents. Then she'd met him and now she wasn't even a shadow of the intelligent girl he once knew. And that was it; he didn't know her anymore. The Gemma he had fallen in love with was long gone. Perhaps the books were there as a reminder to her of what might have been.

He looked up and saw her standing in the doorway of the bedroom.

'Come in here.' She beckoned him over to her.

'We have to get going, Gem.' Reminiscing about her made his voice softer.

'Just come in here for a minute.' She beckoned him to the room with her head.

He did as asked and when they were in the bedroom, she showed him Prayer's mobile phone. Temple took it.

'It's locked, I've tried it,' said Gemma. She then nodded towards a small pink case on wheels. She put it on the bed and unzipped it.

'Look. These are her things. Prayer's things.' They stood beside each other and gently turned over the clothes that were in the case. There were the usual things girls have, leggings and tops. Temple couldn't help but compare them with those of China Lewis. No Primark here; there were jumpers from Ralph Lauren, Burberry, Tommy Hilfiger. Gemma took a jumper and held it up, burying her face into it, inhaling deeply.

'She's ours,' Gemma whispered as her gaze went beyond, her mind fixed on some place in the past as if she was in a trance.

'She's not, Gem,' Temple said gently, watching her. 'All we did was make her. She belongs to the two people who brought her up. Her parents. We've had nothing to do with that. They made the girl you described to me. They've done all the hard work. I only wish she'd stayed where she was. We have to find her for them too. We have to get her home to them.' His comment broke her gaze and as Gemma stood still clutching the jumper, Temple continued to look through the case.

'She'd started asking about who her father was. I hadn't got round to telling her about us.'

'How much does she know?'

'Not much. I haven't told her your name yet.' She looked at him. 'You've got a daughter, haven't you?' she said quietly. He replied without looking up.

'Yes.'

'Her name's Daisy, isn't it?'

He looked back at her. 'Yes, how do you know?'

'I've seen her on Facebook; I do a bit of looking around on there. Found your wife. She's pregnant, isn't she? I see what she says and posts, the pictures and that. Your little girl's pretty.'

He'd told Leigh numerous times not to put things on Facebook and to set her page at maximum privacy. He told her that anyone can look at what she put on there if she wasn't careful, and find out things about them that they could use or trace them with. And here was Gemma proving the point. She'd been looking at their life, or rather Leigh's life; a life Leigh was doing her best to make sure he wasn't part of anymore. He wondered if Gemma knew that. She hadn't said. He couldn't believe Leigh wouldn't have shouted her divorce across Facebook. He changed the subject.

'Is there a brush, something with Prayer's hair on?'

'Over there, why?'

'It doesn't matter.' He walked across the room to get it from a table near the bed. Gemma then realised why he'd asked for it. Her face cracked and she was suddenly in floods of tears. He went over to her and her body crumpled into his as he held her to him. The last time they'd been this close was a lifetime ago and he'd never envisaged their separate lives coming together again. So much had happened to them.

But as he held her and felt the sobs wracking her body, any thoughts he had of Gemma setting him up disappeared.

Her face told him everything he needed to know and as he felt her body next to his again for the first time in years, he knew every emotion she displayed now was genuine.

This is how she'd been when he'd told her it was over between them all those years ago. This was the Gemma he recognised, the Gemma of old, before the drugs, the booze and the men. After a minute or so he shook her gently.

'I need you strong now, Gem, come on. Get yourself together. We'll get her back. You and me.' She looked at him through her tears and believed him. Temple had no idea how he was going to get Prayer back, but right then, he knew he had to make Gemma confident in his ability to do so. The least he could do was give her hope that she would see Prayer again.

* * *

He drove them both to Marlborough Road. The tears wiped away, Gemma had put her hard face back on. She was different, some other person he couldn't emotionally connect with. The old Gemma he knew was gone again. Whatever it was that had unlocked as he'd held her, that softness had now disappeared.

She directed him to Sloper's property, which was a 1930s white semi with a garage to one side. He quickly sized it up, looking at the neighbouring houses. Temple then drove to the Manchester Road area and before dropping Gemma off, she pointed out one of the girls Sloper ran. Before he went, he checked his phone. He remembered when he last worked with Sloper that he was using at least two phones and he only had a number for one, his work phone.

'Give me all the mobile numbers you have for him. Get the girls to ring him and say you need to see him, make sure he comes down here. Make up some shit so that you keep him with you for at least half an hour. Text me as soon as he turns up. Do it now.'

She did as instructed and Temple drove off back to Marlborough Road alone and parked down the street a little way from Sloper's house. He put another mobile number for Sloper that Gemma had given him into his phone. He had no choice but to sit and wait for Gemma to get in touch. Within the hour, she texted to say that Sloper was on his way to them. He waited until she confirmed that Sloper had arrived before he got out of the car and walked up the street to Sloper's house.

Looking up, he saw an alarm on the outside. To the side of the house was an attached garage. Before going further, he flicked the video recorder on his mobile and used it to film the front of the house and his movements. Going round to the side of the garage, he quickly pushed through a tall gate to the back of the house. Temple tried the handle of a door to the back of the garage, which was locked. He continued down the side of the house to the kitchen door. It was double-glazed. He went back to the garage door, which was half-glazed with small panes of glass. He'd soon find out if the alarm covered the garage. Covering his hand with his coat, Temple broke the window, reached through and turned the key, letting himself inside. All was quiet.

Luck was with him and the connecting door from the garage to the hallway was not locked. He knew the alarm would sound as soon as he opened the door. If it went off, he knew that he would just have to ignore it. It remained to be seen what the neighbours did. Slowly, he opened the door and stepped inside. He looked into the hallway; he could see a motion sensor in the corner of the ceiling furthest from him. As soon as he moved forward he knew the alarm would sound. He walked down the hallway. There was nothing. Sloper hadn't set the alarm.

He made his way through the house, talking into the camera on his phone as he did so, giving a running commentary as he looked in each of the rooms, into the kitchen, inside the fridge, the oven, through drawers, an understairs cupboard – anywhere he thought Sloper would hide money. He went upstairs into the bathroom and rattled the bath panel. It was solid and fixed with no signs of it being disturbed. He lifted the lid on the toilet cistern. There was nothing there. He was trying to second guess where someone like Sloper might hide his money. If he was dealing in drugs as Gemma said, he knew he would have a stash somewhere.

He moved on to his bedroom. Again, he searched through drawers, under the bed, until at last he found what he was looking for. Hidden behind a chest of drawers, a safe had been built into the outside wall. Temple moved the chest away from the wall to get a full look at it. It had a numbered digital keypad.

'The bastard.' Temple couldn't help but curse him. He'd almost expected the money to be hidden in a drawer somewhere, behind a cistern, under a bath, like a chaotic drug dealer. But he conceded now that Sloper was smarter than that. From what Gemma had told him, Sloper had been at it for some time and therefore was good at what he did. What was to stop anyone doing what he was doing now, breaking in and rifling through his house? Sloper would have thought of that.

He was hoping against hope to find the money he'd stolen from Gemma's flat still here. Sloper was bound to run a more sophisticated operation after all this time. But he needed to find the money to barter with Gary Lewis for the girls. It was Temple's only hope of getting his hands on that sort of cash.

He knelt down in front of the safe. It was a four-digit code. Temple hoped that Sloper would be like most cops and used the only four-digit number they were unlikely to forget: their collar number. Temple knew Sloper's collar number was 326. He tapped 0326 into the keypad. Nothing happened. He then tapped the number in reverse. It opened.

Inside he could see a number of see-through plastic bags, some containing money and some drugs. Temple stood back, and with his phone recorded the room, the safe with the door closed and the safe with the door open and the contents visible. He pulled all the bags out of the small space, along with a silver-coloured watch, a modern-looking Rolex.

He then examined the bags, laying them out on the floor, videoing everything in proximity to the safe. Looking through the bags, the drugs looked like tabs of heroin. He left these sealed and put them back in the safe. The five bags containing money he opened. The notes were arranged in bundles of a hundred £10, £20 and £50 notes and there was a grand or two in each bag.

He opened all the bags and arranged the money on the floor before taking photos. He counted £7,000 and had the video rolling as he put the Rolex back in the safe and closed the door. Speaking to the camera, he took the money and put it in the pockets of his mac. He hoped it would be enough to buy the return of the girls.

Going downstairs and making his way back outside, he took a photo of the front of the house. Once in his car, he found the photo and attaching it to a text message, he sent it to Sloper.

CHAPTER 32

Temple had changed out of his jeans into his army combats and the grubby woollen overcoat. It would be dark in an hour and he wanted to make sure he blended into the down-and-out world of the dossers and drug-takers of Swindon, although there wouldn't be many of them with over £7,000 in their pockets. He decided to keep the money on him, ready in case he could trade it for the return of the girls. He desperately wanted a call from Gary Lewis. He had money, now he just wanted to be told where to go.

Parked up in Old Town, Temple rang Paul Wallace. He arranged to meet him outside St Mark's Church. Wallace had told him that he had gone in there when he arrived and it seemed as good a place as any to ask for his help. As he suspected, Wallace had been in the town centre doing his usual circuit looking for Megon.

Paul Wallace approached him, slightly out of breath but pleased to see him. He'd raced across town following Temple's call. It was late afternoon and the sun was fading, bringing a chill wind into force. Wallace noted Temple's shabby-looking appearance, quite different to when they'd met before. Wallace sat beside Temple on a bench in the grounds of the church.

'I didn't know you were a religious man,' panted Wallace as he got his breath back from his march across town.

'I'm not. There's been some developments and I'm going to need your help.'

'Anything you want, of course I'll help,' Wallace said eagerly. 'Have you heard anything about Megon?'

'I have. I don't know where she is at the moment, but I'm hoping to get word from a contact later today. She was, maybe still is, in Swindon. She was with another girl. The same girl I told you I've been looking for—'

'What? Where are they? Are they in trouble?' Wallace interrupted, unable to contain himself, his eyes wide.

'Look, I've told you, I don't know for sure and I don't want to get your hopes up. Can you be in Swindon later tonight?'

'I'm due back on the last train, which leaves at ten tonight. But if Megon's here and you've got a lead I'll stay out all night – as long as it takes.'

'I'll be around the town. Listen out for your phone – I'll need you to act quickly.'

'I'll stay with you. This is fantastic news!' He leapt up and stood in front of Temple. It was the best news he'd heard in weeks and he was excited – Megon was here, she was in Swindon, he was going to find her. He might be able to take her home with him tonight. His mind was racing ahead, thinking of reuniting her with Leonie and her sisters. They would all be together again. And soon.

Temple saw the change in him; he'd come alive. But he needed Paul Wallace to remain calm. What he had in mind was risky but it was all he could think of that might give them a chance to rescue the girls. He had to have Paul Wallace's help; he knew he couldn't do it alone.

'Look, there's something else, something I need to tell you. I'm not meant to be here. I've been taken off the job so to speak, which is why I look like this, because I can't be seen to look like I'm on duty. But I want to help you and there's a chance we could get Megon back. So we're probably going to have to do this together.'

'I'll do anything to get her back, you know that.'

'You might have to.' Temple sighed. 'Paul, you might want to sit back down. The sighting of Megon confirms she was here last week. Hopefully they haven't moved her already.'

'What do you mean, "if they haven't moved her" – who's "they"? Where is she? Tell me!' Having sat down at Temple's request, Paul Wallace leapt back up on his feet. His emotions were going wild; he thought he was going to find her and here was Temple telling him that she was being moved around. By who? Who had his little girl? What did Temple know?

'Sit down, Paul. I need you to be calm, I need you to be able to take this information in and stay calm, otherwise you can't help me. You'll be no good to me.' Temple knew this was a huge gamble and at the moment, it wasn't paying off. Reluctantly, Paul Wallace sat back down, looking at Temple intently.

'Just tell me what the hell's going on.'

'Megon's in some trouble. She's been caught up in drug dealing, probably with dealers from the estate back in Hackney. She's been ferrying drugs and money from London to Swindon and anywhere in between. There's a name for it, county lines, you'll have seen it in the newspapers. Drug dealers in London, or elsewhere for that matter, it's all around the country. They advertise their goods via text to their client base and wait for their orders. The buyer responds and the dealer arranges with the courier to make contact with the buyer and arrange where they can pick up the drugs. This way, the dealer is not involved in the transaction. When the courier has sold all his drugs, he goes back to the dealer, gives him the money and goes out again with more drugs, waiting for the dealer to make contact. The dealers are using kids now as couriers. Kids like Megon.'

'County what? Lines? What does that mean? And you're saying that Megon is a courier, is that what you're saying?'

'Lines means phone lines, mobiles, and the kids being sent out into the counties, out of London. Yes, Megon's been couriering. They attract the kids at the school gates, on estates, with promises of making money, big money. They use kids because they're easy to manipulate, scare and control. They're also less likely to be suspected of carrying drugs because of their age, and therefore not come to police notice. And because they're kids, if they do get lifted, they are unlikely to be prosecuted.

'And yes, she probably has earned herself a few hundred quid and she thinks it's lucrative. Then at some point, they'll be set up, robbed and they won't be paid anymore; they'll be working for free because they're in "debt" and have to work for nothing to pay back what they lost, only they didn't lose anything, it's just another form of control to make them frightened. Fear is a powerful motivator, especially for kids.'

'Why haven't I heard of this? And where is she then?' Paul Wallace held his breath. One minute he was near to finding Megon, taking her home, and the next he was being told of a new nightmare scenario of her being mixed up with drug gangs and drug dealing.

'I don't know where she is. She was with the girl I've been trying to find, China Lewis, the girl whose photo I showed you. China and Megon ran off together after they lost some drugs and money – now I suspect that people are holding China and another girl to get their money back. It's what drug gangs do, a vendetta kidnap. So there's every possibility they've got Megon too. I have a small chance of being able to get to China and hopefully Megon tonight.'

'What if it doesn't work?' Wallace was hanging on Temple's every word. His mind had pictures of Megon walking through the streets with drugs, being held against her will, kidnapped. How the hell had she got into this?

'Then we'll have another conversation. I'm hopeful, but as I say, I will need your help. We might just be able to pull it off.'

'I want my Megon back. I don't want her put in any danger.'

'She's already in danger, Paul. I'm going to do my best to get her back. I've got a vested interest in it too. The people who have China and Megon also have another girl I need to find.'

Paul Wallace let the information Temple was giving him sink in. He'd read about drugs gangs, he even knew of them on the estate and around where he lived, but that was the extent of his experience. He'd not touched drugs as a kid and he'd done his best with his own kids to make sure they weren't interested. He hadn't realised just how prevalent and embedded the problem was for children at such a young age.

Of course he'd heard about youngsters being offered drugs at the school gates, but being enticed or coerced into dealing – that was new. And they'd done this to Megon; his sweet little girl had succumbed to this. Why hadn't she turned to him, told him, asked him for help? The thought of her being threatened and involved with such people turned his stomach. If they laid a finger on her, he'd kill them.

'Just tell me what you want me to do.'

* * *

The boy was glad to be back on the train to Swindon. He was wearing Katya's school blazer and because of his small size, it was a little too big. He kept his hand in his pocket, where he felt the knife Lordon had given him. He felt all around the handle of it, becoming familiar with its grip and feel, the curves of it, how it felt in his hand as he constantly gripped it, released it and gripped it again. It kept him alert; the train was warm and stuffy and the journey felt long.

He had no idea that he was being watched, that he'd been spotted at the train station and followed onto the train. All he could think of was getting back to Lordon and completing another task. It was draining. He was tired and needed to sleep. The sheer effort it took to be alert all the time and aware of his surroundings – who might be watching him, who might be after what he was carrying – was taking its toll. He hadn't been alert when the men had stopped him and slashed him in the street. He'd been lucky then, he'd been able to run away, his small stature making him particularly nimble.

His wound had been itching today but Lordon had told him that was a good sign that it was already starting to heal and not to scratch it in case it broke open. Instead, he pressed it, which gave him a little relief. He was sitting next to a dozing woman and as he looked sideways and watched her head nodding, the motion of the train and the quietness of the carriage settled on him in a comforting way, and for a moment he felt safe. He felt his eyes begin to close and for one quick minute he drifted into a half sleep, only for his eyes to snap open at the sudden realisation of it. He was desperately tired but he had to stay awake. He pressed his fingers onto his wound through the jacket. The pain of it would keep him alert.

As the train stations rattled by and an announcement came that Swindon was the next stop, he gathered up the rucksack that he had stashed underneath his legs and stood up, straightening the jacket and buttoning it up. The woman continued to nod in her seat. His hand checked again on the outside of the pocket for the feel of the knife inside. He would tap his pocket many times for reassurance that it was still there as he stood and waited for the train to stop after it crawled into the station.

At last it ground to a halt and he waited while the passengers in front of him pressed the button for the door to open. He could now step into the cold fresh air. It was a little too cold and he shivered at first, keeping his hand gripped around his rucksack, once again checking for the feel of the knife through the jacket pocket. He mixed in amongst the other passengers as they moved off the platform and into the street.

Not long now and he'd be back. He could sleep. He walked down the road, focusing on getting back, completely unaware of the man following behind him. By now, he'd put the rucksack on his back and looked like any other studious pupil from an expensive day school with his red and gold blazer. He reached the trap house and let himself in through the front door. He pushed the door behind him but before he heard the familiar sound of the catch closing, the door was pushed back open and he felt himself being lifted off the floor from behind.

Suddenly realising someone had come in behind him, he yelled out. He was no match for whoever held him. His rucksack was now off his shoulders and on the floor in the hallway. An arm was around his throat and he yelled out in pain again as his wounded arm was yanked behind his back.

Lordon appeared from the kitchen as the boy was being carried down the hallway by a large, strong man. The boy could see from Lordon's face that this was trouble. As Lordon backed into the living room, the boy was flung forwards across the room face-first onto the settee opposite the door. The man who threw him there now stood filling the space in the doorway, holding the jacket. He was looking at it, looking inside for something. And then he found it. Katya's name. Then he turned to them, holding the jacket up in his fist.

'Where's Katya? Where's the girl whose jacket this is? Where is she?' he demanded as his hand went to his pocket. He drew out a gun and pointed it at Lordon. Lordon was quick to speak, holding up his latexed hands.

'She's on a delivery! She's on a delivery, I swear! She's not here. She'll be back.'

'Where's she gone? Where's the delivery? Take me there.'

'I can't, I don't know, I mean I don't know where she's gone.'

The man pointed the gun, moved forward past Lordon and looked into the kitchen. The work surfaces were full of the drugs he was cooking and cutting. The man grabbed Lordon, forcing him further into the living area.

'You're dealing this shit so you know where it's going. Where is she? Where did she go? If you don't take me to her I will shoot the boy right now in front of you. I'll blow his fucking brains all up the wall.' The man moved his arm so that the gun was pointing at the boy. The boy was now sitting up, frozen, white-faced and wide-eyed, transfixed by the barrel of the gun. Lordon instinctively knew the man would shoot if he didn't do as he asked. He knew the look in the eyes.

'All right! All right! Stop, stop. I'll take you. I'll take you.' In the living room, the boy remained still and said nothing, watching what was happening. Lordon took off his blue latex gloves and threw them onto the floor as the man grabbed the collar of his jumper and threw him out into the narrow hallway. Neither Lordon nor the boy could match the man's strength or sheer presence, and putting a gun in their faces ensured they did exactly what he told them.

'You are going to take me to her. If you run, I'll shoot you in the back. Take me to her and I'll let you go.' He shoved Lordon towards the front door; he fumbled with the latch to open it. They both went out, the door remaining open behind them. The boy was left shaking, his trousers wet through between his legs.

CHAPTER 33

Temple went with Paul Wallace to a local café where they ordered tea. As they sat in silence, Temple sent Sloper another text; this time it was a photo of his living room. Ten minutes later, he sent Sloper another containing a photo of his bedroom. While he was likely to have dismissed the first photo, Temple thought the others should have him rushing back home. Temple liked the thought of Sloper being in a panic about someone poking around his house.

Just as he sent the third photo, his phone rang. It was Gary Lewis. Temple got up and went outside, leaving Paul Wallace sitting at the table.

'I've set up the meet,' Lewis said.

'Where and who with?'

'It's at eleven-thirty tonight. I'll let you know where later.'

'Who am I dealing with, Gary?'

Lewis ignored the question. 'We'll do an exchange by car – you bring the money, they'll bring the girls. They want ten grand.'

'That's way more than they lost.'

'That's what they want. They want their money back and potential earnings from the girls.'

'There's three girls, Gary, I want them all for that money. They're all reported missing to the police.'

'You can have two girls for that, the ones you mentioned. China and her friend, the ones who lost the money.'

'I told you of another, the one they took in retaliation; she's also been reported missing. The heat won't be off, Gary, until all three are returned. Make sure she's there.'

The phone line went dead in response. Temple still had no idea who he was dealing with. That bastard Lewis was enjoying this. He went back inside the café and sat down opposite Paul Wallace, who made no effort to question him.

Temple jabbed his thumbs on his phone to send Sloper a further text; this time it contained a photo of the money and drugs laid out on his bedroom floor. After a minute went by he received a response. It had had the desired effect. It was from Sloper.

'Who are you?' Sloper had asked.

Temple responded. 'You lost something?'

'We need to meet.'

'Yes we do.'

'Where?'

Temple replied, telling Sloper to meet him in an hour in a Swindon pub. He turned to Paul Wallace.

'Right, I have the makings of a plan and this is what I want you to do.' Wallace listened intently. When Temple finished telling Paul what he wanted from him, they went back over it again and he answered his questions.

Wallace had no idea if what Temple was suggesting was going to work, but for some reason, he trusted him. If what he said was true about Megon being caught up with drug dealers, he knew he needed Temple's help. Without him, he had no hope of finding Megon. The thought of losing his daughter when he was so close to finding her choked him.

'I really need you to hold it together now, Paul, we need to pull this off. Follow my lead, confirm what I say to Sloper. Be ready to have an answer for anything he asks. Remember what I've told you. Remember we're doing this for Megon, to get her back safely and quickly.'

They went out to Temple's car and he drove them both to the pub where they were to meet Sloper. Once inside, Temple looked round; there was the normal Thursday night trade and as it was early evening, it wasn't too busy. He indicated to Paul Wallace that they'd take a table near the back where they could see who was coming and going. They didn't have to wait long. Eager to see who was sending him text messages of the inside of his home, Simon Sloper arrived early.

From his vantage point, Temple watched as Sloper came into the pub. Slowly, his beady eyes scanned round, searching the faces of the people at tables, at the bar, walking around, until suddenly he saw Temple sitting at a table with some guy he didn't recognise.

At first his eyes brushed over him, as if he hadn't seen him, discounting him. Then, after a double take, he fixed on him. In one look Sloper knew it was Temple he was after. Temple saw Sloper's jaw tighten as he came towards him, manoeuvring his bulk around the tables and chairs until he stood in front of him. By now, Sloper's breathing was shallow and fast.

Sloper had been expecting a welcome from some of his Eastern European colleagues – when he saw Temple, it was almost a relief. But he had better things to do than have Temple give him the runaround and he wanted the contents of his safe back.

'*You?*' he spat. 'It was you sending me texts. You fucking twat.' Sloper stared down at Temple, who remained seated. Temple responded calmly. Paul Wallace didn't move but fixed his eyes on Sloper.

'Sit down, Simon.'

'I haven't got time for this bollocks. What the fuck are you playing at?'

Temple was unmoved and repeated himself. Slowly and calmly.

'Sit down.'

Sloper pulled a chair away from a table opposite and sat facing the two of them.

'What the fuck's going on? You're a fucking clown, Temple.' Sloper's tone was low and menacing. He leaned forward as far as the bulk of his large stomach would allow. '*You* – or someone – has been in my house. Now, you're going to give me the fucking money back.' Sloper looked from Paul Wallace back to Temple. 'And who the fuck is *this*?' His breathing was heavy. He put his mobile on the table in front of him. Temple leaned forward to put his face close to Sloper. He spoke quietly and purposefully.

'You, Simon, have been caught. This is DI Paul Wallace from the Met Vice Squad. They've been running an operation on some London traffickers who have led them to Swindon, and during the course of their investigations they've come across you. There's been a job running on you, watching you, gathering evidence on you, on your activities in Swindon, for months.'

Sloper was quick to react. 'Fuck off! You're fucking suspended, I heard that in the canteen earlier and Clive Harker confirmed it when I rang him.'

'Clive Harker doesn't know about this operation. Clive Harker *thinks* I'm suspended. I work for Buller. I've been working for Buller since the Met approached the force asking about you. I was working for Buller when we worked on the Ashton-Jones murder investigation. I was watching you then. Clive Harker doesn't know because, as we all know, Clive Harker is your friend, so it was always important that he didn't know. He has no idea about this operation. He has no idea what we've been gathering on you. If you put a call in to him now to help you, you'll bring him down too.'

Sloper looked at him, quickly processing what he'd heard. Temple didn't give him time to answer. If this was going to work, he didn't want to give Sloper too much time to think about it. He pressed on.

'The operation has been run from the offices that I share. It was made to look like I was on a disciplinary. Clive Harker gave Buller the ideal cover by initiating the complaint against me. The complaint never went to the IOPC but Buller used it as my cover. The other officers in my office, they've all been working on this case too. If you look over your shoulder, you'll see DS Sam Mendoza. He's been working on it; he's part of the team too.'

Sloper turned and looked behind him. Sure enough, Sam Mendoza was sitting across the room at a table and acknowledged Sloper with a slight nod. Sloper shifted in his seat, his breathing a little faster. Temple saw he'd started to sweat. He could see him turning it all over in his mind. It was Paul Wallace's turn.

'We know all about the girls you run, the money you've got, the drugs, the deals – we've been watching you for about ten months now. A bent cop. Nobody likes a bent cop. We've also been talking to Gemma.'

'Gemma's a fucking whore,' Sloper retorted. 'No one believes whores.'

Temple cut in quick. 'Gemma, as you know, is Harker's daughter, Simon. Put in a call to Harker, go on. Ring him up. That's what you usually do, isn't it? He usually comes to your rescue. Only this time, he won't know what you're talking about. Who do you think he'll believe when he reads Gemma's statement? A statement that goes back years, that will tell him of years of your dealings on the streets of Swindon, deals with the drug dealers, the pimps. Who do you think he'll want to believe? She knows it all. She'll tell her dad how you pimped out his own daughter when he thought you were looking out for her. What do you think he'll say then? Who do you think he'll believe with that statement and all the evidence that's been gathered about you?'

Sloper looked between the two of them. He scanned their faces, looking for chinks in their armour, looking into the backs of their eyes for anything he could exploit or deride. He sat back in his chair and looked over their heads at the wall. Temple watched him, looking for any sign or gesture of surrender. The bullish attitude Sloper had when he approached them was turning into something else.

Sloper's hand moved for his mobile on the table. Surely after all he'd heard, Sloper wouldn't ring Harker? If he did, Temple knew his gamble wouldn't pay off. As Temple watched him, he'd almost stopped breathing. Then he started to see darkened marks appearing through the cheap suit under Sloper's armpits. He had a sweat on. Sloper believed every word. Temple kept the pressure on. It was like a high stakes game of poker.

'We have times, dates, faces, names. Now you know we've been in your house, Simon; we installed covert surveillance months ago. We know about the money and the drugs you've got stashed there. We've also been all over your phones. The investigation's nearly over now but there's a couple of things outstanding that we're going to give you an opportunity to help us with. Something so we can say that you've been helpful to us in our enquiries, as the other officers sweep up a couple of other characters. It might help you in mitigation.'

Sloper had turned very red by now, as if his blood pressure was pushing at its limits. He was having difficulty controlling himself. Beads of sweat had appeared on his top lip. His hand involuntarily wiped across his mouth to make the telltale signs of his discomfort disappear. His shoulders moved as his breath became quicker and more shallow. Temple thought he was on the verge of a heart attack. Eventually he spoke.

'What do you want?' There was no trace of contrition in Sloper's voice.

'You took some drugs and money from Gemma Harker's flat last week – correction, *your* flat. That's right, isn't it?'

'Go on.'

'We know you did. And Gemma's made a statement to that effect. She knew it was there, saw it herself and then, when she returned with two girls, it was gone. You see, your actions in taking the money and drugs set off a chain of events. The two girls who took refuge at Gemma's flat had to run when you took the money and drugs because they'd lost it. You know as well as I do what happens to people who lose drugs and money. You knew exactly what you were doing in taking it.

'Next we get a police report that one of the girls is missing. The girl with her has been reported missing from London. In addition to that, the people that have been pissed off by having their drugs and money stolen then kidnap a different girl from Gemma's flat in retaliation. So we've now got three girls, one of who's been kidnapped and two who are running in fear of their lives, possibly being held too. You caused all that.'

Sloper sat opposite, his eyes flicking downwards and back to Temple, taking in what was being said, trying to think ahead, think his way out. His heart was banging. How come he hadn't spotted them if they'd been watching him for months – how come he hadn't seen it?

It was true the Met were good, but as Sloper's mind sped over the deals he'd done, he couldn't believe he wouldn't have spotted something. And fucking Gemma, that bitch who he had kept out of the hands of dangerous pimps over the years, had opened her filthy mouth.

Temple was watching him and knew he had to continue to pile it on.

'We now have three vulnerable teenagers in the hands of ruthless dealers and we want them back. Whatever else you are out here to the scum you deal with, you're still a cop. We're giving you a chance to redeem yourself and get the girls back. We want them out of the way before the investigation goes any further. I particularly want the girl taken from Gemma's flat. You're going to make some phone calls and we're going to find them – alive.'

Temple's mobile rang; he could see it was Gary Lewis. He answered the call but before Lewis could utter a word, Temple stopped him.

'Wait,' he said into the phone. He looked directly at Sloper and muted the call. 'My colleagues sitting outside want to know – am I taking you in now or are you going to be cooperative?'

The last thing Sloper wanted was to be taken into custody. His best chance of getting himself out of this shit was on the outside.

'I'll make some phone calls,' he said. 'I'll help.'

'Wait,' Temple instructed Sloper.

Temple stood up, moved away from the table and continued his phone call with Gary Lewis, leaving Paul Wallace to supervise Sloper.

'What do you want, Gary?'

'The meet – be in the Greenbridge area and I'll ring you again.' Lewis then ended the call. Temple was left looking at his mobile. He knew he couldn't trust the bastard. He wouldn't know until later whether he was just pissing him around. He'd make sure Lewis was arrested as soon as they had the girls. He wouldn't be so arrogant in custody. He went back to Sloper.

'Start ringing,' he nodded at him.

* * *

With his hand fixed hard on Lordon's shoulder, the man followed at arm's length behind him as they walked through the streets of Swindon. Lordon had no thoughts of running; a bullet in the back was something he knew he wouldn't survive. He might, however, survive if he could just reunite this angry man with Katya. He didn't care about losing her – there were plenty more to recruit out there. He just didn't want this kind of trouble. The sooner this was resolved the better. He could then resume business as usual. That was the most important thing.

They walked in silence in the dark until Lordon reached the address where he had sent Katya with the drugs. Another nondescript low-rent Victorian terrace, it had been used as a trap house in the past and had been passed on to another 'set'. Lordon approached the door and, looking down at his feet, he banged on it with his fist. The door was opened.

Before anyone knew what was happening, the man thrust Lordon forward with all his might, using him as a battering ram to force both of them in through the door. The momentum of the action pushed the door wide open and the man behind it fell to the floor. The man maintained his grip on Lordon, his hand now tightly around the back of his neck like a vice. In his other hand was his gun, the barrel of which was now against Lordon's temple.

'Stay down!' The man kicked at the legs of the guy scrambling on the floor trying to get to his feet, his angry, loud command adding to the confusion of the sudden intrusion. The guy stayed on his knees, sliding along the hallway on the laminate flooring, briefly looking up and seeing a quiet Lordon with a gun held to his head.

They all burst through a door into a living room at the end of the narrow passage, the man on the floor scrabbling through on all fours. The gunman stood still, his thick body filling the door frame with Lordon standing in front of him, the gun barrel pressed hard into the skin on the side of his head. He looked at the startled men in the small room. There were two sitting on a settee looking up at them and one standing. They had initially jumped when the intruders burst in and were all now stock-still, all eyes on the man with the gun. The man who was knocked to the floor at the front door slid across the room, his back against the wall.

'You tell me where Katya is or I spray his brains all over you.' The gunman looked around at the startled men. 'And then I'll spray your brains all over him.' He gestured to the man on the floor. They were silent and still, their eyes fixed on Lordon and the gun. Lordon spoke.

'I sent a girl here. Her name was Katya, she had a delivery. We just want to know where she is. This man has come to collect her.' Lordon was trying to stay as calm as possible. He spoke slowly and clearly.

As he finished, a noise came from a room beyond. It was the sound of a toilet flushing. Still no one moved in the room as they all seemed to be waiting for something. After twenty long seconds, the door opened, Katya walked through and froze at the sight that greeted her.

‘Come here, Katya.’ The man spoke softly, still pressing the gun into the side of Lordon’s head. Lordon felt the pressure of the barrel increase and spoke quietly.

‘Just everyone be calm, be calm. No one move. Katya, come over here, let me swap places with you.’

‘Come here, Katya, we’re going home.’ The man’s softly spoken voice was at odds with the gun he was holding. Katya held drugs in her hand and, not taking her eyes off the gun, she put them on a low table in the room. She moved slowly and walked towards the man with the gun. She didn’t know him but she knew he’d been sent for her. She stood next to Lordon. Suddenly the man pushed Lordon away. He fell into the room and into another man who had been standing stock-still. With Katya in his grip, the man turned on them.

‘You scumbags. You filthy pieces of shit. You think I’m going to let you go? You think this is over?’

He released a shot, which embedded into the wall opposite. The noise in the confines of the small room stunned them and had them involuntarily ducking their heads and falling to the floor. Screams were heard from a room above. He let another shot go into the room, which he aimed at another wall.

‘I know every one of your faces. I will come back and you will all pay with your lives for this.’

Now conscious of movements behind him coming down the stairs, the man took Katya by the arm and turned. Suddenly, at the bottom of the stairs were two girls. As soon as China and Megon saw the man with the gun in his hand, they screamed. He looked at them. Two terrified scrag ends in cheap tracksuits. With him and Katya barring their entrance into the living room, their only alternative was back up the stairs or out the front door.

‘Go, get out,’ he barked at them, flicking his head towards the front door. Looking at one another for a second, both took the opportunity being given to them and ran out into the dark of the night.

CHAPTER 34

Brian Porten walked down Fleming Way in Swindon. The darkness of the street at night was diluted by the street lights and bright headlights from the cars going by. He walked along the pavement, facing towards the oncoming cars, his shoulders hunched up. He was going towards the centre of town. He knew what he had to do tonight; he couldn't go back empty-handed. There should be enough litter around the streets to keep him occupied. He felt the chill of the wind when it blew into his face so he made sure his coat collar was turned up and pulled his cap down, firmly fixing it onto his head.

He hummed to himself as he walked, no distinct tune, just a low hum to keep himself company in his head. The streets were becoming all too familiar to him; he knew all the little side streets, the alleyways, little dead ends, the building recesses the sleepers used to keep themselves sheltered. Just as litter swept along by the wind gathered in crevices, so did they.

He looked at the grey hue of the buildings and their outline in the skyline in the semi-darkness. They didn't look too much better in the light, he concluded. It was all stark, boxy, drearily utilitarian and concrete. As he walked, from his pocket he took out his handkerchief and wiped it across his mouth. Returning it to his pocket, he kept it in his hand, his fingers keeping the feel of the cotton cloth against his skin. It soothed him; like a baby with a comforter, he needed to have the cotton material close to hand. It helped him to keep clean; the very fact that it was white made him feel clean.

The people that he looked upon had no cleanliness. Their filthy appearance was something that constantly needled him. He wondered how they didn't smell their own and each other's stench. Perhaps it was only the clean that could smell their engrained body odour and piss-stinking clothing.

Soon he was where he wanted to be. He could see them. He slowed down, his step becoming more relaxed, his stride less urgent. He couldn't see their faces; they were wrapped up against the cold with all manner of hats, balaclavas and woollen scarves around their heads. They wore old military-type coats or puffa-style jackets to keep warm, along with their blankets and duvets.

He walked slowly now, his eyes taking in the numbers of them, how they looked, what they were drinking, whether they were talkative or part-comatose already. Some were invisible; they had already made their beds for the night and were under a pile of blankets, faced away into doorways, the world shut out. He wouldn't disturb the sleeping; he didn't know how they would react to being suddenly woken, and besides which, they might pull a knife on him or be way too drowsy to understand what he was saying to them anyway.

Just around the corner, away from the main area and sitting in a door recess, was a man, alone. He had a woollen hat pulled down on his head and at the sight of him, Porten knew he had all the information he needed. He had to be in his early to late sixties, the long, wiry hair coming out of the beanie hat he wore was an indication of the length of time he'd spent on the streets.

As did his profuse facial hair; his fringe, beard and eyebrows created almost a natural home-grown balaclava, with his thick, purple nose the only unprotected protrusion. The man wore matted gloves with his fingers coming through the ends. His boots were worn and scuffed and he was wearing a threadbare green parka. His legs were pulled up and he was rubbing his hands and rocking his body in little sideways movements to keep out the cold. Yes, he would do.

Observing him, Brian took out his handkerchief and wiped it slowly across his mouth, feeling the soft cotton against his lips. He approached the man, standing over him as he spoke.

'You look cold, mate,' he said in a gentle voice. He waited to see if the man would respond. He replied, but not immediately.

'It's getting in my bones tonight,' the man replied in muffled tones. 'This helps though.' He pulled out a small bottle of cheap vodka from the inside of his coat.

'Yes, that will do it. Something nice to keep the cold out. Take a good swig of that and you'll have a fire inside.'

The man did exactly as suggested and put the bottle up to his mouth. Porten watched the man tilt his head back. As he emptied the liquid into his mouth, he saw him gulp. The liquid poured over the man's Adam's apple like a waterfall over a fixed rock. Having quenched his thirst, he sat the bottle back in his lap. A minute or so later, Porten encouraged him to take another, deeper swig. If he was coming with him, he didn't want him talking or seeing where he was being taken.

He seemed fairly pliable. Porten continued with the small talk and, little by little, found the man engaged with him. They chatted tentatively at first but gradually Porten made sure his conversation fell in with the man's and was agreeable.

It was all lip service on Brian Porten's part; he didn't care what circumstances had brought this man to the streets so he didn't enquire. He didn't care to ask when was the last time the man before him on the pavement had actually sat in a room, in a chair, with a fire, food on the table, listening to music playing. Simple, basic pleasures that were denied to the man in front of him. No, Porten didn't care. The man was sitting in the street creating a mess. He was an eyesore. He had to go.

'If you want a bed for the night and some more vodka, I can offer you one. It's not much mind you but it's better than sleeping in this doorway and it'll be much warmer. A lot more comfortable. And don't worry about me, I'll just drop you off and then I'll be gone.'

The man looked up; they'd found some common ground in the small amount of time they'd been speaking. He knew he had to be careful but he was tired and so cold that he was numb. He'd only spent six months on the streets but he'd learned a lot in that time. He'd had to learn who to trust, where he could sleep and where he couldn't, where he could find the cheapest booze, free blankets and clothing.

He hadn't always been homeless; he'd had a good job and a nice rental. He'd passed people like him on the streets himself then. He'd been employed, had a salary paid into the bank every month and then suddenly redundancy hit and it was all gone. There was no money for the rent.

He hadn't given street sleepers the time of day, not one kind word, not one penny when he was earning. Yet here was this man, a complete stranger, out late at night like a kind Samaritan offering a place to stay, a warm place with some vodka. It was too good an offer to refuse.

After the man had drunk some more vodka, Porten helped him to his feet. He was stiff with the cold and a little slow, so Porten walked along by his side as he shuffled along. Not talking much, he walked the man slowly to his car. There was no CCTV here in this side street and so neither of them would be seen as they walked alongside one another.

Porten followed the same well-used plan. As he drove out of Swindon away from street lighting, the landscape became darkened. The only light came from car headlights of the oncoming traffic. The dark also helped to disorientate; Porten navigated a few bending and winding roads that gave no indication of location and before long, his passenger had no idea where he was or where they were heading to.

The sudden warmth and the vodka worked together, and for the first time, the man began to thaw. He was quickly rendered sleepy as the car heater blasted out. Porten checked him at intervals, looking across, watching his head nod with the bumps and turns in the road until, not long after the journey had started, a deep snore sounded.

By the time he pulled up at the abattoir, the man was in a deep slumber with his head hanging forward and his bristly chin resting heavily on his chest. Porten turned off the engine and waited to see if the lack of motion and noise of the car jolted the man awake, but he was snoring loudly. Porten was relieved to get out; the heat in the car had made the smell of the man cook and he took deep breaths of the cold air. He unlocked a side door of the abattoir and ensuring that everything was ready and in its place, went to fetch the man. He could see him still sitting in the passenger seat.

He went back to the car and opened the passenger door. The man was sleeping so deeply he was oblivious to what was going on around him. This was always a tricky moment, waking someone from a deep sleep, but it had to be done. The man woke easily enough; he was groggy and disorientated so Porten guided him towards the side door, and once through, sat him on a chair. Before the man could shake himself awake to register what was happening, Porten applied the pistol to the side of his head and fired. He was gone.

Porten manoeuvred the dead man into his large freezer room. Then he left, driving back to Swindon. To get another.

CHAPTER 35

Amy Davidson was sick of waiting on everyone else. She'd reported her friend China missing days ago and no one was doing a thing to find her. She'd also rowed with her parents last night as they no longer wanted her to see China, telling her that China was no longer welcome and if she showed up as she generally did, that she could no longer stay over. Her friendship had brought trouble with China's brother visiting them and threatening them, and trouble with the police. The family was no good. Enough was enough.

Truth was, Amy's parents were frightened for their own daughter's safety in her association with the sister of a known drug dealer. They didn't want her mixed up in that world and if China was no longer on the scene, no longer invited in and to stay over as she had been, then all this trouble would go away.

China was a nice enough girl; she was respectful and caring when she stayed with them and Linda Davidson liked and felt sorry for her, knowing what sort of background she had. Amy hadn't let her parents know the extent of her knowledge about China and her family. If she had, she knew they would have stopped her from seeing China years ago, never mind having her stay over. But it was because of the things Amy knew about her that she felt she had to look out for her and look after her. She knew all about China's brother Gary Lewis and her useless mother. The pair of them were evil.

China's mother Barbara did nothing but live for drink. She didn't care what happened to China and Amy hated her for it. Her mother neglected her so that she didn't eat properly and was malnourished. She stole clothes from shops because her mother was too drunk to register she'd grown out of the ones she had or that they'd simply become worn out from wear. China was thin, small and looked younger than she was, and so was a perfect drugs mule.

Long before that, when he was only a boy himself Gary would deal in drugs and use China to deliver them around the town. He would send the shy seven-year-old China with packets of heroin into homes and to street corners and alleyways to the desperate, who waited for her like she was their lifeline. He'd sent her into these contaminated places full of crack heads and their dangerous hallucinogenic minds without a thought for her safety. Most were so pleased to see her that they were kind to her, but some were not.

As China grew older, her brother made her go further than the streets of Swindon and she found herself on trains or being taken in cars to different towns where she would go and make her deliveries. She'd had to carry the drugs inside her using condoms in case she was stopped by police.

When she was older, China confided in Amy about the men that Gary Lewis would take to the house. He would take money off them and wait in the kitchen as they went up to China in her bedroom for sex when she was only twelve. When China told Amy of these things, it made her so angry.

China was assigned a social worker but she hardly saw them from one year to the next and even when one did visit, they were different to the last. On these occasions, Gary Lewis made sure the house was unusually clear of the vodka bottles and they just managed to put on enough of a show to warrant a sufficiently good report to keep social services from being too frequent visitors.

No one, it seemed, could see what was going on. Amy couldn't tell her parents because she guessed rightly that they would put a stop to China coming round and that was the last thing Amy wanted. There wasn't any teacher at school that could be confided in, and if she did tell anyone, that might end with China being taken into care and being sent miles away to keep her from her family. She didn't want that either. They decided that when they were old enough to leave school and get jobs, they would get a flat together and then she could be away from her mother and her brother. They would live like sisters, like they did when she stayed over. They could lock them all out then and China would be safe.

The only person China could rely on was Amy and now Amy had waited long enough. She had told the police and they said they were doing something, but she wasn't sure what. It couldn't be much because China still hadn't returned. Amy was beginning to think it was down to her to go out and find China; she had to take matters into her own hands as she felt she would instinctively know where her friend was if she just got out there and started looking. Yes, she would go out and find China herself.

It was nearly 10 p.m. and from her bedroom, she could hear the television in the sitting room downstairs. Her parents thought she was in bed but she was now dressed in her jeans, jumper and a short faux-leather jacket. She was tying her trainers on and thinking about the best way to get out of the house unnoticed. She decided to go out through her bedroom window, which led onto a garage roof, and from there ease herself off onto the top of a wheelie bin.

She had done this a few times with China when they had wanted to go out late and unnoticed. She made her bed look as though she was sleeping in it by moulding her duvet cover into a body-shaped mound in case either of her parents looked in on her. It looked convincing enough in the dark of her room.

She then opened the double-glazed window and slipped out onto the ledge. She pushed the window closed before easing down onto the flat roof of the garage, being careful not to thump down onto it. She looked around for any neighbours watching her and crept across the roof to where the wheelie bin was situated. She sat on the edge of the roof. She was still and listened out for anyone moving inside. Then she jumped down onto the top of the bin.

Silently, she ran down the residential street until she reached the end and then with her heart beating, she put her hands in her jacket pockets and slowed to a brisk walk. She was going to find her friend. Just being out in the darkness of the night, she already felt an affinity with China and almost knew she would see her that night. She would go to their usual haunts, the town centre, near some pubs and clubs. When she found her, she would take her back to her bedroom. It was no use relying on anyone else to find her.

CHAPTER 36

Paul Wallace studied Sloper as he sat across the table. They were still in the pub, which was now filling up with payday revellers. There was a group dressed up in Halloween costumes standing at the bar and the place was becoming noisy. Sloper was looking intently at his phone as his thumbs punched out a text message.

Paul wasn't exactly sure what was going on between Sloper and Temple; all Temple had said was that he wanted Sloper to think that Wallace was a detective working out of London and told him what to do and say if Sloper asked for any ID which, thankfully, so far he hadn't. He was so far out of his depth but he knew he was doing this for Megon. Somehow Paul knew he just had to keep up the mien of how a hard-nosed surveillance detective would be, but he was finding it difficult faced with Sloper in Temple's temporary absence while he went to the toilet.

Paul saw the beads of sweat that continued to appear on Sloper's forehead and top lip, and watched as he wiped them away with the back of his hand. Sloper's shirt buttons were also straining against his bulk and as he sat with sweat pooling on a ledge under his chest, wet patches formed on the tight material as it stretched across his stomach.

Sloper finished with his mobile and looked across to Paul.

'So, who's overseeing this investigation in force?' asked Sloper.

Paul kept his best poker face while his mind ran through a list of possibilities. He wasn't familiar with policing ranks and there was only one he could think of. He hoped Temple would appear soon.

'The chief, the chief constable.' He could see Sloper was trying to weigh up his options and the significance of what he had said. He must have said the right thing.

'What exactly started the enquiry?'

Paul was relieved to see Temple coming towards him.

'I'm not going to discuss the case with you any further,' he said. 'There's still a lot we need to do, like finding the girls. I think you need to concentrate on that.'

'Have I missed anything?' Temple looked across at Paul, who shook his head. 'What news have you got for me then, Si?'

'My sources say the girls were at a house in Swindon but they've gone. They've done a runner.'

'What house in Swindon? You better get back onto your sources and find out where they've gone.'

Temple's phone rang. It was Gary Lewis.

'We have a change in venue for the meet,' he informed Temple. 'Be at the twenty-four-hour Tesco, in the car park, far end.' Temple knew he was likely to receive a call changing the venue and that this might be one of many calls until they eventually met, as Lewis would be wary of allowing Temple to set an operation to trap him.

'You got the girls?' asked Temple.

'We've got the girls if you've got the money.'

'All three of them?'

'All three of them.'

'What are their names?'

'I don't know the others but there's obviously China.'

He felt sure Lewis was lying to him. 'Tell me the other girls' names before we meet; I want to know that you've got them.'

'I'll text you. Just be there with the money.'

Temple looked between the phone in his hand and Sloper. He couldn't tell who was lying to him – Sloper or Gary Lewis – but one of them was. He was conscious of the money he had in his coat. If he met Lewis, there was every likelihood that he would be set up and mugged for the money. But what if Lewis did have them? He could be so close to getting them back. But why would Lewis be reluctant to name the girls if they were with him? It would be easy enough. Temple had to face it; it probably meant Lewis didn't have them. And now Sloper was telling him the girls had run. His plan was falling apart.

They had to get out of the pub; it was too noisy, he needed to think. And he hadn't finished with Sloper. Temple stood up.

'Come on, we're going.'

* * *

Across the road, the three of them sat in Temple's car. With Paul Wallace sitting beside him, turning around in the driver's seat, Temple continued his questioning of Sloper who was in the back.

'So what are your contacts saying then? Where are they?'

'The person I was talking to said that the two girls had run out of the house where they were.'

'I'm after three girls. China Lewis – who I think you'll know – a friend of hers, Megon, and another girl, whose name is Prayer, taken from Gemma's flat in retaliation for your actions. Who took Prayer from Gemma's flat?'

Sitting in the back of the car, Sloper was tightly contained. Taking him out of the arena of the pub and into the intimate and close confines of the car had been a good move. It was as if everything was suddenly condensed and Temple was able to see that Sloper knew much more than he was saying.

Sloper continued to work out how he could get out of his predicament. Sitting in the back of the car, he suddenly had a plan he could try if all else failed. Temple repeated his question.

'Well, who took Prayer from Gemma's flat?'

Sloper looked back at them. 'Look, the girl's sick.'

'What? What do you mean by that?' asked Temple.

Concerned for Megon, Paul Wallace turned to question Sloper then. 'What girl are you talking about?' Temple flicked Wallace a look of caution. His plan was hanging by a thread; the last thing he needed right now was Wallace to be exposed as the imposter he was.

'She's not well apparently. They knew I took the money so they went round to the flat. They were going to take Gemma. When they saw she had a visitor, a young girl, they took her instead. The girl Prayer, she's ill.'

CHAPTER 37

Amy Davidson reached the centre of town. In the run-up to Halloween, it was busy with revellers in and out of costume. Amy was trying to remember anything that China had told her in the past of where she went when she stayed out. There had been so many stories, so many things she had told her over the years. She could be anywhere; she might not even be in Swindon. But Amy felt she was more useful out here, looking for her friend than sitting in her bedroom waiting for someone else to do something.

She went towards a street vendor, the sweet smell of frying onions drawing her there as it might draw China, she thought. There were a number of people around the white van who were either eating or ordering. None of them looked familiar and none of them stopped to notice her.

People were spilling out of the pubs and there were so many of them that it made it difficult for her to look around. As she walked on, she looked through the crowds, trying to see if China was amongst them. She tried to recall anything that China had told her – didn't she say she used to hang around just outside the Brunel Centre? She couldn't remember, but now she made her way there.

She kept looking, her eyes following any girl that remotely resembled her friend with her white-blonde hair. She kept walking. She knew it would be darker around the Brunel Centre but she had to go there. She was sure that China went there.

Amy was there now, under the part-glass roof, following the buildings right round until she had the glass walkway in her sights. She could see small groups of people huddled together on benches or hunched down in shop doorways. Her pace slowed as she approached them, looking at them quickly before going onto the next. Every small pocket of sheltered spots seemed to have someone in them.

Suddenly, only yards away from her, she saw a bob of white-blonde hair duck out by the side of another figure. Then she was gone, hidden behind a column of darkness. Was it China, was it her? It was her – Amy knew it was. She practically skipped over to where she could see two figures hunched down. It was her. It was China. She half shouted her name.

'China! Oh my God, where have you been?' She was overjoyed at seeing her again. Amy's arms were outstretched as she threw herself at her friend. China was momentarily shocked to see her and also concerned that her noisy greeting would draw attention to them.

'Amy, what are you doing here?' China whispered, enveloped in her friend's arms but looking over her shoulder to see if anyone had taken any notice of them.

'I've come out looking for you. I rang the police but they haven't done anything. You've been missing for days and I was worried sick.' Amy was looking at China all the time she spoke, taking in her appearance, how she behaved. 'Are you all right?'

'We got caught up in some shit, didn't we, Megs. This is Megon. She's from London, she's been with me. We've been caught up in stuff and it went wrong.' China had wrestled herself from Amy to put her arm protectively around Megon. 'She's had a hard time; it was awful for her.'

Amy felt a stab of jealousy seeing China being so protective of Megon. She'd come out into the night to find her and she seemed more concerned about another girl. They were normally so close and it was the first time she had seen China caring for anyone but her. Just in those first few moments she could see there was a bond between China and Megon.

'We managed to run tonight but there was a man with a gun, so they'll be after us. There's no police about so we're just keeping down until the morning.'

'What do you mean there's a man with a *gun*? What man? Where have you been?'

'We were being held. It all went wrong. We trusted someone and we shouldn't have. It's all right, Megs, I know Gemma Harker. I'll get her back for this, the bitch. We got set up. We were robbed; she took our money. We trusted her and she robbed us.' Megon just sat staring ahead as China spoke.

'Come back to mine, I've come to take you back.' Amy eyed Megon, not sure that she wanted to extend the invitation to her too, but she could see that China was comforting her and wouldn't let her go. Reluctantly she said, 'Megon can come too.'

'But what will your mum say?'

'They're asleep. We'll go in over the garage roof; they won't even know that we're in until the morning.'

China immediately warmed to the plan. Amy's bedroom was a safe haven compared to a recess in the Brunel Centre at this time of night; it would get them off the streets until the morning and it would be safer with the three of them walking back.

'Come on, Megs, we're going back to Amy's.'

Megon had no wish to go back to someone else's home; she wanted to go back to her own. She felt frail and her mind had already started to block out the things that had happened to her. It was a coping mechanism to trauma that she was glad of. All that mattered was that she was out of that room.

She was sick of being with strangers and people she didn't know and who didn't know her. She wanted her parents, her mum and dad; she wanted to be cared for. She'd trusted China before when she'd persuaded her to go back to Gemma's flat and that had all gone wrong. Here was another girl, another person China knew, offering them a bed for the night. How did she know she could trust *her*? Megon trusted China but this could be like Gemma all over again, another trap.

She knew her dad was on the streets of Swindon looking for her and she wanted to find him and go home with him. Without him, she couldn't see how she could be safe. He'd protect her all the way home. He'd keep her safe. At least out here she was free, not trapped in another house. No, she felt safer on the streets, where there was space to run and where her voice could be heard if she screamed for help. She didn't want to be trapped again. Not in another stranger's house, another bedroom.

'I'm going to look for my dad,' she said, extricating herself from China's arm. 'He was here looking for me and if I find him, I can go home. I have to go home.' China could see she was beaten.

'I'm not leaving you behind – we've got to stick together. They'll be looking for us. It's dark now; it'll be better in the daylight. You'll be safe at Amy's with me.'

'If we split up it might be better. You've got somewhere to go now and I can go home. If we're together, it's easy for them. At least if we're in different areas it'll make it harder for them to find us.' It took all she had to say it but she believed it; she'd be better off without China.

There was a certain logic to what Megon was saying, but China still didn't want to leave her friend behind. Megon wouldn't be persuaded; even Amy tried to get her to go with them but she was adamant that in the morning she would look for her dad and he would take her home. All she wanted was to see him and go home to her mum and sisters. After everything that had happened to her, that was all she wanted. And as she saw it, all that was between her and what she wanted was a few more hours of darkness.

CHAPTER 38

'So where is she, Si?' Temple was hanging off Sloper's every word. His mind was racing. He was trying to keep his emotions in check. He wanted to turn round and put his fist in Sloper's face. He wanted to ask him why he'd exploited rather than protected Gemma all these years. It could have been different. As Harker's friend, Sloper could have mediated between Gemma and Clive Harker, he could have brought them together, but instead he'd seen an opportunity to use her, use Clive Harker for his own ends. Temple kept thinking of her standing in his kitchen pleading with him: *'You're the only one who can help me.'*

During the hours he'd spent with Gemma that night, he'd been saddened by the waste. It wasn't just the loss of her once pretty face, it was also the life she had led; the waste of potential of the person she could have been. She had been set for better things; she had had such a bright future. She could and should have lived a very different life, been someone else other than who she currently was. Surely he could do this for her, bring Prayer back? He knew he had to do everything he could. He couldn't let her down again.

'Start the car. I'll take you there,' Sloper said.

Temple pulled away. As they drove to Sloper's instructions, Temple continued to question him.

'If you knew Prayer was ill, why didn't you get her help?'

'I was trying to find her on the night I saw you in Swindon. They rang me, told me they had taken her. Because they took her from my flat where Gemma lives, they thought I knew her.'

'They thought she was one of your street girls, didn't they? That's the bit you've left out. Because we know you run street girls, we've seen them. So what do you know about Prayer?'

'I've never seen her. All I know is that she was at Gemma's. Next thing I know, I get a call saying they've taken her. Later I get a call saying she's not well. They said she keeps having fits.'

Temple didn't recall Gemma saying anything about Prayer being ill or having fits. When they had both looked through her case at the flat, he hadn't seen any medication and Gemma hadn't mentioned any either. Temple's gut wrenched with the realisation. They must have drugged her and she'd had a bad reaction. She was fitting due to some shit they'd given her and they were panicking. He had to find her fast.

'Did they say if they'd given her anything to make her fit? Have they given her drugs, or that new synthetic shit Spice and the like they dole out now?'

'No, they said they hadn't touched her.'

Temple lost it. 'And how would you know? Why would you believe these pieces of shit? And who the fuck are "they"? Who are we talking about – who took Prayer?'

'I thought you said you had them under surveillance?' Sloper looked at Temple in the rear-view mirror. Temple knew he'd let his emotions get the better of him. The plan was hanging by a gossamer thread and he was jeopardising that. He had to think fast.

'We were watching *you*. Not this crew who took Prayer, or I wouldn't be asking you where she is. Who took her? Give me a name.'

'Names don't mean anything. These Eastern Europeans are all on a dozen or more aliases. They probably can't remember what their real names are, they've assumed so many different ones. You only know these people by their faces.' Sloper shot Paul Wallace a derisory look. 'You lot should know that. That's why they're so hard to track. They're very organised, not like our home-grown lot. The place is swarming with Eastern Bloc villains. They just take advantage of their freedom to come to the UK and they set up here.' As Sloper spoke, Temple watched him in his rear-view mirror. He was looking around, out of the windows.

He knew it wouldn't be long before Sloper would start to question the surveillance job and he knew he was going to struggle to keep up the pretence. They were in his own car, with no radio contact; Sloper would shortly start to look for signs that they were being followed, that they were part of a large operation. It was getting desperate and he didn't know how much longer he would get away with deceiving him.

'Just tell me where I'm going, what road I'm aiming for.' Temple wanted to know his destination as quickly as possible. If Sloper suddenly realised he'd been mugged and there was no surveillance operation, Temple knew he'd be left with nothing for his efforts. At least if he told him where he was going he'd have somewhere to start from.

Paul Wallace suddenly put his finger to his ear and started talking.

'Yes, just follow. The subject's taking us to the victim.' Temple looked across at him and they met each other's gaze. Watching Bond films had given Wallace the idea. Undercover operatives touched their ear before speaking into a covert button on their cuffs. Temple held his breath. This surely had to be it, Sloper would suss them; it had been a desperate effort that was just about to fail. Then Sloper spoke, giving Temple directions to Penhill. Temple drove on. He hadn't suspected. When they arrived at their destination, Sloper finally directed him to pull over.

'Where is she?' Temple looked down the dimly lit street with a mixture of terraced houses and flats.

'You'll find her at number thirty-six.'

They were parked some hundred yards away from that address. Temple got out alone, telling Paul Wallace to keep Sloper in the car. As he walked, he made a quick call to DS Sam Mendoza, as he knew he would need him for backup if Prayer was there. It was fairly quiet in the street at that time of night, with no traffic and just the faint noise of music and televisions from inside the houses. His heart pounded as he walked and he felt tense. How reliable was Sloper's source? What if she wasn't there? The thought of Prayer being kept against her will and being drugged sickened him but at the same time sent a surge of anger through him so strong that he could think with perfect clarity.

Temple found the house and banged on the door. From inside he heard footsteps on a hard floor coming towards him. He was within inches of whoever was behind the door and could sense them put their hand on the latch to open it. Just before they did, they called out.

'Who is it, man?' a voice with a foreign accent asked. Temple replied in a low voice.

'It's me, man, let me in.' Without waiting for a reply, Temple took a step back and, sizing up the door and with his anger driving him on, he drew his knee up and used his foot as a battering ram against it. He kicked at it again. The door started to give way but not completely. He followed it up with a shoulder barge and the door opened. As he went through with his own momentum, the sudden opening of the door startled the person behind it. Temple turned and grabbed a young, wiry-looking male, pinning him to the wall.

'I've come for the girl, where is she?' The man looked back at him and tried to resist. 'Don't fuck me about. The girl is ill, where is she?' he shouted. He badly wanted to hurt the man. He again pushed him back hard against the wall and drew satisfaction that the back of the man's head hit the wall with an eye-popping thud. It must have registered Temple's intent that he would stop at nothing. The man caved.

'Upstairs,' he spat.

Temple pulled the man towards him, then pushed him up a steep stairway. With his head still ringing, he offered little resistance but Temple gripped the stair rail as he was wary of being kicked back down. When they got to the top of the tiny square landing with two rooms either side, the man went left into a bedroom and Temple followed.

Curled up on a mattress on the floor with her back to him lay a girl. Just as Temple caught sight of her, there was a commotion downstairs. He went back out onto the landing with the man. DS Mendoza appeared at the bottom of the stairs along with a uniformed constable.

'Take hold of this one, Sam. There might be some more out the back.' Temple pushed the man towards the stairs, resisting an urge to kick him as he went, slowly making his way down towards Mendoza who waited at the bottom. Temple went back into the bedroom and turned his attention to the girl on the mattress. He crouched down by her side. The mattress was on bare boards and it was filthy.

Wearing jeans and a jumper, the girl was on her side, lying with her back to him, stock-still. He could just make out that her eyes were open, staring ahead of her. He said her name and she responded. She had been here for days and now someone was saying her name. No one here knew her name.

'Who are you? How do you know my name?' she demanded, immediately turning round. Her dark hair fell away from her shoulders as she moved and propped herself up on one elbow. He could see the resemblance to both Gemma and his mother in her. The combination of all of them making up the girl in front of him suddenly struck him.

He saw her eyes and read her instincts – she was ready to fight, she was just working out what she had to do. He had to check himself not to take her in his arms but she had no idea who he was at that moment. The only thing he could think of was to reassure her the best way he could.

'I'm Detective Inspector Temple. I'm a police officer and I've come to take you home.'

CHAPTER 39

Temple was prepared for the worst; his mind had been working overtime as he knew how young girls were treated in these situations. They were beaten, plied with alcohol and drugs and raped into submission by their captors and sometimes tortured to send a message to those who slighted them.

In some cases, they were killed; murdered as an example to all. Sloper had told him she was sick, that she was fitting. Temple looked around the room. There was no evidence of the usual drug paraphernalia. From the quick look Temple had of her, Prayer didn't even look ill. In fact, as he continued to assess her and the surroundings, there was nothing to suggest that this was someone who was sick from a drug overdose.

'Prayer, I've been told that you're ill. Do you need me to call an ambulance for you?'

'I'm not ill,' she said simply and as if she was a bit put out. 'I did it to scare them and to make sure they left me alone. And it worked.' As she spoke, she sat up facing him.

'*What* worked? What did you do?'

'I pretended to have an epileptic fit every time they came near me. I'm not stupid. I'm lying on a mattress, I'm a girl in a house full of men, so I knew what was coming next.' She said all of this matter-of-factly. His fears that this experience would have badly affected her seemed unfounded at the moment as she gave the distinct impression of being no more than indignant and seriously pissed off.

'Have they hurt you in any way? Did they hurt you when they took you or since you've been here?'

'No. I read the newspapers. I've read about girls in these situations. It's horrible what they have done to them. I decided a while ago that trying to repel men in that sort of situation might help, so I decided to pretend I was fitting. I scared *them*,' she said with some satisfaction.

Temple had sat down on the floor next to her. He watched her as she spoke, taking in how she looked and what she sounded like, trying to gauge if she was in shock or hiding anything. Her attitude dumbfounded him. She was calm and well spoken; her voice was level as though she was talking him through her latest school project.

There was a confidence in her that made her seem different from other teenagers he'd experienced. Despite never meeting her before, he felt an immediate connection to her. He wondered if he would have felt it if Gemma hadn't told him she was his daughter.

'OK, I was a bit scared but I think my survival instincts must have kicked in or something, adrenalin, I don't know. Their stupid Halloween masks frightened me a bit at first, but I think that was more for Gemma's benefit.' She looked up to his face. 'Gemma's my birth mother. I was with her when they came into her flat and brought me here.'

'I know. I've seen Gemma, she's very worried for you – we all were.' He'd been so tense and so sure that this was going to have a bad ending that he couldn't believe the composure of the girl in front of him. 'I'm going to call Gemma now and tell her that we've found you. Look, I'm sorry that this has happened to you, but this could have had a very different outcome.' She nodded silently and gave him a slight smile. The relief flooded through him. She was going to be all right.

'That was a pretty smart thing you did, and it probably saved you from God knows what – well, it seems you know what it saved you from. Come on, let's get you out of here. Put your shoes on.'

He admired her presence of mind to deal with the situation in the way she had. He was finding it difficult not to put his arms around her and draw her to him. He felt ridiculously proud of her; she had been held here for over forty-eight hours and she'd held her own, she'd come through relatively unscathed against these bastards. He thought of her parents and said a silent 'thank you' to them for the way she had been brought up. She might have his genes, but he knew he could claim no credit for this remarkable girl.

'I did drama at school, which I was pretty good at. Who'd have thought it would come to such good use.'

Temple helped her up. She was nearly as tall as him with her shoes on. They went downstairs where Mendoza had been joined by a few more uniformed colleagues who were handcuffing and arresting three males. Prayer identified her abductors amongst them.

While they were still in the house, Temple called Gemma and told her Prayer was safe. She demanded to know where he was and despite him trying to persuade her otherwise, she immediately made the short journey by car to collect her. He knew he had to keep Gemma on side and so had acquiesced to her, but he had to keep her away from Sloper – and Mendoza and the other officers for that matter if Gemma was to keep Prayer's existence from her father. They would need to take a statement from Prayer later, but for now he knew that some food and a bath was probably what she wanted. When Gemma pulled up outside in the middle of the road, Temple went to her, leaving Prayer inside. He had to restrain her from rushing to Prayer.

'Stay here. Don't go in the house, there are police officers in there – they'll know you and they'll put two and two together. She's fine, Prayer's fine. I'll fetch her. If you want Clive to have no knowledge of Prayer, you have to stay here. I've already told the DS that she was visiting you and that she comes from the Midlands.'

Her face was tense. 'Are you sure she's all right? I need to see her.'

'Yes, she's fine. I'll get her now and then I want you both out of here.' Conscious of the close proximity of Sloper in his car further down the road, Temple wanted Gemma and Prayer away as fast as possible, but he also needed to contain them and keep them safe. He knew Gemma wouldn't go to a police station, and not wanting them to go back to her flat, Temple told Gemma to go back to his house. It was far from ideal, especially with Ben there, but Temple would be back with them possibly within a couple of hours.

'And, Gem, don't tell her about me. All that can wait. After we've taken a statement, we need to get her back to her parents. There'll be a lot of explaining to do. I've woken Ana and she'll be waiting for you. I'll see you when I've finished up here.'

As soon as she saw her, Gemma's relief was evident as she drew Prayer into a tearful hug, wrapping her arms around her. Temple ushered them both into Gemma's car and reminded her again to meet Ana at the cottage. When they left, Temple went back inside where he was met by Mendoza.

'Do you want to tell me why the victim has gone off with Gemma Harker?'

'She was in Gemma's flat when she was abducted; wrong place, wrong time. They went there for Gemma and took her instead. They're both witnesses. We'll take statements in the morning. The girl's assured me that nothing's happened to her. As I told you, she lives in the Midlands. She pretended that she was fitting upstairs which scared them and meant they kept their distance from her.' Temple hoped to divert Mendoza's attention from making any connection between Gemma and Prayer.

'Smart kid.' Mendoza said he would arrange a video interview for Prayer in the morning, but Temple cut in.

'I'll take the statement from her.'

'Not wishing to state the bleeding obvious, but you're suspended from duty. I know I said I'd help you with Sloper, but I had no idea it would lead to all this and nicking people for human trafficking. I've got three slimy bastards on their way to custody when all I came out to do was sit in a pub to give you some cover. What's going on with Sloper?'

'Sloper's caught up in all this. I found drugs and money at his home that he'd robbed from dealers when he found it in his flat. Gemma Harker lives in Sloper's flat. The girl we've rescued just got caught in the crossfire of him trying to give these bastards a lesson. Sloper's up to his neck in all this. I'd let you have him to take into custody but there are two other girls that he might be able to help us find. The guy with us in the pub is a father desperate to find his daughter and Sloper might just be useful. I've told Sloper that you're part of the job we're doing on him but he's going to suss us pretty soon, if he hasn't already, so I haven't got long, an hour tops, probably less.'

'Where's the drugs and money?' Mendoza asked.

Temple was grateful for his colleague's help but he couldn't allow himself to trust Mendoza, even though he wanted to. He wanted to hand Sloper over to Mendoza, along with the money he had hidden in his coat and the photos he had taken of the drugs and money in situ at Sloper's house. He could hand it all over and drive off and help Paul find Megon. But what if it all went missing? What if Sloper made some phone calls when he got to custody and it all suddenly somehow disappeared? He couldn't risk it. Along with Gemma, he had all the evidence that he needed to ensure that there was no way out for Sloper.

Rumours had always circulated about Sloper, about him being bent, but with the help of Clive Harker, he had always managed to shrug them off. There'd always been a bad smell about him, but because of his association with Harker, and because Harker had always been held in high regard, the rot never seemed to be exposed. With Harker as top cover and with Sloper deceiving him with regards to Gemma, Sloper had enjoyed carte blanche in Swindon. Even with everything he had, Temple couldn't risk that happening again.

With Gemma on her way back to the cottage with Prayer, he knew he needed to keep everything close, he knew he had to keep control of it all. If he could only find China Lewis and Megon to confirm Gemma's side of the story, he could wrap it up.

Temple knew he owed Mendoza an explanation. 'I know where it is and I'll keep it that way until I can find these two girls. Then I'll bring Sloper in. I've got everything recorded on this.' He held up his phone.

At that moment, Temple's phone signalled an incoming text. He looked at it. It was from Amy Davidson. 'I've found China.'

CHAPTER 40

Locked arm in arm, Amy and China turned in to the road where she lived. They were keeping each other warm against the cold of the night. Amy was glad to have her friend back and had been telling China of her encounters with the police. In the end, she had been the one that had found China, not the police with all their interview suites and partnerships with social workers and protocols for this and that.

She had had to go out onto the streets and do what she had asked to be done when she reported China missing. She went out looking for her and she'd found her. That's all she had asked of the police, and yet it had taken *her* to do their work for them. Pleased with herself, Amy had sent a text to Temple. She didn't need his help anymore.

As they walked back to Amy's, the friends vowed to each other never to break contact again. China said that she would always let her friend know where she was in future. It was because they were talking they didn't see the car in the darkness.

As he watched them approach, Gary Lewis sprang out of the driver's seat and appeared in front of them. They both stopped when they saw him but it was too late. He had the back door of the car open.

‘Get in,’ he ordered, his voice with its usual menacing tone.

‘Fuck off,’ Amy instinctively replied, her shrill voice ringing out in the quietness of the night. She was nearest to him, her arm locked tightly with China’s. They were a hundred yards away from her front door and she was determined to get there.

‘Shut your fucking mouth, bitch, and get in the car,’ he hissed as he put his face against hers, their cheeks touching. She went to pull her head away in disgust but he clamped his hand around the back of her neck. Her arm tightened around China’s. ‘Now, get in.’ His voice was loaded with threat. China had already started to push Amy towards the open door of the car.

‘No, we’re nearly home, we’ll get my dad.’ Amy was resisting the push from China to get into the car.

‘I know where your family live, Amy. If you don’t get in this car now I will set fire to your house. I’ll set fire to it with your mum and dad asleep in it. They won’t get out and it’ll be all because you didn’t do as you were told. I’ll do that to teach you a lesson. Now, get in the car.’

China pushed her from behind and they both fell into the back of the car. Lewis shut the door behind them and got into the driver’s seat.

* * *

Megon shivered against the cold. She didn’t want to walk around in the dark in case the dealers were out looking for her, but she was cold to her bones just sitting in the recess where she had sat with China just half an hour before. It didn’t take long for the cold to take hold; never mind the wind and rain, the cold crept up through the ground. She knew she’d be warmer walking, but sitting here, she remained out of sight. She was hidden here. A few more hours and she could walk in the light and find her dad.

There weren’t many people in this part of town at this time of night. A group that had been not far from here when they arrived had dissipated. When she peeked out of the recess she could see someone tucked into a doorway further away, their heaped blankets shrouding them. She was also trying hard to stay awake. She was finding it hard to battle the cold when she felt so tired. She knew that she should just give in and sleep. If she could just sleep, before she knew it, it would be morning and she could move more easily.

She wondered if she should have gone with China and Amy. She'd be in the warm now, lying on the floor in Amy's bedroom, on carpet, with a pillow perhaps, cosy. It had started to rain and she wished she'd gone with them. It was very fine rain but dense and despite being in the recess, the rain still found its way in and soon her clothes were wet. It wouldn't take long before they were saturated. She kept vigilant; vigilant against the cold, the wet, against falling asleep and against anyone approaching her and attacking her. It was exhausting.

A man had walked slowly past a few minutes ago and spotted her but he'd moved through without bothering her. From what she could see of him, he was older, not young like the dealers who were after her.

Brian Porten was taking his time. There were hours before daybreak and he wasn't going to take any chances. He was keeping his coat collar up and his hat on and although many parts of the town centre were heavily regulated by CCTV, he still managed to avoid it and get round in the few pockets it didn't cover.

He had passed what looked like a young girl sitting in a recess of a utility doorway. She was small but still in the way. Still part of the growing problem. Fitting into ever smaller gaps and nooks and crannies, soon there would be a build-up, like he'd seen with the shop doorways. He could nip this one in the bud. Wipe it out. Get rid. As he'd walked around the area that night, the wind had blown in all manner of litter. It was too much for him to tackle on his own; the problem was becoming out of control. He'd ended up trying to chase loose newspaper sheets and discarded paper bags. It was winding him up.

He wondered how much trouble it would be to take the girl off the streets. His mind worked quickly; his car wasn't far from the spot where she was. All he had to do was get her to the car. Once inside he would be able to contain her. If she became troublesome to him on the journey, he could control her easily enough. It might just be better to incapacitate her as soon as she got in the car. Then he'd have no concern. He quickly flipped the ideas around in his head, looking for the pitfalls, anything he'd failed to consider. Planning was everything; it was the secret to his success.

Yes, he'd try it. It was dark enough around there for her not to be able to identify him if it went wrong, if she wouldn't go with him, if she put up a fight. He would make sure he changed his voice for the short exchange they would have. Disguise himself as best he could, just in case. Stoop a little more. Draw his scarf up to his chin, pull his hat down to shadow his eyes, ensure that all she would see was the middle section of his face. Make it as difficult for her as possible to identify him. He started to walk back, to see if she was still there. Yes, he could see her.

CHAPTER 41

Temple sent a text back to Amy asking where she was and if Megon was with them. He then went back out to the car where Paul Wallace was waiting with Sloper. Since receiving Amy's text, he was feeling more upbeat. As soon as Amy told him that they were safe, he would hand over Sloper into custody. When he knew where Amy was, he could reunite Paul with his daughter Megon and see and speak to China for the first time since she was reported missing. He was now just one text away from wrapping the whole thing up. Then he'd go after Gary Lewis.

Sloper had watched as marked police cars stacked up down the road. Not quite able to see what was happening, Sloper knew he should have paid more attention to what Gemma was up to; he hadn't anticipated her turning the flat into some sort of refuge for young girls. He had no idea why the girl Prayer in particular was so important to her, but it had certainly got Temple exercised. Sloper could see him walking back to the car.

Now, his survival instincts were kicking in. Self-preservation was what it was all about now and he knew he had to avoid custody at all costs if he was going to have any chance of getting himself out of this. He needed to get out of the car, out of the grip of Temple and this DI Paul Wallace from the Met. Away from any surveillance team. He had yet to spot the surveillance team, which meant they were either extremely good and a notch up from any other squad he'd known or they were actually alone and not being followed.

He'd done as asked and helped them to find one of the girls. He'd taken them directly to the premises and helped them detain individuals. He had no doubt now that Temple would want to take him to Swindon police station and book him in. He was going to avoid that at all costs. Temple sat in the driver's seat of his car.

'All good in here?'

Paul Wallace answered him. 'Yup. Just waiting for you to return.'

'I'm just waiting for a text and we'll be off.' At that moment, his phone rang. He could see it was from Gary Lewis.

'You're supposed to be meeting me in Tesco's car park. I've got the girls – have you got the money?'

'Who do you think you've got with you then, Gary?'

'I've got my sister and Amy Davidson. It's going to cost you.'

'I need proof first. If you've got Amy Davidson let me speak to her.' Temple hoped to catch Lewis out, knowing he'd received a text from Amy just minutes earlier, but the next voice he heard was definitely her. How the fuck had that happened?

'Amy, you texted me to say you had found China?'

'I did, I found her in town. On our way back home Gary Lewis stopped us and forced us into his car.'

'Where's Megon? Is she with you?'

'No, she wouldn't come. She stayed behind.'

'Where is she?'

With that Gary Lewis resumed his call.

'I told you I had them. Now you've got ten minutes to get here.'

'Put Amy back on the phone, Gary, I need to speak to her.'

'You'd better be here in ten minutes with your money, then you can talk to her all night if you like.' Lewis terminated the call.

In the car, Paul Wallace had just heard a one-sided conversation. 'What was that about Megon?'

'We need to go to the Tesco car park.' Temple started the engine.

'Was there any news on Megon?'

'Yes, we have to go and pick up the girls she was with.'

'So where is she?'

Temple was keen to stop the questioning that he knew Sloper would be listening to. He wanted to get him into custody but now he didn't have time if he was going to meet with Gary Lewis to get the girls back. And he was conscious of the fact that he only had Paul Wallace's support on the premise that he would find Megon. Now it seemed she was lost again and he wanted an explanation. The sooner he got to Gary Lewis the better.

Temple gestured to Paul Wallace that Sloper was still sitting in the back of the car and was listening to their every word. Temple reckoned he could be with Gary Lewis in minutes and that there was nothing to be gained from any other action in that time. The sooner he could question Amy and China as to Megon's whereabouts, the sooner they could find her. At least they would have a location to go to next. Temple looked forward out of the windscreen and drove at speed to meet Lewis.

CHAPTER 42

With his coat collar pulled up, Porten started to approach the girl sitting in the dark. She had her back to him as he was walking towards her. She was sitting on the ground leant up against the wall, with her legs outstretched and her feet on the other side of the recess. It was such a small space, like a small cupboard without a door. And it was so dark. He passed no one and he knew there was no CCTV in this particular spot. In his mind he had plotted their course back to the car to remain invisible. The only thing he had to do was persuade the girl to go with him.

They were more difficult, the young girls. But it wasn't impossible. He'd done it before, but with men it was easier. They weren't as suspicious of him. He had to be a bit more sophisticated with the girls. A bit more contriving. He knew what he could do. Yes, it just might work again.

Megon's whole body was shaking with the cold so much that it was becoming difficult to control. She knew she only had a few more hours to daylight and then she could move in relative safety. At least there would be safety in numbers as more people were about and she could more easily avoid being spotted by the dealers. She figured they wouldn't dare take her off the street in broad daylight, not when she could scream for help.

Despite her coldness, her senses were acute. She instinctively felt someone coming towards her. Her ears strained for the sound of their feet against the cold, wet ground. Yes, there they were. Footsteps. Coming her way. Someone would pass her any minute now. She sat and waited for a figure to go by.

She felt the shadow of their presence loom over her, and instead of them moving on as she expected them to do, the footsteps stopped. She turned quickly and looked up, suddenly aware of her vulnerability and her disadvantage as she sat on the floor.

Looking down on her was a man. He was wrapped up against the cold and wet and she could barely see his face. He was standing so close to her that she had to strain her neck to look at him. Once she'd established his presence, she locked her eyes on her feet against the wall opposite her, hoping that by ignoring him he would go away. She was suddenly aware that she was backed into the recess with no point of escape, should she need it. Almost tearfully, she acknowledged that she might again need to fight and scream.

Instead of going away as she'd hoped, he started to speak to her. His voice was soft and the accent was from somewhere up north.

'I've been speaking to a man and a woman who approached me. I think they were looking for you. The man said they were looking for a young girl with dark hair. I can't remember what they said your name was now as I wasn't paying enough attention. Are they your parents?'

Megon knew she had seen her dad searching for her; perhaps he was there with her mum too. But they wouldn't be out this time of night surely? Or would they be thinking this is exactly the time they might find her? They could be close by, in the next street.

'They showed me a photo. Let me see . . . yes. It looked like you. I can see the likeness.'

The man still peered down at her and Megon's curiosity was sufficiently roused to look up at him.

'When did you see them?' she asked, blinking up at him, feeling the rain on her face.

'Less than an hour ago. They were in the main concourse, talking to people out walking by, mainly the drinkers at this time of night.'

He was well spoken and from what she could see of him, he didn't look like a tramp or a nutter. Her eyes skimmed over his clean white trainers.

'I heard them say they would be moving on to another part of town, to see if they could find you. Do you want your parents to find you? Do you want me to go and tell them where you are? They showed me the picture of you.'

Megon desperately wanted to see her mum and dad. The thought of her mum coming out to find her too made her heart break. She had been so ill, she had never meant to cause her any worry. She thought she was earning money, good money, to help with their situation.

In two weeks she had earned £400. She hadn't had a chance to spend it; she had hidden it in a zip-up pocket of her jacket. But that was lost to her now. It had been taken from her when she lost the drugs and money. When she had been stripped of all her clothes. That's why she was so cold; all she had on was a thin cotton tracksuit and a scruffy pair of cheap pumps that she'd found at the last house.

'Have you really seen them?' she asked, blinking at the raindrops.

'I think I have, yes. Shall I take you to where they are?'

'Yes, please.'

'Of course. Come on, up you get. Come with me.'

Megon was so stiff from the cold that she found it hard to move. As much as she wanted to get up quickly, she found it hard to bend her stiff limbs. Slowly, she stood up. Her sodden clothes clung to her. She was wet through. Her hair hung down and stuck to her face. She was so cold she could barely walk.

'That's it, slowly does it.' The man was encouraging her to walk. 'Let's go down this way.'

All she could think of was at last seeing her parents. She thought of them putting their arms around her, she thought of that first hug and how warm she would feel. This man was taking her to them. He had seen them, spoken to them, knew they were looking for her. At last they would be together. What was it people said? The kindness of strangers.

'Where did you say you saw them again?'

'They were in the main concourse but said they would move up towards the outlet village, ready to catch the morning commuters. If we go down this way there's a shortcut and we'll be able to just drive a short way to where I think they said they would be. It's not far now. You'll soon see my car and I'll take you straight to them.' All the time he spoke he kept his voice soft and even, making full use of the Geordie accent. It had been a good choice. Very non-threatening, soothing even.

She started to move a little quicker, the blood circulating through her cold body with the motion of her steps. It was still dark and the man was guiding her through unlit walkways. They had passed no one. They then appeared at the end of an old, empty cobbled street, which was shut off at one end by bollards. He could see his car. He just had to get her a few more steps down the dead end road and into it. They were nearly there. Just then, Megon caught her foot on a sharp stone. It felt as if it had cut through her pumps it was so hard. She wobbled and grabbed out to steady herself, having to hold onto the man's arm.

'That's it, you hold on to me. We're nearly there. That car over there's where we're going.'

They made the last few steps along the road and reached the car. Just as Megon put her hand on the door handle to open it, a voice in the distance bellowed out.

'Oi!' She looked up and saw the unmistakeable outline of one of the dealers. Although it was dark, she still knew it was the man with the clouded eye and scar on his face. He was running fast towards her.

CHAPTER 43

Temple pulled into the car park at Tesco. It was a 24-hour store so he made his way to the more remote part at the end and saw Gary Lewis's car parked up.

'I'm just going over to see Lewis and I'll be back.' He left Paul Wallace with Sloper in the car. As Temple walked over to Lewis's car, he made a call to Mendoza. He could now clearly see Lewis in the front seat and two girls in the back. He leant down by Lewis's open window and looked inside. He saw Amy and China sitting in the back.

'How are you, girls?' For the first time, Temple had China Lewis in his sight.

Amy spoke up. 'We're OK, I just want to go home. We were going home when this arsehole stopped us.'

'I need to speak to you both – where's Megon?'

'We left her in town, she wouldn't come with us. She wanted to wait until morning and then go looking for her dad. She saw him looking for her in Swindon so she knows he's about. We tried to get her to come back to mine but she wouldn't.' China told Temple where they'd left her. She was smaller than he had imagined but he could see that her attitude made up for what she lacked in size.

Gary Lewis was listening to the exchange. 'This is all very nice, but if you want them out of this car, you're going to have to stick to the arrangement we have.'

'I have the money, Gary. Let the girls out of the car.'

'I need to see it first.'

Temple opened the inside of his coat and showed Lewis a wedge of notes. 'It's here. Let them out.'

Lewis clicked the central locking and Amy and China got out of either side of the car.

'Stand over there, girls, out of the way,' Temple instructed them. He knew he had to play for time and he started to get the money from his coat.

'You know how much. I said ten grand,' Lewis chirped.

From the corner of his eye, Temple could see a dark blue saloon slowly approaching. Suddenly the car moved forward quickly in front of Lewis's car, effectively blocking him from moving. Lewis started gesticulating from behind the windscreen. The car turned on flashing lights in the grill and Lewis knew then it was an unmarked police car.

Mendoza walked towards them with another officer and directed Lewis to get out of his car. Lewis refused, clicking on the central locking and glaring out of his window at Temple. The officer accompanying Mendoza drew his metal baton and smashed the driver's window. With Lewis trapped in the car, the officer barked at him to get out. Threatening him with being tasered if he didn't let himself out of the car, Lewis saw the futility of his situation and dropped the central locking. He got out, swearing at Temple as he did so.

Mendoza read him his rights and Gary Lewis was arrested and put into the police car. While this was happening, a marked patrol car had turned up and Temple walked the two girls over to it. Amy relayed her address to the driver, Temple opened the rear door and they both sat inside.

'Now both of you go home and stay there. I'll go and find Megon. Then I'll come back and see you both and take a statement.' He spoke to the driver. 'Make sure they go inside.'

Temple walked back to his car. Finding Megon had to take priority over ensuring Sloper was taken into custody. And he was indebted to Paul Wallace; he'd kept his side up and they still hadn't found Megon. He owed it to him to keep looking until they found her. He got into the car and anticipated his question.

'We're going to find Megon, they've told me she's in town.' He drove back to the town centre. Sloper had been fully expecting to be handed over when he saw the patrol car pull up in the car park. He didn't know what was going on, but all the time he could stay out of custody and remain at liberty, he could plan and think. They were now going back into town. If he could just get back home, if he could just make a few phone calls. But for that he had to get away from Temple. Away from this surveillance job.

And suddenly Sloper started to join the dots. They hadn't had any comms for some time now. The DI in front seemed to have an earpiece in at one point but that seemed not to be working anymore. They didn't appear to be part of a surveillance unit as they hadn't been approached by any other cars or officers. Sure enough, Mendoza was in on it and he worked with Temple at HQ – but there was something about all this that wasn't right.

He'd be in custody now if this was a job, not being driven around. He'd helped find the girl who was ill, so why hadn't he been arrested? They hadn't asked him for any further help. What was Temple up to? Before he could think further, Temple started talking to him, looking at him in the rear-view mirror.

'So, who does the drugs money you took belong to? You haven't given us any names yet. Who are they?'

'Like I said, names won't be any use to you. They change their names, they have no names, no one knows who they're dealing with. All deals are set up in person, face to face. Whatever name they give you isn't their real name, it's just something to call them at any given time. You're not dealing with people with identities. They morph. It's easy for them. Not having a name or a number keeps them safe.'

'They have telephone numbers.'

'That's as far as they go and even then, those aren't widely circulated and they chop and change them regularly. As I said, deals are done in person, so everyone can see who they're dealing with.'

'So, tell me about the faces. I followed someone from Swindon station with a girl and then I saw you coming out of a house where I lost him. Whose face was that?'

'Yes, that would have been a dealer, although not a foreigner. He was showing a girl the ropes that night, taking her through the routine.'

'We're just going to search for a girl called Megon and you're coming with us. If we can't find her on the streets we're going to use you like a bloodhound and you're going to take us to all the trap houses and dealers in Swindon until we find her.'

Temple parked up. Paul Wallace was ready for the search for Megon. He'd rung Leonie and told her he wasn't going to make it home, that he was staying out to look for Megon. He didn't tell her about Temple as he didn't want to get her hopes up unnecessarily. The next time he went home, he wanted it to be with Megon.

He'd put all his trust in Temple. He had become so desperate to find her that he'd trusted him eagerly when he'd said he may know her whereabouts. Paul had nothing else to hang on to now. He had to believe he was going to find Megon tonight.

They split up for the search, Temple taking Sloper with him one way, Paul Wallace another. He was well used to this and could cover the town in a few hours. She was on the streets of Swindon and now he was going to find her. Friends she had been with had left her in town so he knew she was there. She was there! All he had to do was find her. Find his baby, his Megon. He started to repeat her name under his breath, 'Come on, Megon, where are you, sweetheart? Come on, Megon, I'm here.'

The rain was getting heavier. It had been a long night, a night Temple thought would never end. He just needed to repay Paul Wallace by finding Megon. He knew he wouldn't rest until she was found. He couldn't return home to see his own daughter before he'd found Megon. They had to find her.

As soon as they found Megon, Temple would take Sloper straight to custody. He had all the evidence he needed. In under an hour, he hoped he'd be there. He just had to help Paul find Megon.

Sloper was glad to get out of the car. When Wallace went off in the opposite direction, he couldn't believe his luck.

CHAPTER 44

Megon had to make a split-second decision. Could she risk getting into the man's car and him not pulling away quickly enough before she was caught and dragged out? No, she had to run. Run away from someone who wanted to help her. She also felt she couldn't risk her kind helper. By the looks of him, he wouldn't be in a position to protect her. He would be no match for Tarek. She'd seen the way he'd attacked China, she'd seen the twisted look on his ugly face. Tarek was now running towards her. She looked at Porten and pleaded with him.

'Find my parents and tell them I'm looking for them.'

Then she ran. She was wet through and the cobbles on the tiny street bit through her pumps and into her feet as she ran as fast as she could. She had been so close to finding her dad and she had been chased away from the man who was trying to help her.

She knew if Tarek got hold of her he would hurt her badly; the image of him with his hands around China's throat was fixed in her mind as she ran. China had also told her he carried a large knife that he used to terrorise girls, cutting their faces, their arms and legs to make them do what he wanted. The fear of that nearly choked her.

She had come so close to being reunited with her parents and now she was running again. But this time she was running for her life. She needed to get out into the town centre, where there were people, perhaps even a police officer, but she could hear him behind her. She needed to run before he caught her. As her heart pounded, she headed for cover into a nearby multi-storey car park. She had a chance of hiding in there.

She ran inside and hid herself behind some parked cars. It was a 24-hour car park, but at that time of the morning, it was quiet. She crouched down beside a car, hiding behind a wheel, trying to still her heart that was banging against her chest from the effort of running so hard and from fear of being caught. The sound of her heart beating filled her head. She had to be quiet and careful, listening and watching on the ground for his footsteps as she literally crawled along the floor. She had to keep moving.

She had made her way from the ground to the first floor where there were only a few cars parked. She made sure she was ducked down behind a wheel, using it to shield her feet from sight. She was terrified of getting caught and wished there were more cars to help her hide.

She knew he'd followed her into the car park. It was merely a matter of avoiding him for as long as she could and then running back outside. It wouldn't be long before the first cars started coming in, and they would provide her with more cover. Perhaps she could even approach someone to help her.

* * *

Sloper went with Temple to where Amy and China had told him they had left Megon. Temple felt sure she would have kept moving around the town and hoped that with Paul going one way and them another, they would find her.

'As soon as we've located this girl, I'm taking you in to custody,' Temple informed Sloper as they walked.

It was dark and dank and the rain sat in pools on the ground. They walked to the spot where Megon and China had been hours earlier, China describing the recess where they had sat. Temple looked up and down the street – there was no one around. He called out her name and drew no response. It didn't surprise him. He hoped Paul had found her by now. Sloper was standing just behind him, outside of his vision. He had only moments to feel the crashing pain before falling to the ground. Suddenly, Temple's world turned black.

Sloper had spotted the half-brick as they approached the recess. It was now or never. He had to take his chance and there might not be another. He brought it down hard onto the back of Temple's head. As Temple fell onto the wet ground, Sloper looked about – there was no one around. Quickly, he crouched beside Temple and rolled him over. Searching his coat, Sloper found a wad of bank notes and his phone and took them. Giving one last cursory glance around to make sure no one was watching him, he stood up and walked away with the brick still in his hand.

Sloper knew there was no CCTV in the area and knew where he needed to go to avoid it through town and back to his home address. He threw the brick into a waste bin, ensuring there was enough distance between it and Temple to make it unlikely that it would be found. He continued on, walking in amongst the early morning workers, away from the scene.

* * *

The pain in Temple's head was like nothing he'd experienced before. His head felt twice its size and there was ringing in his ears. The searing and sharp nature of the pain made him feel overwhelmingly nauseous. He lay on the wet ground with the rain pouring down on him. He couldn't lift his head in order to get up. He felt so sick. He knew if he didn't move and he vomited, he was likely to choke to death. But he couldn't help himself. He couldn't get up. He managed to turn his head to the side before he was violently sick. His world went black again.

When he came to, he was sure he could feel motion and yet he couldn't quite understand how. He was definitely moving and he was in a vehicle. He was in an ambulance. Suddenly, the feel of it was making him feel sick again. All he wanted to do was sleep. He wanted to go back to unconsciousness. There was no pain there. But it seemed as though a fight was going on between his mind and body. Half of him wanted the safe blackness of unconsciousness but the same mind wanted him to waken. He wanted to be left out of it. He couldn't care less. He felt so sick and in pain, he only wanted to be left alone. Right then the pain was so bad, he didn't care if he lived or died. He wanted relief from it in whatever form that took.

Then suddenly a kaleidoscopic jumble of pictures flashed in his mind. He hadn't put his little boy to bed. He had to get home. Who would look after him if he wasn't there? He thought of him alone with no one to care for him. The pain was back. It was sickening. He felt as if he wanted to vomit.

He saw his mother, dead on a makeshift bed. He saw Daisy, his lovely Daisy. She was giggling and he held her, her arms around his neck. Then he could hear voices. He tried to prise his eyes open but they were nailed down. Still the images went round and round in his mind, like a mad merry-go-round, going faster and faster. The pain, the sickness and the images were forcing him to a consciousness that he didn't want. He wanted the pain to go away. To leave him in peace.

Slowly he forced his eyes open. It was a mammoth effort. And that simple act of his eyelids flickering open seemed to turn a screw, increasing the pain in his head. It was warm, too warm. It was dark. He realised that he wasn't in an ambulance. He was in a car. He was facing the windscreen and the darkness and the rain were broken by shards of light from oncoming car headlights. He closed his eyes against the piercing pain.

CHAPTER 45

Paul Wallace was in the town centre. Like all the other times since he'd started coming here, he could almost feel Megon's presence. 'Where are you, Megon?' he continued to chant to himself, to her, as he walked.

He knew he would have to ring Leonie in a few hours and he wanted to give her good news. He wanted to tell her he'd found Megon; he wanted her to hear the sound of Megon's voice again. He couldn't bear the thought of going home without her. Another journey home on the train on his own.

It would be daylight in an hour or so, then he would be able to find her, he was sure of it. Her friend said they had left her in the town centre, so where was she? She wanted to find him and he wanted to find her. Where would she go? Would she be at the railway station? Would she go there, would she wait for him to find her there? He'd been around the town and couldn't see her. He would try the station and if she wasn't there, he'd come back.

* * *

Megon's heart refused to be silent. It continued to bang in her ears, making it difficult for her to listen. She no longer thought Tarek was on the same parking level. She was going to move down to the ground level so that she could make her way out. Perhaps he had given up on finding her. Perhaps she'd managed to shake him off. She just needed to get back out into the town centre.

She dared to raise her head enough to look through the windows of the car she was hiding behind. She scanned round as far as she could see. No one. It seemed like she was alone. Quietly, she started to move across the back of the car. There was another car that she needed to get to in order to make her way down. She'd thought about going down the stairwell but the thought of him being there, being caught with him in such a confined space, scared her. At least out here there was room to run. If he caught her in the stairwell, she'd be trapped.

She had to make a run for the next car. As silently as she could, she broke cover and ran across to the rear of it. Her heart pounded but there was nothing. No movement, only hers. Again she peeped up to the windows to scan the rest of the car park. Nothing. From there she could run down the exit slope to the next level. She had to do it. She could get out of there.

She hesitated. Her fear of him finding her checked her resolve to run. She was literally petrified of him catching her. She was in a quandary. Stay until there were more cars and people about, or run now and risk him catching her? But her dad was out there. He was looking for her.

She made her move, running as fast as she could. Looking all about her she ran, fixing her sights on a car in the distance. All around her there was silence. She now found she was close to the exit itself, it was just beyond the car that she was going to make for. *Run, run, keep running,* she told herself. *Don't stop, keep going.* She ran as hard as she could. All she had to do was go under the barrier – she was nearly there. Suddenly from behind her, he shouted. Where had he come from? He was running after her now. He felt close; he was fast.

She slowed to go under the barrier. He was swearing at her now. She was so frightened she didn't know whether to surrender or run. She kept running, out into the street as fast as she could with him chasing her. It was starting to get light but it was dull due to the rain that fell on her, soaking her. Her fear was starting to paralyse her; the adrenalin was ripping through her but she was becoming breathless. Her legs wanted to go faster than her lungs would allow. Her fear was both telling her to run faster and telling her to stop and plead for him not to hurt her.

She was only a few strides ahead of him now. He had her in his sights; if he put his arm out he could almost grab her hair. She was slowing. He'd make her run, exhaust the bitch. Then there'd be no fight in her.

She was crying now, crying with fear and the thought of giving up. The pain in her lungs was tearing her chest apart. She started to scream, the fear of him catching her making her shriek loudly.

'Megon!'

A voice from across the shopping concourse shouted her name. She instantly recognised it and looked across. She could see him. Her dad.

Paul Wallace was making his way to the station. As he walked through the Brunel Centre, a girl came running across out of nowhere, screaming. It was Megon. It was her. He instantly ran towards her and saw she was being chased by a man. She'd seen him and called for him.

'Dad, Dad, help me!' Fear was etched on her face as she ran to him with her arms outstretched like she had when she was a baby. There were tears streaming down her cheeks. The man behind her had slowed but was still in forward motion. Paul saw him and momentarily ignored Megon. Running towards her, his focus was on the man who had obviously been terrorising his daughter.

'It's all right, it's all right now, love,' he called out to her. 'Come to me.' No sooner was she in his arms than he turned to the man behind her. He broke from her arms to confront him. His elation at seeing Megon and now seeing the need to fiercely protect her made his anger boil inside him.

'Come here, you scum, come here.' He moved to run towards him but the man had already decided to run away. 'Fuck off then!' Paul shouted after him. 'Fuck off, you bastard!'

He turned back to Megon and pulled her to him. They clung to one another. 'Oh, Megon love, where have you been? It's all right now, love, you're safe. You're back with me, you're safe.' He repeated it over and over as he landed kisses on her head. She started to sob. She had all but collapsed in his arms from exhaustion. He had to tell Temple he'd found her; he dialled his phone. There was no answer.

CHAPTER 46

The motion of the car and the nauseating searing pain in his head had the obvious effect and Temple was sick. Being in no position to move or help himself, the vomit covered the front of his clothes, the footwell in front of him and the dashboard. Brian Porten looked across at Temple in disgust.

The dirty bastard. He knew the bloke wasn't right when he picked him up; he couldn't speak properly and he had blood from a wound at the back of his head. He was unsteady on his feet, but all this had lent itself to him being easily manoeuvred and malleable to get him in the car. Fuck knows what the bloke had eaten but now Porten was looking at it.

Porten unwound the window against the stench. He'd have to clear it up as soon as they got to the abattoir. It wasn't something he could leave, for God's sake. As he looked across at him, he could see Temple's head lolling forward, jerking with every bump in the road. He looked totally out of it, the filthy bastard. But they were nearly there.

Porten pulled up at the abattoir and round to the big roll-up doors at the back. He got out and let himself in through a small door to the side. It was dark inside as he found a chair and positioned it near the door. He had the captive bolt pistol ready. Porten went back out to the car.

As the car door opened, Temple fell against it. He felt a man's hands on him. He was saying something to him but he couldn't work out what it was. He could feel fresh air on his face and the man's hands pulling at his coat collar, encouraging him to get out of the car. He could smell the stench of his own vomit, the remnants of which were dribbled down his chin and the front of his coat. He spat some more out on the ground.

As he got unsteadily to his feet, he slowly opened his eyes. He was away from light now but prising his eyelids open felt like lifting heavy rocks. His head continued to swim as a noise beat between his ears. Even so, encouraged by the man taking him by his arm, he took awkward steps towards a door.

Inside, Temple was guided towards a chair to sit on. His double vision made it hard for him to place his hand on it to help position himself and he nearly fell to the floor as he misjudged the edge of it. His hand was placed onto the back of the chair and he was then able to turn himself enough to be able to sit down before his legs buckled from under him. His legs wouldn't work; they felt like jelly. Temple leaned forwards, putting his head between his legs, and was sick again.

Brian Porten went back outside. The bastard couldn't stop being sick and Porten now had the contents of Temple's stomach on his clothes. He took his handkerchief out and carefully wiped his mouth. Looking down, he saw vomit on the arm of his coat where he'd helped him out of the car and he now had splashes of it on his shoes from where the vomit had hit the concrete floor. Disgusted, Porten took his coat off and dropped it on the ground. He then took off his shoes. He would do what he needed to do and then tidy up afterwards. He would incinerate both later.

For the first time while he sat, Temple looked around with something resembling clear vision. He had no idea where he was, what this place was even, or why he was there. He'd thought he was in an ambulance at one point but realised he'd been confused. Why had he been brought here? Seeing he was alone he stood up, checking his steadiness. He could move a little better now. His legs were still rather shaky but they did at least seem to want to coordinate at last.

He could see a large steel door and staggered towards it. It might give a clue as to what this place was and why he might be there. He opened the sliding door. A rush of freezing cold air escaped towards him. He opened the door further and looked inside. All he could register was the headless corpse of a man hanging from a meat hook.

CHAPTER 47

China lay awake, looking at Amy sleeping. She hadn't slept since they'd both climbed through the window of Amy's bedroom and snuggled down in her bed two hours ago. They'd giggled at the police officer who'd sat shaking his head at them from the patrol car as they scaled the garage and watched as they climbed through the window.

Amy had slept almost immediately, content in the knowledge that China was safe and back with her, lying next to her.

China's head was still full of everything she had encountered and she was trying to make sense of what had happened over the course of just one week. It had felt like one nightmare day after another, but here she was, safe at last. But she couldn't sleep. She was missing Megon. She liked Megon and really hadn't wanted to leave her. Still, China couldn't force her to come, and besides, she could tell Amy hadn't been keen on the idea.

It hadn't been the first time she'd seen a bit of jealousy flare with Amy when she'd seen her in the company of someone else. But Amy didn't understand; even though she had only known Megon for a couple of weeks, they'd shared experiences that China never had with Amy.

Megon knew what it was like to run drugs and money. She knew how easy it was to get trapped. It was like quicksand. One minute you're walking, sure of yourself, the next you've fallen through a hole into an entirely different world and you're sinking, drowning, and no one can help you.

They thought Gemma Harker was helping them. She said she would help them. If they hadn't trusted her they would have been fine, delivering the drugs, collecting the money, getting more, earning. They had been set up by that bitch, she was sure. Lying there going over it all, she could see it now. Getting them to go to the shop with her, leaving their stash in her flat. She should have known better. Christ! What had she been thinking? No wonder the drugs and money were gone when they got back. They'd been so naive.

Megon had been so scared when they ran. She'd told her what had happened to her, holed up in a shitty room while a stream of men were shown in. China had fared a little better, but Megon wasn't used to this life. She shouldn't have left her on her own to run and she shouldn't have left her all on her own a few hours ago.

She looked at Amy; she knew nothing. She had a mum and dad who looked after her, a lovely home where she felt safe. She was spoilt by China's standards. She knew nothing of what it was like to rely on yourself for your own survival. Or for your survival to be in the hands of strangers.

China couldn't lie there any longer. She had to make sure Megon was OK. Slowly and quietly, she slipped out from the warmth of the duvet and silently put her clothes on. It was nearly 6 a.m. and still dark. No one was stirring in the house. With her pumps in her hand, she left Amy's bedroom and crept downstairs and out the front door. Sitting on the step outside, she pulled on her pumps and went back into town to find Megon.

By the time she reached the place where they had parted, the rain had stopped. There was no sign of Megon, but on the ground near to where they had been, she saw a pool of blood. This was where she'd left her and now here was blood.

She looked around, panicking. Was Megon hurt and hiding somewhere? She ran around looking in shop doorways. She started to call her name.

It was just beginning to get light but the street sleepers were not stirring. She knew Megon had only been wearing her tracksuit and had no blankets to keep out the rain. She would have been cold and wet. Maybe someone had attacked her? Maybe she was lying wounded somewhere. Perhaps the dealers had found her.

China padded quickly through the Brunel Centre precinct, her feet pounding heavily on the pavement. She was oblivious to everything around her, such was her focus on finding Megon; the shops went by in a blur. She didn't look at the faces of people she saw. She was only interested in finding Megon. She was fearful for her and also angry at the thought of anyone attacking her friend.

Suddenly, she felt pain as her head was pulled backwards. From behind her, someone had grabbed a fistful of her hair and she was stopped in her tracks. Her hands instinctively closed over the hands that were holding her hair.

'Hello, little China.' He'd put his mouth to her ear and the sound of his accent chilled her like ice running down her spine. Tarek was grasping her hair, pulling it so hard she felt the roots of it straining on her scalp. She feared it would suddenly come away in his hands. She was stock-still. How come she hadn't seen him – where had he come from?

'Don't scream or do anything to draw attention to yourself or I will drop you right where you are with my knife. You thought you'd got away from me, didn't you? You don't think I'd leave it like that, do you? You didn't think I'd let you go? You're going to come with me and we're going to be friends, great friends. Come with me. That's it, walk with me.' He put his lips to her cheek and she felt his tongue slowly lick her. The hatred rose up in her.

Using the pain of her hair pulled tightly in his hands, he moved her back through the precinct to where his car was parked. With her hair as a lever, he'd slightly lifted her so that she had to walk up on her toes. This prevented her from kicking out at him. He clicked the car open with his key fob and opened the boot.

'Get in.'

'What?' She quickly looked about her for someone, anyone, but there was no one there.

'Get in.' He pushed her head forward with his hand and let go of her hair so that she could climb up into the boot of the car. When she had climbed inside, he slammed it shut and drove off.

CHAPTER 48

Temple stood for a few seconds, blinking back the shock of the hanging corpse, thinking he was not quite seeing straight. He still had a sickening pounding in his head but he could clearly see a headless corpse in front of him. He quickly closed the steel door and looked around him. He was still alone but he could hear the sound of a car door closing outside. He went to reach inside his coat pocket for his phone but it wasn't there.

He didn't know where he was, or the identity of the man who he'd thought was helping him. But one thing he could be sure about: he'd brought him to a place of death, where the corpse of a man was hanging like any other piece of dead meat. And if the man in the fridge had walked through the door as Temple had, what was coming next?

Temple knew he had just seconds to make a decision before the man came back inside, but his mind wouldn't work fast enough; he had to battle through a constant ferocious thudding noise for clarity. He was in no fit state to fight. He felt ridiculously weak as his legs struggled to keep him upright. He was sick, he couldn't think straight and he couldn't run and hide.

So this is it, he thought. *This is how it ends.* In a dingy abattoir, hung from a hook, where no one would ever guess he was there. He started to think of Daisy, Ben and Prayer. Daisy had Leigh to look after her and Prayer, well, she might never know who he was and she had two parents to look after her. But Ben, what would happen to him if he didn't emerge from this? Ben would be orphaned. The thought of that stung him. Ben was still so young. He wouldn't know his mother and he wouldn't remember Temple for sure. He had to think of something.

He went and sat on the chair as if he'd not left it, putting his feet astride the vomit he'd left on the floor. As he did this, Porten came back inside. Temple leant forward in the chair and noticed that as Porten walked towards him, he had no shoes on.

Still bent over, Temple's eyes followed him as he walked towards the empty animal pen. As he turned back to him, he could see that in his hand there was a pistol. There was only one thing left that Temple could do and that meant letting him get as close to him as possible.

'Come on, mate, see what I've got for you here,' said Porten as he looked at Temple bent over with his head forward. The dirty bastard was still looking at his own vomit. Well, as soon as he sat upright, he would put the pistol to his head and pull the trigger. Porten put his hand on Temple's shoulder.

With all the effort he could muster, Temple managed to raise himself slightly and with his hands gripping the legs of the chair he was sitting on, he let out a roar as he suddenly stood and swung the chair at Porten.

The action caught Porten completely unaware and as the chair crashed against him, the pistol flew from his hand. The side of his body had caught the full force of the metal chair. Knocked sideways, Porten struggled to maintain his footing and as he staggered, he saw the pistol slide away from him across the concrete floor. Temple kept the chair in his hands and swung it again, crashing it against Porten's outstretched arm, which broke with a crack as he fell to the floor.

Temple was about to bring the chair down onto Porten's head when he was suddenly aware of movement behind him.

Fearing the man was not working alone and that he was about to be attacked from behind, Temple's strength suddenly deserted him. He'd put so much effort into swinging the chair that his legs were again unsteady. He knew he wouldn't withstand another assault and was resigned to defending himself as best he could.

'What the fuck's going on here?' It was Mendoza, along with two other officers in uniform. Temple had never been more relieved to see him, to see anyone. He felt a ridiculous urge to hug him.

'I don't know.' He was breathless as he threw the chair away to the side, looking down at Porten on the floor. 'But he should be able to tell us. I think I was just about to join the other poor bastard in there.' Temple gestured to the steel door of the large fridge. Two uniformed officers had gone over to assist Porten, whose arm was badly broken. Mendoza followed Temple's eyeline. He walked over to the fridge and opened the door.

'Shit!'

Behind him, Temple's legs finally gave way and he slumped onto the concrete floor.

CHAPTER 49

Temple was sitting in the back of an ambulance with a paramedic looking at the wound to his head, with Mendoza standing outside sucking hard on a cigarette. It had been over an hour since Mendoza gatecrashed Porten's abattoir and there had been a lot to do. Brian Porten had been arrested and taken away.

The light would be up soon on the godforsaken place and they would be able to start searches of the outside. Mendoza called in all available units and locked the place down while putting CID and forensics on notice for a 7 a.m. start. Although still shaken, Temple helped Mendoza put things in place before finally succumbing to the ministrations of a patient paramedic.

'So how did you find me?' he asked. Mendoza was trying to blow the smoke away from the back of the ambulance. Temple had no choice but to sit while the male paramedic saw to the wound at the back of his head. He was being thorough but taking way too long for Temple's liking.

'We picked up Sloper, who was walking back to his place alone. When we searched him we found he had your mobile on him, which had blood on it. I figured you wouldn't have given that up without a fight and that the blood on his hands was yours. He said you both argued and that he'd hit you, and having walked off, he had a touch of the seconds and went back to help you. How true that is I don't know. But he said when he went back he watched some bloke helping you into a car. When I told him he was lying, he gave me the registration number of the car. We ran it through and it led us here.'

'Did you find any money on him? He took it out of my coat pockets.'

'No money, just the phone.'

'Then he's dropped the money somewhere. Where's Sloper now?' Temple was facing away from Mendoza as the paramedic continued to examine him, lifting his eyelids and shining a light into his eyes.

'I gave instructions for him to be delivered to the cells, along with all the other people as you blazed through Swindon last night.'

'Did he ask to make a phone call?'

'I don't know. The priority was finding you. I'll give them a call and find out. As soon as they book Brian Porten into custody, the place will be full, thanks to you. We've not found out much about him at the moment. There's an address that'll need searching, we'll take the car away and turn this place over to forensics.' Mendoza threw his spent cigarette on the floor, crushing it with his foot before calling his phone.

'Has he said anything?' Temple asked.

'No, he confirmed his name and that's pretty much it. No explanation as to what he was doing bringing you here. As you say, you were probably going to be next to get a bolt in the head and end up on a hook. We've got to try and find out who the poor bastard is in the fridge. This is going to excite the top brass when they get in this morning.'

'They won't thank me for this lot. All they'll be thinking is pound signs. The bean counters will be rolling their eyes.'

Mendoza cut short their conversation as his call was answered and he questioned the custody sergeant about

Sloper. It was a brief exchange and at the end of it Mendoza bent down to retrieve the cigarette stub, putting it in his pocket.

'They had to call an ambulance to Sloper as he was complaining of chest pains. He's in Great Western Hospital. He didn't ask to call anyone.'

Temple started up. 'Christ, take me over there. He won't have had chest pains, that's his way of getting out of the cells. Have you finished with me yet?' he asked the paramedic impatiently.

'You might have to go in,' he replied. 'It's a nasty gash and you'll have been concussed. It might be a good idea to have an X-ray just as a precaution. You've taken a bit of a bashing.'

'Can you blue light me to the hospital now?'

'You're not an emergency.'

'I have to get over to the hospital. You tell me I should go there so either you take me or I'll get him to take me. Either way, I need to get there fast.' Reluctantly the medic agreed to take Temple using his blue lights.

When the ambulance pulled up outside the hospital, Temple made his way to the lifts and the cardio unit. Once there, looking up at a whiteboard, Temple saw Sloper's name. He was directed to a small room in a corridor and as he approached, Temple saw there was no police presence outside the door. Before he went into the room, he knew. The bed was empty.

Temple looked round and found the men's toilets. Sloper wasn't in there. After speaking to a doctor and ensuring that Sloper wasn't elsewhere, they concluded that he had discharged himself without anyone knowing. He called Mendoza.

'Sam, he's not here, he's gone. Get them looking for him. Who knows how long he's been gone from here – no one saw him leave. There were no police guarding him. Come and get me out of here.'

Mendoza alerted the control room; it would be an embarrassment if they couldn't locate Sloper and fast. Temple knew there was enough evidence to convict Sloper but that was largely dependent on Gemma making a statement. Thinking of her, he wondered if Sloper had, after all, called on the services of the one man who had his back. Harker.

* * *

Having retrieved his car with Mendoza's help, Temple made his way to Wanborough to Clive Harker's house. It was just before eight and the tree-lined road was quiet. He parked up outside at the bottom of the driveway. Harker's silver Mercedes C-Class was still on the drive. Temple walked up the incline and knocked on the front door. After a few seconds, it was opened by Clive Harker. Temple could just see that behind him, Harker's wife Rita was standing in an internal doorway, wondering who was calling at that time of morning. As soon as he saw who was knocking, Harker moved to close the door behind him, barring the sight of Temple from his wife. There was no reason for Temple to be on his doorstep.

He was instantly needled. What's more, he needed to get into the office; his mobile had been going mad with texts about a murder in an abattoir.

'What the fuck are *you* doing here?' he said in a low drawl, knowing that any higher pitch would have his wife up behind him, opening the door.

'We have to talk.'

'I don't think so. You're suspended and at a disciplinary hearing on Tuesday. We have nothing to talk about. And you look and smell like shit. Now fuck off.'

Temple expected the abuse so ignored it. 'Have you seen or heard from Simon Sloper today?'

'No I haven't and if I was you I'd get myself off my drive and go back under your stone until Tuesday.'

Again, Temple ignored him. 'You don't know, do you?'

'What are you talking about?'

'You don't know about Sloper.'

'What about Sloper?' Harker was clearly narked.

'Sloper's been arrested. You really don't know do you?'

Harker looked back at Temple. He didn't like being doorstepped at the best of times and especially not by Temple. Neither did he like being caught unaware of information about someone he considered to be his friend. Temple continued.

'He was taken into custody in the early hours and then when he started complaining of chest pains, they took him to hospital where he disappeared. He's on the run. All the contacts you must have and they haven't told you. I'm here because we need to discuss what I know about Sloper. The man who you're relying on in my disciplinary hearing. Only, you might not be so keen to associate yourself with him now.'

'What are you talking about? What's he done?' Harker was interested. His voice had lowered further.

'I'll come to that. The last time we spoke, you gave me some career advice. "Get another job," you said. Well, I'm here to give you some. You and Sloper are tightly aligned and he's on the run. So he won't be the star witness you were relying on at the hearing on Tuesday. But more than that, people will be wondering just how much you knew about what he's been doing. Because there's another angle to this: Gemma.'

At the mention of her name, Harker almost flinched. The last thing he expected was for Temple to mention Gemma. It was the second time he had caught Harker unawares and Harker didn't like it. Temple was watching him and, for once, was taking pleasure from Harker's obvious discomfort.

'Gemma?' It was all Harker could say. His thoughts were still trying to work out what on earth this unexpected and unwelcome visit was about. Could it be true that Sloper was on the run? If it was, why hadn't he been told? What the hell was going on?

'Yes, Gemma. She came to me for help and made disclosures about Sloper. She told me he'd been running girls in Swindon, taking drugs money from dealers, playing them off against one another. I found the drugs and money at his house, and located the girls. So I see it like this: you need to distance yourself from Sloper pretty fast. All the times in the past when he's relied on your help, this time it's different. You can't help him now, and besides which, if you do, not only will you be helping someone who is corrupt, you'll be going up against your own daughter.'

Harker's mind was calculating. If what Temple was saying was true, he'd need to do some serious damage limitation. If Temple had his facts right, Sloper, the man he had relied on to look out for Gemma, had let him down. Their friendship was well known and there had always been rumours about Sloper. Yes, Sloper had always had a tendency to bend the rules to breaking point and he did himself no favours, but he'd been a useful person to have in his armoury and he'd always thought that Sloper was sloppy rather than devious. He never had him down as bent. But he didn't know anything about this. If this was true, this was serious corruption.

Temple was right though. If this was true, he would need to move fast or he'd be tainted by association. Thirty-two years in the force and a reputation second to none for it to come to this. Corrupt by association. He knew how it worked – the canteen gossip, the long looks of mistrust until he'd find himself shut out, with operational meetings taking place discreetly without him because no one would be sure that they could really trust him. Sloper would taint him. But why did it have to be Temple telling him this? Why was he the messenger?

'Why are you of all people here? Why would you want to help me?' asked Harker slowly.

'Because you can help *me*. You're going to go and see Buller this morning; you're going to tell him that we were working together unofficially, trying to get to the bottom of Sloper's corrupt behaviour. You're going to get the charges against me dropped and I'm going to be reinstated. And you're going to undo your lie and give me the credit I'm due for the Ashton-Jones murder.'

'How the hell do you expect him to believe that?' Harker balked at the idea.

'I've already paved the way with Sloper. When he pops up he's already primed. Gemma came to me when she got caught in the crossfire of Sloper's actions against Eastern European dealers, and she told me he was up to his neck in it. I told him he was under surveillance, that I'd been watching him during the Ashton-Jones murder. I told him I was working for Buller.

'Not true of course, just me hoping that he'd believe it and tell me what I wanted to know. He knew I found drugs and money at his house and he believed me when I said I was part of the surveillance operation looking at him. Although I told him I was working under Buller, I could tell Buller that I was doing this under your instruction. As I see it, you've got only marginally less trouble than I have, and I'm offering you a way out.'

'Why? Why would you do that?'

'Because I'm in the shit. You and Sloper put me there and only you can get me out. Because you were taken in by Sloper. You turned a blind eye and if you hadn't, you would have found out that, far from looking out for Gemma, Sloper was abusing her himself. And because I want this, this feud, this vendetta that exists for you against me to stop. Because you're in a position to keep making things difficult for me. And I don't deserve to lose my job over a lie, which, as you pointed out, was exactly what was going to happen on Tuesday. It was going to be a sham, a kangaroo court for what was already a foregone conclusion.'

Harker had to concede the truth in all he said. And what was it Temple had said about Gemma, that Sloper had been abusing her? He'd trusted Sloper to look out for her, to let him know where she was, how she was. If he saw him again, Harker knew he'd kill him. And after everything that had happened, Gemma had turned to Temple and he'd helped her. Harker was grateful to him for that. Many would have turned their back on her, saying she deserved all she had coming to her. Despite everything, despite all the hurt she'd caused him, Gemma was still his daughter and Harker still remembered their better times.

Temple resisted the urge to tell him about Prayer; he felt he had to heed Gemma's request not to tell him. Harker would find out about the drug trafficking as the cells were full of traffickers; he'd see Gemma's involvement for himself but there was nothing to connect Gemma to Prayer, even with them both as witnesses. It would be her decision as to when and if she informed Harker that Prayer was his granddaughter. He hoped in time Gemma would make contact with her parents again.

Temple turned to go, but Harker had one last question. 'How is Gemma?'

'She wants to turn her life around. She's got a purpose.'

CHAPTER 50

Temple arrived home to find the cottage in silence. There was no one at home. A quick text to Ana located them all out having a walk around the stone circle and then the gardens of Avebury Manor. He told her to enjoy it and not hurry back. He could imagine that Gemma and Prayer had a lot of talking to do and the gardens might be the perfect place to do that.

He had a quick shower, put some logs in the grate and lit a fire. He settled down to outline a statement for Gemma for when she returned. He knew he would have to sit down with Prayer and do the same. He would then have to talk to Gemma about getting Prayer back home and what they would tell her parents about what had happened to her. After he'd written a couple of pages, tiredness got the better of him and he fell asleep in a chair by the fire, his laptop by the side of him.

He woke to the muffled sound of voices coming from the kitchen. They'd come back and found him sleeping so went into the kitchen and closed the door. He found them sitting round the small pine table, hot drinks in hand, with Ben driving his favourite tractor on the tiled floor. It was a strange picture, with Gemma sitting there next to Prayer. She looked up at him as he came in and he could see the gratitude in her eyes. She was a different Gemma to the one who'd turned up a few nights ago.

He showed her the statement, asked her to go through it and add any more information she could think of. While Gemma scrolled through and read the document, Temple asked to see Prayer in the other room. She went with him; they closed the door on the kitchen and sat near the fire in the hearth.

It was surreal having her sitting there. He wondered if Gemma had told her of him. She was wearing the same jeans and jumper that he'd found her in, but she looked somehow fresh. Perhaps that was the power of designer clothes, he wondered, and remembered rifling through her case. Like many teenage girls, she seemed older than her sixteen years. He stoked the fire as he spoke.

'Have you been in touch with your parents yet?' he asked her gently. 'Are they going to come and get you?'

'I've called them. I've told them that I'll be catching the five o'clock train this afternoon; Gemma's going to drop me off. They'll meet me at the other end. I want them to stay there, I don't want them coming here.' She was looking into the fire as she spoke.

'What will you tell them?'

'I've decided not to tell them about what happened. If it goes to court, I'll deal with it then.'

'If I've anything to do with it, Prayer, it will go to court. It might be best to tell them now.' He couldn't see how she could keep this from them; she would need support at court and there was always a chance that the press would pick it up and report it out of the area. She looked at him.

'If I tell them what happened, they'll never let me out of their sight again. Besides, no harm came to me.'

'It could have been very different. But for your presence of mind, it could have been so much worse.'

'And you getting me out,' she said slowly, looking at him.

'Just doing what they pay me for,' he replied.

'No, if I tell them, they certainly won't let me see Gemma again. And it wasn't her fault.'

'You want to see Gemma again?' He was surprised.

Prayer met his gaze. 'We're going to stay in touch. We're linked to each other after all. She's told me about herself. She's not lied to me. She came from a good home like I do. She's done bad things and she's made mistakes. I understand why she did the things she did. I understand why she gave me up. She says that, now I'm in her life, she wants to make me proud of her. It's given her the reason she needed. I'm not going to turn my back on her, not now.'

'I'm sure she will.' He was concerned for Prayer. He didn't know what Gemma had told her but he wanted her life to stay on its original track, before she knew Gemma. He didn't want it skewed by association with Gemma in any way. They'd got away with it this time – but only just.

'So, what are your plans? Next week, next month, next year?' He tried to lighten the mood.

'Well, I'll be going to college for my A-levels, of course, and then I'm going to university to study law. I'm just trying to decide which one to go to. My parents have said they'll fund me. They've set money aside in a trust. I want to be a lawyer.'

'That's very good of them. Why law?' He felt so grateful to the people who'd looked after her all these years and who would continue to. He suddenly thought of Gemma when he'd first met her. She had only been a few years older than Prayer was now. He suddenly understood Harker's rage at him that night so long ago. If only they'd never met, Gemma would have had such a different life, such a good life. But then he wouldn't be sitting there looking at Prayer. At least something good had come of it all.

As he looked at her, he could never imagine the bright, confident girl sitting before him taking her life off a cliff as Gemma had done. But as he knew, it could easily happen if she just met the wrong boy. 'I like law because it's complicated. I like unravelling things.'

‘Let me give you some advice, Prayer. Don’t deviate from your plan and never let a boy or man get in the way and throw you off course. It’s a fantastic plan. You’ll make everyone really proud of you. Gemma was at university, did you know that?’

‘I know, she told me.’ She looked back at him. After letting silence settle between them, she spoke. ‘I’ve worked it out, you know. She hasn’t told me, but I’m right, I know I am. I know who you are.’

CHAPTER 51

The press conference was heaving. Reporters were elbow to elbow, calibrating their cameras, balancing on one knee as they squeezed together, trying to keep it friendly and not get in each other's way. They worked in the mixture of excitement and tension that was building in the room. There was press interest from around the world as well as the usual domestic suspects. They had almost set up camp outside Swindon police station with their satellite wagons. For a brief moment in time, the eyes of the world were centred on Swindon. It was sensationally macabre, an editor's dream. 'HANNIBAL HALLOWEEN HORROR' the headlines screamed from the scant details already given.

DCS Clive Harker sat alongside DCC Buller and amongst the many clicking camera shutters, they outlined how Porten had pleaded guilty to multiple counts of murder of street dwellers and had sold the meat he had butchered from their bodies before incinerating their remains. They detailed how Porten had come to their attention, the involvement of Temple and DS Mendoza and how they had a lot of work still to do as early indications were that Porten was prolific. There was a collective closing of camera shutters at that point.

It was understood that, due to the number of years over which this had occurred, they could not be sure how many murders may have been committed. They didn't know if they ever would be. The identities of many of the people he'd murdered were unknown. Enquiries were ongoing and if anyone had any further information about anyone they suspected could be one of the victims, they were to call a dedicated line. Now behind bars, Porten was to be the subject of numerous psychiatric reports before sentencing.

Alongside Buller and Harker sat a representative from Public Health England, to reassure the local populace that it was unlikely there was still human meat in the food chain and that, as unpleasant as this was, there was no actual danger to the health of unwitting consumers. The press conference was over.

* * *

In his cell, Brian Porten was bewildered by it. He still firmly believed he was doing society a favour by taking homeless people off the streets, and nothing could shake him from that view.

'Where was the harm?' he said to the psychiatrist. 'Really, where was the harm? Who missed them?'

In light of their premature deaths at his hand, the homeless murdered by Porten were given an almost martyr-like status from the red tops. The case sparked widespread alarm and uproar. How was it that people could just disappear off the streets without anyone knowing? How could Porten have operated for so long without anyone being aware? Why wasn't he stopped before? There were calls for a registration system for homeless people to keep tabs on their whereabouts, ensuring it didn't happen again. Even an 'adopt a homeless person' initiative gathered pace on a crowd-funding website.

In the midst of all this, DS Sam Mendoza handed in his resignation and was working a month's notice. Despite his efforts in coming to Temple's rescue and being the arresting officer for Brian Porten, there was no going back for him. The odds were stacked against him. It was either resign or be fired, and he knew what would look best on his next job application. Temple had tried to persuade him otherwise but he was adamant it was time for him to cut his losses and go.

'At least this way, I go out on a high. My name's all over the papers and I got to nick a serial killer. I've already put it on my CV. This'll be good for me. I've already made various contacts with some ex-Met. They've got some private security firm running in Belgravia, providing services to the rich and don't-want-to-be-famous, so hopefully that'll work out. It's like the Wild West up there, so there should be plenty of work.'

'Stay in touch. I could do with a good contact. And thanks, Sam.'

'I'll let you know how it is on the outside.'

Temple was in his office. He was moving and had to clear the misper files from his desk and inbox. They were going to someone else who was in the shit to look at. The other guys in the office were envious. They couldn't quite work out how he'd managed it but suddenly the disciplinary hearing against him was dropped. They called him Harry Houdini. His fed rep inspector Bob May said that, in all his time, he'd never seen anything like it.

'You had one foot out the door, in fact – no – your foot was the only thing left in,' he told him over the phone. 'Everything was against you. Then there's a "closed-door meeting" and all's forgiven. I can't find out what happened. You'd better watch your step in future. My experience is, if they didn't get you this time, they'll get you next time and hard. They've got long memories. That's my advice.'

Temple knew he was probably right. There was unlikely to be another situation that presented itself as this one had. It had been a pretty close call. Temple hadn't told anyone about his bargain with Harker, nor would he. For his part, Harker had persuaded Buller that he'd always suspected Sloper and had used Temple in a covert capacity with the Ashton-Jones case to provide the cover required to see if his gut instinct was right. At the end, things had moved too fast, he told Buller, for them to stop and risk everything and they'd had no choice but to carry on, hoping for the right result. Harker told Buller he knew it was messy and unconventional and he wouldn't do it again. He hoped the end justified the means.

'But you encouraged me to suspend Temple,' Buller said, testing Harker's explanation of events. 'You showed me a tape of him taking DNA kits from custody.'

'I did, sir, yes. It had to look real. We had to maintain cover. I called the sergeant to escort him off the premises if you remember. I knew if I did that, it would be all around the force within the hour, which of course, again helped to ensure the operation remained covert.' When his own reputation depended on it, he found it easy to lie.

Buller had looked at Harker a little too long with his small pig-like eyes before giving his opinion.

'I'm having trouble believing a fucking word of it, Clive. I don't know what's gone on here and I'll probably never know, but what I *do* know is that a detective sergeant is on the run from custody.' Buller knew that he'd been used. He was angry. The only saving grace was that Sloper, a bent cop, had been winkled out of the force.

'Never,' he said, 'use me like that or leave me on the outside again, Clive. And, Clive,' Buller knew when to take advantage of a situation, 'you owe me for this. And I'll be collecting.'

It was never a good thing to owe a chief officer, particularly one in charge of discipline. But Harker felt he could make up the lack of trust he knew Buller felt towards him now; he would rather that than the alternative of having a whole department or force distrusting him. Besides, right now, despite Buller, the chief constable thought the sun shone out of his arse. The cells were full with a serial killer and human traffickers, and that all equalled community confidence – policing gold.

* * *

Temple had his warrant card back and was going back to the main CID office. And there was a glimmer of hope: there was a vacancy on the Major Crime Unit and he'd put in an application for it. He didn't know how far his favour would stretch with Clive Harker but he thought he'd try it out and see. He knew it wouldn't last long. He was an unforgiving Scot after all. But he needed Harker's endorsement for his application and now was the best chance he'd ever have to ask for it.

Feeling his mobile vibrate, Temple looked at his messages. It was a text from Amy Davidson. She was asking if there'd been any update on the enquiry into China Lewis. She had reported China missing again when she found she had gone from her bedroom after she woke up. That was nearly a week ago.

Temple had ramped it up. Gary Lewis had been arrested and questioned and teams had gone into known trap houses looking for China, disrupting drugs gangs and county lines operatives as they scurried away, temporarily giving Swindon a wide berth but only until the heat was off.

In amongst all the activity, a drug dealer named as Lordon Hayter had been found badly wounded. A strange scene greeted the officers when he was discovered sitting at his kitchen table, which was awash with blood. Both of his hands had been hacked off with a cleaver and lay in front of him on the table. The hands were still wearing blue latex gloves. It had taken them a while to realise he also had a gunshot wound to the leg. The bloke was barely alive. But despite all the efforts to find her, no one had seen China. Temple couldn't stop thinking about her. She had to be somewhere, she couldn't just disappear.

He'd seen Megon and taken a statement from her. He'd listened as Megon had quietly described China and how she'd looked out for her.

'She was fearless,' she sniffed, her tears brimming in her eyes and running down her cheeks. 'She tried to look out for me. She tried to keep me safe but it was no use against them.

She stood up to them though, she wouldn't let them beat her.' Megon gasped her way through her tears. Temple felt wretched for her. He could see that Megon was broken by China's disappearance.

'You will keep searching for her, won't you? You must – she's out there with them. That scum with the clouded eye. They'll know where she is. You must find her,' Megon pleaded.

Temple promised that he'd keep looking until he found her, like he'd promised Amy. He tasked himself with leaving no stone unturned. But he still couldn't find her. It was as if she'd vanished off the face of the earth. Even after turning the trap houses over, there was no trace of her.

To put China in the public consciousness, he involved the press. The local papers were now running an ongoing campaign to find her – 'CONCERN FOR MISSING TEEN' with the photo supplied by Amy. The nationals had picked it up but only in terms of a column filler, because it was Brian Porten who was stealing all the headlines at the moment and had done for days as the grim story continued to unfold. China had been relegated to the inside pages.

CHAPTER 52

When Fin Chadwick thumbed through the *Wiltshire Daily Record*, he missed the headlines. But he didn't miss the photo of China Lewis. Her face leapt out at him and kicked him in the guts. He would never forget her. He hadn't been able to. She'd haunted every minute of his day since. Her face was different of course; the picture he looked at was of a live girl, young, pretty with blonde hair and a pout. The face he'd seen had been set in the grimace of a violent death. But it was her. He was sure about that.

His mouth went dry. Snatches of words that he'd read penetrated his panic. *Concern for her safety. Hasn't been seen for a week. Fourteen. Whereabouts unknown.* He closed the paper. He couldn't read any more. He suddenly leapt up like a scalded cat and paced the Portakabin. It wasn't hot and yet he wiped at the beads of sweat that had appeared on his brow. So, she was a local girl. *Fuck.* Too close to home. Too close to him. He probably knew someone who knew her. *Oh God.*

Well, he could tell them where she was. He was in no doubt that was the girl he had found in the boot of the car in his yard, the girl he had removed and buried in the woods. But how could he possibly tell them where she was? How would he explain it?

He'd only found her; he hadn't murdered her. Now the police were looking for her. *They should have found her in the car before they brought it here*. If he went to them now, they would never believe him. He wanted to tell them where she was. But he couldn't. How could he?

She haunted him like a ghost. The look of terror on her face. The sickening loll of her head when he'd moved her had turned his stomach. It revealed a wound to her neck that was so deep, it had almost cut her head from her body. And as he'd moved her, he'd struggled to keep the two parts together, terrified that if he didn't support her head, it would fall to the ground. Although she was dead, he knew he just had to keep her head in place.

He'd never forget standing over her as he laid her in the grave he'd dug for her. She'd been such a pitiful sight. She was so small. He knew he would never get rid of the sight of her. He'd never get the cuts and bruises on her body out of his mind. He knew he'd never be able to forget her face. *Her face.* That terrible look of fear. He'd felt ill ever since. He couldn't eat and he'd barely slept.

Perhaps he should just pick up the phone and tell them where she was. Perhaps he could do it anonymously. What could he do? There she was in the newspaper, everyone asking where she was and he knew. He *knew* exactly where she was.

They would never believe him. He'd have to stay quiet. There was nothing to lead them to him. He'd wait until they found the murderer, then he would help them. Until then, he'd have to try and blank out her face from his mind.

Only he knew she wouldn't go away. It was no good. Her face never left him. If he shut his eyes, she was there. He couldn't stop thinking about her from the minute he woke. She was constantly with him. She was tormenting him.

He thought of her lying in the grave in the woods. What if they didn't find who killed her? What if the trail went cold and only he knew she was there? How could he keep that terrible secret to himself for the rest of his days? Knowing she was lying out there, under the darkness of the trees. He could still feel his sweat and hear the sound of the shovel as it sliced through the earth. He knew he would never forget anything about that night for as long as he lived. It had been his own personal horror show ever since. It would send him mad.

He looked back at the newspaper he had discarded. Maybe there was something. Someone. One person he could call. The only person likely to believe him. He paced around, thinking, his mind speeding through scenarios, trying to work it out. How to reveal the girl's whereabouts and avoid being labelled a murderer. No, it wouldn't work. No matter which way he turned it, he couldn't see a way through. He couldn't go to prison. Not now, not at his time of life. Not for something he hadn't done. Not for murder.

He took a deep breath. He had to do it. It was the only way. He had to find peace again. Get her face out of his mind. He flicked back through his newspaper and found the printed mobile number. He dialled and waited for the phone to be answered.

'Hello, DI Temple?'

CHAPTER 53

'I know you did your best,' Paul Wallace tried to reassure Temple. 'You helped me to find my Megon. I'll always be grateful for you listening to me and helping me.'

Temple had the phone pressed to his ear. 'It was more a case that you helped me, Paul. We had China. They were all together. I don't know why she didn't stay with her friend Amy Davidson. It's not what I wanted for her. It's a tragic outcome. How is Megon? How did she take the news?'

'She's heartbroken. China was her friend and she can't believe she's dead. She doesn't want to go out. She has nightmares, the most awful night terrors. The news about China has broken her. The doctor's recommended a counsellor, which might help. She won't really speak about what happened to her but the main thing is she's with us, back safe. She's alive. We'll look after her.'

'She's a good girl, she'll get her strength back. She gave us lots of valuable intelligence about the bastard. And at least we've got him. He was picked up yesterday. Tarek Sulaj is now in custody.'

They said their goodbyes. It was small comfort that Sulaj was in custody for the murder of China. Like Amy and

Megon, Temple would never forget her. He'd never forget the sight of her in the shallow grave dug by Fin Chadwick.

* * *

Temple couldn't quite believe it when Chadwick rang him.

'You need to get a team and go out to West Woods. The girl that's missing, China Lewis, she's buried there. I'll show you.'

He'd known Chadwick on and off over the years. He'd sailed close to the wind in some of his dealings but it was always petty stuff, a bit of handling, nothing exciting. But his call changed that. Chadwick took them to a spot in the woods and stood by with Temple while a team of four officers with shovels set about moving the earth. As soon as they found her, Temple arrested him and had him taken away.

Temple stayed and watched as the scene was unearthed; watched as they slowly removed the soil until only China was left in the grave. With other officers, he looked at her tiny, naked body, laid out by Chadwick, her head to one side, pushed that way by the weight of the soil. The deep slash in her throat was evident, as were the cuts and bruises. The violence meted out on her tiny frame made him feel sick. They had just about caught the body in time before it started to putrefy. Before the evidence was lost.

Then the forensics arrived, put up the tent, their lights, put on their suits and, clicking their cameras, they moved in to recover all they could. Temple stayed, silently going in and out of the tent, not wanting to leave her alone now he'd found her. Not until she was taken out of the ground. Taken off to the morgue.

Chadwick had been interviewed and his story checked out. The two officers who had found the Audi were adamant that there was no body in the car but as Chadwick described how she was found, the officer conducting the search had to admit he'd never searched the boot of the car. Chadwick was charged with unlawful burial and released from custody.

Amy had described China telling her about the guy with one eye; Paul and Megon had first-hand sighting of him and could put him in the town centre in the early hours of the same morning that China had left Amy's. No one had seen her since. The battle scars he was so proud of marked him out and once put on notice to find him, officers quickly picked Sulaj up on a cross-Channel ferry. He was still carrying the knife he'd used to kill her.

Temple felt he'd let China down. He turned the events over and over in his mind. He'd found her once, her and Amy, he'd rescued her from Gary Lewis's car. If Sloper hadn't coshed him that night, he would have gone back to Amy Davidson's and taken a statement from them both. He could have made arrangements for China to be safe. He was sure they would have found Megon and there would have been no need for China to go out and look for her.

He'd so wanted to get China the help she obviously needed, she'd been through so much, but instead she'd run into Tarek Sulaj. If only he hadn't been left on the ground for Brian Porten to find, he felt certain China would still be alive. But then he wouldn't have discovered Porten's evil and twisted actions at the abattoir, which would have left Porten free to continue killing. It was a bitter payoff. The press had wanted to interview Temple, they wanted to declare him 'the hero cop' for stopping Porten in his tracks, but he knew he was no such thing. Given a choice, he'd rather have saved China Lewis and left Porten for another day.

* * *

It was a beautiful scene. A horseshoe-shaped bay with endless golden sand and turquoise waters. Ko Sukorn was idyllic. He especially liked the sunsets. There was something about watching the sun go down here that really settled a sense of peace on him. It was like watching a phenomenon.

This was a place where he could leave the other world behind him. He looked out to sea and felt the sand beneath his feet. A soft, warm breeze off the lapping shore welcomed him back. After the long journey, he was home.

Barefoot in the sand, he turned away from the sea and into the vegetation of the tall palm trees. He found the familiar track and made his way towards a typical wooden house, albeit it was larger than most. He wondered how near he could get before they would see him.

He loved Thailand. It gave him his freedom. This time, it had given him his life. For this he had to thank Bangkok. He loved its chaos, its vibrancy, the noise, the smell. Most of all, he loved its street life. The food sellers, leather sellers, gold sellers, the sex sellers. If you knew where to look, as he did, it would cater for your every need. But after being there a while, he found out there was more it could offer. He discovered that there was a street in Bangkok where you could enter as one person and by the time you'd walked to the other end, you were someone entirely different. At least, that's what your passport said. When you know these things, a whole new world opens up.

As a consequence, he could move about as Edward Read, John Herriott, Robert Cardman or Simon Dew. He had passports for all these names and identities. Luckily, they had been safely hidden to enable a quick getaway. He had managed to order his ticket with EVA Air on his phone in the back of the car when he was with Temple. When he left the hospital, he was in a taxi to Heathrow within the hour. He was in the air before they even knew he was missing. Sweet.

He always knew it would come: a time when he would be unlucky. He had hoped he could last out a few more years, rake in a few extra grand, but it didn't matter. His freedom was far more important. He could always make more money. The trick was knowing when to get out. And having a plan for that eventuality.

'Ah, Mr Edward, you're back!'

Sloper walked towards the open arms of a tiny Thai woman. He easily morphed from Simon Sloper into Edward Read – until he got tired of being him. That's what he loved about this place.

* * *

Prayer Taylor lay on her bed. She couldn't help but go over events, even though over a week had passed. She could do this in the confines of her bedroom without being watched over by her parents. To them she had to appear as normal as possible; she didn't want them to know anything untoward had happened to her. As far as they were concerned, she had met her biological mother and they could now move forward.

She hadn't told them anything of what had really happened. She hadn't told them of the night that men in grotesque Halloween masks had burst into Gemma's flat and abducted her. How they had driven her to a flat and taken her to an upstairs room and pushed her inside. She hadn't confided to anyone how terrified she'd been on that journey, how she knew that she had to keep her wits about her in order to survive. Something had kicked in that night, something she hadn't known existed within her.

They'd told her to undress or they would do it for her. It was then she knew she had to do something to save herself. And that had worked. But now she felt the need to go over the events again and again. From when he'd found her. Rescued her. Her biological father. She couldn't stop thinking about him. Thinking about *them*, her real parents. They weren't real, the people she lived with. She felt she no longer belonged to them.

CHAPTER 54

Temple pulled up outside the lychgate. His mobile buzzed as he locked the car, but he ignored it. He wanted to go inside the tiny cottage where he could see the welcoming lights and spend some time with Ben before he went out for the evening. As soon as he crossed the threshold, Ana was waiting for him.

'I've been trying to get through to you. I rang and texted you. There was a message from Richard here when I got back this afternoon. On a piece of paper through the letterbox – he must have called by. Now where have I put it?'

As Ana looked around, Temple looked for Ben, distracted by the need to spend time with him. He had to get Richard a phone and show him how to send texts.

'OK, I'll look at it later.' He found Ben, took him for his bath and read him a story before showering and changing to go out with Callie.

As he drove back to Huish, his thoughts were full of her. They'd spent last night together. After the last few days, what with finding China and Sulaj being arrested, being with her was just what he'd needed. Every murder investigation he encountered seemed to take something from him, something he never quite recovered. Every time he altered a little. That was certainly the case in respect of China, but being with Callie last night had made all the difference to how he'd felt today.

And he was becoming more and more enamoured of her. She'd made a big impression on him in a short space of time. He couldn't understand why she was still single, but he was glad she was and glad their paths had crossed. He had started to tell her about his mother, about Leigh and Daisy. She knew about Ben of course, but not all the circumstances.

Over dinner tonight, he planned to tell her about that and about Prayer. He'd made so many decisions recently and was feeling much more positive about the future. He didn't want to hide his past from Callie and felt it was only fair to tell her everything – that way, whatever the outcome, she would have had it all.

If she felt she didn't want a relationship with him once she knew, then at least he'd know where he stood. He felt confident though; she seemed to take the news of Leigh's pregnancy in her stride. It hadn't seemed to faze her at all. The sooner she knew everything the better. And if she knocked him back – well, he'd deserve it.

He was also pleased that he'd made the decision to step back from Op Acre. He was sure it was the right thing for him to do. In fact, he knew it was – ever since he'd made the decision, he'd felt as if an enormous weight had lifted from him. His life felt lighter. It started to make sense. Things had to change, and when he looked back, the murder of his mother had impacted in one way or another on most of his life and on Daisy. Well, no more.

He would tell Richard that they should stop the quest the next time he saw him. The peace of mind he had found since making his decision and coming to terms with the fact he would not know the identity of the killer was a peace worth having after all these years. He was no longer going to let a killer control him or impact on the people in his life. The collateral damage was too great. He'd make a point of seeing Richard in the next few days and agree with him to put an end to it, for both of them.

The car rumbled over the cattle grid and he pulled up at the front of the house. He heard his mobile sound an incoming text. Temple pressed the horn and Callie waved from a window, indicating she'd be out. As he waited, Temple looked at his phone: there was the text that Ana had sent him earlier to tell him of the message Richard had left him and another now from DC Paul Wright. He had forgotten to read Richard's message before he came out, not wanting to be late for his date with Callie.

He looked at Wright's text. Clicking on it, he saw that there was a photo attachment. He wondered at first what it was on the screen. He tilted his phone on its side for a better view. The screen showed an image with four lines of numbers contained inside symbols arranged like a series of spikes, like bleeps on a heart monitor. The spikes were of varying heights. Then he realised what he was looking at.

It was the DNA sequence from the blue T-shirt. He'd almost forgotten he'd asked Paul Wright to see if he could get it for him. After all this time, there it was. He now had the DNA profile from the blue T-shirt. He recalled the words on his mother's death certificate: *'Unlawful Killing. Killed by person or persons unknown.'* He was holding the killer in his hands. Temple felt the hairs on the back of his neck bristle.

Looking up, he saw Callie heading towards him. He closed the message and quickly opened the previous text from Ana, relaying the content of the note left by Richard.

'Hoped to catch you in. Need to see you urgently. New development.'

Callie sat next to him in the car and he kissed her. 'Change of plan,' he said to her. 'There's something I need to do.'

THE END

DI TEMPLE BOOKS

Book 1: WATCH HER DIE
Book 2: DEAD OF NIGHT

Thank you for reading this book. If you enjoyed it please leave feedback on Amazon, and if there is anything we missed or you have a question about then please get in touch. The author and publishing team appreciate your feedback and time reading this book.

Please join our mailing list for free kindle crime thriller, detective, mystery, and romance books and new releases.
http://www.joffebooks.com/contact/

Our email is office@joffebooks.com

http://joffebooks.com

We hate typos but sometimes they slip through.
Please send any errors you find to
corrections@joffebooks.com

We'll get them fixed ASAP. We're very grateful to eagle-eyed readers who take the time to contact us.

45712489R00190

Printed in Poland
by Amazon Fulfillment
Poland Sp. z o.o., Wrocław